The Murder at Red Oaks

by

Kay Pritchett

Mosey Frye Mysteries

The Murder at Red Oaks

Cover Art by *Teddi Black*

The Wild Rose Press, Inc.
PO Box 708
Adams Basin, NY 14410-0708
Visit us at www.thewildrosepress.com

Publishing History
First Edition, 2025
Trade Paperback ISBN 978-1-5092-6284-7
Digital ISBN 978-1-5092-6285-4

Mosey Frye Mysteries
Published in the United States of America

Dedication

In memory of Hope Christiansen,
my friend and faithful reader

Chapter One

Jeremiah Java Café
Monday, March 15, 2010, 8:00 a.m.

Mosey saw little appeal in the exterior of the Jeremiah Java Café. The wooden steps leading up from the gravel parking lot were warped and splitting. The floorboards on the small front porch—actually, more of a stoop than a porch—sagged quite a bit. Not to mention, the paint on the clapboard siding was half peeled off.

And yet, as she stepped foot into the small, three-room building, all thoughts of the shabby facade vanished from her mind. She caught the screen door just before it banged and, searching for a spot away from the loud chatter of farmers, lost herself in the heady aroma of freshly brewed coffee. Not just any coffee, mind you, but a rich concoction created from Aaron Willoughby's special blend of beans, imported to Hembree from some distant corner of the world. The exact place of origin was a little hazy in her mind. But regardless, the beans had managed to find their way to this outpost on the Mississippi River, where they were blended, roasted, and ground right there on the premises.

Through his expert knowledge of blending, Mr. Willoughby had achieved something quite magical, indeed, a real curiosity to his customers. Nobody had managed to sneak a peek at the recipe, but those conversant on exotic varietals argued heatedly over the infinite possibilities. Hugh Jessup, her husband Robert's colleague in Anthropology, had a good bit of experience in coffee-growing climes. Every so often he would proclaim he'd cracked the code, only to retreat when jubilant Aaron, his broad smile breaking into laughter, would say, "Nope, not quite, Dr. J."

Mosey, on the other hand, didn't care much about the origin of the beans, the percentages of this and that, the method of roasting, and whatever else contributed to the superbly complex cup of coffee she was about to sample. What she relished was the aromatics, the body, the aftertaste, and the finish of what she'd come to regard as the best cup of coffee in the world.

While waiting for a table, she sniffed again and this time noticed the warm scent of homemade biscuits wafting from the kitchen. She was hoping to snag a spot near the kitchen door, which matched up perfectly with the front door and back door as well. You know, that's why they call them shotgun houses. A person positioned on the front porch has a clean shot straight through the house. At least that's the lore, but Mosey had stumbled upon a more likely explanation, i.e., that "shotgun" actually derived from the Afro-Caribbean word *to-gun* or *tog una*, meaning "places of talk or assembly."

At one time, this shotgun house on the edge of a cotton patch belonged to Mosey's boss John Earle Shepherd of Shepherd Realty. But a couple of years back, he ended up selling it to Lenna King Fortney, who owned Hembree's premier accounting firm along with a bunch of other businesses that you simply would not believe. Her position at the firm had given Miss Lenna, as she was called, an inside view of the commercial goings-on in Hembree and Dent County. And whenever an awesome deal would go up for sale, she'd snatch it up before anybody else had a chance to think twice. The Jeremiah Java was one such acquisition. And while keeping a tight rein on the credits and debits, she'd had the good sense to leave the day-to-day operation to Aaron and his wife Sue, Aaron being the expert on all things coffee and Sue, the best biscuit maker in the county.

The café's offerings were slim. Just coffee, hot chocolate for the children, and biscuits, either plain or filled with one of a long list of tasty options, like bacon, ham, sausage, and fried chicken. Fried oysters, too, when in season. But Mosey wasn't really here for the biscuits. She was here for the coffee. And to be honest, maybe not even for the coffee as much as for the special way it was served, in small green enamel coffee pots set on trays lined with white paper doilies. The waitress would set the tray on the table, and lifting the miniature pot in one hand, the white porcelain cup and saucer in the other, she'd fill the cup without spilling a drop before setting it neatly on the tray. Whether requested or not, fresh cream in tiny jars and sugar in small covered bowls were placed on the tables and attentively refilled. No matter how limited the choices, whatever was on the menu was prepared and served to perfection.

That particular morning, Mosey wasn't breakfasting alone. Her best friend Nadia Abboud, manager of Abboud Antiques, would be arriving any minute. She and Mosey were going down the road a short distance to take a look at Red Oaks Manor, whose owner, the aforementioned Lenna Fortney, was thinking about retiring and putting her home up for sale. But before making any definitive move, Miss Lenna, astute business woman that she was, would naturally want to have all the relevant information at her disposal. Hence, she'd reached out to John Earle, knowing she could rely on him for a professional assessment of the house's value.

Red Oaks would sell for a bundle, and everybody knew that, seeing as it was fairly large, beautifully kept, and rather unusual. It came with its own mausoleum, a lovely structure, macabre, uh-huh, but made of priceless marble with a high-pitched roof and an oval arched doorway. Not especially roomy, the mausoleum currently held the coffins of six family members, including Lenna's parents and paternal grandparents, her husband, and her ward, Kemena King, known affectionately as Miss Kimmy. Two more occupants would fit into the space, and everybody assumed, of course, that Miss Lenna would be one. Who would occupy the other spot was anybody's guess, considering that the bloodline had petered out and there was very little chance of Miss Lenna contemplating nuptials. It could have been donated to the town or the King's church, or it might have been used for her devoted cook Miss Willie White, who was like a member of the family. But Miss Willie, so Mosey had heard, had no desire to be shut up for all eternity in a mausoleum with the Kings. And now, with Miss Lenna considering selling the house, the fate of the mausoleum hung in the balance. Indeed, this was an uncomfortable situation and certainly one Mosey hadn't experienced previously in her limited time in real estate. Before speaking with Miss Lenna, she wished she'd thought to seek the advice of John Earle's trusted assistant Saffron Smiley, if not John Earle himself.

That worrisome thought occupied her mind as she glanced around at the clientele, checking her watch periodically, and putting off the waitress, who had asked several times if she was ready to order. At last, the screen door opened and in came Nadia, looking quite professional in her gray linen jacket and matching blouse, even if her long, dark hair was a little wind-blown. By comparison, Mosey felt sort of shabby in her casual jeans and cotton jacket. She supposed she might have dressed better for Miss Lenna, but oh well, too late now.

"Well, it's about time." Mosey frowned as she tapped her watch.

"Sorry, so sorry."

"Now please don't tell me you couldn't get away," she cut in before Nadia could explain. "You haven't even gone to the store."

"For heaven's sake, Mosey." Nadia set her tote on the sparkling white laminate table top. "I got a call from Aunt Paula and—"

"Oh, never mind, let's order. I'm starved to death." Mosey waved to the waitress across the room. "Lula, we're ready when you can."

Lula approached with her order tablet in hand. "Yes, ma'am, what can I get for you ladies?"

"Coffee and a biscuit," Mosey said, "plain with butter and fig preserves on the side."

Nadia took a seat and leaned against the backrest of the chrome and vinyl chair. "Coffee, and let's see…" She eyed the list of specials scrawled on the blackboard behind the counter. "I'll take a biscuit with bacon and Swiss."

"Coming right up." Lula tucked her tablet in her

apron pocket and hurried away toward the kitchen.

As soon as Lula had gone, Mosey said, "Okay, what do you know about the place?"

"Red Oaks? Not much. I've been there a couple of times, haven't you?"

"Once, a long time ago. The Kings aren't exactly what you'd call hospitable, are they?"

Nadia shrugged. "Oh, they're nice enough. But come to think of it, shouldn't we be talking in the singular. Everybody's dead except Lenna."

"Yeah, I know. The mausoleum is full of Kings."

"And a Fortney."

"I was wondering just now how the mausoleum might affect the property value. Not sure I'd want a bunch of moldering bodies close to the front door."

"It's not that visible. And I suppose you could move the bodies if you wanted to."

Mosey shivered. "What a thought."

"It happens all the time. Just yesterday I saw a tent set up in the cemetery. They were exhuming a body, relocating it somewhere, I'd imagine."

"My lord!" Mosey exclaimed before quickly turning her attention to Lula, who had arrived with the coffee.

Lula filled Mosey's cup, then Nadia's.

"That smells absolutely heavenly." Nadia breathed in deep, a gentle smile playing around her lips.

"By the way," Mosey said to Lula, "we were just talking about Miss Lenna's place. You haven't heard her mention what her plans are, have you?"

"Plans?" Lula tilted her head.

"I heard she was thinking of retiring."

"If I were Miss Lenna," Lula said, "I'd be thinking about it, too. Why would she wanna work? Surely, she doesn't need the money."

"Maybe she likes to work," Nadia chimed in. "I like to work."

Lula laughed. "It takes all kinds. I'll be right back with your biscuits."

"Besides"—Nadia turned to Mosey—"what's she gonna do if she doesn't work? She's not that old."

Mosey reached for the cream and poured a generous amount into her cup. "She could start by sprucing up the place, getting rid of all that creepy stuff."

"What creepy stuff?"

"All that stuffed stuff."

"Mosey, your vocabulary leaves much to be desired."

"Oh, please."

"If you're referring to the mounts, they haven't been called *stuffed* since the nineteenth century. They're mounts. And I've looked at those. Museum-quality. Doc Fortney was a bona fide taxidermist."

"Well, he was a veterinarian by trade." Mosey sipped her coffee. "You wouldn't think he'd wanna sit around looking at a bunch of dead animals."

"Taxidermy is a craft," Nadia said, exasperation in her tone. "I thought the animals were rather artfully done, the deer in particular."

"You aren't thinking of buying one, are you?"

"What if I am? I've had quite a few customers express an interest—"

"Around here, I guess so. Without a critter's noggin' on your wall, you're nobody," she said with a shiver.

Nadia set down her cup and looked Mosey in the eye. "Are you feeling all right?"

"Of course. I'm just remembering that antelope head

you convinced me to put in Waite House for the staging."

"Yeah, and that old guy kept it, didn't he?"

"Yeah, I reckon he did."

Lula arrived with Mosey and Nadia's order and set a covered basket between them. "I'm leaving you some extra biscuits. Let me know if you want anymore."

"Thanks, Lula." Mosey dropped her napkin in her lap, then split open the biscuit. "Oh, my goodness," she said as she caught a whiff of tasty goodness. "We should come here more often."

"Wow." Nadia sliced her bacon and Swiss in half. "I wish I had Sue's recipe."

Mosey spread butter on her biscuit, then preserves. "Getting back to Red Oaks, what about the mausoleum? You think it'll hurt the sale?"

"I don't know. It wouldn't bother me, not if I wanted the house. There're a lot of little family plots all around here. What's the difference?"

"Yeah, I guess there isn't a big difference."

"I would think the lake might be more of an issue," Nadia said.

"Why the lake?"

"Who wants a lake right at their back door?" She waggled her head.

"I wouldn't mind having my very own lake for swimming, boating, fishing."

Nadia arched an eyebrow. "You know what happened to Miss Kimmy."

"Oh, lord. They ever figure that one out?"

"She drowned."

"Yes, but didn't somebody question that, saying she was a good swimmer or something?"

"Well, even good swimmers can drown," Nadia

argued.

"But her boyfriend—what was his name?"

"Merritt...Merritt Trumble." Nadia took a bite of biscuit and wiped her mouth.

"That's right. Wasn't he sort of bent out of shape? I mean, didn't he spread some rumors about Lenna?"

"Now that you mention it, seems like he did cast aspersions. But I seriously doubt she had anything to do with it."

"She's not a very likeable person. Kinda bossy."

"Yeah, so I've heard."

"I wonder what ever happened to Merritt?"

"He's around," Nadia said. "In fact, seems like somebody mentioned him just the other day. He's working for his daddy's architectural firm in Mound City. You know," she added, "if I'd been Kimmy, I don't think I'd have liked having Lenna for a guardian."

"Huh, me, neither. In fact, I'm not really looking forward to this appointment."

"Why? If you get the listing, well, money in the bank, considerable money."

"I suppose." Mosey took a sip of coffee and checked her watch. "We need to get over there soon as possible. I promised Saffron we'd get there early, before Lenna left for work."

"I suppose we could wrap these up and take 'em with us."

"I'll ask Lula for a to-go box." Mosey waved at Lula, and she came right over. "Would you bring us a to-go box, please, ma'am, and some paper cups for the coffee?"

"What's your hurry?"

"We're running a little late. We've got an

appointment with Miss Lenna."

"You'd better get going, then." Lula frowned. "I see her drive by here about this time every morning."

Lula soon returned with boxes and two cups filled with fresh coffee.

"Thanks so much." Mosey placed a twenty on the table.

Nadia added a ten. "Keep the change."

"And sorry for the rush." Mosey waved back as they left through the screen door.

Chapter Two

Red Oaks Manor
Monday, March 15, 2010, 8:45 a.m.

Mosey pulled into the circular brick drive at Red Oaks and stepped down from her truck. "I feel terrible about this, Nadia."

"Why?"

"We should have gotten here sooner."

"Lenna's her own boss, isn't she?"

"Yeah, but you know how it is. People establish a schedule and prefer to stick to it." As they neared the front of the house, Mosey spotted a car and added, "Looks like she's still here." Mosey stood looking around at the surroundings. "You know, this place doesn't look a thing like a manor house. But then again, I'm not exactly sure what a manor house looks like."

Everyone in Hembree called a house a house, but not the Kings, who apparently fancied themselves a notch above the rest. But maybe they *were* in a position to draw that conclusion. If anyone in Hembree other than the tax assessor was aware of who had what, she imagined it was the Kings. "I think you're right about the mausoleum, Nadia." She peered at the small structure set a good distance from the house. "It fits in pretty well. I sort of like the looks of it, actually. Imagine how incredible that view is on a misty day." She paused momentarily to capture the details for her property description. "Would you call that Gothic?"

"Well, it doesn't have any external buttressing," Nadia replied with a chuckle. "But the vertical proportion certainly looks Gothic."

"External buttressing, indeed." Mosey laughed and walked on, turning her eyes toward the entrance to the three-story home. "It's funny, isn't it, how Gothic and Victorian seem to blend."

"Not a bit funny if you're aware of the history. The Victorians were quite interested in the Middle Ages."

"Is there anything you don't know?" Mosey asked, half serious. She always counted on Nadia to fill her in on one thing or another, and rarely did she ever let her down. "I just love having an encyclopedia for a friend," she said with a grin.

"Thanks!" Nadia rolled her eyes.

As they came to the door, Mosey was about to ring the bell but noticed an envelope clamped to the mailbox lid. Intrigued, she took a closer look. "Says 'welcome.' You think it's for us?"

"How should I know? Open it and read it."

Seeing that the envelope wasn't sealed, Mosey opened it and read the contents. "That's strange. It's typed." She held the pale cream stationery up for Nadia to see.

"What does it say?"

" 'Come in. The door is open.' " Mosey dropped the note in the box.

"That's weird," Nadia said. "Wonder what's up."

"I don't know, but I suspect we'll find out soon enough." When she turned the knob, the door swayed open practically on its own. She walked into the foyer, a large space with a wide staircase winding up. As she approached the steps, she noticed a niche to one side of the landing. "Nadia, look at that."

"It's a coffin corner," Nadia informed. "Wonder if they keep a family coffin in the attic."

"What a thing to say."

Not sure whether to call out or continue into one of the rooms, they hesitated in the foyer, their eyes darting around the opulent space.

"Let's go that way." Nadia gestured toward the parlor. "I think I see a light."

They entered the parlor where, by the dim light of a crystal sconce, Nadia, apparently, was able to make out an unsettling scene. "My word, Mosey." Nadia covered her mouth.

A bit slower in processing the surroundings, Mosey glanced from one part of the cavernous space to another and, bringing her eyes to rest on a large object in front of the bay window, muttered, "What *is* that?"

"Can't you tell?" Nadia inched toward the object, the true nature of which she'd managed to decipher.

"It's dark in here," Mosey grumbled. "I can't see a thing." But as her eyes adjusted to the darkness, she, too, realized that the bulky item stationed near the window was, in reality, a coffin resting on a bier. With the help of faint sunlight, she distinguished the silhouette of a head reposed on a small white pillow. In an instant, she gasped, "Miss Lenna! Oh, my lord! It's Miss Lenna!"

"I think she's dead, Mosey."

"Oh, no…"

Nadia opened her eyes wide and blinked a couple of times. "Poor woman. That's what she gets for picking you as an agent. Too late now."

"What?" Mosey cast a glare at Nadia. "It's not my fault!"

"Not her fault," Nadia muttered sarcastically.

"You can't possibly think—"

"No, I don't think—But, Mosey, really. You walk in, hoping to list the place, and a dead body appears right in front of you. What a coincidence!"

"Oh, Nadia, cut it with the snark. Miss Lenna is *dead*."

"Okay, you stand there gawking"—Nadia pulled out her cellphone—"but I'm calling 911." When the dispatcher came on the line, she calmly said, "Yes…we have an emergency at Red Oaks on Little Smith. I can't tell you the exact address."

Mosey shot Nadia a sideways glance. "It's 1099 Little Smith."

"Hold on a sec. What?"

"1099 Little Smith," Mosey repeated.

While Nadia talked to the dispatcher, Mosey took some deep breaths, then scanned the area for any clues that might shed light on the bizarre spectacle. Without getting too close, she carefully observed the body and then looked around the room for possible clues. Grabbing a pad and pencil from her tote, she jotted down the hour, knowing from experience that Lieutenant Olivera would want to know the exact time they'd arrived. Likewise, he wouldn't want anything disturbed. And with that in mind, she decided to stay put, fighting off the temptation to inspect the body for signs of whatever brought about Lenna Fortney's demise.

At a half room's distance, she could see the body wasn't laid out in contemporary clothing but in a long dark gown with lace trim around the neckline. She wore satin slippers of the same dark shade. The overall appearance of the body implied the work of a funerary professional, and yet it was doubtful that an undertaker had prepared the corpse. The air carried a distinct odor of decomposition, suggesting decay had already set in. The flesh, however, was still lily white, leading Mosey to believe Miss Lenna hadn't been dead for long, a day at most.

Recalling that even a faint smell of decay could be harmful, Mosey rummaged in her tote for her handkerchief and placed it over her nose. She glanced at Nadia, still on the phone and, motioning for her to follow, headed out of the house. Reaching the porch, she breathed in the fresh air.

Nadia stepped out behind her. "Should I close the door?"

Mosey shrugged. "Better leave it open. One less set of fingerprints. Olivera won't be pleased we disturbed the crime scene." She waved her handkerchief in front of her face.

"Well, good grief. How were we supposed—?"

"You know how he is," Mosey cut in, "or maybe you don't."

"Oh, who cares." Nadia dropped her phone in her tote. "They're sending an ambulance, by the way. Where you want to wait?"

"Here's good." Mosey took a seat on the cool stone steps.

Nadia sat down beside her, and they waited for the ambulance to arrive.

Minutes later, the ambulance pulled into the drive and came to a screeching halt in front of the house. Two paramedics jumped out and swiftly made their way toward the entrance. "Is she inside?" the more senior member of the team called out.

"Yes," Mosey responded, "but I'm afraid it's too late. I'm pretty sure she's dead."

He paused at the steps. "We'd better have a look. Where did you say—?"

"She's in there." Mosey gestured in the direction of the parlor. "But Lieutenant Olivera isn't going to like it. I'm telling you, he's not going to like it one bit." She cut off, feeling Nadia's elbow hit her ribcage. "Hey!"

Nadia scrunched her nose and raised an index finger to her lips. "For heaven's sake, Mosey, let them do their job."

Minutes later, when the vehicles of the police and coroner pulled in, Mosey and Nadia walked down the steps to the drive.

Lieutenant Gus Olivera, sporting a dark blue cotton blazer with khaki trousers, tipped his signature fedora as he approached. "Ms. Frye…Ms. Abboud."

"I asked them to wait, Lieutenant," Mosey said, "but a lot of good it did."

"What have we got?" He advanced toward the steps.

"Well, Lenna Fortney, dead in a coffin in the parlor."

His eyebrows lifted. "Dead? Are you sure?"

"Well, no, I'm not positive, but she certainly looks dead, doesn't she, Nadia?"

Nadia nodded. "I'd have to agree, but we didn't disturb the body, didn't take a pulse or anything."

"So, you haven't touched anything. Good." He pulled out his pad and pen and made a note. "If you wouldn't mind waiting over there, I'd like to take a look around." He then directed himself to Sergeant Springer, who was standing near the SUV. "Go ahead and set up the cones, Springer." With those words, Olivera entered the house.

Eads McGinnis, the coroner, then ascended the steps with a camera case dangling from one shoulder and an instrument case from the other. As she passed, she nodded to Mosey and Nadia. "You two find the body?"

"I'm afraid so," Mosey responded with a sigh.

After Eads had gone inside, Mosey spoke to Springer and Reagan, who were placing cones along the edge of the drive. "Sergeant Springer…Sergeant Reagan."

"Ms. Frye," Springer said. "You ladies find the body?"

"We sure did."

"If you don't mind my asking, how did you happen—?"

"—to be out here?" Mosey cut in. "We were summoned, well, I was summoned. Actually, it was John Earle I believe who received the call."

"I see." He walked toward the porch with a cone in each arm. "Reagan, bring some more cones over here, would you?"

Reagan grabbed a couple of cones and joined them at the steps. "Where you want these?"

"Right along there. From that tree"—he pointed— "all the way to the end of the curve."

The door creaked and Mosey looked around as the paramedics came out. They descended the steps and headed toward the ambulance.

"That was a waste of taxpayers' money," Mosey commented to Springer as the paramedics got in their vehicle and pulled away.

"Well, you never know, Mosey. She might have been alive. It's hard to tell sometimes."

"Huh. It was clear to me. I could smell it in the air."

"Decomposition?"

"Yeah, unmistakable."

"How many bodies does this make, Mosey?"

"Let's not even go there." She knew exactly how many homicides she'd "worked," but to her great relief, most of them hadn't involved close contact with a corpse. Even so, she had to face the fact that she was getting a reputation, as Nadia's snarky remark made abundantly clear.

She and Springer chatted back and forth until Olivera came out, pausing in the doorway to take off his mask. "Springer, you and Reagan get masks on and raise the windows on the first floor."

Springer nodded and, after masking up, entered the house.

"And you ladies"—Olivera turned to Mosey and Nadia—"I'd like to get some information. Shall we sit over there?" He gestured toward the lawn furniture near the towering red oaks that gave the property its name. After they had seated themselves around the small wrought-iron table, he said, "If you don't mind, I'll record this." He looked at one, then the other.

"Of course." Mosey glanced at Nadia. "You okay with that?"

Nadia agreed with a nod.

"Very well. I presume you are here to list the property." He cast a discerning gaze over Mosey, his olive complexion impeccably groomed as if he'd just stepped out of a barber shop.

"Yes, that's what I was hoping, but I didn't get a

chance to speak to Miss Lenna, I mean, before we came out."

"No?"

"It was John Earle who received the call, and I assumed it was from her. I guess it could have been from her secretary. It seems she was thinking of selling the house when she retired and wanted to get started on the preliminaries."

"Preliminaries?"

"Well, yes. Most people do what they can to increase the value of the property, which could mean sprucing up the place or even replacing the roof. You know, some folks like to consult with an agent about bumping up the market value."

"I see." He thought for a second, then looked at Mosey again. "But you must have spoken with her about the appointment. You had an appointment this morning, didn't you?"

"Yes, but Saffron set up the appointment."

"So…you hadn't spoken with Ms. Fortney at all?"

"Correct."

He turned to Nadia. "And Ms. Abboud, I suppose you are here to—?"

Nadia, who'd been staring off across the front lawn, turned her head. "Actually, Lieutenant, I did speak with Ms. Fortney a while back about some of the furnishings. She wanted to get an estimate on the value of a large dining room suite and a couple of other items. Then, when Mosey mentioned she was driving out, well, I thought I'd tag along, snap a couple of pictures."

He sat back, shading his dark eyes from the sun. "When did you speak to Ms. Fortney?"

"Last week, Thursday, I think it was."

"Did she know to expect you this morning?"

"I suppose so." Nadia shrugged. "I called and left a message with her secretary at the accounting firm."

"So, she knew to expect both you and Mosey this morning?"

They nodded, and then Mosey posed a question of her own. "Lieutenant, what do you suspect, if you don't mind my asking?"

"Well, keep this under your hat"—he cleared his throat—"but it looks like she might have been strangled."

"Strangled!" Mosey gasped. "Good lord!"

"But, obviously," he said with a shake of his head, "that didn't occur today. Dr. McGinnis will have to determine time of death, but she suspects the victim has been dead for a day, more or less."

"So, yesterday morning?" Nadia said.

"Which means, of course, that the perpetrator could be long gone," Olivera added.

"Oh, my. I suppose he or she would have arranged all that." Nadia gestured with her head toward the bay window, beyond which the crime scene lay.

"Yes, he or she *did* go to an awful lot of trouble, didn't they?" Olivera commented.

"I've never seen such a thing," Mosey exclaimed. "It's all so…intentional."

"Indeed. That's a very good word for it…intentional. Macabre, too, and utterly theatrical," Olivera added, awe in his voice. "And straight out of the Victorian era," he said as he turned to Nadia.

"I didn't get a chance to examine any of the furnishings, Lieutenant, not closely," she responded, "but the catafalque looked Victorian, as did the coffin.

It's bronze, I believe, and that hexagonal shape isn't used much anymore. A rather expensive piece, I'm thinking."

"Catafalque?"

"Some call it a casket bier, since most regular biers, at least the old variety, had wheels that allowed the casket to be moved from the house to the church, which might have been some distance away."

"So the casket—"

"Properly speaking, Lieutenant," she explained, "that's a coffin, not a casket."

"Didn't know there was a difference." He looked perplexed.

"Well, most people wouldn't, but in my business, terminology—"

"Yes," he cut in, "I can imagine that in your business…"

"Sorry," Nadia said, "I didn't mean to rattle on."

"No, actually, I appreciate whatever help I can get. I suspect this is going to be a tough one."

"Why's that, Lieutenant?" Mosey asked.

He paused, drumming his fingers against the tabletop. "We haven't been able to pick up much so far."

"Well, you weren't in there more than a few minutes."

"True, and the surfaces I examined were wiped clean."

"But surely—"

He stared at Mosey but said nothing. "By the way," he turned to Nadia, "while I've got you here, I wonder if you wouldn't mind filling me in on a couple of things. For example, let's say the 'props,' meaning the catafalque and coffin, are Victorian. How might I, uh, track down the source?"

"I could help you with that, but, you know, my first thought is they were already on the premises."

"Here at the house, you mean?"

"Well, probably not in sight, but it wouldn't be that unusual in a stately house like this for a family coffin to be kept in the basement or attic."

"That's interesting. Didn't know that."

"Interesting?" Mosey said.

He looked at Mosey. "Well, not just anyone would have known about a coffin in the attic, now would they?"

"No, I see what you mean."

"Oh, and another thing." He turned back to Nadia. "Did you happen to notice the white gloves on the shelf underneath the coffin?"

"What gloves?" Mosey cut in.

"Five pair of identical white gloves. I didn't see them at first, but Dr. McGinnis called them to my attention."

"That's odd," Nadia said.

"How so?"

"There ought to be six, a pair for each pallbearer."

"Hmm," Mosey said. "Wonder what happened to the other pair of gloves."

Chapter Three

Red Oaks
Monday, March 15, 2010, 9:45 a.m.

Once Mosey and Nadia had left Red Oaks, Olivera put on his mask and retreated inside. "Springer," he yelled as he entered the foyer.

Springer appeared from the library. "Yeah, Chief?"

"You get the windows up?"

"That was the last one. The sashes are broken on a couple. We had to prop 'em open."

"You'd think in a place like this, everything would be shipshape." Olivera looked up at the chandelier, then toward the stair rails ascending and twisting to the upper floor.

"These old places are hard to keep up, Chief. In fact, I'd say it's been a while since this one got a good once over."

Olivera casually ran his finger across the console by the stairs, wiping away a thin layer of dust.

"Yep," Springer continued, "hard to keep a place like this clean." He looked around the foyer, then back at Olivera. "What next, Chief?"

"Where's Reagan?"

"I left him in the kitchen."

"Let's see if Dr. McGinnis has finished up, and if

she has, go ahead and take the body out."

They entered the parlor, now brightly lighted, where McGinnis, having completed her examination of the body, was gazing at a mount of a prowling coyote, one of several taxidermy animals stationed in front of a grand fireplace.

"Amazing," McGinnis said, "the delicate execution of the mounts."

"Indeed, I've never seen so many outside of a museum." Olivera checked out the free-standing mounts and then shifted his attention to the specimens displayed in tall wooden cabinets on either side of the fire surround. He peeked into one that was filled with birds. "Yes," he said, "all delicately executed." He paused to marvel at a stunning bird menacing a smaller one valiantly guarding its nest. "And rather dramatic, isn't it?" He moved on to the cabinet on the other side of the fireplace, where a mix of creatures returned his gaze with shimmering glass eyes. He recognized a barred owl, a couple of mourning doves, a squirrel, and a rabbit. Spotting a small furry creature with puffy cheeks and two prominent front teeth, he turned to McGinnis. "What's that?"

She approached the case. "A gopher. You've never seen a gopher?"

"I guess I'm just a city guy."

She leaned in to get a better look. "You know, these mounts were quite popular with the Victorians, sort of a status symbol."

"I imagine they didn't come cheap."

"Actually, they were the handiwork of Lenna's husband Jim Fortney. He was a veterinarian and, supposedly, not at all a fan of hunting. I've heard it said

24

he took up taxidermy to settle his nerves."

"Really?"

"Lenna, rest her soul, was quite a handful."

"How's that?"

"Bossy, controlling…"

"Enough to get her killed?"

"Well, it wasn't he, if that's what you're thinking. He died some years ago."

He looked back at the lifeless victim a few feet from where he was standing and, shifting his attention to her face, noted the deep frown lines in the forehead and the unappealing shape of the jaw. "Did they have kids?"

She shook her head. "Nope, Miss Lenna lived here all by herself after her husband died. But at one time, she had a ward, Kemena King, who was her cousin, her much younger cousin. When Lenna's father died, the responsibility for Kimmy, as she was called, was passed on to Lenna. But a couple of years later, Kimmy died, too."

"Did you know them well?"

"Not that well, but I've been here before."

"Did the place look like it does now?"

"I don't really remember. I was just a kid, but I do recall seeing the animals."

"I bet you had nightmares." He chuckled.

"Most likely."

He turned away from the coffin to face McGinnis. "So, what do you make of it?"

"I'll stick with what I said before. Strangulation, likely."

"Manual or ligature?"

"I want to get a better look at the bruising before I say for sure."

"What about time of death?"

"Definitely not today. Some hours ago, twenty-four maybe."

"So, we're looking at Sunday morning, more or less."

"About that."

"See anything else?" he asked.

"Unfortunately, the crime scene has been wiped down rather well."

"And with all this dust, new fingerprints would be hard to miss."

"True."

"So what about that?" he said. "Why would a woman of significant means keep such a messy house?"

"I wouldn't say messy. Dusty, but everything looks in order."

"Nadia Abboud said the coffin looked like an antique to her. Original Victorian."

"Could be," she said. "I imagine everything here is original to the house."

"Ms. Abboud thought the coffin might have been kept in the basement or the attic, re-used, I suppose."

"I've heard of that," she said with a nod.

"And how would that work?"

"Well, if the family paid a good price for a handcrafted coffin, they would use it for the wake but wouldn't put it in the ground. The better coffins were for display." She bent slightly to take a look at the platform. "In fact, this same catafalque might have been used for generations. The coffin is old-fashioned, but exactly how old it is, I couldn't say. I imagine Nadia would know."

"I always assumed coffins were for burials."

"Yes, the less expensive ones."

"You know, come to think of it"—he scratched his head—"I noticed what looked like a mausoleum off to the left of the house."

"And?"

"Well, I don't know for sure, but I suppose we should take a look." He checked his watch. "First, let's get the body out. I'm anxious to see what the autopsy can tell us." He strode through the foyer to the porch, where Springer and Reagan were waiting. "Springer"—he pulled his mask down—"if you'd help Dr. McGinnis, and, Reagan, let's close the windows before we go. By the way, you men didn't happen to see a key lying around, did you?"

Reagan slipped his hand into his pants pocket and brought out a key chain full of keys. "I figured you might want these, Lieutenant." He tossed him the keys. "They were hanging from the kitchen door."

"They look old."

"They *are* old. Looks to me like a set of old skeleton keys. Not sure what the big one's for, but the middle one fits the kitchen door."

"Huh. Let's see if it works for this one." Olivera inserted the key. "Fits. That's good."

McGinnis came out on the porch. "So you found the keys to the house?"

"Sure did. Reagan ran across them in the kitchen. You ready to move the body?"

"I am."

While McGinnis and Springer headed for the SUV and Reagan went back in to close the windows, Olivera proceeded toward the small structure he'd guessed to be a mausoleum. It was a short distance away in the shade of a stand of cypresses. Reaching the door, he found it ajar, but before going in, he inserted the largest of the skeleton keys in the lock. It fit. Then, pushing back the door, he came face to face with a room full of coffins, lined up on racks along both sides of the narrow space. All of them bore a striking resemblance to the coffin in the parlor.

His eyes drifted to the marble floor. Unlike the coffins, the floor was clean, too clean, in fact, as if someone had recently mopped it. He walked out and waved to McGinnis, who was pushing a stretcher toward the house with Springer's help. "Hey, Dr. McGinnis, could you step over here for a second?"

Leaving Springer to handle the stretcher, she called out as she approached, "Shall I get the camera?"

"Take a look first, if you don't mind."

When she reached the door, he pointed to the keyhole. "The largest of the keys fits, but the door wasn't locked. In fact, it was ajar."

"You'd think they would have kept it locked."

"Yeah, seems that way, doesn't it? But my knowledge of family mausoleums would fit in a thimble." Going inside, he took a small flashlight from his pocket and flashed it across the floor. "Looks almost too clean, especially considering what we saw in the house."

"Hmm. So, you're thinking somebody cleaned it?"

"Right, and for some particular reason." He ran a beam of light across the top of the coffins. "Why clean the floor but not the coffins?"

"Well, if the perp came in here, he wouldn't have wanted to leave footprints."

"Of course."

"So I'd better get some pictures."

While McGinnis ran back to her vehicle for the camera, Olivera scanned the walls, floor, and ceiling, but, finding nothing, stepped out on the walk that led to the porch.

Chapter Four

As soon as Olivera returned to the station, he sat down at his computer and began typing up the handwritten notes he'd made at the crime scene. As he recorded the names of the victim, her late husband, and her ward, it suddenly occurred to him that he hadn't asked McGinnis about the young ward's death. He called out for Springer to come in.

"What you need, Chief?" He paused at the doorway and rubbed a finger along the top of the partition. "You know, this place could use a cleanin', too."

"Yeah, I suppose so. Have a seat, Springer."

Springer settled his substantial figure into the metal chair beside the desk and extended his chubby legs in front of him.

Olivera leaned away from the computer. "When we were at Red Oaks, Dr. McGinnis was filling me in on the victim's background and happened to mention that her ward Kemena King died young. I forgot to ask *how* she died. You know anything about that?"

"Yeah, I remember that. Sure do. I reckon it was a good ten years ago."

"You remember the circumstances?"

"Oh, yeah. It was kind of a big deal. She died in a boating accident. At least I think that's what they decided, but there was a lot of talk around town."

"What kind of talk?"

"Oh, I don't know." Springer rubbed the back of his neck. "Some people didn't think it was entirely straightforward, like maybe it wasn't just an accident."

Olivera leaned closer. "You mean, like somebody else was involved?"

"No, I don't think anybody was involved exactly. It was more like the boat was not working properly and she should have been told. That sort of thing. You could ask old Dr. McGinnis. He must have been the coroner on the case."

"I think I'll ask young Dr. McGinnis first. Likely she'll remember. Another thing, Springer." He gestured toward the evidence board on the partition by the door. "I can't imagine that puny little evidence board is going to work for this particular investigation."

Springer sat up straight and glanced around at the board. "Why you say that, Chief?"

"Because, well, there's just not enough room." Admittedly, he had little evidence so far, but he had a hunch that, before he closed the case, he would have a great deal, certainly more than the evidence board would accommodate. He rocked back in his high-back Executive. "We don't have anything bigger? Before it's over and done, we'll have enough to fill, gosh, I don't know, three or four of those."

Springer tilted his head. "Well, I don't know. They been working for us so far."

Olivera, feeling a little out of sorts, got up from his chair and walked over to the window. He stuck his hands in his pockets and looked back at Springer. "I can't quite put my finger on it, but for some reason, I have this nagging sensation that this is going to be huge. I don't know why."

Springer scratched his head. "Well, I can think of a couple of things. I mean, can't you? You know, Lenna Fortney was a big deal around here. Now, poof, gone in a second, and she wasn't all that old. That's gonna stir things up, don't you think? Well, I mean it could."

"I reckon so." Olivera shrugged. "How old was she, by the way?"

"I think she and my momma were in high school together, so that'd make her about fifty-five, sixty."

"Yep, not that old, not really. From what I saw, I would have guessed older."

"I'm pretty sure she was about Momma's age."

"Well, I guess people age in different ways."

"But you know, Chief, when a big business woman like Miss Lenna dies, things start to change hands. Like, I mean, who's gonna take over the firm and all those little businesses? For years, she's been making the decisions, lots of decisions that affect people's lives. Who'll make 'em now?"

"Gosh, it really never occurred to me...I mean, I wasn't aware of all that."

"But you see, it's not exactly something that catches your eye. The accounting business isn't as in-your-face, let's say, as a cotton gin or a towboat. The whole accountant gig isn't carried out under the lights. It's a bit more behind the scenes, if you catch my drift."

Olivera patted his chin a couple of times and, turning away from the window, faced Springer. "That's a valid point. Yep, it is, indeed." He walked back to his chair and sat. "And, if you think about it," he continued, "from that backstage perspective, so to speak, they must be able to see things that others don't. Well, since a person's financial affairs for the most part remain private. And you know what else?"

"What?" Springer raised an eyebrow.

"In a small town like Hembree, I bet King Accounting has a pretty good handle on the financial affairs of a lot of businesses. Wouldn't you agree?"

"Of course it does. As far as I know, that's the only accounting firm around here."

"So think about it. With Lenna Fortney no longer around…"

Springer tilted his head. "Yeah, Chief, that's what I was getting at."

"So you were, Springer, so you were." Olivera reared back and gazed off into space, unsure of the direction he and Springer were headed with their speculations. He picked up a pencil off the desk and stuck it back in the pen holder, then looked across at Springer, who appeared to be somewhat lost in thought as well. "So, what about that evidence board?" He gestured toward the board.

"Well…" Springer let out a sigh. "I reckon I could put up another one if you think you need the space. Want me to bring—"

"But it's not really set up for that, is it?" Olivera expressed his disapproval with a half frown. "Oh, well, I suppose I could ignore the writing."

"Writing?"

"Yeah, right there in the center." He pointed toward the middle of the board. "*Conclusion.* Maybe use one board for physical evidence, one for people of interest, and one for conclusion."

Springer raised and lowered his brow. "Not ideal, but it'll have to do till I can get a bigger board."

"Yeah, let's do that. Bring me two more."

"Right...one each for physical evidence, people of interest, and—"

"Conclusion."

"Right, conclusion," Springer repeated, then added, "though it's hard to imagine where this is going."

"Now, don't go jinxing it, Springer." Olivera felt a twinge of discomfort and gave his shoulder a little rub.

"Whatcha mean *jinxing it*?" Springer shot him a quick look, slightly reproachful.

"Well...I didn't really mean jinxing it. I'm just feeling a tad bewildered, and I'd rather not start out that way. I'd prefer to start on a more positive note, like, well, let's think the whole thing is going to unravel right before our eyes." He smiled as he splayed his hands.

Springer shook his head. "Not meaning to rain on your parade or nothin'—"

"I know, I know. I guess I'm just trying to look on the bright side. To be honest, thinking about all the possibilities—"

"Possibilities?" Springer cut in.

"Yeah, I'm thinking the people of interest alone could be huge. Family, friends, associates..."

"You're thinking Miss Lenna knew the perp, are you, Chief?"

"Oh, yeah." If there was one thing Olivera was sure of, it was that no stranger had committed this crime. Well, unless someone she knew had masterminded the whole thing and hired another person to execute it. But setting that thought aside, he felt confident that at least one or two people from Fortney's close circle would have vital information. At least that.

"You sound pretty sure about that." As Springer spoke, he absentmindedly rubbed his hands against the fabric of his khakis.

"Well, think about it. No stranger would have gone to all that trouble. I mean really, who does that?"

"The staging, you mean?"

"But besides that, who would have known?" Pausing, Olivera opened the bottom drawer and grabbed a bottle of water. He unscrewed the cap and took a drink. "I mean, wouldn't you need to know a good bit about the family, the place?"

Springer's lips parted, but before he could get the words out, Olivera added another twist to the mystery. "Oh, and what about this? That coffin in the parlor looked just like the ones in the mausoleum."

"Seriously?" Springer gaped.

"Somebody went to an awful lot of trouble. And another thing, think about the timing. The perp must have planned every little thing to perfection, so he'd have ample time to commit the crime, set up the scene, tidy up after himself, not only in the house but in the mausoleum before Mosey Frye arrived." He drank again from the bottle before setting it on the desk. "I figure he had to have known about the appointment, otherwise...You know, he even left a message stuck to the mailbox, telling them to go ahead in. Who could have known all that, planned all that? Yeah, this wasn't any spur of the moment deal, Springer. Pulling together the props, I mean the gown and slippers, the coffin, the catafalque."

"Catafalque?"

"The platform the coffin was on."

"Catafalque," Springer repeated. "Well, I can't argue with any of that. Kinda gives you the creeps, don't it?" He stood bobbing his head. "Somebody went to all that crazy trouble and then scooted out of there ahead of Mosey and Nadia."

"And where to start—family, friends, associates? Who would have done all that?"

"It's almost like he did it for her benefit, but she was dead. Didn't see any of it. What a waste."

"No, I think he did it for his own benefit. I'm thinking somebody with a hefty grudge, somebody who seriously despised the woman." Olivera sat tapping his chin with his fingers. It was unnerving to think that so much seething hate was out there in his little town, and he was going to do his best—

"If there's a person out there who hated her that much"—Springer cut into his thoughts—"it'd be awful hard to keep that under wraps. Somebody has to know."

"Yeah, probably so. And you know something else I've realized? If someone, say, Lenna Fortney, stirs up animosity in one individual, you can bet they'll stir it up in lots of others. I wouldn't be surprised to learn that a number of people had it in for her. And that reminds me of something. People kill with guns, knives, blunt instruments. But strangulation, especially with the hands, suggests the offender knew the victim. And driven by rage, hatred, some deep emotion, he decided to squeeze the life out of her, or him. It'd be like, in this case, he was saying to the world, I eliminated Lenna Fortney, removed this vile individual from the face of the earth. She's no longer alive, because I dealt with it."

"Lordy!" Springer shuddered. "Somebody hated her that much?"

"Yeah, I believe they did." Olivera gave a couple of enthusiastic nods. "And here's another point to consider. I think the perpetrator actually wanted the body to be discovered, wanted it to be viewed. Think about it. Isn't that the opposite of what most killers want?"

"Course." Springer nodded, mimicking Olivera's enthusiasm. "I agree with everything you've said, Chief, but you've got to realize—"

"Realize what?" Olivera glimpsed at the computer screen, then turned back toward Springer.

"As I was saying before, Miss Lenna was well known around here. If she had a row with somebody, it's likely it would have been noticed. People gossip. You know that, Chief. What I'm saying is that if somebody wanted to take her out, they'd have to consider the consequences. I mean, they wouldn't want to come under suspicion."

"Yeah, somebody might automatically suspect them, and knowing that—"

Springer tapped him on the arm. "But you know what they could do? They could try to come up with some kind of sneaky distraction plan, like try to shift the blame onto somebody else."

"Which would make our job all the harder." Olivera nodded. "We'd have to look for the likely killer without losing site of a possible frame up. But Springer"—he twisted toward the partition door—"I'm afraid we may be getting ahead of ourselves."

"We are?"

"Yeah. I don't want to get too deep into motive before I get a better grip on the physical evidence. You know what I mean?" Olivera stood and reached for his hat.

"You leaving, Chief?" Springer stepped back, clearing the way for Olivera's departure.

"Yeah, I need to get back to the morgue, see if Dr. McGinnis has come up with anything."

"You reckon she has? It hasn't been that long."

"But hang on tight, you and Reagan both. We may need to head over to the crime scene this afternoon. And this time, I plan on thoroughly examining the mausoleum and the rest of the house. We didn't pick up much this morning. Surely there are footprints, fingerprints, other than the victim's. I'd like to gather as much physical evidence as possible before I start interviewing people of interest, which is going to eat up quite a bit of time."

"Won't be pleasant, if you ask me," Springer commented.

A tad perplexed, Olivera asked Springer what he meant.

Springer shook his head, hesitated, and then continued. "Those folks over at the accounting firm... Well, let's just say it ain't gonna be smooth sailing."

Olivera didn't really know the people Springer was talking about. He'd never even set foot in the place. "Tough customers?"

"You could say that."

Olivera adjusted his hat and buttoned the top button of his sports coat. "I guess I'd better get my act together, then." He checked his watch. "It's after eleven. I'll be in touch after lunch."

As he headed off to Delta Infirmary, Olivera decided to drive by King Accounting, though he wasn't exactly sure why. He doubted he would recognize any of the employees who might be entering or leaving the building. He'd had no occasion to go there, for personal or professional reasons. He was relying mainly on McGinnis to fill him in. She was sure to know something about the people who ran the firm. In any event, he wanted to take a look at the storefront so as to get a better mental picture of the business.

He pulled up to the building and, as he stepped out, looked both ways along Lee Street. The office of Frye, Frye, and Humphrey was a few doors down, and, boy, oh boy, he'd certainly crossed that threshold more times than he could count. As a matter of fact, he was already feeling an itch to go there again to visit the intriguing head of the firm, Carlotta Humphrey, though he somehow doubted he'd make it there ahead of Mosey Frye, who he confidently assumed had a scheme of her own in the making.

He chuckled. It was interesting how that relationship, which had started out rancorous, was beginning to seem downright advantageous. During the last case, i.e., the whole Morris House affair, he'd come to regard Mosey as an ally. Feeling in his jacket pocket, his fingers touched his lucky charm, the poker chip he had taken from a table drawer in the Morrises' secret cellar. He retrieved it from his pocket and examined it closely. When he'd first run across it, he'd thought it was ivory but soon realized it was crafted of bone. With a satisfied smile, he gave it a good rub. As pleasant as it was to have something a tad magical within reach, he'd come to realize that the true magic resided not in the charm but in Mosey. Her extraordinary knack for detecting the darker side of Hembree's citizenry never ceased to amaze him.

He dropped the chip back in his pocket and got on with the task at hand—to gain a better understanding of

King Accounting, a place he'd passed a hundred times but had never really stopped to look. He walked over to the brass plaque beside the door. Below the name of the owner, the names of the other partners were listed: Edward T. Neville, James Fortney, Sarah J. Williams, Harvey C. Smith, Anne Graham Bentley... Quite a business, it seemed for a small place like Hembree. The door was solid wood without a single window to sneak a peek through. But that made sense when you thought about it, especially considering what he and Springer had been chatting about earlier. Indeed, accounting carried with it a sense of privacy as well as a certain gravity. It was as if Hembree's financial health was somehow configured within their clever calculations, like a secret code waiting to be deciphered. In reality, he didn't have a clue about what accountants knew or didn't know. But he could imagine how fascinating it must be to have complete knowledge of the assets of a person—or a town, for that matter. It'd be more or less equivalent to knowing the ups and downs of a place. And all of that, neatly organized in books. Well, probably not books anymore. Computers, more likely.

It suddenly struck him how much McGinnis had helped with the technology during the Sunny Banks investigation. The data she'd retrieved from Johnny Eldridge's computer turned out to be quite valuable. And now, as he envisioned the numerous files he would have to browse and the daunting number of email messages he would have to peruse, he murmured a quiet prayer, hoping he could count on McGinnis's support again.

He checked his watch. It was almost eleven thirty. The Tavernette was right across the street. Should he go ahead and grab a bite to eat? Save his visit to the morgue for later? Maybe he ought to call McGinnis, see if she would like to join him. Nope, he didn't want to distract her. The sooner he knew cause of death, the better. He would order a sandwich at the bar and head to the morgue after lunch.

Chapter Five

Jeremiah Java Café
Monday, March 15, 9:45 a.m.

When Mosey and Nadia pulled out of the driveway at Red Oaks, it was almost ten o'clock. They drove straight back to the Jeremiah Java, where Nadia had parked her SUV. In a rush to get to the store, Nadia jumped in and zoomed off, but Mosey, noticing the parking lot had cleared out a bit, decided to step inside to have a quick word with Aaron or, if he wasn't available, then Lula. It occurred to her that one of them might have spotted something relevant on the road or, passing Red Oaks, might have seen a car parked at the front. Or perhaps someone dropped by the café for a coffee at an unusual time of day. She was hoping for something, anything that deviated from the norm. But how could she inquire about the goings-on up and down Little Smith without revealing prematurely everything she knew? Uh-huh, that was a problem, because Olivera had explicitly instructed her and Nadia to keep it all to themselves. And if she wanted to avoid losing the man's trust, it simply would not do to announce the murder at the Jeremiah Java Café.

Standing in the parking lot, she lifted a forearm to her nose and sniffed, then repeated the action with the other forearm, checking to see if she'd carried away the stench of the parlor. Just then, the café door creaked open, and Lula emerged onto the porch.

"Mosey, you okay?"

Mosey turned to see Lula's elegant figure leaning casually against a post. "Why, of course I am. I was just checking to see if I smelled like cigar smoke. I had this jacket on last night over at Al's."

"I totally get you." Lula laughed. "I come away from there smelling like a chimney every time. Those dudes puffing away right at the entrance…"

Mosey walked toward the porch. "Speaking of which, you weren't there last night, were you?"

"At Al's? Yes, as a matter of fact I was."

"Does it creep you out, driving on this lonely road at night?" Mosey asked this as she climbed the steps. "You hardly ever see a soul, and when you do—"

"You sure you're all right?" Lula frowned and looked down her nose.

"Well, I've been hearing rumors lately."

"What kind of rumors?"

"I'd better not say. I wouldn't want to get somethin' started that's not true." Mosey stared off in the distance, gazing one way and the other up and down Little Smith.

"But Mosey, I work here. I come here every day. If something's going on, I have a right to know."

"Well, if you put it that way," Mosey granted.

"Nothin' to do with drugs, is it?"

"In Hembree? I don't think so, but you never know. You haven't seen anything, well, unexpected, have you?"

Lula frowned again. "What sort of 'unexpected'?"

"Any cars passing by, people you don't usually see

43

out here? Or people dropping by the café at an unusual hour?"

"Let me think." She looked down at the porch floor, then up at Mosey. "We don't get a lot of through traffic. It's the regulars I see mostly. But there was a man in here the other day I hadn't seen before."

"So, I guess you don't know his name."

"Actually, I *do* know his name."

"Who was it?"

"I heard Aaron speak to him, called him Mr. Patterson…something like that, then shook his hand and said he was glad to see him. He ordered a cup of coffee to go, then headed out. He wasn't in here more than five, ten minutes. Seemed like he was in a hurry. I watched him drive off. It's a little eccentricity of mine, looking to see what kind of car people drive."

"So what was he driving?"

"A fancy new ragtop, fire engine red."

"Did you recognize the make?"

"Naw, but I could ask. Aaron seemed to know the guy."

"That's okay, don't bother him. But I tell you what, if you see anything that strikes you as peculiar, would you mind giving me a buzz?"

"You aren't tracking down some murderer, are you?" Lula looked askance. "I heard all about that business up at the Bilyeu place." She paused as a pensive look crossed her face. "I reckon it's not the Bilyeu place anymore."

"Actually, A. B. Bilyeu is staying there right now," Mosey said, "he and his nephew Cecil DeGroat."

"Huh. I thought the last Bilyeu died…Sister Clare."

"She did, but her New Orleans cousins inherited the

place, and they've started fixing it up."

"I think I know who you mean. Just the other day, an old guy and a young, snooty-looking fellow with a ponytail—"

"That would be they," Mosey said with a nod.

"They been in here 'bout every day. They aren't the ones—" Lula stopped, her eyes filling with apprehension.

"Oh, no. They're okay. A little on the secretive side, but I'm pretty sure they're okay." Mosey checked her watch. "I'd better get going, but, like I said, if you see anything that strikes you as out of the ordinary—"

"I'll let you know, sure will."

Mosey, thinking she'd invested enough time and with little return, hopped in her old truck and wheeled off toward town. "A guy in a red ragtop, Patterson," she said under her breath. She couldn't think of anyone right off who matched that description and, for sure, a fancy convertible would have caught her eye. "Maybe Nadia will know."

As Mosey was driving back to town, she decided she would stop by Shepherd Realty. Her listing had flopped, at least temporarily, but there might be a chance to negotiate with the heirs of the deceased. Unfortunately, her clients, when alive, didn't have a habit of staying that way for long.

Mosey, what the heck's going on now, child?

"Daddy, I was hoping to hear from you," she said, responding to the voice of her late father Ellis Frye. Though she alone could detect her father's presence, a time or two she'd received a funny look from a bystander. She'd kept this paranormal phenomenon under wraps for quite a few years until, finally, she stumbled upon the right moment to tell Nadia, who hadn't really understood a word she'd told her but, as a supportive friend, had somehow managed to embrace the idea.

Mosey cast a sidelong glance at the spot where she imagined him to be. "Daddy, it's Miss Lenna. Nadia and I found her dead in the parlor at Red Oaks, looking every bit as hateful as she did in life."

Don't speak ill of the dead, Mosey.

"Sorry." She'd gone and stuck her foot in it. "I didn't mean—"

You never do, do you? But one of these days, that mouth of yours—

"I apologized, didn't I?" Which is more than Miss Lenna ever did. "I feel sorry for Olivera."

Ha-ha-ha. Now I've heard it all.

"Just think, Daddy." She glanced away from the road ahead to take another look at the seat beside her. "Imagine the list of suspects. Half of Hembree would have liked to throttle that harridan."

A sad legacy to leave behind.

"Yeah I suppose so."

Strangled, was she?

"She sure was."

By hand or instrument?

"Olivera didn't say—probably didn't know."

Yeah, they'll have to check the bruising.

"But, Daddy, can you believe it? It's all started up again, and this time I didn't even have a chance to list the place."

Any idea who might have done it?

"You're asking me? If anybody would know—"

Don't look at me. He let out a chuckle.

Mosey froze but then laughed right out loud. "Daddy, you kill me."

The chuckle echoed, then gradually faded into nothing. Her daddy had departed back to wherever he'd come from, leaving her to work through the mysterious death of Lenna Fortney, a woman of standing but not at all liked among the locals, and for good reason.

Mosey didn't really know much about Fortney firsthand, but over time, she had formed an opinion based almost entirely on hearsay. Lenna had apparently been dissatisfied with her position as head partner at the accounting firm and was constantly looking for new ways to increase her already enormous wealth, which led her to buy up numerous little businesses in and around Hembree. When she thought about it, Mosey really did feel sorry for Olivera. She seriously doubted he knew much about the complex inner workings of the Hembree business community. If Fortney's demise was somehow connected to her business dealings, and Mosey had a hunch that it might be, she wondered if Olivera could even begin to understand the true motive driving the crime.

Though no expert herself, she was pretty sure she had a better chance of working it out than he did. If she could just figure out how to go about it, where to start. Her stepaunt Carlotta Humphrey's door was always open, though Mosey was a little embarrassed to impose on Carlotta again. She'd done it so many times before. There was also Dot Cowsley, always anxious to hear Mosey out and offer advice if she could. But then again, she'd bent Dot's ear a thousand times. Who else might be able to give her a little direction?

Upon her return to town, she drove straight to

Shepherd Realty and, pulling into the parking lot, stopped alongside Saffron's car. "The saints be praised!" she muttered. John Earle's jeep stood right next to it in the space by the entrance. Must be a sign. And that's exactly where she'd start…with John Earle. It was he who'd sent her out to Red Oaks in the first place, and now she would deliver the outcome of the errand to the man himself.

As she strolled down the brick sidewalk to the quaint cottage-style building, she enjoyed the delightful array of blooming plants that adorned the path. The tulips were in full flower along with sunny daffodils, elegant daylilies, and fragrant hyacinths. As she made her way toward the door, a gentle breeze lightly brushed against her face, carrying the delicate scent of the lemon-yellow primrose that thrived in the shadow of the building.

Passing through the door, she caught a glimpse of a bowl of camellias on Saffron's desk. "Oh, my, what a nice change of scenery."

"Huh?" was Saffron's greeting.

"Well, after what I've just come from."

"What happened?" John Earle asked, curiosity in his tone. He stood and offered Mosey the stool he'd dragged up to Saffron's desk.

Mosey took a breath and let it out. "I don't know how to tell you this."

"Spit it out, girl," John Earle said.

"Brace yourself."

"I'm braced."

"Miss Lenna is dead."

"No"—his jaw dropped—"surely not."

Mosey nodded. "I saw her with my own eyes."

"I can't believe it." He dragged up another stool for

himself.

"What happened?" Saffron said.

"It was just awful, unbelievable." She slid onto the stool. "Nadia and I got to Red Oaks for the appointment. I was about to knock on the door. But then I noticed a note on the mailbox and I read it."

"What'd it say?" John Earle asked.

"It said to come on in, the door was open."

"You mean it wasn't locked?"

"Right. Closed but not locked."

"So, what'd you do?" Saffron asked.

"We did like it said and went in. Everything was dark. The lights in the foyer and up the stairs were turned off, but a faint light was coming from one of the front rooms. So, we walked that way, and just as we passed the threshold to the parlor, get this, we saw a coffin, all set up, like for a wake."

"No way," John Earle exclaimed.

Mosey slowly shook her head. "Just like I'm telling you. There she was, Miss Lenna, all laid out in the coffin, dead as a dodo."

"Dead and already laid out?" John Earle said with a tone of disbelief.

"She was, but it was pretty clear…" Mosey's voice trailed off as she hesitated, feeling uncertain about getting into the grim details.

"What?" Saffron urged her to continue.

"Well, it seemed clear to me, from the smell, that the body hadn't been embalmed."

Saffron covered her mouth and nose, as if she were smelling what Mosey and Nadia had smelled.

"Good god a' mighty!" John Earle got up from his stool and started to pace.

"Nadia called 911, and we got out of there as soon as we could. Before long, the paramedics showed up, and a little later, the police and the coroner. We stayed outside with Springer and Reagan while the others masked up and went in. After a while the paramedics left. Then Olivera came out and told us Miss Lenna had been strangled."

"My lord." Saffron crossed herself. "It's not safe living in this town anymore. If a powerful woman like Miss Lenna isn't safe, who is, for the love of—?"

"Oh, Saffron," Mosey said with a dismissive wave of her hand, "this was no random homicide. Whoever did it, knew her, and I'd say—"

"What?" Saffron urged.

"Well, it's my guess he or she *despised* her."

"Despised her?" John Earle paced back toward Saffron's desk and perched on the stool.

"Either that or despised something she did or was going to do. Or I suppose fear could have been the motive. Miss Lenna was a formidable woman, to put it nicely. I've heard her called worse, haven't you?" She looked at John Earle.

"Yeah, I guess so," he muttered, lost in thought, as if he were trying to figure out who could have been responsible for such a horrendous act. "Did Olivera have any idea…?"

"I don't think so, but when Nadia and I left, they were still poking around the place. And, by the way—" She stopped, suddenly remembering what Olivera had said about not saying a word to anybody. "Olivera told us to keep it quiet."

"Well," Saffron said, "I bet it's circulating online right now. How you gonna keep something like that under wraps?"

"Yeah, I imagine you're right about that. But I don't want Olivera pointing a finger at me. So be careful who you tell, and for god's sake, don't say I told you."

"The people at the accounting firm have to be told, don't you think?" John Earle said. "And don't the police have to get in touch with the next of kin?"

"I wonder who that would be," Mosey said. "She doesn't have any family left, does she?"

"Maybe a cousin or two. Not sure. She's got a nephew by marriage over at the accounting firm."

"Who's that?"

"What's-his-name." John Earle snapped his fingers. "Bud Fortney, Jim Fortney's brother's boy."

"Oh, yeah." Saffron nodded. "I know who you mean. A young fellow."

"Yeah, he's been at the firm a year or two."

"How do they track down next of kin anyway?" Saffron asked.

"Damned if I know," John Earle said.

"I don't know, either," Mosey said. "But around here, it ought to be simple enough. Most anybody on the street could tell you that."

Saffron scooted back in her chair and took a long look at Mosey.

"What are you looking at?" Mosey asked.

"You."

"Yeah." John Earle focused his attention on Mosey.

"You must have some theory," Saffron said.

"Not yet. I'm thinking this is going to be a tough one."

Chapter Six

Shepherd Realty
Monday, March 15, 10:45 a.m.

Mosey sat at her desk, pondering the situation. What she'd said to Saffron was true. She didn't have a single theory, not yet, as to who might have sent Lenna Fortney prematurely to her grave. Despite her time in years, she seemed to be in excellent health. She still worked fulltime at the accounting firm as well as keeping a watchful eye on a number of other companies. That might be a good place to start, she thought, with Fortney's business affairs. The firm was right on the Square, only steps from Frye, Frye, and Humphrey. If anything of a visible nature was involved, surely Dot Cowsley or Carlotta Humphrey would have taken notice.

While mulling over the situation, Mosey mentally strolled from one shop to the next until she ended up at the Tavernette. She'd wager the people who worked there, Ms. Tisdale at the hostess station, Clinton at the bar, Ruby and Miffy in the dining room, knew more about the carryings-on in Hembree than people would imagine. Even though Fortney didn't appear to be a regular, the staff might have overheard chatter about either her or her business dealings. Surely some of the King personnel stopped in from time to time. As soon as the news of the head partner's demise got out, Mosey felt certain tongues would wag. And she would make darn sure that she was there to listen.

Hearing a ring, she fished her phone out of her tote and checked the name on the screen. "Robert, what's up?"

"I was hoping you could tell me. I was just over at Red Oaks with the students from my eight thirty class. I was planning to stop by the place, have them take a look at the mausoleum, but crime scene tape was stretched all across the front of the house. Didn't you have an appointment with Lenna Fortney this morning?"

"Indeed, I did. Nadia and I, actually. " She stopped, suddenly feeling the need to swear Robert to secrecy. "You can't mention this to anyone, understand?"

"Of course, but what?"

"Lenna Fortney is dead," she half whispered.

"Dead? What do you mean dead? I talked to her just—When was that? Saturday?"

"Then you might be one of the last people to have seen her alive. I'm figuring when we found her, she'd been dead a while."

"What do you mean *when you found her*?"

Robert's question came across as a little naïve. "Robert, of course, I found her. Who else?"

"I see what you mean."

"Well, to make a long story short, when we got there, nobody answered the door, but it was unlocked, and we went in. She was in the parlor, strangled, according to Olivera."

"She was just lying there on the floor?"

"No, she was in a coffin."

"Hey, hold on," Robert interjected, sounding a tad

perplexed. "Just to be clear, was there some kind of gathering going on, I mean, like a wake or something?"

"If there was a wake underway, nobody showed up, other than the deceased. Poor thing, lying there all alone, dressed in black, head to toe. Prettiest little black satin slippers on her feet."

"Mosey, you are making this up."

"Good lord, no! Who could dream up such a thing?"

"You and Nadia."

"No, Robert, it all happened just like I said. Ask Nadia if you don't believe me."

Robert gasped.

"What?"

"I just had the most terrible thought. What if, instead of you and Nadia, *I'd* shown up with the students?"

"Oh, Robert, that would have been—Gosh. I guess it's a good thing we arrived ahead of you. But what were you doing at Red Oaks?"

"My eight thirty is doing a service-learning project. They're cleaning old gravestones at the Civil War Cemetery. In fact, I just got back to campus. We were going to have a look at the mausoleum. I spoke to Fortney, and she said it'd be okay."

"Really?"

"Yeah, some of the students are looking for projects, and I thought maybe they might want to clean the mausoleum."

"So, you'd already mentioned it to the students?"

"Yeah, they thought it was a great idea."

"Well, you can tell them to forget it. I'm sure Red Oaks will be off-limits for a while. You know, I was hoping to list the place, soon as Fortney decided what she wanted to do. She was thinking about retiring."

"Well, she didn't mention it to me."

"Why would she?"

"Well, I don't know," Robert said. "She might have mentioned it in passing."

"You know, Nadia and I were wondering what would happen to the mausoleum, I mean, if she sold the house. Reckon she'd have the coffins moved?"

"Possibly. Hmm."

"Hmm, what?"

"I was just thinking," he said. "Fortney being the wealthiest woman in Hembree, if not in Dent County, heck, in the Arkansas Delta…"

"How do you know that?" Mosey asked.

"Well, I don't really know, but based on her donations to the college—"

"Really, like how much?"

"I couldn't tell you exactly how much, but millions."

"Millions? That's a shock."

"Yeah, I guess the people at the college were surprised. She has a reputation for being tight-fisted, but she certainly wasn't with us."

"You know what I'm thinking?"

"What?"

"Maybe this evening, we can put out heads together, try to figure out what this is all about. Between you, me, Nadia, and Hugh, maybe we can come up with a few ideas."

"Not sure I like the sound of that," Robert moaned.

She was about to say *why not,* but didn't. It was easy to guess the answer, knowing that her sleuthing didn't sit well with her over-protective husband. But before she could come up with a reasonable retort, he continued.

"You well know what happened at Morris House."

Mosey sighed loudly. "Robert, I have no intention of going back to Red Oaks. But it makes good sense to think through things in a case like this where knowledge of the community is indispensable. Maybe we can help Olivera. He'll never figure it out on his own."

"Oh, Mosey, give the guy some credit."

"I do, he's learning, but I bet he has no idea who Lenna Fortney even was. And he wouldn't have a clue about her little empire."

"Well, you can fill him in when you talk to him. Has he interviewed you and Nadia?"

"Briefly, but there wasn't much to say. I imagine he'll call us in for a formal statement."

"So there's your opportunity."

Mosey didn't accept or reject her husband's suggestion. She just remarked that she needed to get back to work and said she'd be in touch later.

She'd learned a thing or two about the repercussions of spying when back in January, Paul Krueger had jumped out of the bushes and conked her over the head with a chunk of wood. She was lucky the incident hadn't resulted in a serious injury. Even so, she wasn't about to confine herself to the real estate business. Solving crimes had become a passion of hers, and this particular crime seemed especially intriguing.

She remained at her desk a moment longer, continuing her imaginary stroll around the Square. She'd come up with two possible sources of information, her daddy's old law firm and the Tavernette. There was also, of course, the accounting firm itself, but she couldn't think right off of any reason to go there. Her and Robert's income taxes were a snap. Hence, they'd never found the need for an accountant. She wondered if Nadia had an accountant. Though they were best friends, they had never pried into each other's financial affairs. Doing that would have been seen as impolite. Of course, in this instance, money wasn't at the heart of it, now was it? It was about getting her foot in the door of King Accounting. She picked up the phone and tapped on Nadia's name.

"Nadia Abboud speaking."

"Hey, it's me. I wanted to ask you something, but before I do, I'm not trying to pry into your business."

"Mosey…"

"This is not a personal matter, so don't take it that way. Do you happen to have an accountant?"

"Not that it's any of your business—"

"I said it wasn't personal," Mosey cut in. "It's about the case, Lenna Fortney, for heaven's sake."

"Well, yes, we do have an accountant, Daddy and I."

"It wouldn't be King Accounting, would it?"

"Yes, as a matter of fact."

"Oh, good. I'm trying to think of people who own a business on the Square, and I was thinking Frye, Frye, and Humphrey, obviously, and the Tavernette, but the most relevant by a mile would be King Accounting itself. But you see, Robert and I have never used them, never had a need, but I thought maybe you and your daddy, with a business to run and all…"

"I see," Nadia replied, sounding relieved.

"It wouldn't really involve that much. Surely you can think of some excuse to drop in."

"I'll think about it."

"Oh, and by the way," Mosey added, "if you're free

for dinner, what about getting together with Robert and me at Al's?"

"You mean you and Robert and Hugh?"

"Sure, why not?—if he's available. I haven't asked him yet."

"Mosey, when are you going to give up?"

"What do you mean?"

"Turning Hugh and me into a couple?"

"When one of you gets married."

"I may never get married. I'm very happy being single."

"You could be even happier being married to a cool guy like Hugh. Unless, of course, you prefer Dave Morell."

"Oh, right. Just what I need. A long-distance relationship."

"Never mind. But you'd like to go to Al's, wouldn't you?"

"Fine. What time?"

"We'll pick you up a little before seven. That okay?"

After Nadia had agreed to a seven o'clock dinner date, Mosey called Hugh, who happily accepted the invitation. Then, with the afternoon free to plan her investigation of the case, she decided to start with the easiest of her options, a visit to Frye, Frye, and Humphrey.

"Saffron," she said as she strolled through the outer office, "I'm heading over to the Square. I might be back after lunch or I might not. With the Fortney deal falling through, I'm sort of at loose ends."

"You'd better not let John Earle hear you say that."

"Why not, pray tell?"

Saffron laid her newspaper down and looked up.

"People are cutting back right and left, didn't you know?"

"No, I didn't. You think my job is in peril?"

"I don't know. Sometimes I wonder if mine isn't."

"Saffron, I've never heard you talk that way."

"Times are hard, Mosey."

"Robert hasn't said a word."

"Course not, over at the ivory tower, I imagine things are just peachy."

"Speaking of which," Mosey said, changing the subject, "Robert told me just now that Lenna Fortney gave millions to the college."

"That doesn't surprise me. With her wherewithal, she needed all the tax breaks she could lay her hands on, and Blanchard seems like an obvious choice."

"Why you say that?" Mosey asked.

"Haven't you ever noticed? Rich folks have a knack for making their presence felt, bending things to their advantage. And what could be a more convenient means than a college?"

"A college? Why a college?"

"Surely you've heard Robert talk about that. Earmarks, whatever."

"Earmarks?"

"Yeah, when somebody makes a donation, but not just a plain old donation, one with strings attached. You know. They say how the money has to be used."

"Wow, you know what?" Mosey felt a surge of excitement. "I've been sitting here thinking this homicide was related somehow to the business community, but it could be something else entirely. Like maybe it wasn't about business at all."

Saffron responded with a half frown.

"What if it's about philanthropy?"

"Now, how you figure that?" Saffron asked.

"Oh, Saffron, you may have hit the nail on the head. You know I think I'll drop by the Development Office."

"Mosey, wait a second. I didn't say the college had anything to do with this homicide. And besides that, you don't want to go bothering the folks at the Development Office. They just lost one of their own."

Mosey let out a small sigh, her spirits falling. "Oh, well, I suppose they did. Poor old Charles. That was a jolt, wasn't it? I wonder if they've replaced him yet."

"I doubt it. Ask Robert. He'll know."

"Maybe. He doesn't seem to get involved in that sort of thing."

"Or Hugh. Ask Hugh."

"Yeah, I reckon. We're meeting Hugh for dinner."

"Uh-huh," Saffron said with a knowing chuckle.

Mosey looked at her askance. "I swanee. I have the most suspicious set of friends known to mankind. If it's not Nadia, it's you, and if it's not you, it's Robert."

Saffron broke into a full laugh. "Mosey, you are easy. We know what you're planning before you do."

"So, what am I planning now?"

"Miss Lenna's not even in her grave, and you've already started pondering who knows what, and I'm guessing your first visit will be to Frye, Frye, and Humphrey."

Mosey smiled, then burst out laughing. "I won't deny it. You win."

Chapter Seven

Delta Infirmary
Monday, March 15, 12:30 a.m.

As Olivera entered the morgue, he held onto his belief that the coroner would have already determined the cause of Fortney's passing. The actual cause seemed obvious. What baffled him was the intricate scene surrounding the corpse. Nonetheless, having worked several apparent homicides with Eads McGinnis, he didn't feel truly confident of anything. It'd be just like her to tell him there hadn't even been a crime. He chuckled as he approached the gurney.

"What's so funny?" she asked as she held out a container of salve for his sensitive nose.

He dabbed salve under his nostrils. "I was just thinking." He grinned.

"What?"

He removed his hat and hung it on the hat rack. "Well, it wouldn't be a total shock if you said there *was* no murder."

"I wouldn't get too comfy with that grin." She stepped away from the dissected corpse.

"Don't tell me—" His grin vanished.

"Gotcha," she said with a laugh.

"Very funny." He exhaled and craned his neck for a

closer look at the victim's throat. "So, what have you determined?"

"I'm still sorting things out. You don't want to be too hasty in the case of strangulation, and in this case, I'm checking a couple of things. Not just the bruising around the neck area but also the damage to the larynx and hyoid bone. The amount of pressure the offender has to deliver is a good bit more than in the case of ligature strangulation."

"What did you find?" Olivera asked, his confidence slipping.

"There's some damage to the larynx." She reached for the x-ray of the larynx and clipped it to the viewing light box. "And as you can see, the hyoid is fractured."

He checked the x-ray, taking note of the fracture. "Manual strangulation, then."

"It might be." She redirected his attention to the upper torso, then pointed toward the bruising. "But look at this."

He examined the bruising more closely.

"What do you see?" she asked.

"A good bit of bruising, perhaps more than you would expect."

"Do you see any fingerprints, or more specifically, thumbprints?"

"No, not really." He glanced up.

"And that's what you would expect to see in a standard case of manual strangulation."

"Yes, of course." He stepped back and, raising his hands, positioned them as if he were about to throttle someone. "Thumbprints, juxtaposed and right above the voice box." He lowered his hands, watching McGinnis as she moved toward the other side of the gurney. He looked back at the victim's neck. "No thumbprints. Interesting. So, are you suggesting—?"

"That this isn't a case of manual strangulation? No, not yet. You see, it could still be manual strangulation if the perpetrator used an instrument."

"But wouldn't that mean ligature strangulation?"

"Hold on," she cut in. "I didn't say it wasn't manual strangulation, but if it was, the perpetrator didn't use his hands."

He peered again at the bruising. McGinnis was right. It didn't resemble the thumbprints one would expect to see if the culprit had confronted the victim directly. "I don't suppose he or she could have approached the victim from behind. If that's the case, we wouldn't be seeing thumbprints, just regular fingerprints."

She gave him a sideways glance. "Does that look like fingerprints to you?"

"No, it doesn't." He took a step back.

"It sort of looks like manual strangulation," she explained, "given the damage to the hyoid and larynx, but the pattern of the bruising indicates that the assailant didn't use his hands."

"Right." Olivera wasn't clear where this was going, but he couldn't deny either her facts or logic.

"What I'm wondering is if he used some sort of instrument."

"Okay."

"And if not a ligature," she continued, "like a rope or a wire, what? I'm thinking some sort of tool. Maybe a pipe. Anything the perpetrator could have pressed against the victim's throat."

He moved closer to the body. "So, manual strangulation is the cause of death, but the killer didn't use his hands. He used an instrument of some kind to press against the larynx, thereby causing damage to the larynx and hyoid."

"I believe so," she said. "And, of course, the next thing would be to determine the weapon."

"What does the bruising suggest?"

"Could be a pipe, and if it is, some sort of residue might be found on the victim's skin. So, that's the next step, to look for microscopic bits of metal or whatever the instrument was made of."

"We *do* need to look for a weapon, then."

"Yes, but given the staging, I somehow doubt you will find it, unless, of course, the killer wanted you to."

"If he wanted it found, wouldn't he have—"

She shook her head. "Not this person, I wouldn't think."

"You know"—he leaned against the counter—"with cases of strangulation, one usually eliminates women, since women, we are told, don't have the hand strength to exert the force needed to cut off air passage. But if the killer used a tool, like a pipe, perhaps a woman, a strong woman, could have done it." His eyes widened.

"Uh-huh, I agree. If you imagine a woman pressing down on the victim with a pipe, gripped tightly, well, she could throw her body weight into it, couldn't she? Even press against the pipe with a knee."

"Or she might do this." He held his arms in front of him at shoulder level, pretending to grip a pipe. "She could hold the pipe against the victim's neck and push him up against a wall."

"Yes, that might work, too, if the killer had particularly strong arms. Not just any woman could pull that off. I doubt I could. But a woman who worked out regularly might."

"Oh, McGinnis," he said with a sigh. "I was hoping you would make this easy for me."

"Sorry, Lieutenant, but we don't want to start out on the wrong foot."

"I know." He took another look at the victim. "By the way, those little red spots around the eyes…"

"Petechiae, ruptured capillaries, blood vessels. The pressure builds up, and they burst."

He nodded. "I've seen that before."

"Expected in cases of asphyxiation in general."

"So, anything else?"

She lifted the sheet. "The bruising you usually see when a victim's been dragged."

He checked the underarm area, then stepped away. "That's it, then?"

"So far, but I'll run a couple of tests to make sure I haven't missed anything. I want to look at the stomach contents."

"What about time of death?"

"Approximately twenty-four hours before the discovery of the body."

"Do you have any pictures for me?"

"Yes, would you like to have the hard copies?"

"Yes, Springer is setting up a bigger evidence board for me." He followed her toward her desk at the back of the room. "The small size I've been using didn't seem adequate, not for this case. We're putting one up for physical evidence, one for suspects…"

"You may need more." She picked up a stack of photographs and handed them to him.

As he shuffled through the photos, he stopped to focus on a close-up of the victim's face, then a full view of the death scene. Moving on, he came to the pictures of the mausoleum. "I see you got some good ones of the mausoleum, inside and out."

"You figure there's a connection between the mausoleum and the crime?" She propped herself against the desk.

"I don't know. We need to get back over there. You have to wonder if what we were looking at was a clean-up. But if the killer did that, then why did he leave the door open?"

"Well, I can think of a couple of things off the top of my head." She walked around the desk and took a seat. "Either he cleaned up but then rushed off, thinking he'd come back later. Or maybe he left the door open intentionally."

"You mean as a sort of tease?" He sat in the folding chair next to the desk.

"Yes, seems possible. Maybe he wanted to prove how clever he was, playing a sort of game of hide and seek, as if to say, 'I'm cleaning this up, taking away the evidence I don't want you to see, but at the same time, I want you to know that I was here.' "

"Sounds pretty darn manipulative. Kinda reminds me of Lenna Fortney, or at least that's the rumor I've heard."

"So, somebody of her ilk, like maybe a corporate type, a co-worker, or even a competitor..."

"Could be. Might figure in the motive. Like two big shots butting heads."

"Yeah, like two big bucks," she repeated. "I've encountered that in the animal world but not that often in the human world. I wonder why that is."

"Oh, well, I've seen it on the debate stage and in the

ballpark, but not often in a police station."

"Yeah." Her eyes brightened. "It's like, in the human world, hierarchy keeps things in check, most of the time anyway. Interesting."

"I've never thought of hierarchy as a particularly good thing, but if it keeps people from butting heads, maybe it is."

"But you know, Miss Lenna was on her way out after running King Accounting for decades. Why at this point in her life would she enter into a power struggle. She'd be sort of a lame duck, wouldn't she?"

"Yeah, I guess so. But then there's the other thing. She must have already named her successor or was about to. And that could have caused an upset at the firm."

"Possibly. You've got a lot to think about, Lieutenant," she said with a half smile.

"First I need to get over to King Accounting, see if I can find out something about Fortney's legacy. Like where did she want the firm to go and who did she want to lead it?"

"I thought you were going back to Red Oaks."

"Yeah, there, too." He looked at his watch. "Shall we try to meet later?"

"Sure. I'll see if I can come up with some more answers."

"You do that, please." He pressed his palms together in a pleading gesture. Then, moved toward the front, grabbed his hat, and left the morgue.

A little while later, he arrived at the police station and found Springer and Reagan hovering near the door to his cubicle. "What's up, guys?"

"Just waiting for you, Chief." Springer got to his feet and followed Olivera in. "You find out anything at the morgue?"

"Looks like we've got time and cause of death." He slipped off his hat and jacket and deposited them on the rack.

"I thought that was clear." Springer pushed the folding chair nearer the desk and took a seat.

"It *is* clear, but you know how it is. You have to wait till all the results are in."

Reagan came in and leaned his lanky frame against the filing cabinet. "What'd Dr. McGinnis say?"

"For the time being, she's saying manual strangulation, but the perp didn't use his hands." He pulled the photographs she'd given him out of his briefcase, then opening the desk drawer, picked up a stack of tabs and a box of thumb tacks. "Might as well start with this." He took a seat and held up a picture of the victim in the coffin. "This, guys"—he looked from Springer to Reagan—"is hands down the weirdest aspect of the deal. Just my humble opinion."

"Yeah," Reagan said with a nod, "I'd have to agree."

"But I don't know." Olivera passed the mausoleum photograph to Springer, who took a look and passed it to Reagan.

Reagan shot him a puzzled look. "What are you saying, Lieutenant?"

"Well, it's confusing, and I suspect that's what the killer wants it to be."

"How's that?" Reagan checked the picture again.

"He left the door open." Springer pointed toward the door, slightly cracked.

"So?" Reagan asked.

"I mean, seriously, who leaves a mausoleum door open?"

"I don't know. Whoever cleaned it, I'd imagine," Reagan replied. "Maybe he left it open to let the floor dry."

"But why scrub the floor but not bother with the dust and cobwebs in the house?" Springer pondered aloud. "Just makes you think, don't it?"

"Does seem inconsistent," Reagan agreed.

"I'm thinking the door was left open for our benefit," Olivera said, "as if to say, 'come in and look around.' I mean, they cleaned the floor to get rid of the evidence but left the door open to coax us in."

"Could be." Springer shrugged. "So, you think the perpetrator cleaned the floor, left the door open to call attention—"

"Right, "Olivera interrupted, "but to what? I think it'd be worth checking it out again."

Springer thumbed through the other pictures on the desk and singled out the panoramic view of the parlor. "That is one spooky looking room."

"Not a fan of taxidermy mounts?" Olivera asked as he filled out a tab for the board.

"I don't mind a buck head or two, but all those birds." He shivered. "It gives me the creeps."

Reagan's eyes widened. "It's like they were alive."

Olivera handed Springer the tab where he'd printed "victim," along with the picture of Fortney in the coffin. "Pin that up for me, Springer."

Springer pinned the picture and tab to the board, then glanced back at the snapshot of the parlor. "Yeah, the eyes, I reckon it's the eyes. Can you imagine sitting in there at night with all those eyes staring at you?"

Olivera handed Springer the pictures of the parlor and mausoleum. "Add those to the death scene."

"By the way, Chief, if the killer didn't use his hands, what'd he use?"

"Dr. McGinnis said he could have used something like a pipe, which broadens the field. I mean, a person whose hands weren't that strong, like a woman, for example, might be able to strangle someone with a pipe. She could throw her body into it."

"Maybe a young woman, strong…"

"For that matter, some men wouldn't have the hand strength to strangle a person," Olivera said. "But they could take a pipe, back the victim up against a wall—"

"Hey, I just thought of something," Reagan cut in. "Maybe the perp caught the victim off guard. She could have been asleep, considering the time of death."

Olivera nodded. "Good point, Reagan. Let's keep that in mind when we go back over there."

"One thing's for sure," Reagan added. "It wasn't no spur of the moment deal. He didn't just haul off and strangle her. It was way more calculated than that."

"So," Olivera said, "we'll be looking for somebody, man or woman, with motive and opportunity, who seems the type to come up with this bizarre scenario, plan it all out, pull it off, just in time for the arrival of Ms. Frye and Ms. Abboud."

"Sounds kinda theatrical, don't it, Lieutenant?"

He glanced at Reagan. "That's a good word for it."

Chapter Eight

Red Oaks
Monday, March 15, 2:00 p.m.

Fifteen minutes after leaving the police station, Olivera was back at Red Oaks with Springer and Reagan. They sat down on the steps to put on gloves and slip-ons. Then Olivera, sliding the skeleton key into the lock, pushed back the door. A wave of stale air rushed out. "Maybe we should crack a window or two."

"Sure, I can do that, Lieutenant," Reagan said as he neared the door.

"But before we step inside," Olivera cautioned, "remember, be careful and only touch what you need to. And let's see if we can scour the place in short order."

"What do you reckon we'll find?" Reagan said, stepping in.

"I have no idea, to be honest."

"Where you figure she was strangled, Chief?" Springer, circling the staircase, stopped to admire the figurines on a whatnot stand near the landing.

"I don't know. Where would you have strangled her?"

"Well, not in this area, for sure."

"Why not?" Olivera peered at the dusty collection Springer was looking at. "It'd be close to the final destination." He motioned toward the parlor.

"True, but it's too exposed, Chief."

Olivera gave a nod and a smile, indicating his approval of Springer's thoughtful approach to the crime scene.

"Somebody might come in the front door," Reagan said, "and there'd you'd be."

Olivera smiled and nodded once more. It appeared that Reagan, too, was acquiring a knack for crime scene investigation. "What about the library or the parlor itself?"

"Same problem, Chief," Springer said. "Too exposed."

As they moved in the direction of the parlor, the floorboards protested beneath their weight, each step releasing a cacophony of creaks that echoed throughout the house.

Reaching the parlor, Reagan pointed to the bay window and said, "You could peek in here through that big window or those over there," he added, gesturing toward the floor-to-ceiling windows across the room.

"Shall we take a gander at the kitchen?" Olivera said.

"Might as well," Springer replied.

They made their way to the far back corner of the house, wandering through the dining area and entering the kitchen through the swinging door. "Hey, this is spacious," Olivera remarked.

While the other downstairs rooms were formal, the kitchen was more serviceable. And unlike the rest, it was light and airy, with white worktops and fixtures and a white porcelain sink. A marble-topped counter ran along the far wall, and above it, glass cabinets stretched to the ceiling. A large wooden table occupied the middle of the room.

"That big table would have been useful." Olivera ran his hand over the rough surface. "Seems like a good place to prepare a corpse."

Reagan grimaced but said nothing.

"I don't think so, Chief." Springer pointed to the row of small windows above the sink. "Too close to the windows. Anybody walking through the yard—"

"Yeah," Reagan interrupted, "but it'd be mighty convenient to the water supply. I mean, to clean up afterwards."

"I suppose." Olivera shrugged and stepped back into the dining room. Springer and Reagan followed him in. "What about this? It's an interior room. Nobody could have seen in."

"True," Springer said.

The oblong dining table with ten matching chairs caught Olivera's eye. He pulled out one of the chairs, crafted from mahogany, and tipped it back. It had curved back legs and straight front legs with bulbous knobs at the feet. He eyed the rounded backrest. "Looks comfortable for a dining chair, doesn't it? Nice support for the back."

"That's a balloon back chair," Reagan informed. "The backrest is round like a balloon."

"So it is." Olivera looked at Reagan. "How'd you come by that information?"

"Momma's got a house full of 'em. Bought 'em at an estate sale."

"Did she now? Maybe I should check out an estate sale."

"They have 'em around here all the time. *The Star*

Shopper is the place to look if you're interested."

"I just might be. It's about time I furnished the house."

"I wonder if Miss Lenna ate her meals in here," Springer said.

"Seems lonely for a single person," Reagan said. "A big table and all these empty chairs…"

"You think the killer would have done it in here?" Olivera glanced from Reagan to Springer.

"What exactly are you getting at, Chief?" Springer tilted his head.

"Well, I guess I'm trying to eliminate rooms or at least pick the most likely spot." He looked up at the ceiling, studying the elaborate fixture from which a large crystal chandelier was suspended. "Cobwebs…"

"Yeah, and dust." Springer dragged his finger through a layer of dust on the table. "I don't think she took her meals in here, not recently."

"Which brings me to another point," Olivera said. "If the killer used the table—"

"—it wouldn't be covered in dust," Reagan interrupted.

Olivera nodded in agreement. "So, let's take a walk through the house. See if we can find any areas that are *not* covered in dust, where the killer might have strangled the victim, then got the body ready for display. He had to remove the clothing and shoes, then dress the body, maybe fix the hair and apply make-up."

"Sounds like all that might have happened in the bedroom," Springer said, "and since Miss Lenna would have used it daily—"

"Yep, sounds like a likely place to me."

They tramped up the stairs to the second floor and,

after a quick survey of the entire area, returned to the room that appeared to be the master bedroom. As they entered, Olivera noticed hints of something faintly floral, perhaps the lingering scent of Lenna Fortney's perfume. "Let's get the photographic evidence first," he said, nodding to Springer.

Springer lifted the camera out of the case and snapped several frames of the room. "You want me to get any close-ups?"

Olivera scanned the room. "Yes, the top of the dresser and nightstand and the bed cover."

"What about the armoire?"

"Yes, inside and out. Might be pertinent, especially since the perp must have changed the victim's clothes."

Olivera approached the bed and gazed up at the elegant canopy suspended slightly below the ceiling and supported by turned columns. The head and foot boards were carved, and the covers were made of a heavy woven fabric. "My lord, the Queen of Sheba could have slept here. I suppose you know what that's called." He glanced at Reagan, who was checking out the marble-top dresser.

Reagan set down the hand mirror he'd picked up. "That's a tester bed, Lieutenant. A pretty fancy one."

"Not sure that would fit in my bedroom." Olivera chuckled. He walked from the bed to the fireplace. It was centered against a wall with wooden shelving on either side. His eyes drifted to a pair of mounted pheasants on the top shelf. "More birds." Though the taxidermy mounts were a tad haunting, the overall look of the room was appealing, restful, with softer colors than the downstairs rooms. "I could sleep in here, I imagine." He turned to Springer. "What about you?"

"Check this out." Springer was staring at something

inside the fireplace.

"What you got?" He strolled over to see what had caught Springer's attention.

"Charred papers." Springer grabbed a large plastic bag from the evidence box and, after carefully inserting the evidence in the bag, handed it to Olivera.

"Humm. I'll have Dr. McGinnis examine them under a microscope. Might be important. When people go to the trouble to burn something…"

After Olivera had checked the furniture, he turned his attention to the floor and the Oriental rug. "Someone gave the rug a good vacuuming, huh?"

"You can still see the marks," Reagan said.

Olivera bent down to check under the bed, then standing, said, "Here, too. It's my guess this is exactly where it happened if it happened in the house."

"So, what are we looking for anyway?" Reagan said.

"Not blood stains. She was strangled. And I doubt we find the murder weapon."

"Murder weapon," Reagan repeated.

"You know, a lead pipe or something that wouldn't break, something you could easily grip and press against the larynx."

"Like a baseball bat?"

"Yeah, possibly."

"Or a rolling pin."

Olivera's brow lifted. "I've never heard of anyone being strangled with a rolling pin, but I guess so."

"Not a fishing pole. That'd be too flimsy."

Olivera nodded. "You've got the right idea."

"How about this?" Springer, still by the fireplace, pointed toward a poker, which wasn't on the stand with the rest of the tools but was propped up against an ash bucket.

"Yeah, that'd work. I was thinking something bigger in diameter, but why not?" Olivera pulled his cell out and tapped McGinnis's number. She didn't answer, and he left a message. "Dr. McGinnis, Olivera here. We're at Red Oaks, uh, checking the victim's bedroom. We've come across a possible murder weapon. What about a poker, like for a fireplace? I'd say it's iron and a good three feet long, about three-fourths inch in diameter. So, uh, give me a call back, please, ma'am, soon as you can." He clicked off and slipped the phone in his pocket.

"So, you think that could be it?" Springer nodded toward the poker.

"Very well could be. We'll see what she says. Go ahead and bag it, Springer. And Reagan, let's get the linens off the bed, see if we can pick up anything." Olivera removed the pillows, checking each for anything the perpetrator might have left behind. Then he and Reagan removed the coverlet, folded it, and tucked it in a large evidence bag. "I'm more interested in the sheets and pillowcases, actually."

"Why is that?" Reagan picked up one of the throw pillows and stuffed it in a bag.

"Time of death. She was murdered yesterday morning early. For all we know, the killer could have surprised her in bed. Dr. McGinnis didn't find much bruising, except around the neck, of course, and under the arms, which would usually indicate that the body was dragged. So the scant bruising suggests there wasn't a scuffle. The victim apparently didn't resist, and being the time of day it was, well, maybe she was asleep. Maybe the perp sneaked in here, grabbed a pillow off the bed and smothered her, then picked up that fire poker and pressed it against her throat to finish the job."

"Sounds like overkill to me," Springer said.

"Yeah, it does. So, if that's what happened, why would he start with asphyxiation and continue with manual strangulation?"

"Nut job?" Springer shrugged.

"Possibly, or maybe he wasn't sure she was dead."

"I don't know, Chief. You got any more theories?"

"For the time being, no. Do you?"

Springer walked around the end of the bed, rubbing his chin and looking from one piece of furniture to the next. "Well, first, all these surfaces are spotless." He gestured toward the dresser, nightstand, and small desk in the corner. "So, either Miss Lenna made a big exception of the bedroom, or the killer did some serious cleaning in here. I haven't run across a mote 'o dust or a hair on anything."

"Continue," Olivera said with a nod.

"Second, the rug has been vacuumed, and like Reagan said, you can still see the vacuum marks, all nice and even."

"Good point." Olivera nodded again.

"Yeah, this is way more thorough than what your average perp would do. This dude is definitely weird."

"Yes, and we already suspected that from the staging in the parlor."

"It's almost like he staged this room, too," Springer continued, "but not in the usual way. Like this man is some sort of over-the-top perfectionist. He wanted Miss Lenna dead, but not just that, he wanted everything perfect, like in a hotel room. You walk in, and it's like nobody was here before you."

Olivera's brow went up. "I'd go along with that.

There's really nothing much of a personal nature in here, not even a brush or a hair pin."

"Yeah," Reagan agreed.

"Let's check the bathroom," Olivera said.

Springer passed through the door on the other side of the fireplace.

Olivera followed him in. "This must have been added later."

"Maybe." Reagan stepped in behind Olivera and looked around. "But some of these old Victorians had baths, I mean, original to the house."

"Huh." Olivera checked the clawfoot tub, which was spick-and-span clean with a white terry-cloth bath mat folded neatly and draped over the side. The mirror above the lavatory was spotless, as was the floor and fixtures. "Clean as a whistle, just like the bedroom," he said. "Nothing on the washstand. Not even a bar of soap in the soap dish. Again, just like in a motel. You'd never know anybody had been here."

They stepped back into the bedroom.

Olivera turned to Reagan, who had gone back to his perusal of the armoire. "You see anything of interest, Reagan?"

"Not really, just a bunch of women's clothes, shoes."

Olivera sighed. "I'm not sure how much we've learned about Lenna Fortney, but whoever killed her, wanted her about as gone as a person can get. Seems a little off. I don't think I've ever investigated a crime scene quite like this."

"Except for that charred bunch of paper," Springer reminded him.

"That's right. And hopefully Dr. McGinnis will find

something on the bedclothes." He gave the room a final once-over. "So, before we leave, guys, I want to check the grounds."

The threesome descended the stairs with the evidence and loaded it into the SUV before heading over to the mausoleum, some fifty yards from the house. Following the stone path, they came to the smallish structure, about ten by fifteen feet, with a large oval arch and a high-pitched roof. The building looked to be of marble. The door, of dark wooden planks, stood open. Olivera, retrieving his flashlight, shot a beam around the interior. There were five coffins in all, stacked on supports, three on one side and two on the other. The occupants' names were chiseled in the marble floor. He put on fresh slip-ons and, stepping inside, noticed that the temperature dropped a good ten degrees. He held up his forearm. "Goosebumps."

"Yeah," Reagan said, looking around, "all this marble."

"These must have been Ms. Fortney's parents and grandparents," he said as he read the names. "And this one"—he pointed—"must be her husband." He checked the names against the corresponding coffins. "So, here's Fortney's ward, Kemena King, birth date, 1982, death date, 2000." Looking up, he expected to see three coffins to match the three engravings on the floor, but, instead, he saw only two. "That's odd. One of the coffins seems to be missing."

"What'd you say, Chief?" Springer asked.

"Take a look."

Springer and Reagan looked at the coffins and engravings. "Yep, one's missing," Springer said.

"Sure is," Reagan said.

"These look to you like the one in the house?" Olivera asked.

"They do," Springer replied.

"You don't suppose—" Olivera rubbed his forehead.

"Surely not." Reagan shook his head.

"I don't know, guys. Looks that way to me. Let's get the measurements and a close-up of the surface. Get pictures of the names, Springer, and then let's check the coffin inside."

After Springer had snapped the pictures and taken measurements, they headed back to the house for another look at the coffin in the parlor.

Inside, Springer said to Olivera, "I already snapped this one, Chief. You want another picture?"

"No, but I'm thinking I need to give Dr. McGinnis a call. If this is, in fact, the missing coffin, surely there is some sort of telltale sign. Hold on a minute." He took out his cell, tapped the coroner's number, then walked back toward the foyer. "Dr. McGinnis, did you get my message?"

"I did," she said, coming on the line. "I was going to text you, but I haven't had a chance. So, bring the poker in. I'd like to get some measurements, see if it fits the bruising. And if it does, I need to check for residue, prints, all that."

"We've taken care of that, but we've just come across something else. We checked the mausoleum, and one of the coffins appears to be missing."

"Missing?"

"Yeah, we found three on one side and only two on the other. But below the two, there are three names. It's my guess the missing coffin belongs to Ms. King, though it's not entirely clear how the names and coffins line up. We are checking now to see if the one in the parlor is like the others."

McGinnis responded with a soft groan.

"Yeah," he said, "bizarre, isn't it?"

"So, if the perpetrator used the coffin that belonged to Miss Kimmy, where's the body?"

"I was wondering that myself."

"This is a bit of problem," she said. "I mean, you'll have to bring the coffin in, or I'll have to drive out there. Actually, I prefer to come out. The chance of contamination would be less. Lock the house up tight, and I'll get there as soon as I can."

"The interior looks pretty clean, but maybe you can pick up something."

"Well, gosh, Lieutenant, if another dead body was in there, surely I can."

Olivera slipped his phone in his pocket and stepped out on the porch. The strange twists and turns of the case were unlike anything he had encountered in his years as a detective. Seriously? A phony wake and now a missing coffin? As he descended the steps, he couldn't help but feel like he wasn't just tracking a murderer. He was trailing someone who was orchestrating a mysterious game with rules only they understood.

Chapter Nine

The Square
Monday, March 15, 11:30 a.m.

Arriving at the Square, Mosey parked down the street from her intended destination. Eager to do a little sleuthing before entering Frye, Frye, and Humphrey, she got out and strolled along, keeping an eye out for police cars. Seeing none, she assumed Olivera was not around. Had he already contacted King Accounting about Lenna Fortney's death? She imagined that he had. As she approached the building, she realized that, if not Olivera, someone had delivered the ill tidings. A wreath of black silk flowers with an elegant black ribbon was on the outer door.

She continued on to the law firm and, at the threshold, came face to face with Dot Cowsley, standing at the bottom of the stairs.

"Mosey!" Dot blurted. "What brings you here?"

Mosey's expression turned serious. "Haven't you heard?"

"Heard what?"

"About Miss Lenna."

Dot raised an eyebrow. "What about Lenna? Everything okay?"

Mosey moved closer and, lowering her voice, conveyed the news as gently as she could. "It's bad news,

I'm afraid."

"Oh, no! What happened?"

"Well, she's dead, apparently murdered."

Dot gasped and covered her mouth. "Surely not."

"I'm afraid so…just this morning."

"Mosey, that is *terrible* news." Dot pressed her palms against her rosy, plump cheeks.

"I know, and as usual, I found the body, well, Nadia and I this time. I can hardly believe it, even though I saw it myself."

"You actually *saw* it?"

"Surely did. She was all laid out, just like at a wake."

"What?"

"Yes, ma'am. She was in the parlor at Red Oaks, resting peacefully in a coffin. Craziest thing you ever saw. Whoever did it must be, well, crazy, a psychopath, something."

"Are you *sure* she was murdered?"

"She was murdered, all right. Strangled."

"Strangled! I can't believe it." Dot leaned against the banister. "Did you call the police?"

"Oh, yes, right away. The paramedics came, then Olivera, then Eads McGinnis. Of course, there wasn't much point to the paramedics coming. There was nothing they could do."

"Let me get this straight. You say, when you found her, she was already in a coffin?" Dot's eyes widened in disbelief.

"Yes, she was, and dressed in a long black gown with black satin slippers. There were white gloves laid out on the shelf below the coffin, you know, for the pallbearers."

"Mosey, that is the strangest thing I've ever heard."

Dot paused. "Now, wait a minute." She stared at Mosey. "Maybe you walked in on a real wake in progress. Maybe she died, well, of natural causes."

"I don't think so." Mosey slowly shook her head. "Olivera said she'd been strangled. And I tell you another thing. She had not been to a mortuary." She raised a forefinger and waggled it. "Most obviously, if you catch my drift. The body had *not* been embalmed."

Dot, still poised on the bottom step, her handbag dangling from her elbow, turned to go back up the stairs. "Mosey, you come with me. I want Carlotta to hear this."

She and Dot slowly ascended the stairs, then crossed the outer office to Carlotta's door, which was partly open.

"Carlotta"—Dot pushed back the door—"sorry to burst in like this, but Mosey just gave me the most *terrible* news. Absolutely horrific." She took a deep breath and stepped in. "I cannot believe it." She shook her head. "I really cannot believe it, and neither will you."

Carlotta took off her readers and rose from her chair. "What in the world?"

Dot approached Carlotta's desk and stood shaking her head and puffing. "Tell her, Mosey."

"I'm really sorry to cause such an upset." Mosey joined Dot at Carlotta's desk, pulling her arms in tight as if to minimize her presence. She disliked being the one to deliver bad news. And besides that, she hadn't anticipated Dot's extreme reaction. The poor woman suffered from atrial fibrillation, and Mosey felt bad about upsetting her so.

Carlotta came from around the desk and gave Dot a looking over. "Are you okay? Come over here and sit down." She guided her to the upholstered chairs positioned around a low round table. "Sit down right here, and I'm going to get you a bottle of water."

"Let me do that," Mosey interjected.

"There's a bottle on my desk." Dot set her handbag on the table and took a seat. "I'm okay. It was just a shock, hearing about Lenna." She shook her head again.

Returning with the bottle, Mosey handed it to Dot. "Can I get you anything else? Would you rather have a cup of tea?"

"No, I'll be okay." She picked up a folder from the table and fanned her face. "Come sit down"—she glanced up at Mosey—"and tell Carlotta what you told me."

Mosey slipped her sweater off and, joining the circle, dropped her tote on the carpet. "Well, it really is a horrific piece of news, not only because it involves the death of someone we know, but the circumstances, good grief."

"So, who was it that died?" Carlotta looked confused.

"Lenna Fortney, bless her heart." Mosey couldn't have fathomed using those words, seeing as the deceased wasn't a person to inspire pity. But in an effort to comfort Dot, she conveyed what compassion she could muster.

"Lenna Fortney?" Carlotta said.

"Yes, I'm afraid so."

"How did she die?"

"Well, it appears she was murdered."

"Oh, my gosh!" Carlotta leaned in toward Mosey. "How did it happen…and when?"

"I'm not sure exactly when, but it appears she died from strangulation."

"That is unbelievable. Lenna Fortney, strangled?"

"That's what Olivera told Nadia and me."

"You and Nadia?"

"We found the body. We'd gone out to Red Oaks this morning for an appointment. You may have heard Lenna was thinking of retiring. She wanted to talk to me about putting Red Oaks on the market."

"Yeah." Carlotta nodded. "I heard something about that."

Carlotta was aware, then, of Fortney's intentions. That was encouraging. She might also know something about her will if she had one and surely she did. "So, that's what I was doing there, and Nadia went to take a look at some antiques Lenna was thinking of selling. If she sold the house, she'd have to get rid of the furniture. She didn't have any family to speak of, no one to pass the family heirlooms to."

"That's true," Carlotta confirmed. "She was pretty much alone in the world, except for her friends and business associates and one nephew by marriage. You know him, don't you? He works at the accounting firm."

"Bud Fortney, right. I don't know him all that well. He hasn't been at the firm very long, has he?"

"About a year, maybe less." Carlotta turned to Dot. "That's right, isn't it?"

Dot, who had let her head fall back against the chair, sat up straight. "Yes, that's right. Bud moved here last summer, I believe. You know he was Jim Fortney's brother's boy, his namesake, in fact. Bud must be about your age, Mosey."

"Yes, he went to Hembree High," Mosey said, "but I didn't really get to know him. Where were the Fortneys from?"

"A little stop in the road on the other side of the river," Dot said. "Bud's uncle, Lenna's husband Jim, was from there, too. After Lenna lost her parents, she didn't have anybody but Jim and Kimmy. You remember Kimmy, don't you?"

"Yes, of course. She was younger, but I knew who she was."

"Well, Lenna and Jim were a close couple," Dot continued, "but she and Kimmy, well, people thought Lenna was jealous of Kimmy."

Carlotta glanced at her watch. "Ladies, I'm sorry to cut the conversation short, but I've got a twelve o'clock appointment at the courthouse."

"Oh, Carlotta," Dot said, "I forgot all about that. We'll get out of your way." She pushed herself up, grabbed her handbag, and ambled toward the door, motioning for Mosey to follow.

"Sorry, Carlotta. I didn't mean to hold you up," Mosey said. "I'll come back another time."

"By the way," Carlotta said to Mosey, "I don't suppose they know who did it."

"No, I don't think so. You have any thoughts on that?"

Carlotta shook her head. "None whatsoever."

Mosey and Dot passed into the outer office, as Carlotta, after slipping a handful of folders into her briefcase, followed them out. "Mosey," she said, "I don't know the Kings or the Fortneys all that well. I was still in Vicksburg when Mr. King died and took charge of the company and a few other matters. Dot can fill you in on that better than I can."

Other matters? Mosey pondered what Carlotta meant. She assumed Dot would have some insight. "Dot, why don't you and I head over to the Tavernette. I'd be happy to treat you to lunch. You haven't eaten, have you?"

Dot looked from Mosey to Carlotta. "Would that be okay? Lunch at the Tavernette might take a while."

"I imagine I'll be at the courthouse close to an hour. Go ahead, you ladies enjoy yourselves. And, Dot, I should be back by one."

"Okay"—Dot took her handbag by the handle—"if you're sure." She glanced at Carlotta, who was almost to the door.

"Come on, Dot," Mosey said. "If we hurry we can beat the lunch crowd."

As Mosey and Dot were leaving the office, Mosey looked back at the old grandfather clock behind Dot's desk and then at the portrait of her late grandfather Amos Frye. His cheerful face stood out against the deep blue background, which drew attention to his twinkling eyes. "I love that portrait of Grandaddy. You know, I wonder why we never hung a portrait of Daddy."

"We should have." Dot looked at the portrait admiringly. "But I don't believe Ellis would have sat for a portrait, impatient man that he was."

"Don't let him hear you say that," Mosey said with a chuckle.

"Mosey, what are you talking about?"

Oops. Mosey had just about let the cat out of the bag. Some time back, she decided never to mention her conversations with her late father to Dot. "Oh, nothing. Sometimes I get the feeling our loved ones never really leave us."

Dot held her bare forearm up to Mosey. "Look at that. You gave me goosebumps."

"Sorry." Mosey chuckled again. "But having Daddy around wouldn't be such a bad thing, would it?"

"Mosey! As I live and breathe!" Dot locked the outer door and, shaking her head at Mosey, followed her down the stairs.

Chapter Ten

Tavernette
Monday, March 15, 12 noon

As Mosey and Dot crossed the bustling Square to the Tavernette, Mosey couldn't resist stealing a quick glance at King Accounting. Just a half hour earlier she had spotted the funerary wreath on the door. "See." She gestured toward the establishment. "They've already put up a wreath, but I don't see a Closed sign. Surely they aren't open."

"They might just be. It's mid-March, and that's an accounting firm, Mosey."

"Yeah, income taxes. I guess they'll have to keep toiling away regardless."

"Which I imagine is what Lenna would have wanted them to do."

As they reached the restaurant, Mosey held the door back for Dot. Inside, they stopped at the receptionist stand, where Ms. Tisdale stood looking over her list of reservations. "You ladies here for lunch?"

"Yes," Mosey responded, "and if you have a table in the dining room, all the better."

"You're in luck. There's just one left. Follow me, if you will." She picked up a couple of menus and headed into the dining room.

Navigating their way through the crowd, Mosey and Dot nodded and smiled as they encountered familiar faces.

"What a heavenly scent," Mosey remarked as they passed near the kitchen door.

Dot's eyes lit up in agreement. "Smells like fresh baked rolls."

Once they'd taken their seats at a corner table, Mosey said, "Ms. Tisdale, you mind if we order now? Dot needs to watch the time."

"Of course. I'll send Ruby right over."

Ruby promptly arrived and took their order, then turning to Mosey, added, "Would you like a drink while you wait?"

"Sure, why not? I'd love a Bloody Mary. Dot, you care for something?"

"Well, I don't know. I have to work this afternoon. Maybe I'd better pass."

"Oh, Dot, come on. Life's short." Indeed it was! And the black wreath on the door of the accounting firm stood as a stark reminder. She leaned back and, gazing out the window, spotted it right across the square.

"All right then," Dot said. "I'll have a Bloody Mary, too. I guess one won't hurt."

Once Ruby left, Mosey reopened the conversation that began at the law firm but was cut off just as things were getting interesting. She was anxious to know what Carlotta had meant by *other matters*. "You know what Carlotta was saying about still living in Vicksburg?"

"Yes, she wasn't here when Mr. King died." Dot reached for a pack of crackers and ripped open the wrapper. "You know, Lenna was still a fairly young woman when she was suddenly left with the responsibility of the firm."

"I wonder what Carlotta meant by *other matters*. I believe she said Lenna was left to handle the firm and some other matters."

"Oh, I bet I know exactly what she was referring to. Kemena King, Mr. King's ward."

"Of course." Mosey nodded. "I bet that was it. I've heard about Miss Kimmy. I imagine everybody in Hembree has heard the story."

"It certainly has become part of the local lore, hasn't it?"

"People have been discussing it for years. Not that I've ever gotten the inside scoop."

"Well, I don't know about the inside scoop." She snapped a cracker in two and popped half of it in her mouth. "I'd better eat a couple of these before the Bloody Marys arrive. I don't like to drink on an empty stomach."

"Me, either." Mosey picked up a pack. "I remember when all that happened. Seems like Kimmy was a good ten years younger than I. What was she—about twenty?"

"A little younger than that. In fact, she had just finished high school and started college. What a pity." Dot shook her head. "A beautiful young girl in her prime…"

Mosey started taking mental notes, trying to get the time line straight in her head. "So, Mr. King died not that long before Kimmy died."

"That's right. It must have been a couple of rough years for Lenna. First, her mother passed on. Seems like she died of meningitis during one of our terribly hot summers. Then her father died. A heart problem, I think it was. Suddenly, Lenna had to take over the accounting firm. But, you see, Mr. King was Kimmy's guardian, and there was no one to look after her but Lenna. When Kimmy lost her mother, she'd already lost her daddy, Mr. King's younger brother. That's when Mr. King brought her to live with him and his wife. Lenna was a grown woman by then, in her early forties, I reckon. So, there she was, saddled with the responsibility of the firm *and* a head-strong youngster."

"Wow, that's a lot."

"Yes, and you know, the Kings spoiled Kimmy to death. Everybody said that. You see, they no longer had a child at home and, well, with Kimmy's being orphaned at such a young age…"

"Seems like a hefty load to bear." Mosey thought of herself in Lenna's place, never having had a child and, like Dot said, being stuck all of a sudden with a willful youngster. "It certainly aged her, didn't it?"

Dot nodded. "Indeed, it did."

"You know, lying there in the coffin, all dressed in black, the color drained out of her face, Miss Lenna looked really old. How old you think she was?"

"Well, a good bit younger than I. I know that."

"I was thinking she was about retirement age."

"No, I don't think she was even sixty. Probably in her mid-fifties."

"Wow. She looked sixty, sixty-five even, if a day. I wonder why she was thinking of retiring so soon, selling the house…"

"That's a good question." Dot paused to glance at Ruby, who was placing two icy Bloody Marys on the table.

"I put a rush on your order, ladies," Ruby said.

"Thanks, Ruby." Mosey lifted her drink and, taking a napkin, wiped off the excess moisture.

"Can I get you anything else while you're waiting for your food?" Ruby tucked the tray under her arm.

"It'll be here soon, won't it?" Dot questioned.

"I'm sure it will."

"Then I think we're fine."

"Just in case, I'll bring you some more crackers." Grabbing the basket, she hurried away.

"By the way," Mosey said to Dot, "you mentioned before that Lenna was jealous of Kimmy. Seems like I've heard something about that. But it doesn't make sense to me that a grown woman would be jealous of a girl."

"Well, I'm no authority on the matter, but what I heard was that Mr. King doted on Kimmy, whereas he and his wife had given Lenna a much stricter upbringing. Being the competitive woman she was, Lenna saw Kimmy as a rival. Then, of course, once Lenna's parents died and *she* became Kimmy's guardian, she tried to rein her in and it didn't work. From what I've heard, they were at each other's throats, and to make it worse, Lenna's husband Jim sort of sided with Kimmy."

"Wow, that's a slap in the face."

"I'm sure it was."

"When was it Kimmy died?"

"Gosh, I don't know exactly but a couple of years after Mr. King died."

"She died in a boating accident, didn't she?"

"As far as was known. At least that was the way it was reported in the paper, but of course tongues wagged."

"Why was that?"

Dot took a deep breath, then sipped her Bloody Mary, as if she were fortifying herself for something awkward. "It was complicated. For one, it seems that the police report, based on what Lenna and Jim told them, didn't exactly match what Kimmy's fiancé had to say."

"Yes." Mosey nodded. "Merritt Trumble told a slightly different story. Wasn't that it?"

"And Merritt didn't get along well with the Fortneys."

"Really…"

"He wanted to marry Kimmy." Dot set down her drink and stirred it with the celery stalk. "He was a little older, already in college when they started dating, and Kimmy was still in high school. All the Kings were professionals, and they wanted Kimmy to go to college. Of course, they did." Dot's voice had taken on a slightly shrill tone, as if professionals raising their offspring to be professionals was a law of nature. "But Kimmy and Merritt were determined to get married, which isn't so hard to understand, given that Lenna and Kimmy didn't get along."

"Yeah, I suppose so. But surely they didn't think Miss Lenna would have had anything to do with the accident."

"Not directly, but what I heard was that Lenna and Kimmy got into a big argument and Kimmy ran off. Lenna knew that the boat was out of commission. It had a leak or something, and she didn't warn Kimmy. Didn't say a thing. I believe that's the story Merritt and his family were spreading around."

"And how would they have known that? I mean, if she got in the boat and took off…"

"I'm not rightly sure. Someone might have overheard the argument," Dot said with a shrug. She paused briefly as Ruby returned the cracker basket to the table. Then Dot reached for a packet and, opening it, continued. "Or maybe Merritt talked to Kimmy before she took off."

"And you said that the police report didn't match up with the evidence?"

"You know." Dot looked thoughtful. "It's been a while, and I'm not sure if I remember this correctly, but seems like Lenna and Jim said they weren't at the house. It happened at the lake right behind Red Oaks. But then somebody said they *were* there and could have stopped Kimmy from taking the boat." She shrugged again. "Or maybe that wasn't it at all. Maybe it was that Lenna said she wasn't aware of a problem with the boat, but then somebody else gave a statement that suggested that she was." She shook her head. "I'm not sure."

"Hmm." Mosey paused to sip her cocktail. She was already starting to put two and two together. Could Merritt Trumble still be carrying a grudge against Lenna? Did he think she was somehow involved in Kimmy's death? She couldn't fathom a guy like Merritt holding onto so much bitterness, but she figured it was within the realm of possibility. At last, Mosey said, "You know, Merritt never married, did he?"

"I'm pretty sure he's still single. It hasn't been that long since I bumped into him."

"Oh, yeah?"

"He's a handsome young man and doing well, working for his daddy's architecture firm in Mound City."

Just then the people sitting two tables over got up and left, and Ruby, after quickly changing the tablecloth, seated a couple who Mosey recognized.

"Dot," Mosey whispered as she discreetly gestured toward the couple. "Isn't that Ed Neville?"

Dot glanced in their direction, then, looking back at Mosey, gave a nod.

"And the other person?" Mosey asked.

"That's Carrie Hadley."

"Who's she?"

"Secretary at the firm," Dot said in a soft voice.

"Oh." Mosey glanced back at the couple. "Are they an item?"

Dot shook her head. "I don't think so."

"Is he married?"

"Divorced."

"I see."

"It's been rumored," Dot continued, "that Ed would take over the firm eventually, but then Bud Fortney came on the scene."

"But Bud's only been there a year, didn't you say?"

"True, but Bud is family, and Ed is not. Could make a difference."

"You know them well?"

"Sort of. I've seen Ed at meetings of the business community for years."

"Does Bud go to the meetings?"

"More recently, yes."

"Do they get along with people?"

"Ed, most definitely. Bud, on the other hand, can be sort of an upstart."

"Really. Did Miss Lenna attend those meetings?"

"Oh, yes, in fact, she was president off and on since she took over the firm. Most of the business people in Hembree couldn't care less, but she seemed to enjoy sitting at the head of the table, if you know what I mean. Carlotta would sooner offer her hand to a hungry wolf. Your daddy wouldn't have accepted the job, either."

"What about Granddaddy?"

"He got talked into it once, but hated it, and said 'never again.' "

"But Miss Lenna liked it," Mosey said with a dip of her chin. "I can see that. She was sort of a control freak, wasn't she? Not to talk ill of the dead, but I can see how she might have given someone reason to strangle her."

"Mosey!" Dot exclaimed. "What a thing to say!"

"You sound like my daddy."

Dot smiled. "Your daddy was a gem of a man, and he knew a thing or two about people, Mosey. You'd have done well to listen."

"I wonder what he thought about Miss Lenna."

"To be honest, I don't think he much cared for Lenna. Too bossy for his taste. But he did like Ed Neville. In fact, he thought the firm would be better off with Ed at the helm."

"You think Ed wants to take over someday?"

"I'm sure he does. Why else would he kowtow to Lenna for all these years?"

"And you think this rumor about maybe Bud Fortney taking Lenna's place has any credit?"

"I don't know, but knowing you, Mosey, I have a feeling you won't stop till you find out."

Chapter Eleven

Morgue
Monday, March 15, 3:15 p.m.

Upon arrival at Delta Infirmary, Olivera got out of the SUV, loaded the evidence onto a cart, and rolled it down the long corridor to the morgue. Pushing open the door, he called out to McGinnis, "Where shall I put this?"

Seated at her desk at the rear of the room, she promptly got up and came toward him. "What is all that?" she asked as she pointed to the large paper sacks with the bed linens.

"We stripped the big tester bed where Fortney must have slept. And keeping in mind the time she died, well, I'm thinking the guy might have snuck in while she was asleep. Could have used a pillow to smother her and then finished the job with the poker. It's worth taking a look, no?" He picked up the bag with the poker and set it on the utility table next to the counter.

"Why would he strangle her with the poker after smothering her with a pillow? Sounds like—"

"—overkill? That's exactly what Springer said, and yes, it matches up rather well with the impression I'm getting of the murderer."

"I see what you mean. Somebody who takes things

to an extreme."

"You'd be surprised how totally spotless the bedroom and bathroom were, especially considering the rest of the place. But if you think about it, that's where he could have slipped up, overlooked a bit of evidence. I mean, if that's where he strangled her."

"Makes sense."

"Even the vacuum marks on the rug were straight as an arrow. Putting it all together, the staging plus the clean-up, I'm thinking this guy must be obsessive. That's about all I have on the profile, other than an apparent hatred for the victim."

"It was carefully planned, for sure, and he must have known a fair amount about the victim's routine. I mean, really, to find the opportune moment when nobody was around...And it would have taken hours to do all that. Strangle her, dress her, put her in the coffin. Then tidy up the place."

"Seems that way, doesn't it? Bringing the coffin into the parlor, setting it all up. You think he might have had help?"

She shrugged. "I don't know, but it certainly would have made it easier to transport the coffin. Speaking of which, you think the coffin was taken from the mausoleum? I've been assuming it was on the premises, likely in the attic or basement."

"Well, it's pretty much like the ones in the mausoleum, the same shape and apparently the same material. You suppose they purchased the coffins when they built the mausoleum?"

"Maybe, if you wanted them all alike."

"So, with an eight-person mausoleum, you'd need to purchase eight coffins."

"People *do* make such arrangements ahead of time. People buy cemetery lots for the whole family, so I don't see why not."

"Seems gruesome, doesn't it—an attic full of coffins?"

"Oh, I don't know. Maybe not to Victorians. They were sort of death-obsessed, weren't they?"

"You're asking me?"

She chuckled and, then, with a hint of seriousness, said, "Yeah, I suppose things relevant to style are not really your thing."

He shot her a quick look, sensing a touch of sarcasm in her words. "Hey, I pay attention to style as much as the next guy." He took off his hat and gave it a spin, then tossed it onto the hat rack.

"Hats, yes, but houses? And by the way," she added, "I don't suppose you've given any thought to buying furniture."

"Don't worry. I'll get around to it eventually." He was feeling just a bit annoyed, and to be honest, Ead's attention to domesticity was beginning to clash with his utter disinterest in the matter. Surely she wasn't planning to move in—or was she? Not a question he dared to ask. It was safer, he figured, to shy clear of the subject altogether. He liked her well enough, and yet the thought of a serious attachment was unsettling.

He cleared his throat and returned to the topic at hand. "Maybe I should reach out to Ms. Abboud. She's the go-to person for everything Victorian."

"Yeah, I suppose," she replied coolly.

He paced around the gurney and, stopping on the other side, looked down at the package with the poker. "You think the dimensions of the poker correspond with the bruising?"

She picked up the bag and examined the contents through the plastic. "It's about the right size, but before I say anything definite, I'll need to examine both the neck area and poker for any residual material. Even a wrought-iron poker would leave filaments on the skin, unless the perpetrator thought of wrapping it in something like plastic, newspaper, whatever. But then, whatever he wrapped it in—"

"I can see this guy doing that, uh, wrapping the dang poker. He thought of everything. On the other hand, it seems like he made his attempts to cover things up rather obvious, like leaving that bunch of charred paper in plain sight." He gestured toward the bag with the paper, still on the cart, then picked it up and laid it on the utility table. "And besides that, there were the vacuum marks and the open door to the mausoleum. It's as if he left little enticing crumbs sprinkled about."

"But you don't know for sure he did that."

"Who else?"

"What about Fortney? It was her house. She was living in it."

"Yeah, but considering her laxness in the rest of the house, why would she be so particular about the bedroom and bathroom, oh, and mausoleum floor? Clean as a whistle."

"Seems inconsistent, but maybe that's just the way she was. I guess you could ask her co-workers."

"Good idea." He pulled out his notepad and pen and scribbled a note to himself. "And you know, I need to get to the firm right away, but I'm thinking this business about the coffin is more urgent. How you want to handle it? Shall we ride out there, or do you want us to haul it in here?"

"I think I should go out, take another look, and try again to collect some samples from the interior. If the coffin had already been used for burial, surely I can pick up some DNA. And something else, what about Miss Kimmy's remains?"

"If the guy is consistent, I doubt we have to look far. He probably left some clue as to their whereabouts."

She looked pointedly in his direction. "You seem confident about this profile."

"Well, there isn't much concrete evidence to go on."

"Be careful, Lieutenant. This perpetrator sounds every bit as controlling as his victim."

"Hmm." McGinnis's comment had conjured up the image of an excessively controlling woman in confrontation with an equally controlling man. The man had taken all he could, and then, boom! Fireworks. Though it wasn't really like fireworks, was it? More like a simmering pot that came to a boil and boiled over. "But he didn't pick up a poker and strike her over the head, now, did he?"

"Nope, didn't do that."

"I'm thinking he crept up cunningly"—he raised his hands as if clutching an object—"smothered her with a pillow, then crushed her larynx with the poker."

"That idea about two perps..." McGinnis leaned against the counter. "It would account for a couple of things, wouldn't it?"

"Indeed, it would." He paused to think about that, then said, "While one guy committed the murder, the other could set up the parlor, I mean, bring in the coffin and all. Then together they could have cleaned up the death scene. It might have happened just that way. And another thing. The effort put into creating the perfect death scene, well, it suggests a flair for the dramatic, doesn't it?"

"Yeah, like a dash of playfulness. Almost like a mischievous kid."

Olivera paced back and forth along the gurney before halting short of the victim's feet and ankles. Peeking out from under the sheet, they looked cold and bluish. He glanced away, letting his eyes settle on McGinnis's youthful face. "So tell me, who the devil is this person, living in little ole Hembree?"

She didn't answer.

He took a deep breath and, after a perfunctory farewell, left the morgue, his plan being to return immediately to the station. But as he was nearing the exit, he turned and retraced his steps to the morgue. He opened the door and reached for his hat, hanging on the rack where he'd left it. "You know what?" His eyes flicked in McGinnis's direction.

She was standing at the gurney and, looking up, glanced toward the hat rack. "I wondered if you were coming back for that."

"Yeah, that, too. But I was thinking about something else. I don't think it's a great idea for you to go to Red Oaks alone. How about we hop in our cars and meet there? You can check the coffin while I look for the remains."

"That works." She pulled the sheet back over the torso. "Go ahead." She looked at the wall clock. "I'll meet you there as soon as I can."

"Should you decide you want the coffin brought back here, I can help you with that."

As Olivera left the morgue again, he felt uneasy. His

thoughts drifted to that slightly uncomfortable moment in his discussion with Eads when it felt like she was nudging him to hurry up and furnish his house. It dawned on him that he was falling into a familiar pattern. Approach-avoidance conflict, he'd heard it called. Some time ago, a therapist at the Santa Clara department had pointed out to him his habit of moving in one direction, only to become stuck, mulling over the pros and cons. Now, in this situation with Eads, it was like the closer they came to settling down, the more he felt like pulling back. Could it be that she'd picked up on that and was testing the waters? Like pressing him to get a move on? Maybe the bareness of his living quarters was about something other than not knowing which couch to settle on. Maybe he wasn't ready to commit to a relationship.

Even so, this silly reluctance was making him anxious. "For land's sake, Gus," he muttered under his breath, "take the bull by the horns. Make up your mind!" Dancing around was not really his style, now, was it? Or at least he didn't want it to be his style. "But for now," he uttered with a shrug, "let's focus on one thing at a time." And true to his word, he banished all thought of his wavering resolve and turned his attention to the investigation at hand.

A bit later, when he arrived at Red Oaks, he walked the front of the property, searching closely as he went for any clue as to where the remains might be. He'd checked every room in the house and nothing stood out. As he'd mentioned to McGinnis, if there *was* a clue, it wouldn't be difficult to detect. Wanting the remains to be found, the culprit would have placed his "signpost" where it wouldn't be overlooked. Certainly, somewhere at Red Oaks, he imagined, and seeing as he hadn't come across it *inside* the house, where else could it be?

With this rationale in mind, he began at one edge of the property and sauntered slowly across to the other, keeping his eyes focused on the ground in front of him. He passed by the large red oaks, the branches of which were just beginning to bud. Once he'd reached the drive at the far end of the lawn, he turned and walked back. After multiple repetitions, he hadn't spotted anything on the well-kept turf. Passing next to the lawn table and chairs where he'd interviewed Ms. Frye and Ms. Abboud, he paused to give the area a close going-over. Finding nothing of interest, he continued his trek, arriving at the porch just as McGinnis pulled up in her van. "You need any help?" he called out.

"Nope, this is all I need." She lifted out a case. "Come across anything?"

"Nothing. Go ahead with your investigation, and let me know if you need me. I want to look around back. And I guess I ought to re-check the mausoleum."

"You have the house key?" she asked, stepping up on the porch.

He felt in his pocket and handed her the skeleton key. "I'll be inside as soon as I finish."

"This shouldn't take long."

"Okay, so, text me when you're ready."

Once she'd gone inside the house, Olivera continued with his inspection, looking around the sides of the property and the back stretch that led to the lake where King had drowned. He surveyed the wide expanse of lawn and spotted a small dock where a boat gently swayed at the water's edge. A boat, aha! Perhaps just the spot to stash the remains. "Oh, my goodness," he mumbled under his breath. "That could be it." He quickened his step, fully expecting to find what he was seeking. He got to the dock and peered down into the boat but saw nothing right way. When he'd first learned about the accident, he'd imagined a small man-powered boat. But this was a runabout with an outboard motor. Of course, he had no reason to believe it was the boat Kemena used the day of the accident. As he lowered himself into the boat, it began to rock, and he held onto the railing. Then, making his way to a seat, he looked forward into the hull but saw nothing apart from the usual gear. He checked underneath the seats but, alas, there was nothing there. He climbed back on the dock and searched carefully along the edges of the walkway. He peered down into the murky water and, seeing nothing, moved away.

From the end of the dock, he looked around for a moment before heading back toward the house. So far, he'd found nothing, and his last hope was the mausoleum. Perhaps the remains were tucked away in a corner he'd somehow missed. Before, he hadn't really looked for anything of the sort, focusing instead on the coffins and the names engraved on the floor. Coming to the small building, he first checked inside and then circled around to the back. The front, sides, and back were completely bare. There wasn't a single flower bed where something might be buried. Grass and a couple of cypress trees—that's all there was.

Feeling frustrated with his efforts, he walked the stone pathway back to the house and sat on the steps to put on his slip-ons. After giving a loud knock to let McGinnis know he was there, he strolled through the foyer and joined her in the parlor. "Well, that was fruitless," he said as he approached the coffin. "You pick up anything?"

"Well, the lining looks clean. I've found a few fibers and hairs. I'm guessing they'll match the hair and clothing of the victim. I'd like to examine them more closely, though."

"Foiled again!" he exclaimed.

She raised and lowered her brow, conveying a comparable level of frustration. Removing her readers, she slipped them in the pocket of her lab coat. "If the person who did this brought the coffin from the mausoleum, he must have changed the lining."

He thought for a moment. "Hmm. And thinking back to what you said before, I mean, about Victorians keeping a spare coffin on hand, maybe this guy knew exactly where to find a fresh lining."

"This is looking more and more like an inside job."

"You mean someone familiar with the layout of the house?"

She nodded. "We're gathering details for the profile, but we aren't gathering evidence, not physical evidence. Everywhere we look we come up empty-handed."

He was accustomed to receiving good insights from McGinnis, so even though he was confused himself, he had a feeling she might be able to shed some light on the situation. "Any thoughts on the subject?"

She stepped away from the coffin and walked toward the bay window, then turned and looked back at him from across the room. "This is nothing new, is it? I mean, to you. You must have encountered cases in your rather extensive experience in which there was little physical evidence. Surely you have."

He gave a half smile. Inadvertently, she had reminded him of their difference in years. He'd been at the job for over a decade, and she was just starting out. He took a moment to reflect as he scrolled through his time on the Santa Clara force in search of a case similar to the one Eads described. And, bingo, he recalled a scenario that matched up perfectly. "Yes." He nodded. "There *was* one in Santa Clara a good while back."

"Okay. So did you solve it?"

"As a matter of fact, we did."

"How did you, without physical evidence?"

"Happenstance, I suppose you could say. We didn't have much of anything to go on except the bullet that killed the man. The case involved the homicide of a fellow officer. Plenty of people of interest were around, folks who might have held a grudge over some case the victim had worked on. But we didn't have anything substantive. No idea at all who actually pulled the trigger. It was a drive-by shooting with no eye witnesses, no one willing to rat out any of the suspects. Of course, at the same time, we were getting pressure from the higher-ups to solve the case. So we put out bulletins asking for information that might lead to an arrest."

"Good idea."

"Yeah, it was at that. As I remember, we got a call that same day from someone who claimed to have overheard a conversation between the culprit and his girlfriend. Apparently, he was bragging about bringing the guy down. The caller seemed credible and recognized a voice when we set up a kind of 'voice lineup.' She also recalled some details about the shooting itself, things she'd overheard the guy say. The kind of gun he said he'd used matched the bullet the coroner removed from the victim. He also mentioned the time of the shooting, which matched the time of death. We brought the guy in for questioning and managed to get a confession."

"Nice," she said with a nod. "So if worse comes to worst, why not? Somebody could have seen something."

"Like what?"

"Oh, I don't know, a car or somebody in the yard."

"Well, it hasn't come to that yet, but I'll keep it in mind. I've been thinking I need to question the people over at the accounting office, especially Fortney's next of kin, who I understand works there. Bud Fortney."

"Yes, but Bud Fortney hasn't been there long. If somebody had a personal vendetta, the senior partners are more likely to know, I'd think."

"Probably so." He gave the parlor one last glance. "Shall we get out of here?"

"Yes, I need to get back to the lab, finish going over the evidence you dropped off earlier."

"Sounds good." He checked his watch. "And I think I'll head over to the firm, try to catch Fortney's co-workers before they leave for the day."

"You didn't want to check the basement before we leave?"

"Not really. In fact, I might ask Springer and Reagan to take care of that."

Chapter Twelve

Al's Supper Club
Monday, March 15, 7:15 p.m.

Mosey, Robert, and Nadia strolled into Al's Supper Club, leaving the quiet outskirts of Hembree behind for the smooth sound of a jazz quartet, just now setting up in the corner. The recent remodel had transformed the space—sleek plexiglass high-tops replacing the worn wooden tables of years past. Managing to snag a corner table, they sat down and waited for Hugh Jessup to show up.

"There he is." Mosey greeted him with a wave as he approached. "Hey, what's up?" He was surprisingly late and seemed a bit down in the mouth—not at all his usual jaunty self.

"Oh, I had a little mishap, you might say." He pulled out a tall stool and, climbing on, brushed his longish red hair away from his face.

"What happened, old man?" Robert's tone was one of concern.

"Yeah," Nadia chimed in, "you look a little dejected."

Rising off the stool, Hugh gave Nadia, then Mosey a peck on the cheek before sitting back down. "I took my service-learning group out to the Civil War Cemetery."

He turned to Robert. "You were there this morning, weren't you?"

"Yeah, we were."

"My freshman seminar wanted to do the same project as yours—the gravestone-cleaning project. So we hopped in the van and headed over. I figured a quick tour would be a suitable start. Most of them hadn't seen the cemetery before. But just as we passed the statue of the unknown soldier, one of the students let out a yell."

"What in the world?" Robert interjected.

"Yeah." Hugh nodded emphatically. "It was pretty unnerving."

"What happened?" Mosey urged him to continue.

"This girl, Allyson Hanson—you know her?" He looked at Robert.

"A new major, isn't she?"

"That's the one. Well, apparently, she'd picked up a bag at the foot of the statue. She must have opened it and looked in. I wasn't really paying attention until she screamed and sort of stumbled backwards."

"What the devil?" Robert exclaimed.

"What was in it, for heaven's sake?" Mosey asked.

"Teeth, hair, and maybe some other items, but after seeing the teeth and hair, I suspected what they were and immediately closed the bag. It was sort of a drawstring pouch about the size of a shopping bag."

"Good grief," Mosey exclaimed. "That makes my skin crawl."

"My lord," Robert groaned. "That's two mishaps for Anthropology in one day." He stared down at the table, then up at Hugh. "I'm beginning to doubt the wisdom of these gravestone-cleaning projects. You know, on our way back from the cemetery this morning, I decided to take a side trip to the mausoleum at Red Oaks. Well, just as we pulled into the driveway, I saw crime-scene tape stretched all across the front of the house. Lenna Fortney had been found dead." He gestured toward Mosey and Nadia. "And these two found her. But, of course, I didn't know that at the time."

Hugh shook his head and cast a reproachful look at Mosey. "I thought you told me the curse had lifted."

"I thought it had—I swear I did."

"Have you guys ordered, by the way?" Hugh said. "I could use a drink."

"Not yet," Mosey said. "We were waiting for you."

Hugh signaled to the bartender, who came right over. "Bring me a scotch straight up. Actually, make it a double."

Mosey looked at Hugh with surprise, seeing as he usually kicked off with a pale ale.

"I'll take a scotch and ginger." Robert handed the cocktail menu to the bartender.

"Gosh, I guess I'm driving." Mosey looked at the bartender. "Antonio, make mine a whiskey sour, and easy on the whiskey."

"Same for me," Nadia said.

He left but soon returned with four waters and a basket of bread sticks.

"Ha," Mosey said to Nadia, "I bet he's wondering why we're going for the hard stuff."

"Wondering?" Nadia replied, skepticism in her voice. "He's probably heard by now. All of Hembree must have heard." She picked up a bread stick and passed the basket to Mosey.

Mosey took one and offered the basket to Hugh. "But finish your story. What'd you do?"

114

"I called Olivera—what else?" Hugh said. "The contents were rather obvious, and running across, well, human remains like that, I wasn't sure what to make of it. First I thought maybe there'd been an exhumation, but that didn't seem to make sense. Nobody deals with remains right there in the cemetery, do they, Robert?"

"I wouldn't think so. Seems like you'd take the coffin straight to a forensics lab or mortuary, depending on the reason for the exhumation. I don't think I've ever been to an exhumation in a cemetery."

"Really?" Nadia asked.

"Well, I'm usually called when bones are found in a ditch or somewhere."

"I saw a few during my grad school days." Hugh picked up a bread stick.

"You did?" Mosey said.

"Some of my forensic classes included practical training, but the exhumed bodies I saw were fairly new. Exhumed for the purpose of collecting evidence."

"But in this case"—Robert nodded toward Hugh—"sounds like these were very old remains."

"Yeah. Makes me think the body had to have been in the ground at least ten years."

Robert took a sip of water, then nodded. "Yeah, about that."

"So," Mosey said, "did you talk to Olivera?"

"I did, and he rushed right over. Turns out he was at Red Oaks when I called—he and Eads McGinnis."

"Well, that was handy," Nadia said.

"Yeah, I guess they were checking the crime scene. You know what seemed a little weird? How everything just fell into place, almost like it was orchestrated."

"Huh?" Mosey said.

"When I told Olivera about the bag of remains, it was like I'd stumbled upon exactly what he was looking for. Weirdest thing. He said they'd scoured the property for some missing remains but came up empty handed. He was about to head back to town when he got my call."

"What missing remains?" Mosey exclaimed, eyes open wide.

"He didn't say. He just said he'd noticed earlier that the mausoleum door was open, and he wanted to check the area again. So, he did, and one of the coffins seemed to be missing."

"Missing?" Nadia said. "Oh, my. You don't suppose the coffin we saw this morning—"

"Gosh," Mosey cut in, "I suppose it could have been, but that is…Good grief! You think the killer used a coffin from the mausoleum?"

"From what I was able to learn from Olivera, it certainly sounds that way," Hugh said.

Nadia looked at Hugh. "The remains you guys found have to be from the coffin the killer used for the staging."

"Staging?"

"When we found Miss Lenna," Mosey said, "she was all laid out in a coffin, just like for a wake, but nobody was there." She turned to Nadia. "You thought the coffin looked old, like an antique, right?"

"The catafalque certainly appeared to be an antique. The coffin, too, but I didn't really get a good look. I think it was bronze and had a lid that lifts off, sort of like the coffins from the late Victorian era." She looked at Hugh. "You know, the six-sided kind, angled out at the shoulder, then tapered toward the foot."

"I bet that's exactly what happened." Mosey jumped in. "The killer"—she stared into space—"must have taken the coffin from the mausoleum, tossed the remains in a bag—the one Hugh's student found—then cleaned it up and used it for Miss Lenna."

"That certainly sounds like a possibility," Robert said, "given what we know."

"This whole thing seems very complicated to me," Hugh said.

"Indeed it does." Robert gave a nod, then glanced up at the bartender, who had set a tray of drinks at his elbow. "Start a tab for us, will you, Antonio?"

"Certainly. Anything else?"

Robert glanced around the table and received head-shakes from the others. "We're good for now." He passed out the drinks and raised his glass to Hugh. "Cheers to getting through the semester with no more hiccups."

Hugh clicked his glass. "I'm not sure I'll get that bunch back to the cemetery." He took a sip of his whiskey.

"And once the news spreads, I don't imagine we'll be doing any more gravestone-cleaning projects."

Mosey squeezed a lemon slice absently into her drink. "Isn't it interesting that the bag was left at the foot of a monument?"

"Really strange," Nadia said. "You'd expect the killer to try to hide the crime, but nope, he's parading it around like some big accomplishment."

"Yeah," Robert said, "and who sneaks a coffin out of a mausoleum and leaves the door open?"

"Obviously the same guy who strangled Lenna and hung around to stage her wake," Nadia said. "This guy is in serious need of attention, a real show-off."

"It seems that way." Hugh took another sip of his

scotch. "I wonder what Olivera is making of all this."

"Surely, he's seeing the pattern," Nadia said. "It's hard to miss."

"I wonder if he's been able to gather much evidence," Mosey said.

"Well, he's got a bag of remains," Hugh said. "That'd be a good start."

"So," Mosey said, "they'd have to be the remains of a family member if they came from the mausoleum. Nadia, you don't happen to know exactly who's buried there, do you? Seems to me they're all Kings except for Lenna's husband."

"That's easy enough," Hugh said. "Just look on the website, you know, the one for locating graves."

"Hey, that's right," Mosey said. "We could put in the names of her immediate family and see exactly which ones are buried there."

"I'm on it." Nadia reached for her cellphone.

"You know the names of her parents, grandparents?" Mosey said.

"Sure do. The Kings have been customers of ours for years. Lenna's parents, paternal grandparents, her husband, and, of course, Kemena King. That would be the lot of them. That mausoleum is small. It couldn't hold more than eight coffins at the most."

"So, with the ones you mentioned plus Lenna, that makes seven," Mosey said. "That leaves one space."

"I imagine, when it was built, they went with the standard for that size, not really knowing who would end up there. For sure, they wouldn't have anticipated Lenna's ward."

"Right, but since Kimmy died unexpectedly and Lenna didn't have any children..." Mosey looked at

Nadia. "You remember when she died?"

"Seems like it was about ten years ago." She keyed in the information and came up with an obituary. "Here it is. 'Kemena King, 1982-2000.' "

"It certainly could be her, then," Hugh said.

"Would so little have been left?" Nadia cast a pensive look at Hugh.

"Well, there's a kind of 'intrinsic uncertainty' involved in exhumation—a phrase one of my professors often used. You can't really know *what* you might find. And if a body is buried in a flimsy casket, after some years you wouldn't find anything except, well, 'soil.' But even so, it would be considered remains. When a body is buried in a metal coffin—" He looked at Nadia. "You said you thought it was bronze, right?"

Nadia replied with a nod.

"Then I would expect something to be left."

"But just teeth and hair?" Mosey asked.

"Possibly." Hugh turned to Nadia. "You don't happen to know anything about the condition of the body when it was found, do you? It was a drowning, right?"

"Yes, but as to the details, I don't really recall." Nadia turned to Mosey. "Do you?"

"No, but somebody has got to know, like Eads's father. He was the coroner. And there would be records, of course. We might be able to check on that, eh, Hugh?"

"I would think so."

Mosey glanced at Nadia, who'd set her cellphone on the table. "Did you find anything?"

"Yeah, just what I expected, Lenna's paternal grandparents, parents, husband, and Kimmy."

"So, just six," Mosey said.

"But hang on a second," Robert said, "we can't be

sure it was Kimmy's coffin that was broken into. Could have been one of the others."

"True," Mosey said, "but if it *was* Kimmy's, that might—"

"What?" Nadia looked at Mosey.

"Oh, I don't know, but I was talking to Dot earlier today over lunch."

"What'd she say?"

"Quite a bit. What I found most intriguing was the part about Lenna and Kimmy. You see, when Mr. King died, responsibility for the firm fell to Lenna. Plus, she was stuck looking after Kimmy, who was rumored to be quite a headstrong girl. And as you can imagine, she and Lenna didn't get along well at all. Dot said Mr. King spoiled Kimmy, and Lenna was jealous." Mosey paused.

"Go on," Nadia urged.

"Well, I'm not sure I quite get that. Kimmy was a kid and Lenna, a grown woman. At any rate, the boating accident occurred a couple of years later, and Kimmy's death was attributed to drowning. But there was a lot of talk around town about the circumstances. Supposedly, Lenna and Kimmy got into an argument, and Kimmy took off in a boat on the lake behind Red Oaks. Some people claimed that Lenna knew the boat had some sort of problem and ought to have warned her. Dot also mentioned something about various versions of the story not matching up. But the gist of it was that Kimmy's fiancé Merritt Trumble was not at all satisfied with the investigation and held a grudge against Lenna ever after, thinking she was somehow responsible for Kimmy's death."

"So, what does all that have to do with anything?" Hugh asked.

"Maybe nothing and maybe everything," Mosey said. "I've just been trying to think who might have had a motive to strangle Lenna, and hearing all that about Merritt Trumble sort of made me wonder."

"You think Merritt could have done such a thing?" Nadia asked.

"Strangle her?" Mosey shook her head. "Not really. But somebody did. It's just as likely, maybe even more so, that one of the partners had reason to want her dead."

"My lord, who?" Nadia asked.

"Ed Neville, for one."

"Why him?" Nadia scrunched her face.

"According to Dot, it's been rumored that Neville has always expected to step into Lenna's shoes, but he might not get the job. It might go to Bud Fortney."

"But Bud's only been at the firm for a short while, hasn't he? Neville's been around for ages."

"I know, and that's exactly what might give Neville a motive. But I was thinking Bud could have a motive, too. Dot says he's an upstart. She knows him from meetings of the business folks on the Square. He could have wanted to take over the firm and saw Lenna as a hindrance."

"Oh, please," Nadia said, "enough to murder the woman? I seriously doubt it."

"Mosey"—Robert's expression turned serious—"you would do well not to repeat any of this. Let Olivera question Lenna's associates. If there are any suspicions being voiced, I imagine somebody will eventually get around to spilling the beans."

"You think?" Mosey asked.

"For land's sake, this is a murder investigation. Most people will answer questions put to them by the police, out of fear if nothing else."

"I reckon." Mosey lifted her glass but didn't take a sip. After a bit, she set the glass back on the table and said, "I sure do wish I knew whose remains those were. Hugh, was the hair recognizable? I mean, long, short, blonde, brunette?"

"I'd say light colored and longish."

"How long?"

"Oh, about like Nadia's."

Chapter Thirteen

Police Station
Tuesday, March 16, 2010, 8:45 a.m.

The next day, as Olivera arrived at the station, he spotted Springer and Reagan eagerly waiting by the partition door. With a casual greeting of "Morning, all," he walked right past them and into his office. He hung up his hat but kept his sports jacket on, anticipating a quick departure. He checked his watch. It was already eight forty-five, and at nine, King Accounting would be opening its doors.

Springer came in, and Olivera wheeled around. "I guess you guys are wondering what I discovered yesterday at Red Oaks."

"Darn right, Chief."

Reagan peeped over Springer's shoulder. "We waited till five, thinkin' we'd see you when you got back."

"And you might have if things had gone as hoped, but that hardly ever happens in this business. Come in, have a seat."

"So, what happened?" Springer asked. He sat in the folding chair, and Reagan leaned against the partition door.

"Nothing, absolutely nothing. I scoured the whole

property, even checked the dock and the boat. There was a small watercraft tied up there. Didn't find a shred of evidence anywhere, unless you count the fact that I did verify there's a coffin missing from the mausoleum."

"Was it the same one Miss Lenna was laid out in?" Reagan asked.

"Maybe, but we haven't been able to verify that, not yet. Dr. McGinnis came out, took a look, but the lining was removed, replaced with a new one, clean as a pin, well, except for a couple of hairs and fibers. Likely the victim's."

"Gosh darn," Springer said, "that dang perp is bound and determined to remove any little thing that might help us figure this thing out."

"Yes and no," Olivera quickly answered.

Springer gave him a puzzled look.

"It's true what you say. He absolutely does his darnedest to clean up after himself, but at the same time, he's a bit of an exhibitionist."

"How you figure, Lieutenant?" Reagan said.

"You know what an exhibitionist is, Reagan. The opposite of what's his name…Paul Krueger."

"Huh?" Springer cocked his head.

"Simple. Some paraphiliacs enjoy voyeuristic experiences, while others prefer to be the center of attention. I mean, they want you to observe them. Get it?"

"Gad," Reagan said. "I don't know which is creepier."

"I'm not sure if Paul Krueger was a true paraphiliac or just a nuisance." Olivera stretched back in his high-back Executive. "But Dr. Wilson seemed to think so."

"So, this exhibitionist," Reagan said," this guy who

likes to be watched…"

"Oh, I was using the term loosely. There's nothing, uh, sexual about this murder, at least not far as we know. But whoever did it, apparently wants some attention. The staging at the crime scene, for one. Then, this business of leaving the door to the mausoleum open. I was thinking all along that the clues he was leaving were too intentional, but after what came up yesterday afternoon—"

"I thought you didn't find anything," Springer interrupted.

"We didn't. Not I in my search of the property nor Dr. McGinnis in her inspection of the coffin, except for those bits of evidence I mentioned before. On the other hand"—he sat up straight—"Hugh Jessup hit the jackpot."

Reagan, who stood casually propped against the door, leaned forward, causing poor Springer, already struggling to fit his ample backside into the flimsy chair, to lose his balance.

"Watch out, Reagan!" Springer yelled out.

"Sorry, I didn't mean to—"

Olivera heaved a sigh. "Listen, guys," he said standing, "I need to get over to King Accounting. It's almost nine o'clock. I was hoping to get there yesterday but Hugh called."

"But, Chief," Springer said, "what *about* Jessup. How'd he get involved in this?"

Olivera adjusted his hat, picked up his briefcase, and moved toward the door. "Not sure of much of anything yet, but Jessup ran across a bag of remains in the Civil War Cemetery. Dr. McGinnis took them to the morgue, and I'm hoping she can tell us something soon."

"My lord, Chief," Reagan exclaimed. "You reckon they're the remains from the missing coffin, I mean, the coffin in the parlor?"

"I fully expect they are. And by the way, we're thinking there's gotta be another coffin somewhere."

"Huh?" Springer said.

"The new lining—where'd it come from?"

"Oh, I see what you mean."

"I imagine it's in the basement or the attic. So I need you guys to get over there, see if you can find it."

"A coffin with a missing lining," Springer repeated.

"Yes, and should you find it, check the area around it thoroughly for prints, any bit of evidence."

"Fat chance we'll find anything."

"You see what I mean about this guy? He's like some depraved prankster."

"A depraved prankster in Hembree?" Springer looked at Reagan. "You better get home and lock your doors."

Chuckling at his sergeants, Olivera passed through the outer office. He paused at Ms. Hill's desk to tell her where he was going. "I don't expect to get into anything deeply, just an initial visit with the associates at the firm. And, by the way, I'm expecting an important call from Dr. McGinnis. Please let her know where I am."

"I got it, Lieutenant." She scribbled his instructions on a sticky note and stuck it to her desk calendar.

He tipped his hat and left through the front door, thinking that instead of driving over, he'd go on foot, the weather feeling spring-ish. He glanced up at the sky and, seeing no sign of rain, took off.

He soon arrived at the Square, which was only a leg-stretch from the station, and, continuing along Lee

Street, passed the door to Frye, Frye, and Humphrey. Spotting Carlotta Humphrey stepping out of her car, he waited, hoping to have a quick word.

"Lieutenant," she said, emerging from between two cars. "Were you waiting to see me?"

"Well, not really, but since you're here—"

"I've got a nine o'clock, but what was it you wanted?"

"You must have seen the news in the paper last night."

"You mean about Lenna Fortney? Terrible news. I swear." She shook her head. "Hembree is not the sleepy little town it used to be."

"If there's anything you might be able to tell me, I could drop by later this morning or this afternoon."

"I don't know I'd have anything to say, but, sure, come on by. Check with Dot. She can tell you if I've got a free spot."

"All right." He casually tilted his hat and took a step back. "I'll get in touch with Ms. Cowsley." He gave a friendly smile and walked on.

Coming to King Accounting, he spotted the wreath and, checking next to the door, read aloud the inscription on the brass plaque: " 'Accounting Offices of Lenna King Fortney, CPA.' " The names of the associates, Edward Neville and Bud Fortney, were inscribed below that of the head partner. "I bet they'll be taking that down soon," he mumbled as he wondered whose name would go up in place of Ms. Fortney's. "Hmm. That's a question I'll need to ask."

He had run over the interview in his mind and had a list of questions at the ready. If possible, he aimed to garner a rudimentary understanding of the business and some impressions of the team. He would also attempt to find out if Fortney might have been involved in any conflicts and, importantly, who would take her place as head partner. Naturally, he would need to follow up with in-depth interviews, but for now, a few basic questions should be enough.

He trudged up the stairs to the second floor and opened the glass door to the office. The receptionist, sporting a fashionable yet somber suit, rose out of his chair. "Lieutenant Olivera," the young man said, "we've been expecting you. Won't you have a seat?" He motioned toward a setting of mid-century modern furniture to the right of the entrance. "I'll let Mr. Neville know you're here."

Olivera, about to reach for his identification, removed his hat instead and took a seat in one of several green leather chairs arranged around a glossy chrome and glass coffee table. Huh, the color of money, he chuckled to himself, as he surveyed the surrounding furnishings. It was all very sophisticated and modern, not at all what he expected. He had pictured something similar to the front office of Frye, Frye, and Humphrey. But whereas Hembree's premier law firm exuded a strong sense of tradition, King Accounting was sleek and contemporary.

He didn't have long to wait. As he was picking up the March issue of *Currency*, a man he assumed to be Mr. Neville came out of the door just past reception. "Lieutenant Olivera?" He walked quickly in his direction and held out his hand.

Olivera replaced the journal and stood, giving Neville's hand a firm shake. "Yes, that's right. I guess you anticipated my visit. I am very sorry for your loss. It must have come as quite a shock."

"Yes, it did." Neville glanced down at the floor.

"We're definitely looking into it, and if I could get some basic information this morning, it would assist me in progressing a bit faster."

"Of course." He nodded. "I am anxious to help if I can."

Neville seemed genuine enough, but as Olivera followed him to his office, he found himself drawing mental comparisons between him and the image he'd been gradually forming of the suspect: somebody capable of throttling an older woman, staging the crime scene, and carting a bulky coffin from the mausoleum to the parlor. Try as he might, he couldn't imagine this guy fitting the bill. He wasn't stocky or even muscular. He was fairly tall, at least as tall as he was, with long legs and a slender build. He noticed his hair, perchance any hairs should turn up on the bedding he and Springer had removed from the master bedroom. It was darkish brown and a bit long for a man, slicked down, and very neatly cropped across the back.

They reached Neville's office, which was quite tidy, especially for a space occupied by a man. The folder holder at the front of the desk was filled with a neat stack of binders. There was also a pen set and a small clock on the desk, as well as a framed picture. He couldn't make out who it might be—his wife, maybe, though he wasn't wearing a wedding band. Everything on the desk was nicely arranged, and the shelves behind the desk were organized as well, with manuals and three-hole binders standing upright and perfectly aligned. With tax season reaching its peak, Olivera had somehow expected a disheveled mess rather than the very orderly sight before him.

Neville settled into a leather desk chair and cordially motioned toward a matching chair on the other side of the desk. "I read what was in the paper. She was found by Ms. Frye and Ms. Abboud, was she?" His voice reflected confusion.

"That's right. They were out at Red Oaks for an appointment. Let's start there." Olivera pulled out his tablet and pen. "Ms. Frye said she was there to talk to Ms. Fortney about the house. Were you aware she was thinking of selling?"

"Well, she had mentioned early retirement and, in fact, we'd put together a financial plan, anticipating—"

"You mean for her personally?"

"Oh, no, no, no. She wouldn't have wanted any help with that."

The emphasis Neville gave to *she wouldn't have wanted any help with that*, further strengthened the perception Olivera was forming of the deceased as a dominant personality, individualistic, possibly with authoritarian traits. "Then you must be referring to the firm."

"Yes, to the firm. As I said, she was thinking of taking early retirement, but before she left, she wanted to get a few things straight."

"Such as?"

"Well, who would be at the helm, for one, as well as some other changes she was thinking of making."

"In personnel?"

He nodded.

"Was all that decided?"

"Not definitively."

"I see." Olivera wanted to ask him directly if he

expected to take over but felt it too soon for that question, so he decided to go another route and ask about the financial stability of the business. "From what I hear, King Accounting is the premier firm in these parts."

"Yes, you could say that. It's well established in Dent County, and we've been here, gosh, I guess more than a half century. The business was started by Ms. Fortney's grandfather. Three generations of Kings have been head partner—"

"—but no longer, I assume?" Olivera tapped his pad with his pen.

"That's correct. Ms. Fortney didn't have any direct heirs. However, her nephew by marriage joined the firm not too long ago. James Fortney is his name. He goes by Bud."

"Bud," Olivera repeated. He somehow couldn't imagine a man who called himself Bud in the midst of all that sleek elegance. "I would like to speak with him, too, if he's available."

"Certainly, shall I ask him to come in?"

"Not quite yet. There was something else I wanted to ask you. Do you happen to know of any conflicts that Ms. Fortney would have been involved in, with personnel or clients?"

Neville swiveled in his chair and thought. "That's a little challenging to answer. You see, Ms. Fortney was guarded in her dealings with people. From what I was able to observe, she got along well with everyone here. If she hadn't, well, I doubt she would have kept them on. Hirings and firings were all under her control, no one else's. As far as clients were concerned, well, I think most of our clients were satisfied with our work. Rarely have we had a complaint, and I can't think of any recently."

"I will be honest with you, Mr. Neville. I don't know that much about the accounting business, but it seems to me that an accountant would know quite a bit about a person's affairs. Isn't that true?"

"Well, to some degree, yes. It isn't that difficult to spot red flags, should there be any. And, of course, a person's business receipts often tell a story."

"If a client were to get himself into trouble, say, some kind of illegal business practice, might the accountant be aware?"

"In some instances, yes."

"Any chance Ms. Fortney was concerned about any of her clients? And in the event that she was, how might she have approached that?"

"You are putting me on the spot, Lieutenant."

"How so?"

"If she'd had suspicions or any evidence of wrong doing, I believe she would have given the client the benefit of the doubt, unless, of course, he or she had been unwilling to cooperate. Anything that might have sullied the reputation of the firm…"

"But do you know of anything?"

"No," he said, then added, "not that I would feel comfortable speaking about."

"Mr. Neville, please keep in mind that this is a murder investigation and withholding evidence is a serious offense."

His brow rose slightly. "Could we put that question on hold for the time being? Give me a chance to look into this with some other members of the staff."

"Okay." Olivera took a breath. "But I recommend urgency. If you consider the nature of the crime, it is almost certain that it was committed by someone who knew the deceased fairly well, I would venture to say. And since she didn't have any family, other than Mr. James Fortney, well, we have to look at friends and associates."

"I understand," he said, his face all shadows.

"So, if you wouldn't mind seeing if Mr. Fortney is available…" Olivera stood and placed his business card on Neville's desk.

"Certainly. If you'd step back into the waiting area, I'll give him a call right now."

Olivera thanked Neville for his time and cooperation and, tapping on the business card he'd placed on the desk, asked him to give him a call should he think of anything relevant to the case. Neville said that he would and, picking up the receiver of his desk phone, punched in Fortney's number.

While waiting in reception, Olivera checked his messages and was disappointed to see that he hadn't received a text from McGinnis. He was hoping by now she had identified the remains. If they were the remains of Kemena King, as he suspected, they shouldn't be all that difficult to identify, especially if dental records were available. But if they were hers, what then? Why wouldn't the murderer have gotten rid of them or at least stashed them in a less obvious spot, instead of leaving them where they were bound to be discovered? It didn't make much sense, did it? Unless, of course, he actually wanted them found. So, if that was his intention all along, seriously, why? Was he trying to establish some sort of connection between the two incidents, Kemena King's accident and Lenna Fortney's murder? What a conundrum! He might need to dig deeper into that angle.

Perhaps the family member he was about to speak with would have some insight into the matter.

A man he presumed to be Fortney emerged from the office across the corridor from Neville's office, but instead of greeting him warmly, as Neville had done, he simply beckoned from the door, signaling him to come in. "Lieutenant," he called out, "you wanted to speak to me?"

Olivera confirmed with a nod. He got up and, skipping the handshake as Fortney had done, simply showed him his ID. "We're investigating the death of Ms. Lenna Fortney, and it's my understanding you are her next of kin."

"Yes, she was my aunt by marriage, Uncle Jim's wife."

"My sincerest condolences."

"Thanks. Come on in if you want." He waved him in with a sweep of his arm.

Olivera went in and waited till Fortney, motioning toward a guest chair identical to the one across the hall, invited him to sit. He settled into the chair and, while taking out his tablet and pen, caught a glimpse of his surroundings. There was a golf bag slouched in one corner and a tennis racket propped against the shelves. Few manuals were on the shelves but ample sports trophies were prominently displayed. "You go in for golf, do you?"

"Oh, yeah." Sinking into his chair, Fortney glanced at the trophies, then back at Olivera. "So, was there something you wanted to ask me?" He spoke curtly, seemingly eager to dispense with the interview and dive into a more important task, like heading off to the course.

"Well, a couple of things. First, I'm wondering if

you were aware of your aunt's plans to take early retirement."

Fortney's brow shot up, as if he were expecting a different type of questioning. "Surely my aunt's future plans had nothing to do with this terrible incident. I mean, I was thinking some lunatic—"

"This early in the game, who knows, but I fully suspect that the victim was known to the assailant."

"You do?"

Olivera nodded. "Typically, well, in instances of manual strangulation, unless the attacker is completely deranged—think serial killer, for example—it's highly likely that the victim was acquainted with the offender."

"I see." He rubbed his three-day stubble. "So, who do you suspect?"

"No one yet. But I wonder if *you* might suspect someone, I mean, someone who might have held a grudge against your aunt. I'm guessing you've had a night to think about this."

Fortney frowned, apparently not sure how to answer the question.

"I mean," Olivera said, "you must know things that no one else knows. Like, you must have heard stories over the years. Did your parents ever talk about the deceased?"

"Not that much, not that I recall."

"And since Ms. Fortney was your boss, perhaps you have formed an opinion all your own, I mean, independent of what you might have thought growing up. If I were in your place," Olivera added in a sympathetic tone, "I'm sure I'd find it awkward, I mean, uh, divulging details about an older family member. But these are special circumstances, mind you. If you know anything that would help solve the case, it's in your family's interest to let us know."

Fortney had been staring blankly at his desk but now cast Olivera a hard look. "But I don't really know anything. Aunt Lenna was a strong-willed woman. Everyone knew that. And because of that, she occasionally butted heads with people." He relaxed a little. "I got along with her just fine. Some people, I guess, took her more seriously, allowed her to get under their skin."

"What about in her dealings with clients? Did you ever observe anything that, well, struck you as a serious difference of opinion, I mean, between your aunt and some client?"

Fortney reiterated the phrase *difference of opinion* a couple of times, then admitted that he'd seen a man by the name of Nate Patterson, owner of a big seed company, leave the office pretty hot under the collar. "But I can't imagine," he chuckled, "old Nate going to such extremes. I asked Aunt Lenna about it, but she didn't seem to want to go into it, not with me anyway."

"Any other instances?"

He shrugged. "Not that I recall."

"Let me ask you about this. Do you plan to stay on with the firm, now that your aunt isn't here?"

"Yes, I think she would have wanted me to stay, my being a Fortney and all."

Olivera thought for a second. "I'm sorry to have to pry into your aunt's personal business, but, your being family, as you said, do you have any idea who her heirs might be?"

"I haven't seen her will, if that's what you're getting at."

"And she never mentioned…?"

"As her only nephew, I imagine I stand to inherit."

"And her attorney would be…?"

"Carlotta Humphrey."

"Carlotta Humphrey," Olivera muttered, closing his tablet. He thought for a second, then opened it again. "You know there is one more thing, though I doubt you know much about it. It happened a while back and didn't really involve your family. It involved the Kings and had to do with an unfortunate accident. Your aunt's ward Kemena King was killed in a boating accident. Do you know anything about that?"

"I heard about it from my parents."

"So, you weren't living here when it happened?"

"Yes, I was in the area. That must have been a few years after I finished at Blanchard."

"Oh, so you went to Blanchard, did you?"

"Yes."

"Then you might have known Kemena, maybe seen her at your aunt and uncle's house?"

"Yes, I knew her, not all that well, though."

"You don't happen to know anything about the circumstances, do you?"

"I'm not sure what you're getting at, Lieutenant. Why—?"

"It's been said," Olivera cut in, "that your aunt and her ward didn't get along well."

"That's probably true."

"You don't think this boating accident might have been avoided?"

"Well, Kimmy's fiancé seemed to think so."

Olivera flipped back to the notes on the boating accident he'd taken the day before. "Merritt Trumble

137

was his name, correct? Were you acquainted with him at all?"

"Yes, I met him, maybe once or twice. He seemed okay to me."

"So, do you think he might have held your aunt responsible for his fiancée's death by drowning?"

"That's what was said, but I don't think anyone took it seriously. Purely speculation on his part."

"Have you seen him recently, let's say in the last few months?"

Fortney, apparently trying to recall, stared straight ahead. "I did see him once, I believe, at an event at the college. My girlfriend works in the Development Office, and we were at a fundraiser for Blanchard."

"Really?" Olivera said. "I recently met the people over there. You must have heard about the death of one of their team. Charles Ashby was his name."

"Yes, actually, Tara Townsend, my girlfriend, took Ashby's place."

"Small world, isn't it, in Hembree?"

Fortney checked his watch.

"Okay, then." Olivera stood and handed Fortney his card. "That's all for now. I appreciate your time and cooperation, and please don't hesitate to contact me if you think of anything that might have a bearing on the case." Halfway to the door, he stopped. "By the way, that client you mentioned, Nate Patterson…"

"What about him?"

"I should give him a call, see if I can find out—"

"I wish you wouldn't," Fortney hastily responded.

"Why is that?"

"It wouldn't place the firm in a good light, well, disclosing information about a client. And I'm sure it has no bearing on your case, Lieutenant."

"You are?"

"Yes, I said that before. Nate's just a good old boy. He would never involve himself…Well, if you knew him, you would never suspect—"

"Not to worry, Mr. Fortney. Should I speak to Mr. Patterson, I won't mention your name."

"Okay, good, but like I was saying, it'd be a waste of time."

After leaving Fortney's office, Olivera swung by reception to get Patterson's contact information. Then, thanking the receptionist, he put on his hat and continued with his day.

Chapter Fourteen

The Square
Tuesday, March 16, 2023, 10:00 a.m.

As Olivera made his way down the stairs toward the Square, he ruminated about the implications of his interview with Ed Neville and James "Bud" Fortney. He reflected on the things he had learned and how they lined up with his initial expectations. Did he actually get any answers to his questions? He wasn't sure that he did. He still didn't know who would be in charge now that Fortney was out of the picture. And besides that, he couldn't say for sure that either of her associates was aware of her decision, if, in fact, the decision had been made. They certainly didn't let on if they did.

On the other hand, he had formed an opinion about whom he'd pick for the job. Ed Neville seemed the perfect type to run an accounting firm. Bud Fortney was a different story altogether. Too immature, too cavalier to be taken seriously as a businessman. Surely there hadn't been any competition between the two. He doubted that Fortney even wanted the job, at least not yet.

There was also the matter of Fortney's will. He had learned nothing of its contents, but at least he now knew the name of her lawyer, which he could have easily guessed. With that thought, he pulled out his phone and punched in the number of Frye, Frye, and Humphrey. He was only steps away from the entrance but preferred to do as Carlotta had suggested and contact Dot instead of barging in.

"Ms. Cowsley, Lieutenant Olivera here."

"Lieutenant," she said happily. "Carlotta mentioned you might call."

"I'm still here on the Square and wondered if now would be a convenient time to speak with her."

"It might be. She has a little time between this client and the next, and since you're right here…But hold on a second."

He waited as Dot spoke with Carlotta.

Dot came back on the line. "She says she has a few minutes if you want to see her now."

"Thank you, I'll be right up."

He dropped his cellphone in his pocket but then took it out again to make sure no texts or calls had come through since he'd last checked. None had, and feeling at ease, he proceeded up the stairs a few feet from where he was standing.

"Ms. Cowsley," he said as he opened the glass door at the top of the stairs. "It's good to see you. How are you?"

Dot stood and came toward him. "I'm fine, Lieutenant, and you? Let me take your hat."

"Not bad, thank you, ma'am."

"You can go on in. Carlotta is all set for you."

Well, of course, he mused to himself. He couldn't imagine Carlotta being anything other than "all set." When had he ever caught her off guard?

The door was half closed, and he pushed it open, showing, of course, the requisite hesitancy. "Might I intrude just a moment?"

"Of course, come in and have a seat, Lieutenant." She stood and removed her readers and, while moving toward the door, waved him in the direction of the upholstered chairs. "I'm going to close this, since I imagine what you have to say may be, well, private."

"Private, you say?" He unbuttoned his sports jacket and took a seat. "I imagine all I know will soon be public knowledge if it isn't already."

She made her way back toward him and slipped into the chair beside the one he'd chosen. "I know what you mean. News travels like greased lightning in these parts."

"Indeed, it does. I've just come from King Accounting but didn't find out much. I was hoping someone could tell me who will be taking over the firm. I don't suppose you have any ideas about that."

"I assume Ed Neville—who else?"

"Well, I thought perhaps Bud Fortney. I suppose Ms. Fortney might have wanted to keep the business in the family."

She frowned. "Bud's a little green, don't you think?"

"Green!" He chuckled.

Carlotta looked back at him with a puzzled expression.

"No"—he shook his head—"I didn't mean to imply...Well, what I wanted to say was that the furniture in the waiting area is green, and it struck me that the color seemed a suitable design choice for an accounting office." Sensing his little joke hadn't landed well, he cleared his throat and moved on. "But let me get to the heart of the matter quickly, since we haven't much time. Mr. Fortney said that you were his aunt's attorney."

"Yes, that's right. And I suppose you're hoping I'd be able to tell you something about who might inherit."

He nodded. "That is exactly what I would like to know if you can tell me."

"This might come as a surprise, but I don't believe any*one* will inherit all that much."

"Any*one*?"

"You must give me your most solemn promise that you will not reveal what I am about to say. Not that I consider it a violation of privilege for me to tell you this. On the other hand, the heirs deserve to know the contents of the will before the public."

"Of course."

"Seriously, now…"

"You have my word."

"Aside from a few relatively speaking small sums for a few individuals"—she looked bemused—"Lenna Fortney has left the better part of her estate to Blanchard."

"Oh, my, that *is* a surprise."

"I imagine it will be, once the will has been read, tomorrow morning, actually."

"Hmm," he muttered as he allowed the strange news to settle in. "Who would have predicted—? Well, on second thought, maybe it isn't that unexpected. It's my understanding that she was quite a philanthropist, according to the newspaper. So, I suppose the house, everything will go to Blanchard?"

"Not quite everything. Not the house. But, yes, the lion's share of the estate."

"I'm trying to imagine what bearing this might have on the case." He leaned forward, tapping his chin with his index finger. Carlotta didn't say anything but seemed to be looking at him intently, as if she were wondering the same and hoped to get an answer. "I'm going to have to think about this."

"If you come up with anything, would you let me know?"

He felt he had to say "yes," given her generous revelation. "Yes, but I have a feeling that *esto va para largo*. Sorry, sometimes my brain just switches to Spanish. I'm thinking I may not know anything, one way or the other, for a while."

"This is the most peculiar murder case I think we've had around here. And it worries me. The perpetrator seems especially dangerous, depraved. Too calculating."

"Yes, I would agree with that. I've seen some terrible murders, serial killings even. Not around here but in California. And this murder is giving off a similar vibe. Definitely calculated, idiosyncratic. It's hard to imagine how it was carried out. And, by the way, this is something that wasn't in the paper."

"Wasn't in the paper?"

"No, it happened too late in the day, but I imagine tonight's edition will carry the story. You see, as Dr. McGinnis and I were finishing up at Red Oaks yesterday afternoon, a call came in from Hugh Jessup over at the college, except he wasn't at the college. He was at the Civil War Cemetery. I think he must have taken one of his classes there on a field trip, and one of the students opened a bag left on the pedestal of a statue. Turns out the bag contained human remains. Well, hair and teeth, nothing more grisly than that. As we speak, Dr. McGinnis is trying to get an identification."

"My lord!"

"Yes, rather disconcerting, isn't it?" He heaved a

sigh and continued. "Shortly before then, Dr. McGinnis and I had already decided provisionally that the coffin in the parlor had probably been taken from the family mausoleum."

"So, you think the remains from the missing coffin somehow ended up at the graveyard?"

He nodded.

"But you don't know for sure?"

"Correct, but I'm hoping to hear something momentarily."

Carlotta heaved a deep sigh. "Very worrying. You don't suppose this person will kill again, do you?"

"I have nothing tangible that would suggest that. In simple terms, it seems likely the killer was driven by a twisted urge to seek revenge against someone he truly loathed. But at the same time, there is something about it that is quite macabre."

"Indeed." She pondered for a moment. "Do you have any idea which of the coffins is missing? I mean, I'm assuming there were several there."

"We aren't sure, possibly Kemena King's."

"Well, if hers is the missing coffin and the remains are hers, that would place Lenna's murder in a slightly new light, would it not? I mean, it sort of dredges up some unanswered questions about Kemena's death."

"I wish I knew more about that."

"I do, too. I'd only been here a year or two when that happened. I moved here from Vicksburg after my mom married Amos Frye, and it took a while to learn who was who. I remember the accident, though. It was the talk of the town for a while."

"Why was that, do you think?"

"Oh, I suppose because Kimmy was a young, pretty

woman, and wealthy, of course. She was Mr. King's ward before he died. But besides that, there was a lot of talk about her relationship with Lenna, who'd become her guardian when King died. The two women didn't get along. Why would they?" She shrugged. "They were opposites. Lenna was the upstanding, responsible type, and Kemena was pretty wild. Be that as it may, Mr. King seemed to favor Kemena, and Lenna was jealous, according to rumor."

"Sounds like oil and water, doesn't it? But just because they didn't get along, to jump to the conclusion that Ms. Fortney might have had something to do with Kemena's death…"

"That's the part I never quite understood."

"Did the police look into it?"

"I'm not sure. If they did, nothing came of it. I imagine the records show that she drowned."

"I've heard that the victim's fiancé disagreed with the findings."

"Yes, Merritt Trumble."

"Do you happen to know anything about him?"

"Not much. I know he still lives around here but not in Hembree. If you'd like, I could see if Dot has his contact information."

He stood. "That would be helpful, and I really do appreciate your taking the time—"

"No problem," she said, standing. "Glad to help when I can."

Together, they moved toward the outer office.

"Dot," Carlotta said, "could you check your contacts for Merritt Trumble? You know who I mean, don't you?"

"Yes, of course." Dot faced her computer screen and pulled up a file. "Let me write that down for you,

Lieutenant." She tore a pink sheet from a pad. "This is not his home address. I don't have that." She jotted something on the sheet. "This is the contact information for the architectural firm in Mound City. But I am sure they can tell you how to reach Mr. Trumble. He works at his daddy's firm."

"Thanks, much appreciated," he said.

"And let me get your hat." Dot rose out of her chair.

He put on his hat and tipped it to Carlotta, who was standing by her office door.

"And don't forget, Lieutenant," Carlotta said. "If you run across anything I should be aware of…"

"Of course," he said as he turned to leave. "I'll be in touch."

Chapter Fifteen

Nadia Abboud's Shop
Tuesday, March 16, 2010, 10:00 a.m.

Mosey didn't really have a good excuse for dropping in on Nadia, but she couldn't resist. The conversation at Al's raised questions about Lenna Fortney's murder but provided few if any answers. Now that Hugh had filled them in on the remains he and his class had stumbled across in the Confederate Cemetery, she felt more anxious than ever to go over the details of the case once more. Plus, she couldn't shake the thought that she and Nadia might be acquainted with this maniacal individual, and the very idea of him or her being loose in Hembree made her seriously uneasy.

It was about ten o'clock when she got to Abboud Antiques and found Nadia rummaging through a box of leftover merchandise from the previous year's Easter inventory. "You setting up for Easter already?"

"Already? Easter is on April 4. That's less than three weeks from now."

"Yeah, I guess it is. But St. Patrick's day is tomorrow. You can't switch out the window quite yet, can you?"

"I know that, but I've got to get everything ready to go. Spring is hard, girl. You've got St. Patrick's Day, then Easter, then Mother's Day, Father's Day…"

"I suppose so."

Nadia pulled a pair of Staffordshire bunnies out of the box and set them on the counter.

"I'm kind of in a lull over at the agency," Mosey continued. "I was expecting to list Red Oaks, but now, lord knows when Olivera will release the property. This could drag on for a while."

"I know you've been giving the case a lot of thought. Any ideas about who might have done it?"

"Ideas? Well, sure, I have some ideas but nothing the slightest bit substantive. I mean, I don't know if we're looking for some totally deranged individual or a more average person who wants us to think he or she is deranged."

"That's a good point." Nadia nodded approvingly. "It's like whoever did it set the whole thing up to deflect attention away from himself and onto somebody else. But seriously, who you think he was trying to shift the blame to?"

Mosey gave a casual shrug. "I can't think of a soul whose eccentricities rise to that level." She threw up her hands. "I mean, on the one hand, we ought to know the person—"

"What do you mean, we ought to *know* him?"

"Yeah, we should, because, well, Miss Lenna lived here all her life. Her business is right around the corner. Her clients are from here. I'm pretty sure in such cases it's highly unlikely the victim didn't know the perpetrator. This cannot be some random killing. I mean, really."

Nadia shrugged. "I guess you're right."

"Of course, I'm right," Mosey insisted. "But the

question is who in Hembree, for heaven's sake, could have planned and carried out this bizarre murder? Our homicides are always sort of spur-of-the-moment, no? Either crimes of passion or necessity?"

Nadia looked pensive. "I suppose so, though a lot of planning certainly went into that Sunny Banks situation."

"Yeah, it did." Mosey thought for a moment and suddenly feeling a surge of excitement, said, "All planned out so as to put the blame on someone else, exactly like this one."

"Oh, my goodness, I think you've hit the nail on the head. Another frame up."

"Yep, another frame up." Mosey nodded. "You reckon Olivera has thought of that?"

"Of course, he has. The man is a professional and a darn good one."

"Hey." Mosey gave Nadia a close look. "When did you develop such respect for Olivera?"

Nadia sighed. "I guess I sort of liked the way he handled that whole business with the casta paintings."

"Yeah, I did, too. You think he's starting to like us?"

Nadia chuckled. "Maybe. He doesn't seem to think of us as dirt under his feet anymore."

"Well, goodness. I'm not sure he ever thought of us as dirt under his feet. Flies in the ointment maybe."

Nadia chuckled again. "He breezed in here from California, acting all high and mighty. But we sure put him in his place, didn't we?"

"That's hilarious," Mosey said with a chuckle, "but you're right, I guess we did. You know he treated us rather decently out at Red Oaks."

"He did."

"I wonder how we might approach this."

"*We?*"

"Well, of course, *we*. You have as much to gain from this as I do."

"Monetarily, you mean?"

"Just think of all those fabulous antiques, taxidermy mounts…"

"Coffins, a catafalque," Nadia added sarcastically.

"You know what would fit great right over there?" Mosey gestured to a nearby corner that looked empty. "A coffin! Just imagine all the cool things you could put in it. My goodness, you could stick it in the display case and fill it up with skulls, bones…"

Nadia rolled her eyes, then let out a chuckle. "Can you imagine the ruckus it would raise?"

Mosey broke into laughter but quickly composed herself when the doorbell jingled.

"What's so funny?" Lauren Wilson had come in and stood glancing between Nadia and Mosey. She had on dark wash jeans and a plain T-shirt under a herringbone blazer, and her long auburn hair was swept up in back and fastened with a tortoiseshell clamp.

Nadia shook her head. "Nothing, really. I guess we got a little carried away." She picked up the box she'd been rummaging through and carried it behind the counter. "Can I help you with something?"

"I hope so. Spring break is next week, and I was thinking this would be a good time to furnish the downstairs rooms, well, minimally, anyway. I'd like to have people over, but I don't have any seating in the living room."

"Well, I have a good selection of sofas, loveseats, too, and chairs of all kinds. Most of them are in the middle room, but that sofa is rather nice." Nadia pointed to the gold tufted-back sofa near the counter.

Lauren looked at the piece.

"Sit down, if you'd like," Nadia said. "It's quite comfortable."

Lauren sat and leaned against the back. "It is comfortable but a tad formal for my taste."

"If you prefer something less formal, I have some options in the next room." She came from behind the counter and headed through the cased opening into the area where most of the sofas and loveseats were displayed. "Would you like something like this, for example?" She shoved back a wingchair, creating a space for Lauren to slip through. "The cover on the studio couch is washable, by the way."

"Well, yes, I can see something like this in the living room." Lauren sat on the piece that Nadia had recommended, a traditional studio couch with a textured slip cover. "But, you know, I have a lot of room to fill. Maybe a sofa, even two sofas, would work better in there."

"What about that one over there?" Nadia crossed to the other side of the room. "This is a sectional, and if you used all the pieces, you could fill up a good-sized room."

"I don't know." Lauren eyed the dark brown sectional. "It hadn't really occurred to me to put a sectional in there. Would that work with the style of the house?"

"You can make just about anything work these days. People like to mix and match styles. But if you want to stick with a Victorian look, why not do something like that?" She indicated a Victorian couch upholstered in a damask print. "The colors in the upholstery would be perfect for a comfy couch to relax on. Wouldn't show dirt."

"That's right," Mosey agreed, joining the conversation. She had quietly entered the room and was observing at a distance. "You could spill a glass of wine on that and it'd come right up. I always think about that. What if I had a party and somebody spilled a glass of red wine…"

"Maroon and orange, hmm," Lauren said. "Wouldn't show dirt. And the colors are beautiful, sort of like the colors in a sunset." She seated herself on the sofa, beaming as if she had found just what she was looking for. "I like this one, I really do. How much is it?"

Nadia checked the price tag. "Fourteen ninety-five. Is that about what you were wanting to spend?"

"Sounds about right. I've budgeted for a sofa and some chairs. What would go with this, you think?"

"Well, depends on the feel you want to create. You could lighten it up with something in a soft gold, or you could create a dramatic look with black and white. You could go with that orangey amber shade if you want a warm, cozy look. But, first, I'd suggest putting it in your space. Then you can figure out what to put with it."

"I could take it on approval?"

"Sure. You're not going to be certain until you see it in your room."

"Okay, then, I'd like to try it."

"Great. I'll write up the ticket," Nadia said, then headed out of the room.

"That was fast," Mosey remarked, stepping closer to Lauren.

"I guess it was if it works. I'm new at this. It's my first house, as you know."

"I hope everything has settled down for you," Mosey said sheepishly, as though she had a hand in the chaos that ensued soon after Lauren moved into Morris House.

"It has"—Lauren smiled—"though at some point I need to go through all those books in the cellar, get them out of there."

"Any ideas about how you'll use the room?"

"I don't see myself using it anytime soon. It's hard to get to, which must have been what Mr. Morris wanted, considering he built it that way. I consulted an architect about that. You know, if the room were more accessible it would add significant square footage to the house."

"An architect, you say?"

"There's a firm in Mound City, Trumble Architecture—do you know it?"

"Yes, of course. The Trumbles have been here for ages, well, not here but in Mound City."

"They haven't sent anyone out, but I'm hoping they will soon. I would hope to get it done in the summer."

Nice timing, Mosey thought. In mentioning the Trumbles, Lauren had given her the perfect segue to the topic she'd been itching to bring up. But just as Mosey was about to respond, Lauren chimed in. "Which brings me to a topic I wanted to ask you about. I believe back around the time the cellar was discovered, John Earle said something about another appraisal?"

"That's right. Would now be a good time for that?"

"Actually, it would. I have next week off, and I could be available most anytime if John Earle would want to send someone by the house."

"Next week? That might be a little soon, but I'll see what I can do. We definitely need a fresh evaluation, and to be honest, a new inspection would be even better. Your architect will have to follow the latest codes, not the ones from when the house was originally constructed. It would be helpful to know how far off the cellar is from current standards, so that's where I'd start. Nowadays, we've got strict regulations distinguishing rooms fit for habitation from rooms used for storage, I mean, like cellars."

Lauren frowned. "This is going to be complicated, isn't it?"

Mosey nodded. "To be honest, building a stairway from the interior of the house into the cellar and reinforcing the walls, well, all that could cost a bundle. Plus, you'd have to add heat and air if you expect to use the room."

"I thought as much, but it seems like a waste not to be able to do something with all that space."

"I agree, and getting it done now probably makes more sense than having it done down the road, that is, if the expense isn't too burdensome."

"Right."

"But never mind all that," Mosey said. "I'll speak to John Earle right away and see when we can send an inspector over."

"I appreciate that, Mosey."

"Well, it's the least we can do, considering we overlooked the existence of the cellar."

"An honest mistake, and we all make them."

The door bell jingled, and they both glanced in the direction of the front room.

"I should probably leave Nadia a check before I go," Lauren said.

Just as she was about to leave, Mosey quickly said,

"If you could spare a minute, might I pick your brain about something that came up yesterday?"

"Sure, what was it?" Lauren sat back down.

Mosey, going over and sitting next to her, said, "Just as I was about to list a new property, well, hoping to list—"

"Oh, Mosey," Lauren gasped, "I read about that in the paper. Robert and Hugh mentioned it, too, in our section meeting this morning. They seemed to know all about it."

Mosey nodded. "That's because Nadia and I were sort of involved."

"Yeah, sounded like that to me."

"You'd think by now I would be expecting it," Mosey gave a nervous laugh, "but one never really expects such things. You see, Ms. Fortney was thinking of taking early retirement and wanted Nadia and me to offer an estimate on the house and some of the furniture. But when we got there, she was dead, all laid out in a coffin."

"Incredible, isn't it? And then that awful thing at the cemetery. Hugh said one of his students found some remains?"

"I strongly suspect they're the remains of the victim's ward Kemena King. Miss Kimmy, as she was called. She died in a boating accident some years ago."

Lauren inched toward Mosey and lowered her voice. "You think there's a connection between the two deaths?"

Mosey leaned in. "It seems that way to me. But what really gets me is all the staging, with the added complication that the killer must have 'borrowed' the coffin from the family mausoleum. But seriously, why on earth leave the remains where they were sure to be noticed? Seems to me there are some really strange angles to all this, and who better to set the police in the right direction than a profiler?"

"Don't think it hasn't crossed my mind. But if Lieutenant Olivera wants a consult, he will need to contact me directly. I can't really—"

"Yes, of course not."

"But informally," Lauren added, "I could offer you an opinion, based on the information I have."

Mosey was so elated she could have done a cartwheel right there in the middle of Nadia's collection of vintage sofas. "Lauren, that would be just amazing. I've been racking my brain. You see, I can't resist getting involved. Can't seem to help myself."

"Have you ever thought of going back to college, taking some courses in forensic science?"

"That would be grand, but how can I? Gotta bring home the bacon, you know, to add a little extra to Robert's paycheck."

"You ought to think about it. You seem to have a natural inclination."

"What about this?" Mosey continued. "Would you be available later on today, say around happy hour? We could get together and run over the facts of the case as we know them. And maybe you could tell us something about the sort of person who might have committed such a crime."

"I think I could manage that. Say, around four at the Tavernette?"

"Perfect. I'll let Robert and Hugh know."

Lauren wrote Nadia a check but then decided to look at some other pieces that might go with the sofa she had chosen.

Mosey let Nadia know about the plan for later on and, getting a *maybe* in return, went on her way to Shepherd Realty. She entered reception just as John Earle Shepherd was leaving. "Hold on, John Earle. I need to ask you about something."

"What's that?" He paused next to the hat rack behind the door.

"I ran into Lauren Wilson just now, and she reminded me about the new appraisal we promised her."

"Yeah, I think we did say something about that. I tell you what. What about calling Gary Adams over at Dent County Appraisals—?"

"But wait a second," Mosey said. "What she really needs is a new inspection."

"I suppose we could do both."

"Good, because she's already contacted Trumble over in Mound City, and I'm afraid this is going to end up costing her a fortune."

"How so?" John Earle frowned.

"Just think about it. It's going to require quite a bit of construction to make the cellar accessible. As is, the staircase leads from the cellar up to a door under the porch. They're going to have to reposition the staircase or extend the flooring above it a good ten feet."

John Earle hung up his hat and accompanied Mosey into the reception area where Saffron sat glancing between the two of them. "I had a feeling," Saffron said, "we hadn't heard the end of this."

"I seriously doubt we'd be held liable for the buyer's damages," John Earle said, "since an effort was certainly made, well, to point out all defects. The problem is that you, Mosey, didn't know about the cellar, but I guess I did. I'd just forgotten about it. It'd been so long since I'd given the house a thought. Then, the Morris sisters didn't mention it. Oh, well, that's water under the bridge."

"I don't think Lauren really expects us to do anything," Mosey said, "other than provide the new appraisal as promised."

"I understand that."

"But now that she has contacted an architect…" Mosey gave John Earle a grim look.

He shook his head. "Should she decide to press it, hold us responsible, good lord…"

"Yeah, that's what I was thinking. I'd hate to drag the Morris sisters into it, but technically they're at fault for not telling us about the cellar. And seeing as you only knew about it by happenstance, I don't think it could be proved—"

"Good point," he cut in. "But let's try to avoid going to court over this. Let's play nice and hope that Lauren will do the same." He propped himself on the stool he'd been sitting on before Mosey's arrival. "Saffron, do this for me, please, ma'am. Get a new inspection as well as a new appraisal. But let's start with the inspection. Check the files to see who did the first one and give him a call." He looked at Mosey. "You know, it might turn out better than you think. With the extra square footage Lauren got for free, she might just come out on the winning end."

"I guess that's possible, though if she hires Trumble to do the work, the cost of a new staircase plus repairs to the room—"

"We shouldn't have to pay for all that," John Earle cut in. "We'd only be held responsible for whatever it takes to ensure the safety of the cellar, not to convert it into a habitable space."

"Hey," Mosey said with a big smile, "that's right. I was thinking—"

"I know what you were thinking," John Earle said. "Are you trying to run us out of business?"

"John Earle, please, I'm just trying to do the right thing by Lauren, and if it doesn't cost us a dime, all the better."

"Well, I'm prepared to pay for another inspection and another appraisal, but that should be the end of it."

"Okay, okay. I'm glad we've cleared that up."

"So, you ladies take care of that, and I will be on my way."

For once, Mosey was glad to see the bossman go. After what Saffron had said the day before, which had planted a seed in Mosey's brain about the possible insecurity of her job, she didn't want to hear any suggestion that her sale had somehow put Shepherd Realty in jeopardy. "Saffron," she said as soon as the door had closed, "I didn't like the sound of all that, and after what you said yesterday morning—"

"What?"

"You know, about job security—yours and mine. Why'd you say that?"

Saffron shrugged. "Business isn't that great, as you well know."

"But I mean, really, we're the strongest real estate firm in town."

"True, but a lot of places are downsizing."

"And all this would come up just as I lose the best listing I've had in a while. Drat!"

"Yeah, I know." Saffron rummaged through her file drawer and, grabbing a folder, handed it to Mosey.

"What's this?"

"Read the label."

"It's the Morris House file."

"If I were you, I'd check the paperwork before I made another move."

Mosey opened the folder that held the forms they'd filled out prior to the sale. "So, what should I be checking for?"

"I'd start with the one right there on top."

"The inspection form?"

"Yes, ma'am."

"Okay," Mosey said as she scanned the form. "But I did this before I sold the house."

"It won't hurt to look again."

Coming to a note the inspector had written at the bottom of the page, Mosey let out a little gasp. " 'There is no access to the area under the porch, and therefore it has not been inspected.' " She looked at Saffron. "Now I remember reading this and pointing it out to Lauren. She said, no problem."

"We don't do sloppy work at Shepherd Realty. You know that."

"My lord, I feel better about this."

"You did your job, and I did mine, so don't go feeling all guilty."

"You checked all this?" Mosey held up the folder.

"Of course."

"Hallelujah! Problem solved. But, Saffron, why didn't you say something when John Earle was here?"

"It won't hurt to let him squirm a little. John Earle has become an absentee boss, and maybe this problem with the inspection will get his attention."

"Saffron, you are a genius!"

Saffron laughed. "Mosey, it never hurts to look

around corners, see what's coming before it gets here. People have been telling me my whole life that I'm overly cautious, but I'm telling you, it doesn't hurt to be cautious. An ounce of prevention—"

"Oh, my gosh," Mosey interrupted.

"What is it?"

"Hold on a second." Mosey pulled out her phone. "I just remembered something." She had forgotten to contact Robert and Hugh about joining Lauren for happy hour. And hoping to catch Robert before his afternoon seminar, she opened her contact list and tapped on his number. "Just a second," she said to Saffron. "I want to catch Robert—"

Robert came on the line. "Mosey, what's up?"

"Can you and Hugh meet for happy hour at the Tavernette, say around four?"

"Sure, but I'll have to check with Hugh."

"Okay. Lauren is meeting us there, and maybe Nadia."

"Okay, I'll walk down to Hugh's office. Four, you said?"

"That's right, and text me soon as you know."

"Sure."

Mosey slipped her phone into her pocket.

Saffron gave Mosey a knowing look and uttered one word. "Mosey…"

Without another word spoken between them, Mosey understood the silent question in Saffron's gaze. "What?" Mosey said.

"You know what."

"Well, I thought it wouldn't hurt to run this whole thing about Miss Lenna by Lauren. She's a forensic psychologist, for heaven's sake. Who better—?"

"Do you really want to go stirring things up?"

"I'm not stirring up a thing, but I can't just sit here, hands folded."

"Mosey, you need to do your job, your real job."

"Look, I don't see anything wrong with getting together with a client, especially a client it'd pay to keep on friendly terms. Besides, I already mentioned it to Lauren, and she seemed fine with it."

"All right, but if I were you, I'd be careful. There's a killer out there, and this is not your run-of-the-mill murderer."

Mosey's eyes widened as she turned to face Saffron. "That's exactly what I was thinking. This is no ordinary killer."

"You can say that again."

"So, who do you think might have done it?"

"Somebody who despised the living daylights out of Lenna Fortney."

"Well, yes, but who?"

Saffron thought a second. "I'd start by asking myself where you might find that sort of person."

"What do you mean *where*?"

"I mean in what walk of life. Rich man, poor man, beggar man, thief, doctor, merchant, Indian chief."

"Hmm. Could be a rich man. Or a poor man. Unlikely a beggar or an Indian chief. That leaves doctor, possibly. I wonder what Eads would have to say about that."

"I'm thinking *merchant*," Saffron said with confidence.

"Merchant? Why merchant?"

"I guess cause I'm thinking *cut throat*."

"Eueue. Cut throat...*crushed* throat. Not a big

difference, is there?"

"When you think about Miss Lenna, what comes to mind?" Saffron asked.

"Money, accounting..."

"Money, money, money. And I'm thinking that if this was about anything other than plain old loathing, it was about money."

Chapter Sixteen

Abboud Antiques
Tuesday, March 16, 2010, 10:45 a.m.

On his way back to the station, Olivera decided to take a quick detour by Abboud Antiques. He'd received a text from McGinnis saying she needed more time with the remains and to drop by around twelve. He entered the store and, seeing Ms. Abboud with a customer, strolled into the room where the bulk of the furniture was displayed, thinking he might as well start there. To his surprise, Lauren Wilson was sitting on a couch on the far side of the room. He waved his hat. "Dr. Wilson, I didn't expect to see you here."

"Oh, hey, Lieutenant." She waved back, looking pleasantly surprised.

He chuckled. "Well, here we are. Two—" He stopped himself, not really knowing how to finish his depiction.

She chuckled. "So what would you call us?"

"Bachelor and bachelorette, I suppose. Is that word permitted...*bachelorette*?"

"I'm sure someone would find fault with it."

"I guess," he replied as he made his way to the couch where she was sitting. "You in the market for furniture?"

"I have just purchased this." She patted the seat

cushion. "Do you like it?"

"It looks comfortable, but I'm afraid my opinions about furniture wouldn't be worth much. In fact, I was hoping to consult Ms. Abboud about a few pieces for my place. Where to start is my problem. I don't have anything in the living room other than a floor lamp I picked up for purely practical reasons. I think I might have mentioned that."

"Yes, I remember."

Neither of them were likely to forget that day in early January when Wilson had come to the station to report an intruder and ended up on the floor in a dead faint. He cleared his throat and added, "I'm not a fan of overhead lighting."

"Really?" she responded, as if the idea somehow surprised her.

"No, don't care for it, especially those fluorescent lights at the station."

"That's become a popular thing to hate…overhead lighting."

"It makes me feel like I'm on stage."

"You wouldn't be an introvert, would you, Lieutenant?"

"I expect I am."

"That makes two of us."

"Which may explain why a year later—more than that—I still haven't taken the time to furnish the living room."

"And now, all of a sudden, you are taking the time." She gave him a sideways glance.

"Yes, and I'm not sure why," he said, though a second later, he realized exactly why he had thought of furnishing the living room and the dining room, too.

"If you own a house, you might as well furnish it, make it comfortable and inviting," she said. "Otherwise, what's the point? You might as well live at the Tavernette."

"Ugh," he muttered at her reference to the Tavernette. "I spend too much time there as it is."

"You and half of Hembree. In fact, I'm meeting Mosey there later this afternoon."

"You are?"

"She wants to run something by me. I saw her here a few minutes ago."

No surprise there, Olivera mused. He'd pondered who would be the first to approach the young Dr. Wilson, he or Mosey Frye, Wilson being the obvious choice with whom to discuss the matter at hand, i.e., the Fortney case. "Why does this not surprise me?" He gave a half grin.

"You're on to her, are you?"

"Dr. Wilson, this is a very small town, and something tells me that you, Ms. Frye, and I will be rubbing elbows often."

"Does that bother you?" She shot him a playful smile.

"It did at first, it certainly did, present company excepted. But now, as time has passed, I've come to view Ms. Frye as more of an asset than a hindrance." He felt proud of himself for confessing his change of heart to Wilson.

"She's an interesting type."

"Ha," he said with a chuckle. "You've already profiled her, have you?"

"In my line of work, I guess it's the natural thing to do. It's hard not to."

"Speaking of which, Ms. Frye can't seem to avoid getting involved, well, in homicides. When I first moved here, I thought she was just a busybody, but to be honest, it's almost as if murder seeks her out."

Wilson looked disturbed.

Olivera continued. "If there's a body to be found, she finds it, not that she actively hunts for bodies, at least I'm assuming she doesn't. And yet somehow they manage to position themselves in her path."

"And in the case of Lenna Fortney, the offender apparently took advantage of Mosey's reputation."

"How's that?" He gave her a close look. Evidently, she had picked up on something he'd missed.

"Well, what you were saying. Whoever killed Lenna Fortney must have drawn the same conclusion, that Mosey is a kind of magnet for murder, ergo, she would be the ideal person to find the body. The perfect spectator, you might say. A good audience for his or her little—" She looked pensive as she searched for the right word. "—spectacle, I guess I would call it. It's as if the killer were directing a play and arranged the whole thing. A very controlling person—"

"Dr. Wilson," he broke in, "would you mind accompanying me to the Tavernette for a coffee?" He glanced at his watch. "I have a little time to kill, and I would love to pursue this conversation, but I fear this is a rather public place to be discussing—"

"Sure. I'm through here for the moment, but you, Lieutenant—"

"No worries," he said with a shrug. "I can drop by anytime. I'm really in no rush." As the words spilled out of his mouth, he realized that they were true. If anyone was in a rush, it was Eads, and feeling the weight of her resolve, he'd decided to go along rather than resist. But deep down, he was still questioning. Did he really agree with her, or did he somehow need to break through the cycle of approach-avoidance? That bit of complexity really got his mind racing, but then the doorbell jingled, snapping him out of it. "Ready to go, Dr. Wilson?"

A few steps behind Wilson, he entered the front room. Not recognizing the person who'd come in, he felt relieved. In fact, he sensed a little warmth rising to his cheeks. Was he blushing? Surely not. He never blushed. He waved his hat in front of his face.

"Are you okay, Lieutenant?" Wilson said.

"Oh, sure. It's warm in here, don't you think?"

"It seems warm everywhere to me. I'm not used to mild winters. I might as well have given my woolens away."

"I guess you're still adjusting. You've been here for, like, three months, right?"

They passed through the door and into the street, and retracing his steps, Olivera, in the company of Wilson, headed back toward the Square.

Within minutes, they entered the bar of the Tavernette, and he looked for a secluded spot where they could converse freely. He motioned toward a booth in the corner. "Is this okay?"

"Sure."

"Would you care for coffee?" he asked Wilson, as she removed her jacket and took a seat.

"I'd prefer a tea."

"Ruby." He signaled to the waitress. "When you can, a coffee and a tea." He slid into the seat across from Wilson.

Ruby gave him a nod and, before long, arrived with

their drinks. "You guys want something to munch on?"

"Like what?" he asked.

"Miffy just pulled a tray of hot scones out of the oven."

"You care for something?" he asked Wilson.

"Well, I don't think I can turn down a hot scone."

"Nothing for me, thanks." As soon as Ruby had left, he reached for the sugar to sweeten his coffee, then passed the bowl to Wilson. "To get back to what we were discussing—"

"About Mosey, you mean?"

"Yes, Mosey. You seriously believe the culprit chose her to discover the body? I mean, it never occurred to me—"

"It's just a theory, but if the profile I'm imagining holds true, the finding of the body and the reaction of the person who found it, well, both could be key elements of the spectacle."

"I suppose that's true of creative types, like actors, musicians, and so forth. But, you see, I'm not accustomed to dealing with creative types."

"That's probably because most homicides are not planned, well, not in the sense that this one was planned. He or she went to a lot of trouble to create a scene, just as a playwright creates a scene, with staging, props, even a costume for the victim. I don't believe he would have wanted the tableau he meticulously contrived to be regarded by just anyone who happened along."

"Hmm." He thought for a moment. "But if that's true, how could he have arranged for her and Nadia's arrival? It's not as if they dropped in on Fortney every day. I don't believe either of them had been to Red Oaks in years."

Ruby arrived with the scone, and Wilson thanked her, then pulled off a piece and offered it to Olivera.

"No, thanks. I don't have much of a sweet tooth."

She popped it in her mouth and chewed, then, wiping her mouth, continued. "Okay, so regarding your comment, the culprit couldn't rely on them suddenly showing up, as he could have done if the chosen spectator worked there or was a regular visitor. But it is possible—" She paused to take a sip of tea. "—that he knew that Mosey and Nadia had an appointment at the house. The victim herself could have mentioned it, or even Mosey or Nadia might have mentioned it."

"So, you're saying Fortney confided in the killer about personal matters, like the sale of her home?"

"That's only one of many possibilities. How news of the appointment leaked is sort of like a pebble dropped into a pond. Maybe Mosey mentioned it to Robert, or Nadia mentioned it to her father. Or, who knows? Maybe someone at King Accounting overheard Ms. Fortney's secretary remind her of her appointment with Mosey and Nadia. It's even possible the killer could have made the appointment himself. Do we know for a fact that Ms. Fortney made the appointment directly? People like Lenna Fortney often have other people make their appointments."

"I guess I need to ask Ms. Frye about that." He took a sip of coffee and thought for a second. "Let me ask you something else. The remains…You heard about the remains, right?"

"In the graveyard? Yes, Hugh and Robert told me."

"Let's imagine that the perpetrator took them from one of the coffins in the mausoleum. Once I'd checked the names on the floor against the coffins, I suspected that the one missing was Kemena King's, Ms. Fortney's ward. She died in a boating accident at the lake behind the house about a decade ago. She was very young and engaged to be married to a young man by the name of Trumble."

"Merritt Trumble?"

"Yes, that's right. Why? Does the name strike a chord?"

"Indeed, it does. I have an appointment with Mr. Trumble."

"Really?"

"The architect in Mound City?"

"I believe so."

"So what about him?" she asked, sounding slightly unsettled.

"As I said before, he was engaged to marry Kemena King and, according to what I've been told, he thought Ms. Fortney might have somehow been responsible for his fiancée's accident."

"I see." She paused to think. "So, you think Trumble could have a motive?"

"Maybe. I haven't spoken with him yet. Actually, I have a couple of people of interest but no suspects per se."

"If you don't mind my asking, who else do you think might have had a motive?"

"Well, two of her associates at the accounting firm, Ed Neville and Bud Fortney, and a client by the name of Nate Patterson, the owner of a local seed company."

"So, why the two associates?"

"This is speculation, mind you, but Neville might have a motive if things were not playing out for him at the firm. You see, with Ms. Fortney's taking early retirement, Neville could be the one in line to take over as head partner. If he had been passed over, well…"

"Okay." She gave a nod. "So what about Bud Fortney?"

"Same thing, more or less. She might have chosen Bud, since he's her next of kin, though he hasn't been at the firm all that long, and he's only related by marriage."

"So, there could have been some rivalry between Neville and Fortney, and either of them could have cause, should he not get what he hoped for."

"That's what I was thinking, but after interviewing the two of them this morning, I'm not sure I can imagine either as the killer. I'm not sure Bud Fortney would have even wanted a promotion. He's still young and doesn't seem that dedicated. But he expected to inherit…" He trailed off, remembering that he had given Carlotta his solemn word not to repeat what she had told him about Ms. Fortney's will.

"Has the content of the will been made public?"

"Not yet, but I expect to know something soon."

"A lot of important pieces are still missing." She sipped her tea.

"I suppose the nature of the crime is pushing me to focus on the kind of person who could have done it."

"Of course. The killer is apparently clever and deranged."

"Or maybe not. It has also crossed my mind that someone is being framed."

"Like who?"

"Merritt Trumble, for example. He's a creative type, he might have had a motive, considering his connection to Kemena King. If it turns out that the victim was, indeed, laid out in Kemena's coffin, it somehow seems almost obvious, too obvious."

"It does, doesn't it?"

"Gossip has it that the two women didn't get along, and supposedly, Ms. Fortney was jealous of Ms. King."

"The idea would be that Trumble, after years of holding a grudge, finally decided to take revenge, strangling the enemy of his fiancée and placing the body in Kemena's coffin." She pulled off a piece of scone. "And, of course, he wouldn't want that implication to go unnoticed, so he carried Kemena's remains to the cemetery, where they were bound to be seen. Sounds sort of like a three-act play."

"A three-act play," he repeated.

"This totally feels like a play to me, sort of like a Greek tragedy," she added. "Imagine Ms. Fortney as the protagonist. And of course in tragedies, the protagonist must have a fatal flaw, right?"

"If you say so. It's been a while since sophomore lit." He chuckled.

"Oh, you remember this. Of course, you do. The tragic flaw, that little weakness that brings the protagonist down. In Fortney's case, it could have been her jealousy toward her young ward, if we can assume the gossip is true. From the antagonist's point of view, Fortney's jealousy was somehow mixed up in the death of his future bride. And who would be more likely to take revenge than he? So, to me, at least, all of that makes sense so far." For a moment, she sat mindlessly stirring her tea. "What I can't account for is the long delay between the death of Trumble's fiancée and the act of revenge. That strikes me as anomalous. Surely his resentment would have cooled by now. Didn't you say it's been ten years?"

"Ten years." He nodded. "It does seem quite a long time to wait—" He paused. "—unless, of course, something else occurred in the interim to rekindle the 'antagonist's' hatred."

"Well, yes, if the old grudge had cooled. But then something else occurred, reawakening his resentment."

"Hmm. I'll have to follow up on that." He took out his pad and, turning to a clean page, scribbled a note.

"And," she added, "since I am anticipating a meeting with the man himself, maybe I can help you with that."

Chapter Seventeen

The Morgue
Tuesday, March 16, 2010, 11:45 a.m.

Around noon, Olivera arrived at Delta Infirmary and briskly walked the length of the long corridor to the morgue. He was eager to hear what McGinnis had discovered about the remains found at the cemetery and was equally keen to discuss Wilson's profile of Fortney's killer.

As he entered the room, he didn't see the petite coroner in her usual place beside the gurney but spotted her at her desk near the back. "Dr. McGinnis." He tossed his hat toward the rack in the corner. "Have you got some results for me?"

"I do."

"Awesome!" He made his way toward the back and sat down on the chair beside the desk.

"As we suspected"—she removed her readers—"the remains are likely those of Kemena King. I got a positive on the teeth from her dentist, who still has a practice here. That was lucky."

"You know, this is all beginning to fit."

She arched an eyebrow in surprise. "How so?"

"I've just been talking with Dr. Wilson—you've met her."

"Yes, of course, I've seen her a couple of times."

"That's right. It hasn't been that long since we were at her house. Well, she's begun to construct a preliminary profile of the killer."

"You mean you've already asked for a consult?"

"No, not really. I ran into her at the antique store."

"The antique store? How did you happen to be there?"

"Aren't you the curious one."

"Sorry, I just couldn't imagine…"

"I dropped by on my way back to the station after interviewing Neville and Fortney. And Wilson was there. She'd just bought a couch, and we got to talking. She'd already heard the news about the murder, the remains, too. Seems she was in a meeting with Jessup and Ellison."

"And based on that, she came up with a profile of the killer?" She sounded skeptical.

"I suppose so. I think it was the staging at the crime scene she found most, well, suggestive."

"Suggestive is right," she said, a hint of disdain in her tone.

"Dr. McGinnis…I am surprised."

"At what?"

"You sound, well, distrustful of Dr. Wilson's findings."

"Findings," she repeated.

"If not findings, what would you call them?"

"Fantasy?"

"Oh, come now. Profiling has been around for a while. I think it's fairly respected, well, perhaps not by some."

"It's interesting, I'll give it that. And occasionally

helpful, but I don't think it's really scientific."

"I don't suppose you would throw out the whole field of psychology—or would you?"

"Well, no, not the whole field, but it is quiet theoretical, wouldn't you say?"

"Yes, I suppose it's somewhat theoretical." He cleared his throat. "But to get back to the subject at hand, I think Dr. Wilson homed in on some rather interesting elements of the crime." He paused to look at McGinnis, who didn't seem to be paying much attention. "She emphasized the creative nature of the crime and suggested I might keep that in mind. You see any harm in that?"

"No, no harm in that."

"I think it's rather clever. I mean, if you think about it, your run-of-the-mill killer wouldn't have gone to such lengths to create a scene, so to speak. She said it reminded her of a scene from a Greek tragedy."

"Indeed," she said with a slight smirk.

"Yes, she likened the victim to the protagonist, and the culprit, whoever that might be, to the avenger. And when I mentioned that someone—you, I believe it was—had brought up the name of Merritt Trumble, I filled her in on that angle, and she had an intriguing idea about a potential role for him. If Ms. Fortney was jealous of her ward and failed to watch out for her as a guardian ought to have done, then that would be Fortney's fatal flaw. Envy is a mortal sin—did you know that?"

She didn't answer, just raised an eyebrow.

"So, to finish, Merritt's part would be that of the avenger of his fiancée, and that would explain the placement of Fortney's body in Kemena's coffin. And getting to the remains, I suppose you could argue that

Trumble, if he actually did it, was trying to suggest a link between the two deaths."

"That's quite a story, but I think it could be a little dangerous."

"What makes you say that?"

"Because you haven't even spoken with Trumble, and you're already thinking he may have committed this horrific crime."

"That's not so unusual. Even the strictest of scientific methods begins with a hypothesis."

"Yes, but a hypothesis must carry with it a very large question mark."

"Of course. I'm aware of that."

"Poor Merritt."

"Oh, for god's sake. But you must admit he fits the role of the creative killer. He's an architect, is he not?"

"Yes, and I'm not denying the possibility—"

"Then, what's the problem?"

"I would start with the physical evidence and go from there."

"I would like to do that, but the killer did such a good job of cleaning up after himself or herself. Speaking of which," he continued, "did you find anything on the poker or the linens?"

"No. If he did use the poker, he must have wrapped it in something that wouldn't have left any evidence on the victim's neck. But the bruising matches the shape of the poker, so we can assume it could have been the weapon. If not it, something much like it. I also checked the linens and found nothing that might not have come from the victim herself."

"So, basically, we have little to go on. Oh, but what about the charred papers?"

"Well, I attempted to capture the contents using a digital camera with an infrared light. But I'm afraid it would take someone skilled in forensic document examination to decipher the writing. If you think it's important, I could see if they have the right equipment at the anthropology lab."

"We could put that on hold for the time being."

"And, by the way, I've taken DNA samples from both Fortney and the remains, just in case."

"Good. We may need it. Anything else?"

"Yes, one more thing. I think we might extend the time of death a little."

"Not Sunday morning?"

"It could have been some hours earlier, say, Saturday night late?"

"Which could be crucial as far as the suspect's alibi is concerned." He thought for a second, then added, "You know, I had something else as well, but I don't know if I dare mention it," he chuckled, "after your reaction to Dr. Wilson's other deductions."

"Oh, go ahead." She chuckled in response.

"To revisit the Greek tragedy analogy, Dr. Wilson thinks the killer might have chosen the audience."

"Audience? You mean Mosey and Nadia? Or you and me?"

"Wilson was thinking Mosey and Nadia, but I guess you and I were spectators as well. I hadn't thought of that."

"Spectators. I've never thought of myself as a spectator." She gave him a pensive look. "But how would the killer arrange for Mosey and Nadia to appear suddenly at the crime scene?"

"I posed the same question. She said that the killer

could have arranged for them to be there, could have even made the appointment himself."

"Well, that should be simple to verify."

"But even if Ms. Fortney did make the appointment over the phone, would they have recognized her voice? I don't think either of them really knew her. Their contact was minimal."

"So, the perpetrator might have imitated Fortney's voice. Interesting possibility. But why would he do that?"

"He wanted the crime scene to be viewed and picked the people he wanted to view it."

"But why specifically them?"

"I'm not sure about that. It almost seems like he was attempting to inject a bit of humor into the situation. Comic relief, I guess you could say. For Fortney's body to be discovered by none other than Mosey Frye, Hembree's absolute pro at finding bodies…"

She glanced at the clock on the opposite wall and, standing, slipped off her lab coat. "Lieutenant, I don't suppose you have had lunch."

"No, I haven't."

"So, what if we grab a bite to eat, and I will attempt to pull you out of the rabbit hole you've fallen into."

Laughing together, they made their way to the front and, once he'd retrieved his hat, they left the morgue.

During a quick lunch at the dairy bar near Delta Infirmary, McGinnis pointed out some of the fallacies of so-called forensic science, as she put it. While readily admitting to her own reliance on fingerprints, bite marks, and the like, she claimed that recent findings were putting even these old standbys in doubt. Olivera listened attentively, as he always did when she offered an opinion on a case. Nonetheless, he couldn't quite put Wilson's intriguing perspective out of his mind. As a matter of fact, he was fairly convinced that Wilson's Greek-tragedy analogy was worth serious consideration.

But while he was weighing McGinnis's scientific method against Wilson's imaginative approach, a strange feeling slowly crept over him, suggesting, if ever so faintly, that the subject under consideration, at least from his point of view, wasn't the evidence so much as the women themselves. Or to be frank, his feelings toward them. Although the delightfully rational Eads McGinnis had managed to hold his attention from the time of her arrival in Hembree, he now felt his interest drifting elsewhere.

Olivera, starting to feel antsy to get back to the safety of his cubicle at the police station, felt a wave of relief as he said goodbye to McGinnis and gave her a quick kiss on the cheek. When he arrived at the station, Springer greeted him as he came in and followed him toward the back corner.

"You've been gone a while, Chief," Springer remarked.

"Yeah, I have, and I've covered a lot of ground." He hung up his hat and slipped off his sports jacket.

"How's Dr. McGinnis progressing with the evidence?"

"She's managed to get through most of it, well, the bed linens, poker, and charred paper. No good leads so far, unfortunately. No prints or fragments. She did have one vital piece of information to share. The remains Jessup found at the cemetery most likely were Kemena King's. She got a match on the teeth. Evidently, King's dentist is still around."

"That's good to know."

"Yes, it is. But it raises a question, like maybe the killer was trying to connect the two deaths, Fortney's and Kemena King's. What's your take on that?"

"Gosh, Chief." Springer took a seat in the folding chair. "Could be, I reckon. I mean, it kinda seems like some bizarre clue, doesn't it?"

"Honestly, I kind of feel like I'm being toyed with a bit. It's as if the culprit were urging us to connect the dots. Which we always do, but the bad guy usually doesn't help us along with that—wouldn't you agree?"

"Heck, yeah. Criminals don't help you crack the case. That's for sure."

"So, what do you make of that—a perpetrator who drops a clue here and there?"

"I have no idea. I've never heard of such a thing, not around here."

"Which brings me to a theory I've been discussing with Dr. McGinnis. I bumped into Dr. Wilson as I was coming back from the Square, and she said the case has some of the elements of a Greek tragedy."

"A Greek tragedy, eh?"

"You see, tragedies have a protagonist and antagonist, and let's say Lenna Fortney is the protagonist." He paused. "Actually, Kemena King might have been the antagonist originally, but forget that, she's dead. So, now the antagonist would be the culprit, but the culprit isn't entirely to blame. The real blame can be attributed to the protagonist's fatal flaw."

"Fatal flaw," Springer repeated, scrunching his nose.

"Yes, and in this case, Lenna Fortney's fatal flaw was her jealousy. Her jealousy led her to neglect her young ward Kemena King. You know, some people held Fortney responsible for King's death."

"Well, I don't know I'd say *responsible*. More like *involved in*."

"Well, okay, involved in—whatever. So now, ten years later, somebody decides to take revenge, and who better than the victim's fiancé Merritt Trumble, which makes him the antagonist."

Springer sat scratching his head for a second. "I think I follow you, but I have to be honest with you, Chief. I somehow doubt any of this would hold water in a court of law."

"Hmm." He rested his cheek against his fist, feeling a tad deflated. "Yeah, Springer," he said with a sigh, "I expect you're right about that. Unlikely to hold water in a court of law, and I suppose it's a good thing it wouldn't."

"You said Dr. Wilson came up with all that?"

"Yes, as a matter of fact she did."

"I thought profilers—well, I don't know much about it."

"I found it intriguing when she explained it. But when you get right down to it, I suppose it's, well, pretty much baseless."

Springer let out a *huh* but said nothing more. Olivera, finding his sergeant's silence a bit bothersome, decided to counter. "Is that all you've got to say—*huh*?"

"Gosh, I didn't mean to upset you."

"Upset me?"

"Yeah, I mean, I'm sure you and Dr. Wilson must be onto something, but if you start talking about Greek tragedy around here, you're liable to lose your audience. No jury in Hembree would know much about any of that stuff. Protagonists, antagonists, fatal flaw…"

"Springer." His mood suddenly lifted. "Well, actually, you caught on pretty fast. And by the way, I almost forgot. There was another thing she mentioned— audience. Dr. Wilson thinks that Ms. Frye and Ms. Abboud's arrival at the crime scene was calculated. Them showing up when they did was part of the plan. The culprit actually picked them to be the spectators."

Springer tilted his head and furrowed his brow. "Seriously, why?"

"Comic relief!"

Springer hung his head. "I don't find it a bit funny."

"You probably wouldn't, but the perpetrator might. Who better to find a body than Mosey Frye?"

"Oh, okay, I can see that. But it still doesn't seem funny. Sort of pitiful."

"What seems pitiful to you, Springer, might seem funny to the deranged fellow who did the crime."

"Now, that I agree with a hun'erd percent. The guy is no doubt deranged, though right smart, finicky, and quite dangerous."

"Dangerous," Olivera repeated, as he tapped his chin in thought. "You don't think he's likely to kill again, do you?"

"Wouldn't surprise me in the least. Me and Reagan were talking about that before you came in. This dude sounds to us like a serial killer. Not that we've ever seen any serial killing around here, but, you know how on TV they don't put all the details in the newspaper, so as to rule out false confessions. There's a lot of detail in this case, like he was putting his personal stamp on it. Isn't that what serial killers do?"

"Some do, for sure." Olivera took a long, deep

breath and let it out. "You're scaring me, Springer." He got up out of his chair. "I think I need to get on down the road, interview the remaining suspects right away. I'm not sure this theory of Dr. Wilson's is helping me solve the case."

"Where you going, Chief?"

"Well, I need to drive over to Mound City."

"Mound City?"

"That's where Merritt Trumble's office is."

"Shouldn't you call first, make sure he's there?"

"I think I'd rather catch him off-guard."

"If he's as calculating as you think he is, he's probably expecting you."

"You're right, he probably is." Olivera chuckled. "Nonetheless…"

"Is he the only one—Merritt Trumble?"

"No, when I was questioning the others this morning—Ed Neville and Bud Fortney—Neville sort of danced around the possibility of a quarrel between Ms. Fortney and a client, but he wouldn't come right out and say who. Asked me if we could put that on hold until he could speak to the other partners. But then Bud Fortney came right out and said that she and Nate Patterson didn't seem to see eye to eye. You know the guy?"

"Nate Patterson? Must be the one who owns the seed company. I don't know him, but I know who he is. The Pattersons have had a monopoly on the seed business in Dent Country for a good long while."

"So, what's that—a million-dollar business?"

"A lot more than that. Ask any farmer and he'll tell you."

Chapter Eighteen

Blanchard College Campus
Tuesday, March 16, 2010, 3:00 p.m.

Mosey wrapped up her tasks at Shepherd Realty with time to spare before meeting Lauren, Robert, and Hugh at the Tavernette. She took a moment to ponder over Robert's revelation concerning Miss Lenna's generous donation to the college. She'd heard plenty over the years about Hembree's grande dame but didn't recall any mention of her philanthropic endeavors. So, yeah, what Saffron said about philanthropy and control struck a chord with Fortney's need to be in command. Intrigued by these thoughts, Mosey had an irresistible impulse to swing by the Development Office and poke around to see what might jump out.

She entered the campus through the wrought-iron arch and headed to Founders Hall, where some of the administrative offices were housed. She made her way to the building key and found the room number of her destination. As she wandered the corridor looking for Room 18, she silently rehearsed what she was going to say. Her usual tactic was to keep it simple, especially when the primary objective was to get her foot in the door. Coming to the entrance, she waltzed right in, taking a quick peek at the desks lined up against the back wall.

To one side, there was a row of straight-backed chairs. Uncertain whether to take a seat or speak to a staff member, she opted for addressing the young woman she assumed to be the receptionist. "Hi. Is this the Development Office?"

"Oh, yes." The woman glanced up from her computer. "Welcome to Development. How can I assist you?"

She seemed pleasant and was attractive—not surprising, since good looks appeared to be a must-have for Development personnel. "I hope so. I'm Mosey Frye, Robert Ellison's wife. He's in Anthropology. Maybe you know him?"

"Yes, of course," she said with a receptive look. "I know Dr. Ellison."

"I keep hearing about the good things Development is doing for Anthropology, I mean, the new lab and all. And Robert mentioned I might volunteer to help with your events. If you need someone, I'd be glad to add my name to the list."

"Certainly. We can always use volunteers. They do a couple of things for us, well, typically, but did you have anything specific in mind?"

"I don't know. What sort of activities…?"

"Some sign up to make phone calls during fundraisers. Also, when we have receptions or other events, we like to have volunteers on hand to chat with potential donors. Our events are catered, so that's really about it."

"Well, I'd be happy to help with either of those. Whatever you need."

"Okay, I'll put you down. Could I get your contact information?"

"Sure, I think I have a business card here in my tote." Mosey reached in and pulled out a card and, as she placed it on the receptionist's desk, said, "By the way, I don't believe I caught your name."

"Tara Townsend." She nodded politely.

"Tara Townsend," Mosey repeated. "I think I remember you. I know you're younger than I, but didn't you go to Blanchard?"

"I did, Class of 2003."

"And aren't you a Beta Nu?"

"I am."

"I helped you guys with rush one year. Gosh, that was ages ago."

"I thought you looked familiar."

"Well, my goodness, it's a small world, isn't it?"

"It certainly is. Sometimes too small," Townsend said with a chuckle.

"I know what you mean. You know, I had no idea you were working here."

"I haven't been here very long."

Mosey found herself unsure about what to say next. Should she mention her involvement in the Charles Ashby case? Probably not. It seemed like throwing a wet blanket over a pleasant interaction. But on the other hand, it felt almost dishonest not to say something. Balancing one against the other, she decided on honesty, but she would be as tenuous as possible. "I was so very saddened by the death of your colleague. Robert told me one of your colleagues—"

"Yes, that was terrible," she said with a shake of her head. "Such a young man. I hadn't started working here yet, but I met Charles back when I volunteered. I mean, before I got the job."

"I know it must have been a shock for everyone concerned."

"Did you know Charles?"

"Not really. I only knew of him, through Robert."

Townsend picked up Mosey's business card and read the contact information. "So, you're with Shepherd Realty?"

"Yes, for going on two years now."

"I think I saw your name in the paper."

"Oh, you mean in connection with the Fortney case?"

"Yes, you and Nadia Abboud found the body. Isn't that right?"

Mosey sighed. "Yes, I'm afraid so."

"And, if I'm not mistaken, that wasn't the first time, well…."

"No, it wasn't, unfortunately."

"I never dreamed a real estate agent—"

"Nor did I," Mosey said, cutting in. "It certainly wasn't my intention to specialize in stigmatized properties, but, sadly, it's turned out that way."

"Stigmatized?"

"Yes, when a property has been the scene of a crime, real estate agents refer to the house as stigmatized. That can sometimes impact the appraisal, well, not always."

"And in this case?"

"Gosh"—Mosey's brow went up—"I haven't really had time to think about that. I was hoping to list Red Oaks, but now…"

"Well, maybe you still can. You see, I know the place. Lenna Fortney was my boyfriend's aunt by marriage. Maybe you know Bud Fortney?"

"Oh, my goodness." Mosey leaned against the edge

of the desk. "I had no idea. Please accept my sincerest condolences. This must be a terrible time for y'all." Mosey felt the blood rush to her face, and at the same time she heard her daddy's disapproving *tsk-tsk-tsk*. "Tara, I am so sorry. I didn't know you were seeing Bud Fortney."

"Yes, we've been seeing each other for about a year."

"Well, he must be very shaken by all this."

"Yes, of course, he's upset, as they all are at the accounting firm. Hard to imagine who could have done such a thing."

"No, it's unthinkable." Mosey took a step back. "I should go and let you get back to work. You have my card, and should you need a volunteer, give me a call. I'd be happy to help."

"Thanks, Mosey. Do you mind if I call you Mosey?"

"No, please do, everyone does." With that, she turned and left. But before she had reached the stairs, the voice that she was expecting to hear came loud and clear.

See where your snooping got you today, girl?

"And how was I supposed to know? I had no idea Tara Townsend was working in Development, and I certainly didn't know she was dating Bud Fortney."

If you haven't learned by now, when in the name of heaven will you? Hembree is a very small town, and you can just count on everybody knowing everybody, if they aren't kin to 'em. How many times have I told you that?

"About a dozen, I suppose."

Right.

"But other than my own personal mortification, I can't see any harm is done."

Maybe not yet, but I have to wonder where this is

going to lead.

"I doubt it leads to anything specific. But who knows, it could have a positive outcome. Tara might have some ideas about this. Or maybe Bud does. This could be exactly the opportunity I was hoping for." And indeed it was. It seemed she'd ventured out on a simple fishing expedition only to end up with a large catch in her net.

You'd better be careful is all I've got to say. The hair's still growing in on the top of your head, young lady, and here you go again. Mosey, really now. Give it a rest. Let Olivera do his job.

"Okay, Daddy, I hear you." She let out a sigh as she climbed the steps to the first floor. Checking her watch, she saw it was close to time to head to the Tavernette. "I bet I could catch Robert and Hugh," she muttered, pulling out her cellphone. She gave Robert a call, but getting his voicemail, disconnected. "He must be in class still. Guess I'll go ahead on my own."

She drove to the Tavernette and, being the first of the group to arrive, headed to the back room, her go-to cozy spot for happy hour. It provided a more intimate atmosphere than the bustling bar, where most people liked to hang out. The dining room was nice, too, but didn't have quite the same welcoming vibe.

"Mosey, you alone today?" Miffy approached with a menu.

"Hi, Miffy. Nope. The whole gang should be here any minute."

"You know, I've seen that nice doctor in here a time or two." Miffy wiped the table. "I forget her name."

"You mean Lauren Wilson?"

"That's the one. She settling in okay?"

"Oh, Miffy, I don't suppose you heard about Morris House."

"Morris House?" She gave Mosey a half frown.

"The house Lauren bought. Remember?"

"I do remember when she came here lookin' for a house."

"Well, she finally decided on Morris House—that big old place at the end of McAllister. You know the one."

"Oh, yeah, where they found Will Grayson."

Mosey nodded. "So, you heard about that. And that was just the start of it, a pretty bleak start. Not long after, they discovered a cellar, a big underground room sort of separated from the house."

"Uh-huh," Miffy nodded. "I know all about that room. Kind of a gamblin' joint it used to be."

"I think half of Hembree knew about the place, but we didn't. Well, I certainly didn't and Lauren didn't. But, anyway, I think she's settled in now. I saw her earlier today at Nadia's looking for furniture for the living room. She bought a very pretty sofa."

Hearing her name called, Miffy laid a couple of menus on the table. "I'll be back when your friends get here. You want me to bring you somethin' in the meantime?"

"Yes, ma'am. Bring me a short draft. I'll get a head start."

"I'll be right back with that."

Miffy ambled off for a bit and, returning with the beer, placed it on the table and ambled off again.

Mosey took a long sip, letting the slightly bitter liquid roll over her tongue. It had an earthy undertone that lingered pleasantly at the back of her throat. She enjoyed her beer and glimpsed occasionally at the townsfolk drifting in, until Robert and Hugh came in with Lauren at their side.

"Over here," Mosey called out, waving.

They slipped off their jackets and hung them on the rack at the entrance before making their way to the back.

"You already ordered," Robert commented as he slid in next to Mosey. He lifted her glass and took a sip, and just as he did, Miffy came up. "I think I'll have one of these, too," Robert said, "or wait a minute." He turned to Hugh and Lauren, who had taken seats across the table. "Shall we order a pitcher?"

"What is that you're drinking?" Lauren said.

"Oh, it's a new local brew," Mosey said. "Red Oaks, they call it, though I wouldn't be shocked if they decided to change the name," she added with a solemn look.

"Not sure I want any of that." Hugh chuckled.

"Oh, come on, guys," Lauren said. "It's not the house's fault." Then turning to Miffy, she said, "Bring us a pitcher of Red Oaks, please, and maybe some of those fried chicken wings?" She glanced at the others and, getting there approval, added, "And you can put that on my ticket."

"Oh, no you don't," Mosey said. "This one's on me."

Lauren turned to Hugh. "So what do I say now? Am I supposed to argue with Mosey or graciously accept her offer to treat?"

Hugh laughed. "I recommend you accept. I think Mosey owes you one."

"I sure do," Mosey said. Then, turning to Miffy, who was looking a tad confused, she added, "Start a tab for us, Miffy, would you? And, yes, please bring us a pitcher and the wings."

Miffy scribbled the order and, tucking her pad in her apron pocket, shuffled away.

Mosey, in mentioning the name of the beer, had brought up the subject that was probably on everyone's mind.

"So"—Robert gestured toward Mosey's glass—"I guess this is another one of Lenna Fortney's little ventures."

"Exactly. The brewery is a bit farther along Little Smith, not far from the house."

"How many businesses did she own?" Lauren asked.

"I have no idea," Mosey said. "I know she picked up the Jeremiah Java Café."

"And the little motel on the road to Mound City," Robert added.

"I've heard rumors she had her fingers in a lot of pies"—Mosey shrugged—"but who knows really. Apart from the brewery, she didn't show much enthusiasm for attaching her name to anything, except, of course, King Accounting, which bears her father's name."

"You're right." Robert nodded, leaning back. "The Kings and the Fortneys owned substantial properties around here, but they always kept a certain distance, expect for the firm. I wonder why."

"It's not that out of the ordinary," Hugh commented. "Entrepreneurs frequently acquire a company and opt to retain the original name."

"Why do they do that?" Robert asked.

"I'm not entirely sure. It could potentially be a legal concern. However, my assumption has been that they simply prefer to keep their involvement under wraps.

Rather commonly, companies we assume are owned by one company turn out to be owned by another, often a larger entity."

"Sounds suspicious to me," Mosey said.

"Who knows," Robert said. "Let's face it. None of us has much of a clue about the business world."

"It's true," Mosey said, "we all have our little niches. Too bad Nadia's not here."

"Yeah, where is Nadia?" Lauren said. "I thought she was coming."

"She might show up. She didn't reply one way or the other."

Hugh turned to Mosey. "But you must know something about the business world."

"Not really. I ignore it as much as possible."

You'd better watch it, girl. That's a client sitting across the table from you.

"Oh, Daddy," Mosey mumbled under her breath. "Is there nowhere I'm safe from these intrusions?" She had to admit, however, that her daddy had made a valid point. The last thing she wanted to communicate to Lauren was any sign of incompetence when it came to real estate transactions.

Robert gave Mosey a nudge under the table.

"I was kidding, for heaven's sake." She gave a wave of her hand. "Everybody knows my first love is psychology, or music—I could never decide between the two—but I'm happily settled into the world of real estate."

"And, hey, I guess it's a bonus"—Hugh chuckled—"that every time you get a listing, you find a body."

"A bonus, indeed. Hugh, you kill me." A smile spread across her face. "This time, it most definitely is not a bonus. I was really hoping to list the property. Red Oaks would have meant a financial windfall."

"How much is it worth, you think?" Lauren asked.

"I don't know. It hasn't been appraised as far as I know. A million or two would be my guess. I don't know how much of the land would go with it. And there's the lake, of course."

Hugh let out a soft whistle of surprise. "A windfall, indeed. Mosey, you must be feeling a little blue."

"I suppose, but I haven't really stopped to think about the financial angle."

"Maybe you should."

"Why?" She looked at Hugh. "There's nothing I can do about it now. But the sooner the police release the house, the better. Who's to say I won't get the listing after all?"

"You have any ideas about who might have done this?" Lauren asked.

"Well," Mosey pondered, "I've been mulling over a couple of ideas. You know, it might have had to do with her business interests. Seems to be the likely scenario. But maybe that wasn't it at all. Could have been her philanthropic interests."

Robert gave Mosey a reproachful look. "Mosey, don't go getting mixed up—"

"Robert, please, I know better."

"No, I'm afraid you don't."

"What are you guys talking about?" Hugh asked.

Neither Robert nor Mosey answered.

"Oh, I know," Hugh said. "The endowment."

Robert lifted his brow.

"Well, I wouldn't worry about that," Hugh said. "The will is being read tomorrow, and what's done is done."

"Wow," Mosey said, "I didn't know. That soon, eh?"

"Yep, I got a call from Dot Cowsley."

"So, you will be present at the reading of the will?" Mosey asked.

"The college president would normally attend, but he's out of town, so I'm representing Blanchard."

"Hey, you know what they say, every cloud has a silver lining." Robert raised his mug to Hugh.

"Yeah, possibly, but there's the little matter of earmarking." Hugh's face fell.

"Maybe it's not even money," Mosey jumped in.

Robert relaxed back and let out a laugh. "Yeah, it might be the mausoleum."

"Or even worse!" Mosey joked. "A truck load of taxidermy mounts."

Chapter Nineteen

Road to Mound City
Tuesday, March 16, 2010, 2:00 p.m.

It was getting close to two o'clock as Olivera got on the road to Mound City. He had already mapped out a plan for interviewing various people of interest and that morning had checked off the first two names, Ed Neville and Bud Fortney. He didn't intend on chatting with Merritt Trumble and Nate Patterson that day, but once he'd heard Wilson's Greek-tragedy theory, he felt eager to have a conversation with Trumble. The architectural firm and seed company were within a stone's throw of each other, and he figured he might as well do both interviews in a single trip.

He came first to Patterson Seed and Feed but passed it by, heading on to Trumble Architects about a quarter mile farther along, close to the city limits of Mound City. He pulled into the gravel drive and came to a halt in front of the building. It was a modern-looking place but small, no bigger than a cracker box. Painted a dark teal color with black trim, it had several narrow windows across the front and an ultra-modern door with tall, black planters on either side. Two cars were parked on the lot, and he hoped that one of them belonged to Merritt Trumble.

He approached the entrance and, pushing through the door, proceeded to the receptionist's desk, which wasn't a desk at all but a waist-high rectangular block crafted of an exotic-looking wood.

The receptionist stood and came toward him. "May I help you?"

"Yes, I would like to speak to Merritt Trumble if he's in."

"Let me see if he's busy. May I have your name, please?"

He handed her his business card. She glanced at it and, picking up the phone, pressed a button. "Mr. Trumble, Lieutenant Olivera is here to see you." As she placed the receiver back on the hook, she pointed down a dark corridor off reception. "He can see you now. Second door on the left."

He nodded and flashed a smile, then headed down the corridor. As he came to the second door, it opened and a man stuck his head out. "Come in, won't you?"

Olivera showed the man his identification and, after they had introduced themselves, Trumble shook his hand and offered him a seat.

The office didn't touch the standard of King Accounting, but it was still nice, with the design features you might expect to find in an architect's workspace. There was an open-to-construction ceiling painted dark gray. A sleek metallic light fixture hanging from the ceiling cast a subtle gleam across the polished concrete floor. To him, it all looked edgy and cold, given his preference for cozier settings. The low reclining chair where he sat was comfortable, probably a good deal more than the smart task chair Trumble occupied. After settling into his seat, Trumble darkened his computer screen and turned around.

"So, Lieutenant," he said, "I'm guessing you've come about the Red Oaks matter."

"Yes, I thought you might have heard about that."

"I read about it in the paper this morning."

"You know, the time of death was actually early Sunday morning or late Saturday." Olivera paused to count on his fingertips. "That's nearly three days already."

"I see. I don't remember reading that."

"Well, I didn't know that myself until today. The coroner is saying late Saturday or early Sunday. Do you remember where you were then?"

He didn't ask why he wanted to know, he just answered the question. "Well, let me see. Saturday night, how late?"

"Close to midnight."

"Saturday midnight...I must have been home by then."

"Can anyone substantiate that?"

"No, I live by myself."

"Were you with anyone that evening?"

"Yes, as a matter of fact, I was here until late, then met some friends at Al's for dinner."

"Al's Supper Club in Hembree?"

"Yes, between here and Hembree."

"Which is close to Red Oaks Manor."

"I suppose so."

"Have you been to Red Oaks recently?"

He shook his head. "I haven't been there in quite some time."

"Which brings me to a time in the past when you might have gone there rather frequently, I would guess."

Olivera, who had been sort of leaning in, sat back, and gave Trumble a long look.

"Sure," Trumble nodded. "There was a time when I went there almost daily. I'm guessing you are aware of that." His expression turned a little grim.

"Well, yes, but I would like to hear your version of the, uh, situation."

Trumble, who was an attractive man, mid-thirties, with longish salt-and-pepper hair and chiseled features, stood and approached the wall of windows across the back of the room. He looked out on a small patio with several Adirondack chairs arranged around a wood-burning fire pit. He stared for a moment before turning back around. "I was very close to Kemena King, Lenna Fortney's ward. We were engaged to be married, in fact. Ms. Fortney didn't make it easy. She did everything she could to break us up."

As Olivera carefully registered Trumble's reaction, he sensed that, despite the passage of time, Trumble was feeling a fair amount of tension still. He wasn't doing anything as obvious as clenching his fists or cracking his knuckles, but he was certainly avoiding eye contact.

"But you were going ahead with your plans to marry, were you?"

"Um, yes, I'm sure we would have."

"And your fiancée felt the same?"

"Yes, definitely. Kimmy was a determined young woman. She wouldn't have been persuaded otherwise."

"But wasn't she underage?"

"No, she was eighteen, almost nineteen. We didn't need anyone's permission. What we did hope for was some financial help till we got on our feet."

"From Ms. Fortney, you mean?"

"Yes."

"And she refused?"

"Flatly."

"So, if not for the accident, you and Ms. King would have married."

"I'm sure we would have."

Apparently, his fiancée's death had been a profound loss for the man, and he didn't seem to have gotten past it. Olivera hated to remind him of that painful time but felt like it was a subject he had to explore. "It's my understanding," he went on, "that you were not satisfied with the investigation."

"Well, in retrospect, I don't know that the police could have done anything more than they did."

"But at the time, you had concerns, did you not?"

"There were some discrepancies."

"Can you be more specific?"

He took a deep breath and let it out. "Lieutenant, do we really need to go over all this?"

"Yes, actually we do, and I will get to that later, but if you wouldn't mind clarifying a few things…Well, for example, the Fortneys claimed they weren't at home when the accident—"

"That's right," he interrupted, "but I had reason to believe they were."

"And how was that?"

"I got a call from Kimmy that morning, and they were all at home. They'd had a serious argument, and she was anxious to get away."

"An argument. What kind of argument?"

He gave his head a couple of hard shakes and glanced toward the ceiling. "Probably more like a shouting match. Her cousin wasn't above, well, monitoring Kimmy's every move. She seemed to think she had a right."

"I see. But going back to this other matter, why would the Fortneys have lied about their whereabouts?"

"I can't be sure. There weren't any witnesses, other than Kimmy. But the fact that I'm pretty certain they *did* lie, makes me think there was something they didn't want to talk about. Like maybe they heard screams and could have gone to Kimmy's rescue."

"You thought them capable of that?"

"I don't know. I was young, angry, distraught." He dropped his head. "Thinking back now, it does seem unlikely."

"Do you know what exactly the police determined?"

"The coroner recorded the cause of death as drowning, but I suspected that something else might have been involved. I've never been able to shake the thought."

"Like what?"

"There wasn't any real evidence to indicate this"— he turned away from the window and faced Olivera— "but I suspected that the motor might have malfunctioned. It's possible she was electrocuted."

"Electrocuted," Olivera repeated with surprise in his voice. "I wasn't aware of that possibility."

"Well, that's what Dr. McGinnis thought could have happened, but he told me that off the record. As he explained it, the autopsy didn't reveal evidence of an electrostatic discharge, but it wouldn't have in any case. If someone had witnessed the accident or heard cries for help, then electrocution could have been considered as the cause of death. Well, nobody was around, supposedly. That's why the accident was reported as a drowning."

"You say the motor might have malfunctioned?"

"Yes, sending a current through the water. You see, Lieutenant, Kemena was an excellent swimmer, and there was no apparent reason for her to have drowned."

"Mightn't she have fallen overboard, maybe hit her head?"

"Probably not. At least there wasn't any sign of a head injury. The only logical explanation was that something happened to the boat. But since they couldn't prove anything one way or the other..."

"The boat didn't sink?"

"No, and the mechanic who checked it out said he couldn't find anything wrong."

Olivera straightened up in his chair, leaned over and stared down at the floor. He was beginning to feel a tad sidetracked. He was glad to hear Trumble's description of the accident, especially since neither McGinnis nor Springer had provided the details that Trumble had now mentioned. But he felt as if the whole story about the drowning was somehow interrupting his opportunity to dig into the other matter, i.e., the potential role of Trumble in Lenna Fortney's demise. He thought for a second, then, in an effort to get back on track, said, "Well, let me take a guess here. Given the not so pleasant history between you and Lenna Fortney, it must have crossed your mind—"

"—that I could be a suspect?"

"No"—Olivera shook his head—"not a suspect, but definitely a person of interest."

"A person of interest," Trumble repeated. "I can see that I might be."

Now that was intriguing. Rather than becoming

defensive or offended, like many people do, Trumble seemed to take it in stride, which made him ponder for a second more. How did Trumble feel about Fortney now? Was he still carrying a grudge? That same question had occurred to him and Wilson. Furthermore, he wondered how much Trumble knew about Fortney's interactions around town, whether she had positive relationships or not, and so forth.

"I don't have an airtight alibi," he added, "but I swear to you that I haven't set foot on the property since the day of Kimmy's funeral."

Olivera had a sudden realization. Like that maybe he had acted too hastily in coming to interview Trumble. He hadn't really thought out how much he was prepared to reveal beyond what the newspaper had reported. Should he provide Trumble with the details concerning his late fiancée's remains? It somehow felt unnecessarily hurtful even to bring it up, but on the other hand...

After a deep sigh, he decided to go ahead and tell Trumble what he knew, thinking that reading it in the newspaper might be worse than hearing it from him. "Something rather lamentable came to my attention yesterday afternoon late. And around noon today, I received a report from the coroner. I'm sorry to have to tell you this, Mr. Trumble, but Kemena King's remains have been disturbed."

"Disturbed. What do you mean *disturbed*?"

"Well, someone must have taken them from the coffin and left them in a small bag on the pedestal of a statue in the Civil War Cemetery." Olivera watched carefully to record Trumble's reaction.

"Somebody opened the coffin?" Trumble looked quite stunned. "Why, for god's sake?"

"We don't know why, but obviously, it sort of implies a link between one death and the other. We suspect, though aren't completely sure, that the coffin Lenna King was laid out in was the same coffin Kemena was buried in."

"What? How horrible."

Olivera waited, then said, "Can you think of anything that might help us sort this out?"

"No. Who would do such a thing? Horrific, absolutely horrific." He stared ahead, looking dazed.

"I'm sorry to deliver such disturbing news, but—"

Trumble took a deep breath, rubbed his face, then smoothed back his hair. "Lieutenant," he said, checking his watch, "I'm afraid I have an appointment in Hembree, and I really need to get on the road."

Olivera stood. "Well, if you think of anything relevant to the case, please give me a call." He handed Trumble his card.

"I doubt that I do, but sure."

Trumble was already dropping folders into a briefcase when Olivera left, closing the door behind him. As he walked out to get into his car, he wondered if Trumble's appointment might be with Lauren Wilson. He was anxious to hear her impressions of the man. He wasn't sure exactly what to make of Trumble's reaction to hearing about the remains. His response to the news of Fortney's passing seemed fairly run-of-the-mill, and of course, he might react that way, considering there was no love lost between the two. He somehow had expected Trumble to have questions, but he didn't. On the other hand, his reaction to the act of desecration seemed genuine, and understandable, given their relationship.

As he drove to the seed company, he put Trumble

out of his mind so as to prepare himself for his interview with Nate Patterson, whom he knew very little about, other than that he had some sort of run-in with the victim. How would this former client be feeling about the victim's passing, he wondered.

Chapter Twenty

Patterson Seed and Feed
Tuesday, March 16, 2010, 2:45 p.m.

Walking into Patterson Seed and Feed felt to Olivera like stepping into the great outdoors. As he wandered into the expansive space, he passed bins brimming with seeds and, further along, pallets holding bags of soil, fertilizer, and mulch. As he neared the back wall, hay bales, stacked up five or six in a column, drew his eyes upward to the lofty, industrial-style ceiling, of old wooden rafters.

An invigorating scent filled the air reminiscent of grass or straw. Not a farm boy himself, he really hadn't the foggiest idea what precisely he was smelling. Could have been rice, soybeans, or oats—something purely organic. Nonetheless, the pleasant aroma made him relish the stroll around as he continued his search for someone to assist him.

Then, unexpectedly, a pair of metal swinging doors burst open and a man emerged, maneuvering a wheelbarrow loaded with sacks.

"Sir," Olivera called out, his voice echoing through the space, "could you tell me if Mr. Patterson is around?"

"You lookin' for Nate Patterson?" The man, whom Olivera pegged as middle-aged and African American, reached in his pocket for a handkerchief and wiped his forehead.

"Yes," Olivera replied, "you happen to know if he's here?"

"You wouldn't be, uh, Lieutenant Olivera, would you?" He set the leg supports of the wheelbarrow down and strode in Olivera's direction.

"Yes, I'm Olivera."

"Whatcha wanna see him about, if you don't mind my asking?"

"A police matter."

"Well, then, you'd better come with me."

Olivera followed the man through the swinging doors into a closed space with low ceilings, more of an office-like area, with an old wooden desk in the corner. Once he had seated himself in a sturdy wooden chair behind the desk, he motioned for Olivera to take a seat in the straight chair across from him. Olivera sat and, imagining that this man must be the person he'd come to see, took out a card and laid it on the desk. "Lieutenant Gustavo Olivera of the Hembree Police Department. Are you Mr. Patterson?"

"I am." He didn't smile or frown, just looked Olivera square in the eye.

"I wonder if I might ask you a few questions related to the recent death of Ms. Lenna Fortney."

"Well, sure. I don't know why you've come to see me, uh, about that, but go ahead, ask."

Olivera hadn't encountered such directness in a while, and it felt almost pleasant, though not exactly polite, not overly so, as his encounters with the average Hembreeite tended to be. "Your name came up in a conversation with another, uh, shall we say, person of interest?"

"Person of interest..." Patterson raised his brow.

"That's right."

Patterson shrugged.

"Well, let me get to the point," Olivera continued. "I understand you're a client of King Accounting."

"That's right."

"And how would you characterize your business with the firm?"

"They keep the books for me and have advised me on a couple of things over the years."

"So, this has been a long-term association?"

"Oh, yeah, going back a long time, when my daddy managed the place and Ms. Fortney's daddy, Mr. King, was in charge of the firm."

"Have you ever had any disagreements with King Accounting or with Ms. Fortney in particular?"

"I think I know what you're getting at." Patterson shifted in his chair. "I wouldn't call it a disagreement exactly."

"What would you call it?"

"Well, it might have turned into a lawsuit, I reckon, but now that Ms. Fortney is out of the picture..."

"Who was suing whom?"

"I might have sued." Patterson sat back and blinked a couple of time. "But I can't say for sure. I haven't spoken with a lawyer."

"What exactly was your complaint?"

"I don't know what the legal term would be. Conflict of interest maybe—*her* interest versus *my* interest." He pointed toward himself.

"Over?"

"This business." He spread his hands as he glanced

around. "It's been in my family for a while, and I wasn't about to sell it, especially not at the price she was offering."

"Ms. Fortney was interested in purchasing Patterson Seed and Feed?"

"Oh, yeah," he said, drawing out his vowels. "What *wasn't* she interested in buying?" He waggled his head.

"Hmm. And I suppose you didn't want to sell."

"Course not, but she was pressuring me to sell and sort of threatening—Well, I don't know."

"Ms. Fortney was threatening you?"

"Yeah, it sort of felt that way."

"I see." Olivera nodded. "So, now that she's 'out of the picture,' how do you expect this will play out?"

"Gosh, I don't know who'll be making the decisions, but I imagine I'll get along with whoever it is."

"You think you and Mr. Neville, for example—?"

"Ah, yeah, we'll get along just fine."

"And if Mr. Bud Fortney should become head partner?"

"I don't really know him, but I expect he's a sensible guy. I don't have a reason to suspect otherwise."

"Ms. Fortney *wasn't* sensible, then, in your estimation?"

He took in a deep breath and let it out. "Not with me she wasn't, in my humble opinion," he added, dropping his voice.

Olivera was beginning to get a vague notion of who this man was, and besides that, how Fortney had put together her little empire. In fact, if she hadn't died when she had, Patterson Seed and Feed might have become her next acquisition. Did Patterson have motive, then? He supposed he did, but if *he* had motive, mightn't there be some others who did as well, and for similar reasons? He studied Patterson's face for an instant. It was a smooth face, not the face of a man given to worry. And it was a gentle face. What lines he had were smile lines. "Mr. Patterson, what you said before seemed to indicate, uh, that Ms. Fortney might have gone on a buying spree."

"Well, I might have exaggerated some, I often do. But, yeah, she bought a few businesses around here, in Hembree and Mound City, for sure."

"And would you say that some of the previous owners were reluctant to sell?"

"Oh, yeah, two or three complained to me about it. They sure did."

"So, you think she might have used high-pressure tactics against her own clients?"

"I was given to understand that, but I couldn't swear to it, nope, wouldn't put my hand on the Bible."

Olivera had a feeling that his "people of interest" list had suddenly lengthened, but somehow, he just didn't want to go there, not yet. Four was enough for the time being. Plus, he didn't think his conversation with Patterson was going to lead to anything tangible. He couldn't imagine that it would. He tried to picture him doing the crime. A stocky man, he certainly seemed strong enough to pick up a body or carry a coffin from the mausoleum to the parlor at Red Oaks. But the thought of him murdering Fortney seemed implausible. If Patterson ever had the inclination to knock a person off, not that he seemed at all the type, he felt relatively sure it wouldn't involve elaborate planning or cowardly tactics. This guy seemed more like the type to pick up a rifle, blast somebody, then boldly deal with the consequences. His Seed and Feed establishment, however, did show a clear appreciation for order, but not of the overly meticulous kind he had observed in the parlor at Red Oaks.

"So, Mr. Patterson," Olivera said, "I'm glad to see you were able to hold onto your business, at least so far, and I wish you luck with that. Just one more question and I'll let you get back to your work. Could you tell me where you were on Saturday night?"

"I was home with my wife and kids."

"And they would back you up on that?"

"They sure would."

Olivera, having already placed his business card on Patterson's desk, gestured toward the card. "You've got my contact information, and I'd appreciate it if you'd give me a call, should you think of anything that might help us figure this thing out."

"If you think I know who did this, I can tell you I don't. Don't have any idea."

Olivera shook hands with Patterson and, making his way through the warehouse and across the lot, climbed into the cruiser and headed back to Hembree.

The drive back was a short one. It wasn't more than fifteen miles from one city limit to the other, and he didn't really mind the drive. There wasn't much fast traffic along the road at that time of day. Mostly tractors and other farm equipment. He didn't even mind getting behind a slow driver, seeing as he was in a pensive mood. He'd made it all the way through his list of people of interest in a single day and was anxious to think through the interviews and record his initial impressions.

But before he had a chance to get on with his day, an unexpected sight caught his attention. Just as he was passing Red Oaks, he noticed a black sedan parked in the driveway close to the front door. He stepped on the brake and made a sudden turn into the drive, bringing the cruiser to a halt behind the sedan. He pulled out his cellphone and, taking note of the license number, tapped on Springer's name.

"Hey, Chief. What's up?"

"Check a license for me, Springer." He gave him the number on the tag.

Springer came back on quickly. "Looks like that's Wilhelmina White's car. You know who she is, don't you?"

"Can't say that I do."

"She cooked for Miss Lenna."

"She's parked in the drive here at Red Oaks."

"Oh, I bet she stopped by to pick something up."

"Okay, Springer, I'd better check to see what's she's up to. Kind of surprises me that she ignored the crime scene tape. It's still up."

"Well, maybe she didn't think it was a big deal."

"Okay. I should be back to the station soon."

"You catch up with Trumble and Patterson?"

"I certainly did. I'll tell you all about it when I get there."

Olivera walked up to the front door and, opening it a crack, called in, "Ms. White, you in there?" Hearing footsteps coming in his direction, he entered the foyer and waited for White to appear.

"Who are you?" She stopped to give him the once over.

"Lieutenant Gustavo Olivera, Hembree Police." He showed her his identification. "I saw your car parked in the drive and thought I'd better check. You know this is a crime scene."

"I know it is, and I doubt I oughta be here."

He nodded as he held the door open for her.

"All right, all right, I can take a hint. I just wanted to pick this up." She held up an old book. "It belonged to my momma, and I wanted it back." She handed him the book.

He opened it and flipped through the pages, which were filled with hand-written recipes and newspaper clippings. "I suppose that's okay." He handed it back.

She looked down at the porch floor and softly muttered, "This is just awful, Lieutenant, just awful."

"I'm sorry, Ms. White. I understand you worked for Ms. Fortney."

"Oh, lord, yes. For years, I cooked for Miss Lenna and Mr. Jim and her momma and daddy before that. I just can't believe she's dead."

"Seeing as I've got you here, I wonder if you would mind filling me in on a couple of things. I'm guessing you must have also known Kemena King."

"Of course, I did." As she scrunched her face, deep creases formed on her forehead and at the corners of her eyes.

"Why don't we have a seat over there." He motioned toward a pair of wicker chairs farther along the porch. "I won't keep you long."

She obliged and, once they were seated, he pulled out his tablet and pen.

He thought for a minute, then looked into her eyes. "You know what I would really like to clear up? I've heard one thing and another about the victim. People seemed to agree, however, that she was a domineering person. Do you think that's an accurate description?"

"Well, yes, Miss Lenna knew her own mind. That's for sure."

"And was that a problem, you think?"

"For her, no. It might have been a problem for Mr. Fortney and Miss Kimmy."

"When Kemena died, there were some rumors that circulated about the family, that possibly the drowning wasn't entirely—"

"Aw, naw," she cut in. "I heard some of those rumors, but nobody who really knew the Fortneys would have believed a word of it. Ms. Fortney loved that girl. She just tried to get her to do right, act her age. Mr. King spoiled Kimmy, and Miss Lenna tried her best to straighten her out."

"At the time, did you ever suspect that someone around the place, a friend, for example, might have been involved or might have known something?"

"May I ask *you* something, Lieutenant?"

"Okay."

"Why you asking me about Kimmy?" Again, her face twisted into a frown. "You think her death had something to do with this?"

"To be honest, there's no hard evidence to suggest that. However, the circumstances are such..." He paused, not sure he wanted to bring up the matter of the remains. "Let's just say that there is certainly reason to suggest that one death might have had to do with the other."

"Well, you know Kimmy died some nine or ten years ago, but I do remember thinking at the time that something just wasn't right."

"Like what?"

"It's hard to put my finger on it, but I think Miss

Lenna might have suspected something. She never came right out and said it, at least not to me she didn't."

"You have any thoughts about what or who she might have suspected?"

"Oh, I wouldn't want to throw a name out. I don't really know anything."

"You think Ms. Fortney might have suspected that someone was involved?"

"Well, maybe. You see, she and Kimmy's fiancé didn't get along all that well, and just as he seemed to suspect the Fortneys, I think they might have suspected him."

"But, as far as you know, they didn't voice these suspicions?"

"That's right, as far as I know. But they might have said something to somebody, though I kinda doubt it. Miss Lenna was a woman of few words. You might say tight-lipped. She was not happy about the engagement, though. I know that."

"I believe you are speaking of Merritt Trumble, are you not?"

"That's right."

"What about other people around at the time who might be able to shed some light on this?"

"Hmm…Mr. Bud Fortney was around some. But you know, the Fortneys weren't that sociable. They pretty much kept to themselves."

"Well…" He took out a card and handed it to White. "I do appreciate your answering my questions, and here's my contact information should you think of anything."

She accepted the card and tucked it into the recipe book. "I'll give it some thought, Lieutenant. I surely do hope you catch whoever did this. Miss Lenna did not deserve to die like that. I'm telling you she was, well…" She broke off and stared down at the floor again.

"I'm sorry for your loss, Ms. White." He was about to get up and head back to the cruiser but, remembering the unlocked front door, asked White if she had the key.

"Yes, I always had a key. I suppose you want it?"

"Yes, I expect I should take it. Was there anything else that you needed to pick up?"

"Naw, just my momma's cookbook." She rubbed her hand across the frayed cover, then slipped it into her tote and brought out the key.

Olivera accepted it and, after locking the door, tipped his hat to White and made his way to the cruiser.

Chapter Twenty-One

Tavernette
Tuesday, March 16, 2010, 4:30 p.m.

Around four thirty, Mosey, Robert, Hugh, and Lauren were finishing their first pitcher when Mosey glanced up to see Nadia waving from the doorway. Getting up from her seat, she called out, "Hey, you closed early. Glad you could make it."

"Daddy's locking up for me." Nadia removed her jacket and slipped into the chair across from Mosey.

"Why didn't you bring him with you?"

"I invited him, but he turned me down." She reached over and gave Lauren a pat on the hand. "We meet again."

Hugh greeted Nadia with a smile and a shoulder hug. "Glad you could make it." He glanced at Robert. "Shall we order another pitcher?"

"I don't know. I'm thinking we might adjourn pretty soon." Robert checked his watch. "It's a school night."

"Oh, Robert, don't be a stick in the mud," Mosey said. "Nadia just got here."

Hugh signaled to the server. "Miffy, we need another pitcher, please, ma'am, and a mug for Nadia." He glanced around the table. "You guys want another Red Oaks?"

"Red Oaks?" Nadia frowned. "Since when are we drinking Red Oaks?"

Robert lifted his brow. "Don't ask us. Ask your friend here." He nodded toward Mosey.

"I guess I was just curious to see how it tasted. I sort of like it, don't y'all?"

"Well," Hugh said, "I guess you'd have to say it's apropos."

Mosey turned to Miffy, who was patiently waiting, pencil poised above her order pad. "We'll take another pitcher of Red Oaks, and we'd better have another basket of wings."

Miffy scribbled the order and, lifting the empty pitcher onto her tray, headed off toward the bar.

"So what'd I miss?" Nadia asked.

"Not much," Mosey said. "Tara Townsend replaced Charles Ashby in Development, and she's dating Bud Fortney. That's about it."

Nadia gave Mosey a half frown.

"Can't you guess?" Robert said. "Mosey went snooping around over at the Development Office, having heard"—he lowered his voice—"about Ms. Fortney's large donation to the college."

Mosey shot Robert an exasperated look. "Well, it wasn't just that. Actually, Saffron had an interesting idea about—"

"—why Ms. Fortney was murdered," Lauren chimed in.

"Really?" Nadia said.

"Well, we're all wondering, and Saffron's idea made as much sense as any."

"What did she say exactly?" Nadia said.

"You know the old rhyme, 'Rich man, poor man.' "

Nadia nodded.

"Saffron picked 'merchant.' She thinks it's all about money and power, influence, whatever you want to call it. She thinks that Miss Lenna was using the college to exert influence on the community. All of her contributions were earmarked and quite generous."

Just then, Miffy arrived with a fresh pitcher of beer and a mug for Nadia. "The wings will be ready in a jiffy. I'll be right back with those."

Nadia filled her mug and, toasting to the others, said, "Good luck to us, I suppose. Looks like this recent murder has managed to involve us all."

"You're totally right," Mosey replied, looking mildly surprised. "Every one of us is involved"—she paused and glanced at Lauren—"except you, Lauren. How'd that happen?"

Lauren laughed. "I don't think I'll remain on the sidelines for long." She glanced at Nadia. "Just between us, Lieutenant Olivera approached me at the shop this morning."

"He did?"

"Yeah, you didn't see him come in?"

"I did, but he disappeared before I could even speak to him."

"He invited me for coffee. We were here earlier. He wanted to pick my brain about the profile of the perpetrator."

"And did he?" Mosey asked.

"Yes, but only informally."

"Which is sort of what I was hoping to do," Mosey said bashfully.

"Well, I don't really mind as long as you understand that I'm speaking strictly off the record. I wouldn't offer a professional opinion before spending some time at the crime scene."

"So, this wasn't an official consult?" Hugh asked.

"No, not official." Lauren sipped her beer. "Based on what I read in the paper and heard from you guys, I was starting to get, well, a vague idea."

"For Pete's sake, tell us," Mosey said excitedly.

"Okay, but please keep in mind that we cannot take this seriously. It may turn out to be completely off base."

"Oh, come on." Robert reached for the pitcher and topped off Lauren's mug. "We are all eager to see the mind of a profiler at work."

She took a sip and, resting her forearms on the table, began to explain again the theory she had described to Olivera earlier that day. Once she had finished, they all remained looking pensive until Nadia spoke. "You know, I can see that."

"How so?" Mosey asked.

"What you said about the protagonist—" Nadia looked at Lauren. "Ms. Fortney, right?"

"Right."

"Well, from what I know about her, I'd say she sounds just like that. She was certainly domineering, and rumor has it she might have been jealous of Kemena. I can see jealousy as her fatal flaw."

"As you said"—Hugh turned to Nadia—"*rumor has it*, but did any of us really know Lenna Fortney? I certainly didn't."

Nadia shrugged. "No, I can't say I knew her except in passing."

"Me, either," Mosey said.

"Fact is *none* of us really knew her," Robert added.

Lauren took a sip of beer. "And that's why I'm

strongly qualifying my theory."

"Not to worry," Hugh said. "We'll put it in brackets."

Miffy showed up with a basket of hot wings, their sauce still bubbling at the edges. As she departed, Mosey called out, "Some more napkins, please, ma'am, when you get a second."

Miffy brought napkins from the nearby waitress station. "Here you go. Anything else?"

"No, that's all, thanks."

After Miffy had left, Mosey picked up the basket and passed it to Lauren. "I guess we can't help ourselves, can we? When something totally mind-boggling goes down, we just can't help trying to make sense of it. Seems like human nature to me."

"And that's a good thing"—Robert grabbed a wing—"as long as we don't get carried away."

"Which is easy to do," Lauren noted. "So let's just say this idea of mine is one of many possible hypotheses."

"Does anyone have any factual information, other than what was in the paper?" Nadia asked.

"Factual," Mosey repeated. "Hmm. Well, I guess we can consider what I heard from Tara Townsend as factual."

"I don't think you finished telling me about that," Nadia said.

"I didn't, did I?"

"So, what did she say?"

"Well, first, she's dating Bud Fortney."

"Yes, you mentioned that."

"And second, she sort of hinted that Bud might inherit Red Oaks. Could be wishful thinking on my part, but she suggested they might contact me about the house."

"Interesting." Nadia helped herself to a wing. "Would that give Bud motive?"

"I guess it could," Lauren said. "People have killed for a lot less."

"I don't see it," Hugh said with a shake of his head. "Way too obvious." He refilled Robert's mug and then his own.

"Yeah," Nadia agreed. "And the MO doesn't suit Bud at all."

"Anybody really know the guy?" Lauren asked.

Mosey wiped her mouth. "We sort of know him by reputation. He's close in age to Nadia and me."

"Did he go to school around here?"

"Yes," Mosey said. "His folks didn't live in Hembree, but he went to high school here and then college. I think he was a few years behind us, wasn't he?"

"Sounds about right," Nadia said, "but we didn't run in the same crowd."

"Yeah, Bud was a little too wild for us, or maybe not wild exactly, sort of high-spirited, not always in a good way."

"He drank a lot," Nadia added. "Didn't seem to study much."

"I get you," Lauren said. "But what about his girlfriend?"

"Tara was younger than us, a good bit," Mosey said. "I didn't really know her at all until I helped Beta Nu with rush one year."

"Beta Nu?" Lauren asked.

"It's a sorority."

"Oh."

"Mosey was a sorority girl." Hugh chuckled. "Can't you tell?"

"Hey," Mosey exclaimed, "what's that supposed to mean?"

Hugh laughed out loud.

"He's just trying to get your goat," Robert said.

"He thinks sorority women are bozos. I know. Well, I'll have you know that we are *not* bozos…most of us."

"I'm kidding," Hugh said. "But you have to admit this Tara Townsend isn't the brightest bulb in the bunch."

"How do you know?" Mosey looked askance at Hugh.

"Because I met her."

"You did?"

"At a fundraiser."

"You can't tell anything from that," Robert chimed in. "Even if a woman is smart, she's expected to act like, well, a bozo."

"That's not kind." Mosey frowned at Robert.

"I'm not saying it's the woman's fault. I guess you'd have to say it's the college's fault. They often invite women to such events to grace the occasion. Look pretty and bat their eyelashes at the rich folks."

"How pathetically sexist," Lauren said.

"Get used to it." Nadia wiped her mouth and, folding her napkin, laid it on the table. "You'll see a lot of that around here."

"So, how'd Lenna Fortney figure in all that?" Lauren asked.

"Like Saffron suggested," Mosey said, "she used charity to her advantage. She had a lot of money and no heirs to speak of, and I guess she saw the college as a way to make her mark on the community."

"In light of what has happened, the reading of the will…," Hugh said, trailing off.

"Yeah." Robert looked at Hugh. "What about the reading of the will?"

"It could tell us a good bit about motive," Hugh said, "especially if it turns out that the principal beneficiary was aware of what was coming his or her way."

"If people get cut out of a will"—Mosey turned to Lauren—"do they kill for revenge?"

"It happens."

"That's never made sense to me. If a person gets cut out of a will, killing the benefactor wouldn't get you a thing."

"Unless what you were after was revenge," Lauren said.

"Huh?"

"Revenge for being looked over."

"Oh." Mosey looked closely at Lauren. "So, does this seem like a revenge killing to you?"

"It could be, based on my limited knowledge of the crime scene. As I said before, if the antagonist wanted revenge, thinking Fortney was responsible for his fiancée's death. But I wouldn't rule out other scenarios. Maybe it wasn't revenge. Could be something entirely different."

"If not revenge," Mosey said, "what *does* it seem like, with regard to motive?"

"Well"—Lauren squirmed in her seat—"I'm rather intrigued by the whole set-up—often referred to as *staging*."

"Go on," Robert said.

"As you may have heard"—she glanced at Robert—

"forensics has become rather precise about pinpointing the various types of tampering that occur at crime scenes. If the perpetrator tampers with the scene so as to throw investigators off by providing them with false evidence, that's staging, properly speaking."

"Hmm," Robert muttered, "I didn't know that."

"Well, most people don't. But in this situation, I think we might be dealing with a different type. It's called *posing* and implies that the perpetrator wanted the victim to be perceived in a particular light. You might expect to see some posing when the offender's intent is lascivious, for example."

"Lascivious," Hugh said. "Now, that's a gruesome thought."

"You mean because of the victim's age?" Lauren said.

"Yeah, but not only that," he continued. "I mean, she didn't seem like the type to inspire thoughts of a lascivious nature."

"No, from what I'm hearing, I suppose she wasn't. But there is another possibility, besides staging and posing."

"What?"

"It's called *undoing*. The offender commits the crime, then suddenly wishes he hadn't and tries to somehow make amends."

"Undoing," Robert repeated. "That's a new one on me."

"Well, it isn't that common, but I've seen a few crime scenes where the offender did something to more or less comfort the victim. Or to let whoever finds the body know that the person was loved, respected, whatever."

"In this case"—Nadia's eyes widened—"that sort of makes sense, doesn't it?"

"You think so?" Lauren asked.

"Well, I'd say the killer went all out to give her a proper sendoff, exactly the kind a King deserved, or at least expected, complete with a fancy catafalque brought in from who knows where."

"Wow, that does make sense," Mosey exclaimed. "We've been thinking this guy was a total eccentric, a demonic killer, but maybe he wasn't so bad after all if he went to all that trouble to give Miss Lenna a proper wake."

"Mosey, he strangled the woman!" Robert said.

"Yeah, he did."

"But see," Lauren intervened, "that's just the thing. All the perpetrators who 'undid' their crimes, did actually kill the person."

"I see what you mean," Hugh said. "It's like he flew into a rage, committed the murder, then regretted what he'd done."

Lauren nodded.

"Makes more sense when you put it that way," Robert said. "But what about Kemena King's remains? You suppose that could have been some kind of undoing?"

Lauren shrugged. "I suppose it's possible, especially if the person who removed the remains was somehow involved in the drowning."

"Wait, let me get this straight," Nadia said. "You're suggesting this guy came back a decade later, collected the remains, and showcased them, like a trophy?"

"Wow, a trophy, huh?" Mosey said. "You mean like Kimmy, the ultimate trophy wife?"

Lauren, surprise on her face, looked at Mosey, then Nadia. "I think you two are onto something."

Mosey's expression brightened slightly, then fell as she gently shook her head. "But if you think about it, that's really sad, really, really sad."

Chapter Twenty-Two

Police Station
Tuesday, March 16, 2010, 4:00 p.m.

It had been a long day, and Olivera was feeling tired when he returned to the station after his jaunt to Mound City. He spoke briefly with Ms. Hill before filling a cup with hot coffee and heading to his cubicle.

"You made it back," Springer said as Olivera passed his desk. "Did you see Trumble?" Springer got up and followed him in.

"Yeah, I did." Olivera set his cup on the desk, hung his hat on the corner rack, and slumped into his chair. "And Patterson, too," he added as he reached for his cup.

"What'd you find out?"

"I'd have to say not much, considering. I spent the entire day interviewing four people of interest, and I can't see any of them as a suspect. Nope, not really."

"Not a one of 'em has motive?"

"If they do—"

"What?"

"—they're pretty darn good at covering it up. I mean, Neville might have motive, should it come out that Fortney was planning to pass him over, putting Bud Fortney in charge. But he seemed like such an upright guy, pleasant, business-like, clean-cut. It's hard to imagine…"

"You crossin' him off the list?"

"I don't know. I'll say this." Olivera sat up straight. "He certainly seemed capable of pulling it off. Everything about him, his office, his manner, suggests a person of above-average organizational skills. But creative? I'm thinking about what Dr. Wilson said about the offender being a person with a flair for the creative, for drama." He shook his head. "I saw none of that. Just a very capable businessman."

"What about Bud Fortney?"

"Ha! Just the opposite. The only thing those two have in common is their office furniture. But even so, Fortney's office didn't give off much of a business vibe. Looked more like a sports locker or a trophy room. I can't imagine how they'll get along, now that Ms. Fortney won't be around to hold things together."

"Maybe they won't. Maybe if Neville takes over, he might decide to clean house, get rid of Bud Fortney."

"Nope"—Olivera shook his head—"I don't see that happening."

"How you figure?"

"I don't know. I just don't see much changing over there."

"You reckon she left the firm to Bud?"

"Possibly. But neither of them seemed to have a clue about her wishes. And neither one seemed the least bit insecure about his position." Olivera rubbed his chin.

"Did they have alibis for the night of the murder?"

"They were both at home…alone."

"Well, that's logical since neither of 'em is married."

"You know, Bud Fortney mentioned that Nate

Patterson had left the office one day hot under the collar. And Neville also made reference to a client issue but wouldn't say who or what. Said he wanted to consult with the others." Olivera took a sip of coffee. "See, that's what I mean about Neville and Fortney. Neville answered my question without revealing anything really, and Bud just blurted it out."

"Yeah, I'm surprised Bud Fortney managed to snag a spot at King Accounting."

"You know the guy?"

"Sort of…from high school sports."

"He went to school here, did he?"

"He lived in Mound City, but he went to school in Hembree."

"You see him as a cold blooded killer?"

Springer laughed. "On the football field, maybe."

"So how you figure—?"

"Family," Springer cut in. "He's a Fortney."

"So you figure Lenna Fortney hired him to please her dead husband?"

"Well, no, not that, but family tends to reflect on family, so it behooved her to help the guy out. He was Jim Fortney's only nephew, and with her not having any family of her own…"

"Yeah, I suppose."

"But what about Trumble and Patterson? Either one seems more likely than Neville or Fortney."

"You think?"

"Yeah, I do. I mean, both of 'em work not far from Red Oaks, and location is a pretty important factor."

"You been talking to Dr. Wilson?" Olivera said.

"No, but everybody knows that from watching TV."

"So, let's say you're right and location *is* a factor,

which would give Patterson and Trumble an easy ride to the crime scene and back. Patterson says he's got an airtight alibi."

"Well, good grief, I reckon that narrows it down a bit. Where'd he say he was?"

"Home with his wife and kids—"

"—who would have been asleep," Springer interrupted.

"Probably."

"If you ask me, 'home with the wife and kids' is *not* airtight. He could have slipped out, driven to Red Oaks—"

"But I didn't see any strong motive. Well, maybe."

"Huh?"

"He said Lenna Fortney was pressuring him to sell her the Seed and Feed."

"Pressuring how?"

He lifted his brow. "He didn't quite explain that."

"Hmm," Springer muttered, staring off.

Olivera looked over at the evidence board. He still hadn't gotten around to posting snapshots of the people of interest. "I've been wondering about all these local businesses that Lenna Fortney owned. According to Patterson, some other people had complained to him about that. I mean, pressuring them to sell when they didn't really want to. Wonder why she—"

"Money laundering!" Springer exclaimed.

"Huh?"

"Yeah, Chief, I bet that's it. Lenna Fortney had so darn much money that she'd started looking for some little cash businesses so she could avoid paying income taxes. You oughta check that out, ask to see the records."

"Springer, you have been watching too many crime

shows. I cannot imagine a smart business woman like Lenna Fortney straying into money laundering. Give me a break!"

Springer hunched over and looked at the floor.

"Besides, how would she launder money through an operation like the Feed and Seed? Wouldn't customers pay with a credit card? Who pays for big quantities of farm products with cash?"

"Oh, well," Springer said, "now that's easy. You just tell your most trusted customers you'll give 'em a discount on cash and carry. You'd see how many showed up with a passel of cash."

"But what about the bank? Wouldn't they get suspicious, farmers coming in asking for cash?"

"Who says they have to come in? All they'd have to do is drive through an ATM and get all the cash they wanted."

"You been thinking about this, haven't you, Springer?"

"Well, me and Reagan were sort of batting around the business angle."

"And what'd you come up with?"

"Number one, when money is involved, and we imagine it is, I mean why else?"

"Yes, I think we can all agree on that."

"Well, that's not what Dr. Wilson said."

"Oh, right, but that aside…"

"So, as I was saying, if money is the thing, you kill to get it, or you kill to protect it, right?"

Olivera thought for a second and then nodded. "I suppose that's fairly accurate."

"Like there's the case where somebody wants some rich dude's money and kills him to get it, or maybe they end up killing him when it really wasn't their intention."

"Yes, I guess."

"And then, there's the other situation, protection, when some rich person is about to lose money he came by illegally because somebody's gonna rat him out."

"Yep, that happens."

"So, in Miss Lenna's case, somebody wanted her money, and they killed her to get it or didn't mean to kill her but—"

"Wait a second, Springer. What about the method? What about the staging? That doesn't sound to me like murder for money."

"Unless all that was to throw us off. We talked about that."

"Yeah, we did."

"So, the method don't exactly match the motive," Springer said, hands splayed.

"Okay, so?"

"It's a frame up, clear and simple."

"And who, pray tell, are we supposed to think committed the murder?"

"Merritt Trumble."

Olivera thought again. "I get it. The creative angle, and I guess you'd have to add to that the business with Kemena King's remains. Could have been to signal a connection between the two murders, like killing Lenna Fortney was revenge for her causing Kemena King's death."

"Right."

"Well, I'd say your theory holds water, Springer, and it sort of matches up with Dr. Wilson's theory. I mean, the part about the fatal flaw, Fortney's jealousy toward Kemena and her refusal to let her marry Trumble.

By the way, I got him to talk about that a little."

"Yeah?" Springer's eyes widened.

"He's still pretty broken up about it but does seem to have taken a more rational attitude."

"What'd he say?"

"He doesn't seem to be holding on to any resentment about the police's handling of the case."

"Yeah?"

"He said he felt like they had done all they could. You know, that was a weird case. They never really came up with an explanation of the drowning. The boat was okay according to the mechanic who checked it out, yet the coroner, old Dr McGinnis, told Trumble 'off the record' that she might have been electrocuted. Seems there might have been a problem with the motor. But Trumble still felt like the Fortneys lied about their whereabouts. He thinks they might have been at the house, heard the screams, but did nothing to save the victim. Sounds pretty cold-hearted if it played out that way."

"Yeah, it does. To let a young woman like that drown. Naw, I don't see that happening. Trumble must have hated Miss Lenna, her husband, too, to think a thing like that."

"Yes, and you think her disapproval of the marriage could have caused such a hatred?"

Springer shook his head. "Not really. Dislike, yeah, but hatred? Hard to imagine. Did it seem like to you he still hates her—I mean, if he ever did?"

Olivera took a deep breath and let it out. "I'd say probably not. But he does seem to feel strongly about Kemena King, like maybe he never got over the fact that they missed out on a life together. When I mentioned the remains, not that I wanted to bring that up, but I sort of had to, he was visibly shaken. Seemed very upset about the remains being disturbed."

"Yeah, a tad mortifying, ain't it? But after so much time has passed…"

"Right, but thinking back on the interview, I'd say that's what I came away with. A guy with a fragile alibi, close proximity to the crime, still carrying a torch for his lost fiancée. But motive? I'm not sure what he had to gain by killing Lenna Fortney."

"Chief, I'd say we got a lot o' work to do."

"Looks like it. But you know what? I think I'm going to run all this by Dr. Wilson. When I talked to her this morning, I'd only spoken with Neville and Fortney. I wonder if she'll think either of these other guys fits the profile she was telling me about."

"The Greek-tragedy theory?"

Olivera nodded, then checked his watch. "But before I head out of here, let's get a start on the second evidence board. See if you can find pictures of the people of interest online. I imagine you can, and I'll start on the tabs for the board. I want to record my impressions while they're fresh in my mind."

Before they left for the day, they put up the information on the evidence boards: shots of Red Oaks, the crime scene, the bedroom, and the mausoleum, on the first board; and photographs of the people of interest on the second board. The third board, where they would eventually post the conclusion, remained blank for the time being.

"We're gonna need a fourth, I'm thinking," Springer told Olivera as he tacked up the last of the photographs. "We gotta have space for the physical evidence."

"Well, we don't have much so far."

"Yeah, but we got the poker, the charred paper. Speaking of which, what happened to the charred paper?"

"Nothing yet, but Dr. McGinnis suggested we ask Jessup to help us with that. And something else. I've got to call Sam McGinnis to see what he can tell us about Kemena King's drowning."

"We got the files, I'm pretty sure."

"Yeah, but I want to see more than the files. I'd like to see what recollections he might have that never made it into the files. You know what I mean?"

"Sure do."

"Okay then, I'm heading out. I have some things I want to run by Dr. Wilson, see how they might fit into her profile." He reached for his hat and made his way toward the back exit but, remembering something, turned and called to Springer. "You know what?"

"What, Chief?"

"It wouldn't hurt to check the alibis."

"Sure wouldn't."

"Why don't you get started on that. Get the addresses for the lot of them. I already entered them in the files. And see if you can verify their whereabouts on Saturday night, say, from around eleven p.m. till Sunday morning. Check to see if there are any recording devices in the area that might have caught them coming and going. You know, some of the businesses near Red Oaks might have outdoor security cameras. Be sure to check with Al's Supper Club, too. Trumble claimed he was there till late Saturday."

"Will do, Chief."

"And check with the Mound City Police and see if

they have any surveillance on the outskirts of town."

"Sure will. Too bad we haven't invested in that around here."

"Yeah, I know. Well, I never thought we needed it till now."

Olivera left the station and, getting into his car, pulled out his cellphone and tapped in Wilson's number.

"Hello."

"Dr. Wilson?"

"Yes."

"Olivera here. I made it through all four interviews today and had some impressions I wanted to share if you've got time."

"Well, sure. I'm at the Tavernette, but I can meet you somewhere if you want."

"Is the Tavernette crowded?"

"Pretty much. I tell you what, we were on our way out. Suppose I meet you at my place or yours, wherever you prefer?"

"Okay, better make it your place."

"Fine. I can be there in about fifteen."

"That works. I'll head there now. Just leaving the station. But take your time."

Chapter Twenty-Three

Morris House
Tuesday, March 16, 2010, 5:30 p.m.

Olivera arrived at Morris House ahead of Wilson, just as darkness was settling in. By the light of the street lamp, he could make out the porch and lawn and, on the edge of the property, the ghoulish thicket where Frank Ferguson had stumbled upon the burial site of a newborn child. Olivera hadn't been back to Morris House since they'd closed the case on baby Jane Doe. The identity of the parents was clear, and neither of them was alive. Plus, the remaining family members showed no interest in continuing the investigation.

As his eyes scanned the front of the property, he couldn't help but wonder what other secrets waited to be exposed. Besides that, there was the complication of the current homeowner Lauren Wilson. He was starting to have some conflicting emotions about Wilson, even though she was a tad young and he felt more or less committed to Eads McGinnis. He and Eads had been dating since a night in early January when the ground-floor corridor of Delta Infirmary turned briefly into a scene right out of a romance novel.

Just then, Wilson rolled up in her sporty convertible, interrupting Olivera's thoughts. He got out of his car and walked over to the gate, where she stood, wearing a big smile and motioning toward her recently renovated house.

"So what do you think, Lieutenant?"

"It's cleaned up very nicely."

"Ferguson did a good job, didn't he?"

"Maybe it's time I had him over to my place."

"Are you really up for that?" She tossed him a skeptical look.

"Of course, I am." Well, yeah, that's what Eads would've wanted him to say. But to be real, getting his house in shape wasn't at the top of his to-do list. How he'd managed to get swept up in the domestic pursuits of the opposite sex, he didn't really know.

"Could have fooled me," she retorted, then laughed.

Chatting away, they came to the threshold.

"We can sit out here if you prefer," Wilson said as she was about to unlock the door.

"Sure, this is fine." He removed his hat and took a seat in one of the rockers near the entrance. "It's pleasant out here."

"Yeah, it is." She opened the door. "And it's gonna be even more pleasant when all those plantings come into bloom." She glanced down at the new bed just beyond the edge of the porch. "Let me get us something to drink. What would you care for?"

"What are you offering?"

"Wine, beer, something stronger. Or maybe you prefer a glass of iced tea. Everybody around here seems to take their tea iced."

"A beer would be fine."

"Okay, let me see what's in the fridge."

She went in, leaving him to check out the changes

to the place. The veranda was clean as a whistle with freshly painted siding and trim, new furniture, and even a couple of large ferns suspended from the ceiling. In her short stay in Hembree, she'd put more effort into spiffing up her house than he had in all the time he'd been in Hembree, which was going on two years. He was pondering what that was all about, when she came through the door with a tray and placed it on the small table between the rockers.

"You've done well for yourself, Dr. Wilson."

"Thanks, Lieutenant, I have quite a bit to do inside, but I wanted to spruce things up as soon as possible, and this seemed like the easiest spot to tackle. I'd like to start entertaining soon. All work and no play…"

"Yeah—" He sighed. "—a little play is important in our profession." He chuckled. "Well, I mean dealing with unpleasant matters continually…"

"This case got you down?" She sat in the rocker across from him and, after passing him a beer, poured half a glass for herself.

He wrapped his fingers around the chilled bottle and, relaxing his shoulders, felt the stress of the day begin to melt away. "That's what I wanted to run by you. I've finished interviewing four people of interest, but I'm not sure my understanding of the case has seriously improved."

"By the way," she said as she held out a bowl of olives, "I've made some alterations to my original deductions."

He picked out a fleshy green olive. "Already?" he replied, surprise in his voice.

"Yeah, I was thinking about the crime scene, at least as I imagine it. And you know, what initially looked to me like staging or posing could just as easily have been undoing. I mean, think about it."

He raised a forefinger. "Now, wait a minute. I was just getting the hang of that first scenario—"

"Sorry, Lieutenant," she interjected with a laugh. "I didn't realize you'd gotten attached."

"I guess I had. I even bounced it off Dr. McGinnis and Sergeant Springer, who weren't very receptive, as I might have guessed."

"Oh, well, I suppose I got a little carried away. But seriously, now that I've had some time to think about it, especially the positioning of the body, well, I guess that and the placement of the remains…Sometimes offenders sort of change their mind after committing the act and do something, even the slightest thing, to *undo* the crime. Let me grab my computer and I'll show you what I'm talking about." She set down her beer and popped back in the house.

To Olivera, this quick change of opinion seemed a little wishy-washy at first. But on the other hand, it was admirable that Wilson was able to keep an open mind. Indeed, refreshing to see a forensic psychologist who, rather than buying totally into her own theory, was willing to consider other possibilities. He liked that. Broad-mindedness was a personality trait he held in esteem. And not only that, she was obviously a bit ahead of the game. He had heard of *undoing* but had never met a forensic specialist who'd had much to say about it. This one was definitely ahead of the curve. And of course she ought to be, right? Coming from a fancy Eastern school and all.

She soon returned and, scooting her chair close to his, opened the laptop and pulled up a layout of crime scene photographs. "Here we go." She shifted the screen in his direction. "So, what do you think of this one?"

The picture she showed him was a close-up of a dead woman covered in a blanket. All you could see was the neck and face. The head and upper torso were surrounded by artificial flowers and porcelain figurines, like a girl might collect.

"Doesn't it remind you of the scene at Red Oaks, Lieutenant?"

"Well, in a way. She's sort of been laid out, like Lenna Fortney, I suppose. The cheeks and lips appear to be freshly made up, and the hair has been arranged around the face."

"Of course, in the case of Kemena King," she continued, "the offender's recrimination arrived rather late, didn't it? About a decade late."

"Yes, too late, for sure, for this kind of undoing." He gestured toward the photograph. "But I guess the term still applies." He looked over at Wilson. "I'd say your observation could be on target."

"I'm glad you think so. I wasn't sure you'd be open to the idea."

"Why not? It makes sense. And it also suggests, as it occurred to me this morning, that whoever killed Lenna Fortney might have been involved in the drowning. Not that he necessarily did the crime, but he might have been mixed up in it somehow. Doesn't it seem that way to you?"

"It does, especially if you consider that both incidents were sort of 'undone.' "

"So you're thinking it was Fortney's killer who took the remains to the cemetery?"

"Oh, yes." She relaxed, leaning back in the chair and

curling her legs up. "In both cases there's a sense of wanting to alter reality, kind of like trying to undo something as final as taking a life."

"And the fact that the coffin was used for both victims certainly links the two crimes." He looked away from the screen as he reached for his beer. "By the way, I hear the reuse of coffins was an accepted practice back in the day."

"Yes, it was."

"So, you're familiar with that?"

"Oh, yes. They would use a nicely finished coffin for the wake, but the container for the burial would be sort of rudimentary, like a pine box. I think the owners of these old Victorians considered it the practical thing to do."

"So if that's true, the offender might have known something about Victorian funerary customs."

"Which certainly narrows down the suspect pool, doesn't it, Lieutenant?"

"Probably," he said with a nod.

"Why 'probably'?"

"Well, there's always the possibility that the offender studied up, I mean, with the intention of throwing suspicion on someone else, someone who really was familiar with Victorian practices." He heaved a sigh and took a sip of his beer.

"You feeling okay, Lieutenant? You're looking a little flushed." She reached over and touched his forehead.

"No, no, I'm fine. It's just that the odds of a set up keep coming up. Kinda makes a rather difficult case seem all the more complicated."

"Well, you could forget about that for the time being

and try focusing on the more obvious possibilities, like, whoever killed Lenna Fortney was involved somehow in the death of Kemena King, and in both cases, there was an attempt to undo what was done." She thought for a second, patting her fingertips against her lips. "It does sound like the same person killed both women, well, if Kemena was actually murdered. But we don't really know that, do we?"

He raised his brow. "At this point, I would say anything is possible." He thought for a moment.

"You know, thinking back to the hypothesis I mentioned this morning, what if the fatal flaw wasn't jealousy? What if it was something else?"

"Like what?"

"Oh, I don't know. The usual motives I guess." She stared off, then looked back at him. "If someone did drown Kemena King, who might that person be? And why?"

He sighed again, raising and lowering his brow. "Who kills eighteen-year-old coeds?"

"Eeewww, that's a gruesome thought. Serial killers? Jealous boyfriends? Jealous girlfriends?"

"As I mentioned to you earlier, she had a boyfriend, Merritt Trumble. Whether he was jealous or not, I couldn't tell you. When I talked to him, the only conflict I could see was between him and Fortney."

"You think he could have done it?"

"Drown Kemena King? I seriously doubt it. I'd say he's still shaken up by her death. He claims Fortney was trying to keep them apart, but Kemena was headstrong and would have married him regardless."

"Yeah, so he says." She rolled her eyes. "Oh, well, it was just a thought. I suppose it's more likely he would have taken out his frustrations on Fortney. By the way, remember what we were saying earlier about the delay, I mean, the years between Kemena's death and Fortney's murder? Did anything come to light that seemed like it might have rekindled his anger?"

"Not really. To me, he appears to have taken a more rational view of the accident, though I suspect he's still carrying a torch for the dead girl."

"How awful."

"Yeah, it is. I suppose if he still loves her, he might also feel some level of contempt for the woman he claims tried to break them up."

She got up, walked over to one of the posts, and, leaning back, folded her arms. "What a bundle of nothing," she said with a shrug.

"Not sure I'd go that far." He stood and, picking up her beer, handed it to her.

"Thanks." She took a sip. "Too bad there's so little hard evidence."

"Well, everything in the house was either spotless or covered in dust, leading me to believe that the perp must have wiped down whatever he touched. But we do have the murder weapon."

"Oh, yeah?"

He nodded. "Apparently, he used a fire poker. Springer spotted it on the hearth in the master bedroom. Dr. McGinnis says it matches the bruising on the neck."

"I see."

"We also picked up some charred paper from the fire place."

"Charred paper?"

"Right. I'll take it over to the anthropology lab, see if they can recover anything."

"Hmm," she muttered. "By the way, what about Kemena's friends? Any of them still around?"

"Could be. She finished high school here before entering Blanchard. I'm guessing Mosey Frye could answer that question."

"I was with Mosey when you called, and she did mention speaking with Tara Townsend at the Development Office. She and Tara were sorority sisters. I wonder if Kemena King pledged a sorority."

"I haven't gotten around to that yet. I suppose I ought to give Mosey a call."

"She's probably home by now."

He checked his watch, then picked up his beer and took a last sip. "Thanks for the beer and conversation."

"Anytime. And, Lieutenant, I'm usually not this scattered, but since I haven't seen the crime scene, it's hard to focus. My imagination has sort of taken over."

"To be honest, I'm having a hard time keeping up with you"—he chuckled—"but you've certainly shed some light on the crime scene. And you're right, I really do need to speak to King's friends. Surely some of them are still around." He set the bottle on the tray, ready to leave, but then paused. "We could take a look at the crime scene tomorrow if you want. I mean, just give it a quick once over, informally. Or would I need to—"

"Sure, I don't see any harm in that."

"Is tomorrow morning a good time?"

"Let me check my schedule. I'll text you tonight or first thing tomorrow, okay?"

"Yes"—he nodded—"and thanks, Dr. Wilson."

Chapter Twenty-Four

Tavernette
Tuesday, March 16, 2010, 6:00 p.m.

When Olivera left Morris House, it was about supper time, and he dropped by the Tavernette for a quick bite before heading home. He parked near the entrance and, going in, came face to face with Mosey Frye. "Now, this is a coincidence. I was just about to phone you."

"Me? Why's that, Lieutenant?"

"You're on your way out, I see." He tipped his hat to Robert, Hugh, and Nadia, who were standing a few feet from the door.

"We are, but I could hang back if you like."

"Actually, I was hoping for a word with Hugh and Robert, too. I don't suppose I could detain you guys for a moment."

"Let me ask." After speaking with the group, then Miffy, she turned back to Olivera. "Miffy says we can have our table back."

"Good, I was hoping to grab a sandwich."

Once everyone was seated around the table, Olivera placed his order and then broached the subject he was eager to discuss with Mosey. "As you might have guessed I can't really overlook the possibility of a connection between the deaths of Ms. Fortney and Ms. King. It's been brought to my attention that you, Mosey, might have known Kemena King."

"Known her? Of course, I knew her, but we weren't friends. Kemena was a good bit younger."

"But perhaps you would have been familiar with her friends, someone she was close to?"

"Not that much"—she shook her head—"but we did belong to the same sorority."

"Any of Ms. King's, uh, sorority sisters still around?"

"As a matter of fact, I spoke with a Beta Nu alum earlier today. Tara Townsend is her name. She works in the Development Office. Seems like she and Kemena were at Blanchard about the same time."

He pulled out his notepad and pen and scribbled down the name. "Maybe I can catch her at the college tomorrow."

"I would think so. And I might mention that Tara told me she's dating a member of Kemena's extended family, Bud Fortney."

"I believe he might have mentioned that." He flipped to his notes from the interview with Fortney. "Yes, Ms. Fortney's nephew by marriage."

"So, you spoke with Bud?"

"I did, and I'm thinking I may need to speak with him again." He looked up. "Thanks for that information. I won't reveal my source, by the way."

"Tara won't mind. She and Bud will do all they can, I'm sure, to see this horrible business resolved."

Olivera turned to Hugh, who was chatting with Ms. Abboud. "Sorry to interrupt."

Hugh glanced his way. "What was that,

Lieutenant?"

"My apologies for holding you guys up, but I need to ask a favor. I don't suppose Dr. McGinnis has contacted you about the evidence we removed from the crime scene."

Hugh glanced at Robert and back at Olivera. "No, she hasn't."

"We collected some charred paper from the fireplace. Not that it necessarily has anything to do with the crime, but given the paucity of physical evidence, I believe we need to take a look. Dr. McGinnis doesn't have the necessary equipment at the morgue, but she thinks you might."

"She must be referring to infrared reflected photography."

"Yes, I believe that's what she said."

"Sure, I'd be glad to help. No problem at all. Will she be dropping off the evidence?"

"I can do that. I'll pick it up at the morgue first thing tomorrow."

"Good, I'm free till around ten. Wait a second, come to think of it, I have a meeting at eight. Could you make it around nine?"

"Lieutenant, you could leave it with me," Robert said. "I'll be around the department all morning."

"Okay, let's do that. I'll leave it with one of you as soon as I can make it to the college. You think you could look into it tomorrow?"

"Sure," Hugh said. "It shouldn't take long. We'll try to have something for you by afternoon."

Hugh and Nadia excused themselves and went on their way, while Robert and Mosey hung back. "We can keep you company if you like," Mosey said, "I mean while you have your supper."

"Oh, that's okay. I have some calls I need to make. But much appreciated, I mean your offer to keep me company and the information, of course."

"Always glad to help," Mosey said as she and Robert got up and headed out.

Soon after his sandwich arrived, and just as he was taking the first bite, someone touched his shoulder.

"How's the investigation going, Lieutenant?"

"Not great," he replied as he gazed up at Carlotta Humphrey. Laying his sandwich on the plate, he rose slightly out of his seat. "Have a seat, won't you?"

"Sure, I hate to see anyone eating alone."

"Well, I might not be good company."

"Why, that's hard to imagine. What's the problem?"

"Sure you want to know?"

Her eyes widened. "Positively." She slipped into the seat next to his.

"But, first, would you care for something?"

"Thanks, but I'm on my way to dinner. I dropped by for a drink at the bar. But continue with what you were saying."

"Well, I find myself in a position of having more theories than facts."

"But it tends to be that way early on, doesn't it?"

"I know we're just beginning—" He sighed. "—but I'm feeling a stronger than usual need to get on with it. I don't have a supervisor, of course, but if I were still in Santa Clara, the super would be breathing down my neck, given the victim's status and the circumstances of the crime."

"I see what you mean." She looked pensive. "Lenna Fortney was, by all accounts, the wealthiest woman in

Hembree." Carlotta stood for a second, slipping off her jacket to reveal an elegant black dress.

"Nice outfit."

"Thanks," she said with a smile. "It's good to get out occasionally."

She didn't volunteer with whom, and of course, he didn't ask.

"But back to what you were saying about more theories than facts. Seems like you'd have plenty of evidence." She gave him that disarming look of hers.

"You would think, but there's very little to go on. The most compelling 'evidence,' if you can call it that, is the profile of the perpetrator. But that's not really clear, either. I spoke with Dr. Wilson off the record. You've heard about her, I assume. The new forensic psychologist at the college?"

"I haven't met her, but I've heard her name mentioned."

"She's given me a lot to think about, maybe too much."

"Too much?" Her voice brimmed with curiosity.

"She's got this theory we've been calling the Greek-tragedy theory. She thinks the 'protagonist,' Lenna Forney, met a tragic end because of some character flaw. You know, the tragic flaw…"

"Yes, I've heard of it. Go on."

"So, in this case, the flaw would be her alleged jealousy toward her ward Kemena King. I've been batting that around and shared it with Dr. McGinnis, who wasn't at all convinced. Springer, too, and he didn't think much of it, either. Springer made the valid point that no jury was likely to swallow such a story."

She shot him a half smirk. "Nah, they wouldn't."

"But just now I spoke with Dr. Wilson again, and she was focused on an altogether different angle. Earlier, she pointed out that the crime scene looked staged, but now, she's thinking the whole business with the coffin and catafalque might signify a desire on the offender's part to reverse what he'd done. *Undoing*, she called it. Sound familiar?"

She frowned. "Undoing? No, never heard of it. But how? Or perhaps more importantly, why?"

"Let's say the perpetrator, uh, went into a fit of rage and killed Lenna Fortney but then regretted what he'd done. Mightn't he try to express his regret by somehow showing respect for the victim? Instead of just leaving her there, he might—"

"—put her in a coffin?" She looked askance.

"I know it sounds extreme, but let's suppose it's not quite as extreme as it seems. According to what I've learned from our local expert on Victorian funerary customs, all the props could have been in the house. Who knows? The catafalque might have been in the attic all along. And we're fairly certain the coffin was taken from the mausoleum right there on the property."

"Hmm, this is beginning to make more sense."

"Let's face it. It's never going to sound entirely reasonable, *pero dentro de lo que cabe…*"

"Come again."

"Oh, sorry." He rubbed his forehead. "My mind sometimes wanders into Spanish, especially when I'm out of sorts. 'All things considered,' I guess you would say."

She thought for a second. "I think I know what you're getting at. I mean about the general scenario. It's rather bizarre, nothing you'd expect to see at a crime scene, but considering the house and the people involved…"

"Exactly. Should your run-of-the-mill victim be found at such a crime scene, well, it really would be bizarre."

"But Lenna Fortney lived out her whole life in Victorian surroundings with the attendant oddities." She sat tapping her chin. "You may be onto something, Lieutenant. And if I were you, I would continue with that. It might just lead you to the killer. And by the way, you know, tomorrow morning, I'll be reading Lenna's last will and testament. It'll be interesting to see the reactions of the heirs."

"Who gets what could have a bearing on the case."

"Why don't you drop by the office, say, around nine, nine thirty. I imagine I'll be finished."

"When is your meeting?"

"Eight, but I'm leaving an opening between the meeting and my next appointment, in the event that, well…"

"I understand. I expect to have a full morning myself. I'm hoping to arrange a meeting with Dr. Wilson at the crime scene, but I'll take advantage of your offer if I can."

"I'm as anxious as anyone to know how the case is proceeding," she said. "I mean, the outcome could change everything. Well, not everything, but should one of the heirs turn out to be—"

"That would be a complication, wouldn't it? You know, if Kemena King hadn't preceded her guardian in death, I'm guessing she would have been the heir to the whole fortune."

"Possibly, since there are so few family members

left. If Kemena were still alive, I suspect the other beneficiaries would have received little or nothing."

"Those names, Kemena and Lenna, seem eternally linked, don't they? By amity or enmity. It's hard to tell."

"To hear Dot Cowsley tell it, the latter. But I've heard another side to the story."

"I have, too, this afternoon, in fact. I ran into Ms. White, Lenna Fortney's cook at Red Oaks."

"Indeed."

"She gave me a different view of Fortney and her relationship with Kemena. She seemed to like Fortney and said right up front that 'Miss Lenna knew her own mind.' I think that's the way she put it. White didn't believe the rumor that circulated after the drowning, well, that the Fortneys might have been involved. She said Fortney was quite fond of Kemena and was only trying to straighten her out."

"And if anyone would know, Willie White would. She worked for the Kings and the Fortneys for a long time."

"So, how do you suppose that rumor about the Fortneys lying about their whereabouts got started?"

"I know exactly how. Merritt Trumble."

"Oh, yes, of course. I heard the same. You know, I spoke with him today. Nate Patterson, too. And Neville and Fortney at the firm. I happened to see White's car at Red Oaks when I was coming back from the Seed and Feed."

"You don't suspect Nate Patterson, do you?"

"No, and he's the only one so far with an alibi."

"None of those men seems like a killer to me."

"You know all of them?"

"I know Neville and Fortney, mainly as business

associates. The other two I know by reputation, but it's hard to imagine…"

He slowly shook his head. "I agree. I suppose that's why I feel like I've made little progress. I've run out of people of interest. But tomorrow is another day, and thanks to Ms. Frye, I've got someone else to speak to. Tara Townsend. Do you know her?"

"Yes, Bud Fortney's girlfriend. She's over at Development, isn't she?"

"Yes, and she was Kemena's friend, a sorority sister. I'm hoping to get her version of what was going on in Kemena's life at the time of the drowning."

"You suspect it was more than an accident?"

"I don't know. I'm hoping to speak to Sam McGinnis. Maybe between the two of them I can get a more solid view of it."

"You haven't said much about Eads McGinnis's role in the investigation."

"Oh, Dr. McGinnis, yes." He felt heat rise to his face. "She's given me the time of the murder and cause of death, but the physical evidence is thin. We did, however, pick up what appears to be the murder weapon."

"Murder weapon? I thought Fortney was strangled."

"She was, but with an instrument. It looks like the perpetrator used a poker from the fireplace." He started to explain but stopped himself. "Not very appetizing conversation, is it?" He glanced down at his half-eaten sandwich. "Sorry. I warned you I wouldn't be good company."

"Not to worry, Lieutenant." She checked her watch and reached for her jacket. "I'd better be going, but I'll see you tomorrow."

"I'll try to make it by nine, nine thirty." He stood and helped her with her jacket.

Chapter Twenty-Five

Shepherd Realty
Wednesday, March 17, 2010, 8:30 a.m.

"I'm kind of stuck," Mosey said to Saffron.

"What ya mean, stuck?" Saffron glanced up from her newspaper to give Mosey a hard stare.

"Stuck," Mosey repeated. "I thought I could see a path forward yesterday, but now, well, I can't figure out what to do next." She was leaning against the counter in the coffee niche, finishing off a cheese biscuit. She was tempted to reach for another but stopped herself. "Time to take off the winter pounds."

Saffron burst out laughing.

"What's so funny?"

"You kill me." Saffron rolled her eyes. "One or two little pounds and you think you got to go on a diet."

"I wouldn't talk if I were you."

"I am just fine with my curves." Her voice sounded a little shrill.

"Speaking of curves, Tara Townsend is a tad curvaceous these days. Have you seen her lately?"

"Not lately."

"She's dating Bud Fortney."

"You're not suggesting…"

"No, I'm not suggesting, but they're engaged, well,

practically, and she *has* put on a bit of weight around the middle."

"You find out anything at the Development Office?"

"Well, just that, I mean about her and Bud being together. And, hey, she sort of hinted that Bud might inherit Red Oaks, and if he did, he might throw a little business my way."

"Wow, that *is* good news. John Earle would be pleased, very pleased."

"Yes, I suppose so, and I could put what you said to me yesterday right out of my mind. By the way, Carlotta is reading the will this morning."

"How'd you hear that?"

"Hugh let it slip yesterday at the Tavernette, well, let it slip. I guess it's no big deal, but folks seem to be tiptoeing around anything related to the murder. If you ask me, nobody knows squat, not really."

"According to the paper, they seem to know a fair amount."

"They know *how* and *when*, but they don't have a clue about *who*, and that's what I'd like to know."

"What about this other business?" Saffron asked as she ran her index finger down the column.

"What other business?"

"The remains found at the Civil War Cemetery."

"Oh, that. Yeah, one of Hugh's students found them. They're thinking whoever murdered Miss Lenna must have left them there."

"Yeah, Kemena King's remains," Saffron mused.

"Seems so. It was her coffin, too, I mean, the coffin at the crime scene."

"Mosey"—Saffron laid the newspaper on her desk—"this whole thing gives me the creeps. I don't know how you can go poking around—"

"Look. I know it's creepy"—Mosey cut in—"but if you're gonna get to the bottom of it, I mean, who did it, you have to shove the creepy stuff aside and go for it."

Saffron gave Mosey a puzzled look. "Doesn't it worry you that whoever did this might come after *you*? I mean, you don't wanna pop up on this lunatic's radar."

"I'm careful. I've learned to play the innocent. Like with Tara Townsend, for instance. I bet she doesn't have the vaguest idea why I went over there. She thinks I came in to sign up as a volunteer, ha-ha."

"Now, I wouldn't count on that. If Tara Townsend was involved in the murder, you'd better believe she's on high alert. And if she sensed something was off, you're in her crosshairs, for sure."

"Oh, my word, Saffron. Now you're giving me the creeps."

"You'd better watch out, Mosey. You have no idea who might be mixed up in this."

"Now, that I can't deny, but I bet you I start to figure it out pretty soon."

With a harrumph, Saffron went back to reading.

"By the way"—Mosey leaned closer to Saffron— "Lauren Wilson has a new take on the murder."

Saffron looked up. "What'd she say?"

"She says she can see a kind of 'undoing' at the crime scene."

"Undoing," Saffron repeated with a perplexed look.

"Yeah, like the guy who killed her felt bad afterwards and set up the whole wake scene as a sort of, well, expression of his regret."

"You mean like restitution?"

"Yes, come to think of it, that's exactly it,

restitution."

"Dr. Wilson has quite the imagination." Saffron gave the paper a shake.

"Yeah, I guess she does, but with this case, maybe it's called for—somebody with an imagination on the order of the killer's."

"I hope Olivera comes up with some hard evidence mighty quick, before you and Lauren Wilson turn this little town upside down."

"Huh, if only someone would listen." Mosey sighed. "You know, I think I'll run over to Nadia's for a sec. Today's Saint Patrick's Day—did you know?"

"Of course, I know. It's Uncle T.'s saint's day."

"Hey, that's right. You doing anything special?"

"I thought I'd drop by the Magnolia, take him some of those cheese biscuits."

"Give him a hug for me, would you?" Mosey said as she wrapped her shawl around her shoulders. "I'll be back soon, should anyone call."

Mosey left the building and, making her way down the sidewalk, headed to Abboud Antiques. She didn't go on foot, as she might have done, seeing the day was warming up and she hadn't much to do. She drove instead for the devious reason of taking a quick ride around the Square, wanting to see if anything was happening. With the reading of the will, some Hembree residents might see a significant improvement in their financial status, a fact that was hard to overlook.

She couldn't rule out the possibility of an impact on her own finances, either, should what Tara Townsend had intimated the day before turn out to be true. Wow, she wondered if Nadia had thought of that. Nadia didn't stand to gain as much as she, but, for sure, there'd be an estate sale, and she might make a killing on the antiques, mounts, and so on.

She shifted into second and, as she turned the corner onto Lee, noticed that the black wreath on the street door of the accounting office was still there. Not seeing anyone going in or out, she poked along toward Frye, Frye, and Humphrey, where the reading of the will was taking place. Then, shifting into first, she slowed to a crawl. Nothing seemed to be going on in the vicinity of the street door. "Oh, shoot," she mumbled under her breath. It looked like she'd arrived too soon or too late. She'd have to hear about it all second hand from either Hugh or Dot.

Then, just as she was about to drive off, Gus Olivera drove past her and pulled into a vacant space across from the law firm. With no place to stop, she drove ahead. But in the rearview mirror, she watched Olivera climb out of the cruiser and head toward the law firm. "Hmm," she muttered, "I wonder what that's all about. The reading of the will, most likely."

She continued on to Abboud Antiques, and parking in front of the store, hurried inside. "Nadia," she called out, "you here?"

"Course I'm here." Nadia emerged from the middle room. "What's up?"

"I just came from the Square."

"And?"

"Well, nothing really, but I did see Olivera going into the law firm."

"So?"

"The reading of the will was this morning at eight. They must be out by now. But what do you think Olivera was doing there? You would think he'd have bigger fish to fry, much bigger fish."

"Suppose so. Did you see the paper this morning?"

"Yes, and I got a rehashing from Saffron just now."

"You think the will has any bearing on the case?" Nadia said.

"It certainly could, but that's not all. It could have a bearing on me. And you, for that matter."

"How so?"

"Weren't you paying attention last night? If Bud Fortney gets Red Oaks, and Tara seemed to think he will, he's likely to want to sell it and hire me as his agent."

"That's right." Nadia's face brightened. "You'd be rolling in it!"

"I really would. Boy, that'd take a load off."

"You aren't worried about finances, are you?"

"Well, I wasn't until Saffron started hinting that our jobs might be in peril. Gosh, I've never been keen on real estate, but I need this job, at least until our college loans are paid off."

"Tell me about it," Nadia said with a groan.

"You, too?"

"Yeah, I borrowed a good bit, not wanting to exhaust my daddy's savings. Blanchard was expensive. I could have gone to the university and spent about half what I paid for tuition, but Daddy wouldn't hear of it."

"Same here." Mosey thought for a second. "I wonder how Bud and Tara are set for money."

"Bud? Better than we are, I would imagine. People tend to do well in his business."

Mosey, pacing from the counter to the showcase, peeped in to check out the St. Patrick's Day display. "Look at that! That's lovely."

"What?"

"That bird thing." Mosey pointed to a half dozen birds perched along the branch of a dogwood in bloom. "I love that. The colors are wonderful…all those shades of green."

"That's taxidermy, my dear." Nadia lowered one eyebrow. "I thought you didn't care for it."

"I don't usually, but that's pretty. Lovely, truly lovely. How much is it?"

"I'd sell it to you for nine hundred."

"What?"

"Taxidermy is expensive, can be, I mean, the world-class pieces bring thousands."

"Nadia, I had no idea."

"If those pieces at Red Oaks are what I suspect they are, the collection alone could bring half a million at auction."

Mosey looked back at Nadia. "I thought old Doc Fortney made those."

"He made some of them, but there were others that looked vintage, nineteenth-century Victorian. They could bring a bundle."

"My word, I had *no* idea."

"They wouldn't bring as much around here, but if whoever inherits them has half a brain, they'll get a big dealer to haul the pricier pieces out of here. I imagine Dallas is where they'll end up."

"Good gracious, this little matter of the will is getting more interesting by the minute. I can't wait to hear from Hugh. He promised he'd let me know." Mosey walked quickly back to the counter and picked up her tote.

"Hold on. Where are you going?"

"Back to the Square. See what I can see."

"You just came from there."

"I know, but I'm anxious to find out about the will. My future in real estate is at stake."

"You're exaggerating."

"No, I'm not. Saffron says that if we don't get busy, we may not have jobs."

"That's crazy. John Earle would be completely lost without you and Saffron."

"Without Saffron, yes. But me?"

"Who better to sell real estate in Hembree than you?"

"John Earle, for one."

"He's not about to give up golf for real estate."

"He might have to. To hear Saffron tell it, the local economy is about to tank."

"Mosey, that is just not true."

"It doesn't really matter if it's true or not, does it? What matters is what people think, and if they lose faith in the economy…Well, I can tell you one thing. They're unlikely to buy a house if the economy goes south."

"Calm down, would you? Have a seat and I'll make us a cup of tea."

"I don't think so, but thanks for the offer. I'll give you a buzz soon as I hear something."

Chapter Twenty-Six

Police Station
Wednesday, March 17, 2010, 8:30 a.m.

Olivera had his morning mapped out. He was eager to find out from Springer what he'd learned about the alibis of Neville, Fortney, and so on. He also wanted to catch up with Wilson and, hopefully, take her over to the crime scene. Then, he'd head over to Frye, Frye, and Humphrey to speak to Carlotta about Lenna Fortney's will. And somehow, between one thing and another, he had to get over to the morgue, pick up the charred paper, and take it to the anthropology lab. And, he'd almost forgotten, he needed to give Sam McGinnis a buzz, see if he could fill him in on Kemena King's drowning.

He lifted his hat to Ms. Hill as he passed her desk, "Happy St. Patrick's Day!"

"You remembered. Thanks, Lieutenant."

"You're a Patricia, so it must be your day, no?"

"It is." She got up from her desk and spun around. "I'm wearing my only green dress."

"Suits you—the color, I mean."

"Thanks, and by the way, Dr. Wilson called. Wants you to phone her back soon as you can."

"Okay, I'll do that right away. I suppose Springer and Reagan are in?"

She nodded toward the back of the station. "They came in bright and early. I suppose y'all have a big day ahead of you."

"That's what I'm counting on." He picked up the note with Wilson's number and headed toward the back. Coming to Springer's desk, he paused, seeing the sergeant hunched over his keyboard, a half-empty mug of coffee near his mouse pad.

"Morning, Chief." Springer glanced up.

"Morning, Springer. You find out anything, about the alibis?"

Springer rubbed his eyes before answering. "Sure did. I spoke to Hannah Patterson, Nate's wife. Said he was home at the usual time and never left till the next morning around seven."

"Anything else?"

"I checked with Al Bergeron at the supper club. He remembers seeing Trumble there and said he could check the surveillance footage if we needed him to."

"Well, if Al says he was there, I imagine he was. But that puts him in the vicinity of the crime. What about afterward? Any way to prove if he went home and stayed there?"

Springer swiveled in his chair to face him directly. "There's a camera in the parking lot of his apartment complex. I already called, and they're checking the footage between eleven Saturday night and nine the next morning."

"Good work, Springer. You get anything on Neville and Fortney?"

"Not sure how we're gonna verify their whereabouts. I could check with the neighbors, but that's gonna stir things up, as you might imagine."

"Yeah, I see what you mean. Hold off on that for the time being. Maybe we can avoid it if a couple of other things pan out."

"What things, Chief?"

"That charred paper, for one." Olivera leaned against the edge of the desk. "I ran into Jessup and Ellison last night at the Tavernette. They have infrared photography that should expose any writing. And that could be major. When someone burns a piece of paper, it's usually because they don't want anyone to know what's on it. Unless, of course, they were using it to start a fire."

"True," Springer said. "Whatever's on it could blow this thing wide open."

"And I want to speak to Sam McGinnis, see what else he can tell me about Kemena King's drowning."

"Makes sense."

"And...I was thinking of taking Dr. Wilson to the crime scene."

"Really?"

"Yes, she had some more to say about the profile, well, changed it up a bit."

"Huh. What's she saying now?"

"You ever hear of 'undoing' in the context of a crime?"

"No, can't say that I have."

"She showed me some examples online. Sometimes the perp apparently regrets what he's done and tries to undo the crime, so to speak. By covering the body, say, or placing flowers around it. Or, you know, the sort of think they do at a funeral parlor."

"Dr. Wilson thinks that's what happened?"

"She does, well, tentatively, and not only in this

case. She also pointed out that leaving King's remains in the cemetery might suggest the same sort of thing."

"So, both bodies were 'undone'?"

"She seems to think so, which implies that the same perp might have been involved in both deaths."

"You mean whoever killed Miss Lenna killed Miss Kimmy?" Springer said with a tilt of his head.

"Possibly. But I want Dr. Wilson to see the crime scene. Right now she's sort of dithering. I figure that if we go over there, she might get a better idea."

"You gonna ask her for a formal consult, Chief?"

"I'd like to avoid that."

"Yeah, how much does a thing like that cost?"

"Around here, not sure. In Santa Clara, it wasn't cheap, I can tell you that." He took a step toward his cubicle but turned back. "And one more thing, Carlotta Humphrey should be reading the will about now."

"Wow," Springer said, "things are coming together. Anything else you need me to do, Chief?"

He tapped on Springer's desk. "Wrap up what you can on the alibis, and if I get too busy around here, I may need you to pick up the charred paper at the morgue and drop it off at the college, but sit tight for now. Oh, and by the way, don't forget about the lining. You and Reagan need to check the attic and the basement for any extra coffins, and if you find one missing a lining, take a good look around. Sure would be helpful if you could find a print."

"I'll add it to the list." Springer let out a sigh.

As Olivera made his way to his cubicle, he pulled his phone out and tapped on Wilson's number. "Dr. Wilson?"

"Lieutenant, glad to hear from you. Looks like I may

have to substitute for Hugh Jessup. He's in a meeting and has been delayed. Not sure when I can leave here, I mean if you still want to drive out to Red Oaks."

"So, Jessup is detained, then. I bet I know where."

"I don't think it's a secret. He mentioned he had to attend the reading of Lenna Fortney's will."

"That's what I was thinking. It's nine now. I would imagine the meeting will be over soon. You go ahead and do what you need to do, and we can drive out to Red Oaks whenever you're free. I was hoping to see Jessup this morning. I need to take some evidence over. Oh, well, I guess it can't be helped. I'll speak to you later."

"Okay, Lieutenant. I may be in class. I'll check my cell when I can."

"Thanks, I'll be in touch."

He disconnected and called Sam McGinnis. "Sam, how's it going?"

"Great, but what about you? I imagine you've got your hands full."

"You'd better believe it. I wanted to get your take on the Kemena King drowning. I know it's been a while, but I thought you might remember something beyond what's in the official report." He pulled out his pad and pen, ready to jot down whatever McGinnis had to tell him.

"Well, I certainly remember the autopsy."

"Anything specific?"

"It was inconclusive. Unexplained bruising but not a lot.

"Unexplained bruising, eh?" He made a note.

"For certain, she died of drowning, but what I wasn't able to determine was what lead up to the drowning. You wouldn't think that a person who was familiar with the boat and the lake would just go out and get drowned, with no apparent cause."

"You said 'get drowned.' You think someone might have drowned her, intentionally, I mean?"

"No, I didn't mean that."

"I spoke to Merritt Trumble yesterday, and he recalls that you suggested electrocution as a possibility."

"I did mention that, as one of a number of likely causes."

"He seemed to think there was more to it than that."

"Well, he probably thinks it because it fit the scenario building up in his mind."

"What do you mean?"

"He was fairly certain that Lenna and Jim Fortney were somehow to blame, that they heard something but didn't come to Kemena's rescue."

"Did you see or hear anything that suggested he might be right?"

"Nothing, absolutely no reason to suspect the Fortneys."

"His version of the events apparently was shared by a lot of folks around here."

"That doesn't surprise me. People prefer a murder to a drowning. You must know that."

"Sort of sick, isn't it?"

"Human nature. People don't mean to cause harm with their groundless suspicions, but sometimes they do. I felt very bad for the Fortneys. I imagine a lot of people never looked at them the same."

"So, that's all you've got, Sam?" He drummed his fingertips against his desk.

"No...I've got a question for you."

"What's that?"

"I'm assuming it's Lenna's murder stirring up these questions about the drowning."

"Yes, at least in my mind. After the remains were found in the cemetery, I had to look at the possibility of a connection."

"Well, the perpetrator would want you to do that, wouldn't he?"

"Maybe."

"I'd be careful, Gus. Sounds to me like he's trying to throw you off the track."

"You think so?"

"I do."

"You ever hear of 'undoing' at a crime scene, Sam?"

"I haven't actually seen it, as far as I can recall, but I read an article about it once."

"Dr. Wilson, the new forensic psychologist, brought it to my attention."

"It's an interesting angle, but I'm not sure I'd go too far astray of the physical evidence."

"Like father, like daughter, eh?" Olivera chuckled.

"We are scientists, are we not?"

Olivera chuckled again and, after thanking McGinnis for his help, clicked off. "Okay," he muttered, "one more call and that's it." He tapped on Dot Cowsley's number and when she answered, said, "Ms. Cowsley? Lieutenant Olivera here. I don't suppose Ms. Humphrey is free yet, is she?"

"Surely she'll be out soon, Lieutenant. I don't believe she anticipated a long meeting, but they got a late start."

"Oh, I see. Well, I might stop by anyway, just in case. I need to get over to Delta Infirmary, and I could swing by on my way."

"That's fine. We'll see you then."

He dropped his cellphone in his pocket and, stepping over to the back window, gazed out at the gravel parking lot. He felt somewhat scattered, with no discernible path to help him distinguish between the fundamental and the trivial. He had no way of focusing on what was important and what was not. He wondered if Lauren Wilson didn't have something to do with that. As he was focusing on one clue, she'd come along and shuffle things around. Hmm. He couldn't recall having ever felt that way after running over the evidence with Eads. He sighed and, reaching for his cellphone again, tapped on her name. "Dr. McGinnis," he said, relieved to hear her voice.

"Yes, Lieutenant."

"I thought I'd call to see if I could drop by for a minute. I need to pick up the charred paper we found at the crime scene. I spoke to Hugh Jessup last night, and you were right. They do have infrared photography, and he said he wouldn't mind taking a look."

"Great, glad to hear that. Are you coming now?"

"Shortly. I need to stop by Frye, Fyre, and Humphrey on the way. I've been hoping to hear something about the will."

"You sound, well, a tad weary."

"I'm okay."

"Well, come on by. I'll be here till lunchtime."

Leaning against the window frame, he stared up at the flickering fluorescent lights. Then, putting the phone back in his pocket, he returned to his desk and took a seat.

"What else?" he mumbled. He'd spoken with Springer, Sam McGinnis, Wilson, and Eads. He couldn't think of anything else he needed to do right away. He felt in his pocket for his keys and, instead, touched the poker chip from the cellar at Morris House, still in his jacket pocket since the investigation. "Mosey Frye," he mumbled, "wonder what she's up to." Likely her thoughts were as much abuzz as his own. He wished he could see into that curious brain of hers, know what she was thinking. Had she zeroed in on a suspect? Had a particular piece of evidence caught her attention? He was of a mind to give her a call, see what she had to say. Nope. He wouldn't do that. He wasn't that desperate.

Just then he slapped his forehead. He had almost forgotten. He needed to speak to Kemena King's cronies. How could he forget that? Tara Townsend…the Development office at the college. He could go by there before or after stopping by the anthropology lab. "Springer," he called out.

"Yeah, Chief."

He grabbed his hat and stepped through the partition door. "Here's the plan. First, a quick stop at Frye, Frye, and Humphrey, then the morgue, then the lab, then Development. Whether I make it to Red Oaks or not remains to be seen. Looks like I'll have to put that off till after lunch."

"Sounds like a lot, Chief. You sure Reagan and me can't help you with some of that?"

"You're pretty loaded up, too, aren't you?"

"Yeah, but—"

"Never mind. Keep working on the alibis. You might check some of the businesses on Little Smith between Red Oaks and Hembree and Red Oaks and Mound City. Conceivably, some of them may have a surveillance camera."

"You know something?" Springer leaned back in his

chair. "If a person needed to travel that road in the middle of the night without being spotted, he might want to take one of the little cut-offs. And if he did, he might end up straying into the field of vision of a trail camera. Lots of folks living on the outskirts got one. I know my niece does."

"My god, Springer, you're a genius."

"Shucks, Chief, not sure I'd claim genius status. You want me to check with the hunters around there, see if anybody picked up anything Saturday night?"

"Yes, please do that. Check the cut-offs in the area. Hopefully there aren't too many of them, and then pick a couple of likely crossings. How big a deal would it be—?"

"Not too big," Springer cut in. "Reagan knows that whole area pretty well. We'll take a look at the map. I bet we can figure it out."

"Gosh, Springer, I am suddenly feeling a lot better."

"Glad to be of service, Chief."

Chapter Twenty-Seven

The Square
Wednesday, March 17, 2010, 9:30 a.m.

Mosey, back at the Square, crossed paths with Olivera for the second time that morning. Her intention was the same as before, i.e., to find out what had come to light at the reading of the will. She wondered what Olivera was up to and lamented the fact, competitive as she was, that he might have discovered the contents of the will ahead of her. Of course, it was a little silly to set her sights on Olivera. She ought to be on the lookout for Hugh Jessup, who had agreed to share whatever he learned at the meeting.

Mosey came to a halt behind a delivery truck that was unloading and waited, hoping to snag Olivera's spot soon as he left. He backed out and pulled away. She waited for a second, then slipped into the space. She got out of her truck and scurried across the street, then quickly ascended the stairs to the law firm. Reaching the landing, she peeped through the glass door. Dot was at her desk, and the door to Carlotta's office was closed. Could the meeting still be in progress? Had Olivera come and left without having spoken with Carlotta?

She opened the door and ventured in. "Morning, Dot."

"Mosey," Dot stood, "what brings you here?"

"Can't you guess?" Mosey walked cautiously toward Dot's desk, almost tiptoeing, as if fearful she might disturb those inside the meeting.

"Oh, I'm guessing you are here to find out about the will."

"Yes, I am. You see," she thought quickly, "I was hoping to list Red Oaks. I told you that, I believe. That's why I was out there, well, day before yesterday."

"Well, I suppose the cat's out of the bag, and there's no putting him back."

"Umm, that sounds grim."

"I suppose it *was* grim news for those who anticipated something different."

"They aren't still in there, then?" Mosey glanced at the door to Carlotta's office.

"No, they've finished. It didn't go on all that long."

"No?"

"Can I get you something, Mosey?" Dot slipped on her heels and pattered toward the coffee niche.

"No, thanks."

"You sure? I've just made a fresh pot of coffee."

"Well, maybe half a cup." Mosey wasn't sure whether to sit or remain standing, but if she was going to join Dot for coffee, she might as well take a seat. She sat at the end of the brown leather sofa closest to Dot's desk and rubbed her hand over the smooth upholstery. "It's always good to come here."

"Yes"—Dot smiled, as she brought in a tray—"this is a rather cozy setting, I mean, for a law office, don't you think?" She set the tray on the table in front of the sofa.

"I do. I wonder if they set it up this way, I mean,

intentionally."

"Of course, they did. Your grandfather Amos was a considerate man. He always tried to put his clients at ease. He played by the old rules of hospitality, reciprocity. He knew those things mattered. These days, people don't seem to realize the power of such things."

"You think Miss Lenna played by the old rules?"

"Hard to say." Dot picked up the cream pitcher and, before serving herself, offered some to Mosey.

"No, thanks, Dot. I think I'll take mine black this morning." Mosey picked up the porcelain cup and took a sip.

"Mosey"—Dot looked at her pensively—"you're an odd duck. Most of the folks around here have given up on the past, but not you. You always seem interested in what happened back in the day. You and Nadia both."

"Yes, I suppose it's true. In this business—" Mosey stopped herself, realizing she'd referred to her sleuthing as a business. She chuckled. "That's funny. I've gotten so tied up in all these criminal matters that sometimes I put my sleuthing before my real estate work."

"Now, Mosey, that is not wise."

"I know it's not, and I got a strong message from Saffron the other day. She thinks Shepherd Realty might be on the brink—"

"What?" Dot cut in. "Don't tell me that."

"Well, Saffron says she's not sure either of our jobs is secure."

"Oh, come now." Dot looked askance. "We're in a little slump, too, but it'll pass."

Though Mosey didn't mind the chitchat with Dot, she was beginning to wonder how she was going to steer the conversation back to the matter at hand. Dot obviously knew the contents of the will. "As I mentioned before, I was hoping Red Oaks might be the lucrative deal to lift me out of it, the slump, I mean. You don't happen to know—"

"Oh, yes, that went to Bud Fortney—who else? He's the closest relative Lenna had, though he's not blood kin."

"Too bad about Kimmy. If she were still around, she'd have inherited everything, I bet."

"You think?" Dot asked.

"Don't you?"

"I don't know. Probably not if she had married Merritt Trumble."

"You think the enmity was that strong?"

"I think so. Lenna really didn't like Merritt, though I've never understood why. He seems like a nice enough fellow to me."

"So," Mosey continued, still focused on the will, "there weren't any big surprises?"

"I don't think so. Everyone looked pretty content as they came out of the meeting. Bud and Ed left together, looking fairly tight. I'm not much of a reader of body language. You know, this gesture means that and so on. I've never understood all that. But they certainly looked chummy to me. And Wilhelmina White, my lord, she was walking on air."

"Willie White?"

"Don't repeat this, Mosey, but Lenna left her twenty-five thousand!"

Mosey let out a whistle. "How nice for her. And I bet she deserved every penny."

"Don't you know it." Dot giggled.

"And I would guess the college received a nice

donation," Mosey said.

"My goodness, yes. And it was stipulated that the new building be named for Kimmy. I thought that was a nice touch."

"Wow, for Kimmy, not for Ms. Fortney?"

"Nope, in memory of Kemena King."

"Now, that's interesting." Mosey tapped her chin. "I didn't expect that, did you?"

"Well, I suppose somewhere in the back of my mind I must have known. All the rumors after the drowning must have stirred up some negative impressions about the relationship between those two."

"Too bad about that. But looks like Miss Lenna came out smelling like a rose."

Dot shrugged.

"Well," Mosey said, finishing her coffee, "I'm glad to hear that, and I hope Tara was right. I'll sit tight and see if I hear from Bud."

"I'm sure you will. A young couple like that. What would they want with a big house like Red Oaks?"

"I love that house, but Bud and Tara may want something entirely different, and with the money from the sale, they'll be able to buy whatever they want. Okay, Dot." Mosey got up from the sofa. "I appreciate the coffee and the chat. I'd better get going."

"Okay, hon, and I'll tell Carlotta you dropped by."

As Mosey descended the long staircase to the Square, she was already planning her next move. She took her cellphone from her tote and tapped the last name in her short list of favorites. "Hugh, glad I caught you. I've just now spoken with Dot Cowsley, and she's told me, more or less, the content of the will."

"Yeah, it turned out great for the college. We've got

the money for the new building."

"Congratulations! Have you told Robert yet?"

"Not yet, but I imagine I'll catch up with him soon."

"So, everyone at the reading seemed content?"

"I would say so. Neville will take over as head partner, but she left a good bit to her nephew, including the estate and a couple of small businesses."

"Wow, sounds fairly equitable to me."

"You don't sound entirely happy, Mosey. What's up?"

"Oh, I am happy, very happy, but I was hoping something might have shed light on the investigation."

"I see. You're thinking motive."

"Who better than a disgruntled heir?"

"Right." Hugh chuckled.

"Oh, my god..."

"What?"

"I just thought of something, but never mind. I'll catch up with you and Robert later."

"Okay. Olivera is coming by with some evidence, so we may know something soon."

"Really?"

"Robert didn't tell you?"

"No, he didn't. You guys call me if you learn anything." She disconnected and, just as she was reaching her truck, saw some people coming out of King Accounting. It was Neville and Fortney, and Neville was patting Fortney on the back. Fortney had a big smile on his face. They looked pleased, for sure. But she could imagine somewhere not so far away, there was someone who wasn't happy because they hadn't been invited to the reading of the will. And she'd bet her bottom dollar that same person—

Before she could finish her thought, a large hand gently rested on her shoulder. "Al, fancy meeting you here. How are you?"

"Not bad," Al Bergeron replied.

"What brings you to our neck of the woods?"

"Oh, I've got some business to attend to."

Though snooping was her weakness, she knew better than to ask a person about his business. An inquisitive "really" was about all she would allow herself. So, she said it. "Really?" then added, "I assumed the supper club was keeping you pretty busy."

"Yeah, it does. And what's keeping you busy these days?" he asked with a knowing smile. "How's the real estate business treating you? My offer still stands, by the way, should you ever change your mind."

"You mean about singing at the club? No, I'll stick with real estate for the time being."

"Okay, well"—he checked his watch—"I've got an appointment, so, I'd better get going."

Mosey waved goodbye and watched as Al crossed the street in the direction of the accounting firm. "Hmm. I wonder what kind of business he has to attend to at King Accounting."

Mosey, came her daddy's voice, *give it a rest, would you?*

"Give *what* a rest?" she blurted out, though it wasn't hard to figure out to what he was referring.

Al Bergeron's business isn't any of yours!

"I know that."

You've spent the better part of the morning sticking your nose in other people's business and not doing a form thing to attend to your own.

"That's not true. I went to Shepherd Realty first

thing, and I'm headed back there now."

With a stop by Nadia's on the way?

"No, I'm not going to Nadia's, but to tell you the truth, I'm not sure where I'm going."

Mosey had made it halfway through the morning bumbling around from pillar to post. She really didn't know where to go next, so where would she go? Would she go to Red Oaks? Maybe stop by the Jeremiah Java on the way? Surely she wouldn't do anything as brazen as stopping by the Seed and Feed or Trumble Architecture. "Merritt Trumble," she muttered as she climbed into her truck. "He wasn't at the meeting, but what if Kimmy hadn't died. They'd be married, and now, with Lenna Fortney gone, the wealthiest young couple in Hembree. Yep, by a long shot."

Chapter Twenty-Eight

Delta Infirmary
Wednesday, March 17, 2010, 9:45 a.m.

After stopping by Frye, Frye, and Humphrey, Olivera drove to Delta Infirmary. He sauntered down the hall and pushed open the door to the morgue. "Dr. McGinnis," he said with a wave of his hat as he spotted her at her desk in the rear of the room.

"You look like you're in a hurry," she said.

"Well, I guess I am, sort of." He deposited his hat on the rack and walked toward the back.

"What's up?"

"I just came from the law firm. Carlotta read the will this morning." He sat down in the chair next to the desk.

"Any surprises?"

"Not particularly. The college received a big donation, enough to cover a new anthropological sciences building to be named for her ward."

"Her ward, not her?"

"That's what Carlotta said."

"That surprises me. You know for years people thought those two didn't get along."

"Well, maybe they were wrong about that. Or maybe they weren't. Hard to know."

"So, what else?"

"Neville will take over as head partner, but Bud Fortney will get the estate and a couple of businesses. So, it seems like Neville and Fortney didn't have anything to beef about."

"You don't seem pleased."

"Oh, it's fine," he said with a shrug. "It's just that my potential suspects are dropping like flies, which brings me to the object of my errand. I think we need to take a look at the charred paper. I spoke to Jessup and Ellison last night. As you expected, they have the equipment and said they wouldn't mind checking for content."

"You might get lucky and find a fingerprint or two."

"Or it might be a bundle of old brochures. Ha."

"Who burns brochures?"

"I don't know. I guess you could use them to start a fire." He shifted in his chair, wondering if he dared mention Wilson's recent thoughts about the crime scene.

"Shall I get the paper?"

"Well, there was one more thing. I know you aren't impressed with Dr. Wilson's theories, but she said something later on yesterday that I thought might be relevant."

"What?"

"She showed me some photographs of what she referred to as undoing."

"I've heard of it."

"You have?"

"Of course."

"So, having seen the crime scene, do you think that's a possibility?"

"Undoing, eh?" she mused as she removed her readers and gazed into space. "I guess she's thinking the culprit felt guilty for what he had done and, wanting to make amends, staged a nice wake for the victim."

"Well, I don't think she would have said 'staged.' If his motive was to throw the suspicion onto someone else, you could call it staging. But if his motive was to express remorse, that's more like undoing."

"Whatever," she said with a shrug. "But it's hard to imagine anyone going to such great lengths."

"I know. Hard to imagine. But there's more. She also sees a connection between the wake and the business with the remains."

"So, both acts are supposedly expressions of regret?"

"Yes, to her they suggest a similar MO."

"Someone who kills, then wishes he hadn't, and—"

"Right."

"But wait a second." She turned to face him. "What regrets would he have about Kemena King's death?"

"You're convinced, then, it was an accident?"

"Oh, I was too young to have much of an opinion, but Daddy was convinced. He wouldn't have signed off on it otherwise."

"Yeah, I spoke to him about that. I suppose with no witnesses and no hard evidence…"

"There was, of course, the unexplained bruising."

"Well, I'm hoping the charred paper will tell us something. I certainly would hate for this case to go cold."

"So, you're thinking of the other case as 'cold'?"

He scrunched up his face. "Sort of. I mean, I didn't at first, but given this new theory of Dr. Wilson's—"

"Wow," she interrupted, "you're really impressed with Dr. Wilson's theories." She crossed the lab to the counter where she'd stored the evidence bag. He followed and waited as she retrieved the bag with the charred paper. "Or maybe it's not the theories but Dr. Wilson herself." She cast him a knowing glance.

"Oh, please"—he rolled his eyes—"don't go getting all jealous on me."

"Me, jealous? That's a novel thought." She chuckled.

"We'll talk about this later, but right now, I think I'd better get this evidence over to Anthropology." He grabbed his hat off the rack and, letting the door close behind him, went on his way.

As he walked the long corridor to the exit, he couldn't help but wonder what Eads was really thinking. They parted on a jovial note, as if neither of them was taking his possible crush on Wilson seriously. But he couldn't shake the feeling that Eads had picked up on his interest in his new colleague, whom, for any number of reasons, he shouldn't be interested in at all. Regardless, he couldn't deny he found her intriguing in a strange sort of way. And though her approach to forensics wasn't always convincing, it was refreshing to see someone who wasn't a bit afraid of their spontaneous inclinations, their imagination. It was as though it was her superpower. But was it a valuable tool or just a big time-waster? Time would tell.

He got in the cruiser and headed for the college, thinking it would be best to deliver the paper to the lab right away. He made his way there and arrived just as classes were changing. He sat tapping the steering wheel at the crosswalk as students and faculty hurried across the street. Observing the crowd, he noticed that some were wearing matching T-shirts in shades of yellow, pink, and light blue. Sorority women, he thought, like Kemena King, Tara Townsend, and Mosey Frye. Ha. He wondered if Eads had pledged a sorority, but somehow doubted that she had. Once the rush of pedestrians had decreased to a trickle, he was able to continue on and find a parking spot near the social sciences building.

Going in through the side entrance, he came to the lab, which was on the first floor. He opened the door and peeked in. Jessup and Ellison were both there, seated on stools near a long counter.

"Wow," he said as he approached. "Quite a lab."

"What did you expect?" Hugh said with a broad smile.

"I guess I've spent too much time at the morgue," he said with a chuckle as he scanned the modern surroundings: white walls lined with lockers, metal tables, counters with microscopes and computers, and bright overhead lighting.

"Yeah," Hugh said, "it's sort of a shame, actually."

"Dr. McGinnis does well, considering." Olivera set his briefcase on the counter and reached in for the plastic bag holding the evidence.

Jessup accepted the bag. "The papers seem to be intact, and I imagine we can pick something up." He looked at Olivera. "You have any idea what it is?"

"Not really. We found it in the fireplace in the master bedroom. It could be significant. We're fairly certain that's where the strangling occurred. And the murder weapon was likely a poker from the fireplace."

"This is all there was in the fireplace?"

"Yes," Olivera said. "Just this small bundle of papers."

"So, unlikely it was being used to start a fire,"

Ellison said.

"That's what I'm thinking. Seems suspicious."

"Well, we should be able to get to this fairly soon," Jessup said. "I'll give you a call."

"Thanks, guys." He shook Jessup's hand, then Ellison's, and left the lab.

It hadn't been his intention to speak with Wilson but, passing a door with her name on it, he paused and knocked.

The door opened, and Wilson stepped out, carrying a briefcase. "Lieutenant, we didn't have an appointment, did we?"

"No, I was just here delivering evidence to Jessup and Ellison but seeing your name on the door…"

"I wish I had time to chat, but I'm on my way to class. I'm a little late, in fact."

"I won't detain you. I'll call later about driving out to the crime scene."

As he finished his sentence, she was already a few feet ahead of him. Stepping onto an open elevator, she waved, calling out, "Great. Catch you later."

The elevator door closed, and he continued out of the building. He could have gotten in the cruiser and driven away but, seeing that Founders Hall was right across the parking lot, he decided to pay Ms. Townsend a visit. This wasn't his first trip to Development, so he knew exactly where it was. He'd been there back in the fall when he investigated the Ashby case. He entered the front of the building and took the stairs down to the basement, then followed the corridor to the office. The door was open, and he went in.

The young woman sitting at the first desk looked up.

"Ms. Townsend?" He removed his hat.

"I'm Tara Townsend."

"Lieutenant Gustavo Olivera of the Hembree Police."

She stood, looking taken aback. "You wanted to see me?"

"I did, if you have a moment."

"Well, maybe we should step in there." She gestured toward a small workroom off the main office.

He nodded and followed her in.

"Should I close the door?" she asked.

"Maybe partially."

"Have a seat, Lieutenant."

They sat opposite each other at a table stacked with binders.

"I wanted to ask you," he began, "about something related to the investigation of Lenna Fortney's murder, well, sort of indirectly related."

"Okay." Her voice seemed shaky.

"You see, I have heard about the rumors that circulated after Kemena King's death, but I haven't been able to speak to anyone who really knew her. I mean, her friends, college friends specifically."

"Well, I was a close friend of Kemena's. She was my little sister. We were members of the same sorority."

"Yes, I have heard that, and I thought you might have some idea about what was going on with her at the time of the drowning."

She paused to think for a second. "You know, when the accident occurred, Kemena was just a freshman here at Blanchard. I was a sophomore. The drowning was pretty awful. All of us were terribly upset."

"Was she popular, I mean, with the other students?"

"Yes, she was a very special person. She'd lost both

parents and, well…My heart went out to her."

"She had a boyfriend, right?"

"She did, Merritt Trumble. He was a little older, and they seemed rather committed."

"It's my understanding they planned to marry."

"Before I say any more, will what I say—?"

"Remain in confidence?"

"Yes."

He nodded. "I believe I can agree to that."

"You see, Lieutenant, I haven't been questioned before. I mean, back then, I wasn't questioned, and I decided to keep this to myself, especially since it was told to me in confidence."

"Is there a reason you shouldn't reveal it now?"

She shrugged. "I guess at this point it makes little difference except perhaps to Merritt. You see, they did plan to marry, but Kemena began to get cold feet. She was only eighteen. When she started college, the whole world opened up for her. I think during the time she was at Red Oaks with her cousins…Well, she told me that her guardian was very protective. Then, the day before the accident, Kemena confided in me that she had decided to break it off with Merritt. She said she was going to put it all down in a letter. And she might have. I don't really know. When she was packing to spend the weekend at Red Oaks, I saw her slip in some stationery and an envelope."

"Hmm. This is certainly news to me." He paused to think. "And I suspect it would be news to Mr. Trumble."

"I suspected as much, I mean I thought maybe she never got around to writing the letter, or if she did, she didn't send it. Maybe she changed her mind. I never spoke to her again after she left campus that day."

"And that was the day before the drowning?"

"Yes."

"So after that, you never said anything to the Fortneys or any of Ms. King's friends?"

"I did mention it to Bud Fortney but not then. Only recently, actually, and he didn't see any reason to mention it to Merritt. We both thought it would be unnecessarily hurtful."

"So, you think Merritt Trumble might still have feelings for her?"

She shrugged again. "It's been a very long time, but he might. It was traumatic for him. He may have never gotten over it."

"You know, there's a couple of other things I would like to run by you, like this rumor about Lenna Fortney and Kemena not getting along. What was your take on that?"

"Oh, I don't think it was a big deal. Kemena was a little rebellious, but a lot of us were. Ms. Fortney might have been stricter on Kemena than my parents were on me, but I think it was because she didn't really know how to be a parent. The whole parenthood thing was sort of thrust on her."

"So, you don't think it's possible the Fortneys were at Red Oaks but didn't come to Kemena's rescue?"

"Oh, no." She shook her head. "Unthinkable. Anyone would have helped Kemena. She was a dear, dear person. No one would have just stood there and let her drown."

He thought for a second. "Yes, hard to imagine." He paused. "Another thing, people have said she was a good swimmer. Can you confirm that?"

"I think she was, well, about like all of us who were

raised on the water. I mean she wasn't an Olympic swimmer or anything, but she certainly knew her way around the lake. She and I had gone out in that same boat a couple of times."

Before leaving, Olivera apologized for dredging up painful memories. Then he thanked Ms. Townsend for her time and her openness, mentioning again that he would do his best to keep the information concerning the anticipated break-up with Trumble under his hat.

He got in the cruiser and made his way back to the police station. He parked around back and, going in, stopped at Springer's desk. "How's it coming?"

Springer, still at his computer, swung around and gave his head a shake. "Reagan and me checked all the car tags between Hembree and Mound City and haven't found a thing, at least nothing pertinent to the case."

"So, none of the pertinent license plates showed up?"

"Not a one, Chief."

"What about the trail cameras?"

"We'll look at those next. But I don't know, Chief. It's hard to imagine that the killer walked the whole thing. Seems like he would have been in his car at some point, wouldn't you think?"

"Hard to know."

"Unless he got somebody to drive him out there, which doesn't seem at all likely."

"No, it doesn't."

Olivera took a breath and let it out. "Dr. Wilson and I are going out there later. I'll keep my eyes peeled."

"By the way, Chief, how'd it go at the law office?"

"Good. But no surprises there. I dropped by the morgue and picked up the charred paper, dropped it off at the lab. Let's cross our fingers that Jessup and Ellison can tell us something soon. Oh, and while I was over there, I spoke to Tara Townsend. She was one of Kemena King's close friends. She was helpful."

"What'd she have to say?"

"She doesn't suspect the Fortneys or anyone really. She seems to think the police reached the logical conclusion."

"Another dead end?"

"Probably, but I feel clearer on a couple of things."

"Chief, it's getting close to lunch time. Is there anything you need right away?"

Olivera thought for a second. "No, I guess not. Let's hold off on the trail cameras till I get back from Red Oaks."

Chapter Twenty-Nine

Jeremiah Java Cafe
Wednesday, March 17, 2010, 12:00 p.m.

Mosey managed to entice Nadia and Saffron to have lunch at the Jeremiah Java, though both considered it a tad far to go, especially since Hembree proper offered several suitable spots to grab a bite at midday. Mosey, of course, said she was sick to death of them all, so as to avoid having to say why she was willing to drive way out on Little Smith, a good five miles away.

The gravel parking lot was its usual chaotic self, crammed with cars and trucks of every description. But Saffron managed to squeeze her sleek black muscle car into a spot at the edge of the lot, practically teetering on the rim of a ditch. They got out of the car and, navigating their way across the lot in high-heeled shoes, managed to reach the front porch without incident. Once inside the wonderful smelling dining room, they looked around for a vacant table but, seeing none, cozied up against the front wall and waited for Lula to come their way.

Lula gave them a wave, and Mosey moved toward her. "How long is the wait?"

"Not along, five minutes." She checked her list. "Those gentlemen over there should be leaving any minute."

"Okay, cool. We'll wait."

Rejoining Nadia and Saffron, she gave them the good news. "It won't be long…no more than a couple of minutes."

"Good," Nadia said, "I promised Daddy I'd be right back."

"I don't know why we had to come all the way out here," Saffron huffed. "Who eats biscuits for lunch anyway?"

"Why don't you get the lunch special?" Mosey nodded toward the blackboard. "Beans, rice, andouille sausage. Uhm, uhm, uhm. Sounds good to me."

Saffron shrugged. "Who do you think you're fooling?"

"Yeah," Nadia chimed in.

"Fooling? Nobody. When Dot Cowsley said what she did about Bud inheriting the estate, and Tara had already said he'd likely wanna sell, well, I was just eager to take another look around the area."

"So, this has nothing to do with the case," Nadia said with a skeptical look.

"Well, not directly, though I have to admit I was wondering if Lula had seen or heard anything. She said she'd let me know."

"Do you really think Lula wants to get mixed up in a police investigation?" Saffron asked, her voice a little shrill.

"She *said* she'd let me know," Mosey repeated.

"Of course, she did, but that doesn't mean she would."

"Well, she did tell me one thing."

"What?" Nadia said.

"She saw a flashy ragtop in the parking lot, a car she

hadn't seen around here before."

"Not Tara Townsend's car," Saffron said.

"Tara has a red convertible?" Mosey said, surprised.

"I suppose she could have borrowed it, but she was driving one, for sure."

"Hmm. That's not what Lula said. She said Aaron told her it belonged to Nate Patterson."

Saffron chuckled. "Nate doesn't drive a convertible. He drives an old beater."

"Well, I don't know, I was going on what Lula told me."

"Listen"—Saffron raised an eyebrow—"Nate Patterson does not drive a convertible, but Tara does, I'm fairly sure."

"Well, I've never seen her in it. Surely I would have noticed."

Just then, Lula approached and directed them to a table in the corner. "What can I bring you ladies to drink?" She slipped out her order pad.

"Sweet tea." Saffron took a seat.

"Water for me—no ice," Nadia said.

"Bring me an unsweet tea with lemon," Mosey said.

"Lula, if you don't mind," Saffron added, "could we order now?"

"Sure."

"I'll take a fried oyster biscuit with a side of coleslaw."

"Ooo, that sounds good," Mosey said. "Bring me that, too."

"What about you, Nadia."

"Bring me the lunch special, please, ma'am."

"Lula," Mosey hesitated, "can I ask you about something?"

"Sure." She dropped her order pad in her apron pocket.

"You remember the other morning you mentioned you'd seen a red convertible in the lot? You thought it might have belonged to Nate Patterson."

"Oh, yeah, I meant to tell you. It wasn't his car. I asked him where he got the flashy ragtop, and he laughed out loud."

"So, who did it belong to?"

"Not sure."

"I told her it was Tara Townsend's." Saffron looked at Lula.

"Well, I'm trying to mind my own business."

"Why is that?" Mosey interrupted.

"The law's been out here day and night."

"Not too surprising," Nadia said.

"Yeah, and they're unlikely to let up till they catch whoever killed Lenna Fortney," Saffron added.

"You reckon they got any leads?" Lula looked at Mosey.

"Don't look at me."

"Well"—Lula bent closer to Mosey—"do *you* have any leads?"

"I might, but I wouldn't want to say, not just yet."

"What?" Nadia asked.

"It's nothing really." Mosey reached for a cracker from the basket Lula had placed in the center of the table.

"Excuse me just a minute." Lula stepped away from the table, responding to a wave from a customer who'd entered the restaurant.

As soon as Lula was gone, Nadia whispered to Mosey, "What's up?"

"Well, don't repeat this." She glanced from Nadia to

Saffron.

"I won't say anything," Saffron said.

"Well, please don't. It's just that I was thinking, after I spoke with Dot, that not everyone may be as content as it seems. With the reading of the will, I mean."

"Who?" Nadia said.

"Merritt Trumble."

"What's he got to do with it?" Saffron said.

"Nothing," Mosey emphasized, "and that's exactly my point. If Kemena were still alive, I bet she would have inherited a good bit. I mean, she was the only blood relative, and—"

"But I thought she and Miss Lenna didn't get along," Saffron cut in.

"I'm beginning to doubt that," Mosey said. "Who names a building after somebody they don't really like?"

"I sure wouldn't," Saffron said.

"But according to what I've heard," Nadia said, "Lenna threatened to cut Kimmy off if she went through with the marriage."

"Yeah, I know. And that's the part I can't figure out." Mosey looked up, seeing Al Bergeron come in. She waved and smiled, and Al waved back as he approached their table.

"Fancy meeting you ladies here," Al said with a big smile.

"We're sick to death of the Tavernette," Mosey said. "Thought we'd try something different. Speaking of which, you were in our neck of the woods this morning."

"You caught me," Al chuckled, "getting my income tax stuff in early."

"Yeah, I saw you heading into King Accounting right after our chat. How *are* things there, by the way?"

"Normal." Al shrugged. "They haven't missed a beat, well, it being tax season and all, it's not really surprising, despite the circumstances—"

"Yeah," Nadia cut in, looking up at Al, "I can't see that anything has changed, not yet anyway."

"You expect something to change?" Al looked down at Nadia.

"Yes, I do. I would think many things will change with Lenna, well, out of the picture."

"Hmm. I suppose you've heard, then."

"Heard what?" Mosey chimed in.

"Neville is leaving the firm."

"What?" Mosey exclaimed. "I thought he was taking over."

"Nope. Bud Fortney is buying him out, selling the businesses he inherited from Lenna to buy Neville's shares in the firm."

"Now, that's just crazy." Nadia shook her head. "I had no idea Bud wanted all that responsibility."

"You wouldn't think so, but I heard his fiancée sort of pushed him into it."

"Tara Townsend?"

"That doesn't sound right to me," Mosey said. "I can't imagine either of them…"

Al's attention shifted from them to Lula, who was coming out of the kitchen door carrying a big tray of food on her hip. She looked at Al, then gestured with her head toward a table in the opposite corner.

"Sorry," Al said, "looks like we've got a table. Nice talking to you ladies, and, by the way—" He paused, looking serious. "—probably not a good idea to repeat any of what I said. I picked that up secondhand, though the source seemed reliable." He turned and made his way toward the table, where the man he'd come in with had already taken a seat.

"Who's that with Al?" Mosey asked.

"I have no idea." Saffron made a space for the dish Lula had lifted off her tray. "Those oysters look delicious." She smiled up at Lula.

"Came in just this morning from the coast." Lula finished emptying her tray and, glancing around, said, "Anything else I can bring you?"

"Thanks, Lula," Nadia said, "looks like we're good for now."

After Lula had left, Mosey gave a sigh. "You know, ladies, I think I'm going to forget all about Lenna Fortney, King Accounting, and the lot of it."

"Ha," Saffron said, "fat chance!"

"I don't know why you'd back away now," Nadia said. "Things are starting to heat up."

"No, no, no. I've had my fill. Soon as I think one thing is about to happen, something entirely different crops up. I'll leave this one to Olivera." She took a bite of her oyster biscuit. "Wow, this is good. How are the beans, Nadia?"

"Tasty." She scooped up a spoon of beans and rice. "I wonder if Bud Fortney is looking for a buyer for the house."

"Hmm," Mosey said. "Who'd have that kind of money?"

"I don't know," Saffron said, "but they could always borrow it."

"I suppose so," Mosey said as she glanced around the room. "Reckon this place is about to change hands?"

"Could be," Saffron said. "Lula probably knows."

"Dare we ask?" Nadia said.

Saffron gestured toward Lula, who was taking Al's order. "You don't reckon Al—?"

"Hey, that's a good guess," Mosey said. "Especially seeing as how he was at the accounting office this morning and now here he is at the Jeremiah Java."

"Plus," Saffron added, "he seems to be the one in the know, doesn't he?"

"He knows more than we do, that's for sure. I just talked to Tara Townsend, and I would have never guessed that she would have pushed Bud Fortney into anything, much less if it required more work." She shook her head. "He just doesn't seem the type."

"I agree," Nadia said. "I can't seem to get past my impression of Bud as a rather cavalier individual. Not a bad person, mind you, but he doesn't seem to take interest in anything really serious, like running a big accounting firm. Wouldn't his salary plus the businesses his aunt left him bring in enough to pay his membership at the country club?"

"You heard what Al said." Saffron gestured toward the table across the restaurant. "Maybe it was plenty for Bud but not for his girlfriend."

"Oh, I don't know," Mosey said. "Tara doesn't seem all that pushy to me."

"Maybe pushy isn't exactly the right word," Nadia said. "I can tell you this. In her line of work, it pays to know how to take advantage of a situation."

"You hear that?" Saffron suddenly glanced toward the screen door.

"Yeah," Nadia said, "sounds like a siren."

As Mosey glanced over, Al stood up from his seat and gazed out the window.

Chapter Thirty

Red Oaks
Wednesday, March 17, 2010, 11:45 a.m.

It was about eleven thirty when Olivera picked Wilson up in front of Social Sciences. All the way to Red Oaks, they conversed nonchalantly about the investigation, him filling her in on his talk with Tara Townsend, and Wilson apprising him of her latest thoughts on the perpetrator's profile.

"I'm glad," Olivera said, "I was finally able to speak to someone close to King other than Trumble, of course."

"So, what did she say?" Wilson asked.

"Apparently, Townsend was with King when she was packing for the weekend at Red Oaks. Said she saw her tuck some stationery into her suitcase. Seems King was planning to write a letter to Merritt Trumble, a 'Dear John' letter. But according to what I learned from Trumble, seems like he never received it."

"That's interesting. Are we sure the letter was actually written?"

"No, we aren't. And considering Trumble's feelings about King, I would say he hadn't a clue what she was planning. He insisted that King would have gone through with the marriage even if Fortney had disinherited her."

"And Townsend didn't tell anyone about King's

intentions?"

"Not till recently. She said the police didn't question her. Nonetheless, she wouldn't have repeated what King told her, considering she had spoken in confidence."

"So, maybe they are both telling the truth."

"Townsend and Trumble, you mean?"

"Yes, it sort of looks that way. By the way, who did Townsend finally tell?"

"Her fiancé, Bud Fortney."

She looked pensive. "If Trumble did know, that certainly blows my theory out of the water."

"How's that?"

"Well, I was sort of thinking about who might have filled the role of Lenna's antagonist, the person who destroyed Trumble's dream of marrying King. But if King rejected him, I'd say it's highly unlikely he'd still be carrying a torch. Nah, he would have been over it by now, wouldn't you think?"

"I would say so. Doubtful he'd be carrying around anything other than a mild dislike for Lenna Fortney. You know, I wonder if she knew of her ward's intention to break up with Trumble."

"Oh...I don't know." She shook her head. "If Fortney had known about that, wouldn't she have mentioned it to the police? I mean, that would have given Trumble motive, no?"

"I suppose men do sometimes drown women who dump them," he said. "But this recent murder...Nope, I can't see him killing Lenna Fortney."

Chatting away, they came to the property and, pulling into the driveway, parked just beyond the big red oaks. They got out and walked to the porch. Once they had put on their slip-ons, he opened the door and ushered

Wilson into the parlor. "As you can see, the catafalque and coffin are still in place. Everything is just as we found it, except for the body."

She looked around the room, then took out her cellphone. "Do you mind if I take a few pictures?"

"Not at all."

She took several shots of the catafalque and coffin, some close up and some at a distance. "Okay," she said, once she'd finished, "shall we take a look at the bedroom?"

"Sure, follow me."

They went upstairs to the master bedroom, and she took a panoramic shot of the room before snapping several close-ups of the bed and fireplace. "So," she looked at Olivera, "the poker was there?" She pointed to the stand where Springer had spotted the poker.

"That's right. We collected the poker, charred paper, and bedding. Everything else is exactly as we found it."

"And Dr. McGinnis has confirmed the cause of death was strangulation?"

"Yes, manual."

"And the poker matched the contusions?"

"Yes. She also confirmed time of death, so this probably was done around midnight Saturday."

"So, the offender would have had plenty of time to clean up the scene and so on."

"Yes, as far as we know, there was no one else around."

"Well, I think it's possible my theory about an undoing still holds. But I have no idea who the culprit might be, at least among the people of interest you mentioned. Mind you"—she raised an eyebrow—"I'm not saying that one of them didn't do it. I just can't imagine what would have kindled the emotions that stirred things up. As I understand it, the only one of the four who had a long-term, contentious relationship with Lenna Fortney was Merritt Trumble."

"Seems that way. I thought something might have been going on at the accounting firm, but after hearing the content of the will, that seems unlikely. Neither Neville nor Fortney appeared to be the least bit discontent. And why would they be? She left them both substantial bequests. I really don't see motive."

"Well, let me think about it." She approached the fireplace. "This is where the weapon and charred paper were found, right?"

"Yes."

"By the way, did Jessup say when he would have the results?"

"Not exactly, but he didn't think it would take long. I should hear something soon."

"Okay." She took another look around the room. "I'd like to see the mausoleum if you don't mind."

"Sure."

Olivera led the way through the house and out to the mausoleum. Just as he was unlocking the door, the call from Jessup came in. "It's Jessup," he turned to Wilson. "Jessup, that you?"

"Yes, and I have good news. We were able to read some of the writing. I can email you a photograph and transcription right now if you want. By the way, we picked up a couple of fingerprints, too."

"Oh, good. Are they clear enough for a match?"

"I think so."

"Okay, great. If you wouldn't mind sending the results by email—"

"No problem."

"Dr. Wilson and I are finishing up at Red Oaks. We'll drop by the college as soon as we get back to town."

"Sounds good. Either Ellison or I will be here."

"Thanks, Jessup."

He and Wilson returned to the cruiser, where she'd left her briefcase and laptop. Once he'd forwarded Jessup's message to Wilson, she opened the attachment and twisted the computer around for Olivera to see. She pointed to a logo at the top of the picture. "Beta Nu. Isn't that one of the campus sororities?"

"It sure is, and Kemena King was a member."

"And check out the salutation."

" 'Dear Tara.' "

She twisted the computer back around and scrolled to the bottom of the letter. "It's signed by Kemena, so we can assume she wrote it, but it's to her friend, not her boyfriend."

"What does it say?"

" 'Dear Tara…This is a hard letter to write, but now that it's clear to me what you've been up to, I have no other choice but to end what I hoped would be a lasting bond, not with Merritt but with you!' " Wilson pointed to the writing. "Look, she underlined 'you' twice. 'I began to suspect,' " Wilson continued reading, " 'you were jealous, but I never thought you'd do this. I won't stand for it. I'm reporting you to the Beta Nu ethics committee, and if you agree to resign, effective immediately, and to leave me and my guy alone…' Whoa!" Wilson exclaimed, "it never occurred to me—"

"Me, either," Olivera cut in. "The Tara Townsend I spoke with this morning seemed like she really cared for

King." He shook his head, feeling quite puzzled.

"But you know, a good bit of time has passed, and back-stabbing isn't all that uncommon among teenagers. Hmm. I wonder if Bud Fortney knew anything about this, I mean, at the time."

"Don't know," he said with a shrug.

"Isn't Bud Fortney older than Tara?"

"Yes, I think so. He might not have been around then. Not sure."

"I think the next step, of course," she continued, "would be to get a match on those fingerprints."

"Agreed. I think I'll forward this to Springer, and while we're waiting, we might as well take a look at the mausoleum."

They walked down the path, and entering the building, she said, "Whoever did this must have moved the catafalque from wherever it was to the parlor, then carried in the coffin."

"Right, and after setting up the wake scene, he or she must have either walked or driven over to the cemetery to leave the remains."

"All that must have taken hours," she said. "Plus, they would have had to know about the props, I mean, where they all were."

"Yes, so this person must have been familiar with the house. Several of the people I've interviewed might have known their way around the place. Fortney, I imagine, being Jim Fortney's nephew, would have been in and out of here for years. Trumble admitted that he'd been here often, 'almost daily,' I think he said. I didn't actually ask Neville about that, but having worked with Ms. Fortney for some years, it's possible he had access to the house."

"But to know about the catafalque and the gown and slippers—? Sort of sounds like a kid thing, doesn't it? I mean, kids playing in the attic…"

"True, but who would have played here as a kid?"

"Bud Fortney, I would imagine."

"Unlikely Patterson or Neville," he said.

"I don't know, Lieutenant, but I think for the time being, results on those fingerprints are crucial. At least that might tell you who wrote the letter and who received it."

He checked his watch, and it was a little after noon. "What do you say we grab a bite to eat on the way back to town. We can continue hashing this over, and hopefully I'll hear from Springer soon."

He locked the mausoleum and the house, and they got back in the cruiser and headed down Little Smith toward town.

No more than a mile down the road, Wilson spotted the Jeremiah Java Café. Olivera had passed it many times but had never bothered to stop.

"What about that place?" She pointed to the café. "I've heard good things about the food."

"Sure, he said, "it looks a little crowded, but we can certainly give it a try." He pulled off the road and, after waiting for a truck to back out, pulled in. "Okay, let's check it out."

Housed in one of those so-called shotgun shacks, it was a place he never would have entered if not for Wilson's curiosity. It looked sort of interesting but not at all enticing as a spot to have lunch. He was a little surprised she wanted to stop there, seeing as she was even less of a local than he. He opened the screen door, and they went in. The inside was a tad more inviting than the outside but not by much. "I guess we're supposed to wait to be seated."

"The food must be good. The place is certainly popular."

"And noisy." He took off his hat and hung it on the rack next to the door. As he did, he caught sight of Mosey Frye, who got up and came in his direction. She spoke to Wilson first, then turned to him.

"The food's great, Lieutenant. You'll love it."

"What do you recommend?" he asked.

"Saffron and I had oyster biscuits, and Nadia had the special."

"You know, come to think of it, I believe Ms. Humphrey mentioned this place just this morning. It's about to change hands, isn't it?"

"I wouldn't be surprised. If Miss Lenna left it to her nephew, he's unlikely to hold onto it. Probably won't keep Red Oaks, either."

"You're expecting to pick up the listing?"

"Could be. I'll keep my fingers crossed. Listen"— she drew closer—"I wanted to mention something. It's probably not important, but it might be. Lula—" She paused as she glanced around. "—she's a server here. Well, the other day, the morning of the murder, to be exact, I asked her if she'd seen anything out of the ordinary, anyone around that she normally didn't see, and she mentioned having seen a red convertible that Sunday morning."

"Really," he said with curiosity.

"Yeah, she did. And I asked her who it belonged to, and she said that Aaron, the manager, said it was Nate Patterson's, which seemed a little strange at the time. But just now, she said it wasn't his. It was Tara Townsend's."

"Okay, and you think—?"

"Oh, I have no idea, but from the newspaper, it sounds like, well, the investigation might be dragging a little and maybe you could speak with Tara, if you haven't spoken with her already."

He cleared his throat. "I appreciate your passing that along."

"No, problem. I'd better get back to my table. We're about to leave. You can have our table if you want."

Mosey, after speaking again with Wilson, returned to her seat. Olivera nodded to Saffron and Nadia, who were looking their way.

As Mosey, Nadia, and Saffron were preparing to leave, the server caught his eye and guided him and Wilson to a table near the one the ladies were vacating.

"Lieutenant," Nadia said, "I've been hoping you'd get back to the store. Sorry I didn't see you yesterday. Was that yesterday?"

"I think it was."

"And by the way"—Wilson turned to Nadia—"I love the new sofa. I'll be back soon to pick out some other pieces."

"Great, so happy it worked out. Come on in whenever you get a chance."

Saffron smiled and nodded to them both, and the trio made their way toward the door, smiling and waving to half a dozen people as they left. Olivera, meanwhile, settled into his chair, and, turning toward the blackboard, looked over the list of biscuits. "Any of that look good to you?"

"Wow," Wilson replied enthusiastically, "I'm game to try the oyster biscuit. Mosey said she and Saffron liked it."

The server soon returned and took their orders for beer and oyster biscuits. As she was about to leave, Olivera said, "Miss, would you happen to be Lula? Sorry…I didn't catch the last name."

"Alcott," she said with a nod.

"I'm Lieutenant Olivera of the Hembree Police, and Ms. Frye just mentioned that you might have seen something the morning of the incident at Red Oaks." He paused, not wanting to get too specific.

"Oh, so she mentioned that to you."

"Yes, she said you'd seen a car."

"Yes, a red convertible. Hard to miss."

"And did you see the driver?"

"No, as a matter of fact I didn't, but Mr. Willoughby said it belonged to somebody he knows, but turns out it wasn't his. It belongs to Tara Townsend, I think."

"Was she here that morning?"

"I couldn't tell you for sure. We stay so busy."

"Sure, I understand." He reached in his breast pocket for a business card and handed it to her. "I would appreciate it very much if you would give me a call, should you think of anything."

"Okay." She slipped the card in her apron pocket. "Not sure that I will, but if I do…"

Once Ms. Alcott had moved away, he lifted his water glass in a toast. "Even if the food tanks, it was certainly worth the stop, wouldn't you say?"

Wilson clinked his glass and let out a chuckle. "Cheers."

Chapter Thirty-One

Police Station
Wednesday, March 17, 2010, 1:00 p.m.

Olivera dropped Wilson off in front of Social Sciences, then waited while she crossed the street and climbed the steps to the entrance. He let out a sigh and drove off, wondering how he was going to deal with this growing, well, temptation. While he acknowledged that she was unpredictable, he found her light-heartedness captivating. And as much as he hated to admit it, he was growing more attracted with every interaction.

Getting to the station and finding Springer and Reagan perched near the door to his cubicle, he invited them in. "Grab us some coffees, please, Reagan."

As Reagan headed toward the coffee nook, Springer gestured toward a printed sheet on his desk. "Chief, I got a match on the prints."

"Wow, that was quick." He picked up the sheet and, entering his cubicle, hung up his hat and took a seat at the desk. He reached in his drawer for a magnifying glass and compared the unknown prints with the known prints generated by the database. "I'd say those are good matches, Springer. What do you think?"

"Really good, considering. I would have never guessed, but the technology is getting so darn good,

Chief."

"Yeah. I bet those would convince Dr. McGinnis."

"If they convince her, well, then."

Olivera looked from the fingerprints labeled "unknown" to the ones labeled "known." "Lenna Fortney," he muttered as he looked at the first of the known prints. "That's not surprising, considering the paper was found at her house. But this second print, hmm. Tara Townsend. Now, that *is* a surprise."

"You spoke to her today, didn't you?"

"I did." Olivera turned to the photographed content of the letter, which he had already read. "You read the letter, Springer?"

"Yeah, I did. Sounds like Kemena King's boyfriend was sneakin' around with her best friend. Some friend, eh? Reagan and me were studying that, and it sounds like there's a big piece of the puzzle missing, I mean, back at the time of the drowning. I never heard a word about a spat between King and Townsend."

"Sounds like Merritt and Tara managed to keep their relationship hidden. But somebody must have known and told King."

"Or maybe she found out on her own."

"Yep, that's possible."

Reagan came in with three mugs and set them on the desk. "What do you make of all this, Lieutenant?"

"I don't know, but this new evidence sure has dredged up some questions."

"I'm wondering who Kemena's real enemy was," Reagan said. "We been thinking it was Lenna Fortney, but sounds like she wasn't the only one. As they say, with friends like this Townsend chick, who needs enemies?"

"It certainly sounds that way from the letter."

"You know what I'm wondering, Chief," Springer said. "You reckon Townsend got the letter?"

"Well, we can't tell from this, can we? She must have handled it at some point, but this print is new. So Townsend and Fortney both must have been looking at the letter recently. What we don't know is who showed it to whom? Did Fortney have the letter and show it to Townsend, or did Townsend have the letter and show it to Fortney?"

"How would Miss Lenna have a letter Kemena wrote to Townsend?" Springer asked.

"I don't know," Olivera said, "but something I learned from Townsend today suggests how all this might have come about. She said she was with Kemena King as she was getting ready to go to Red Oaks for the weekend, and she packed some stationery, saying she was going to write Trumble a letter, a 'Dear John' letter. If this is the letter she wrote—not to Trumble but to Townsend—maybe she never got a chance to send it."

"You suppose it was at Red Oaks all along?" Reagan said.

"Or maybe," Springer interjected, "Townsend was at the house and saw the letter—back then, I mean."

"That's possible, too, but that wouldn't explain the fingerprint. Both Fortney and Townsend had to have handled the letter recently. But regardless of who had it, why would they have been looking at it and, besides that, who burned it?"

"If Ms. Fortney had the letter, why'd she wanna show it to Townsend?" Reagan asked.

"Yeah, after all these years..." Springer added.

"Indeed, why would she?" Olivera said, pensively.

"I think we have to think about it this way, I mean, how could the content of the letter be used to, well…?"

"Maybe Miss Lenna found the letter only recently," Springer interjected, "and, after reading it, wanted to ask Townsend about it. The drowning has always been a big mystery and reading that letter—"

"So, you're thinking King and Townsend got in a squabble over Trumble, and Townsend drowned her?" Olivera said. "Wow. Of course, if Townsend got into a squabble with King the day of the drowning, she wouldn't have wanted me to know that, would she?"

"If Townsend didn't want anybody to know it," Springer said, "she wouldn't have shown the letter to Lenna Fortney. Fortney must have had the letter and showed it to Townsend."

"Then what?"

"Well, Miss Lenna might have showed her the letter and threatened to show it to the police."

"And then," Reagan chimed in, "they fought over the letter. And maybe Townsend pushed Fortney."

"But according to Dr. McGinnis," Olivera said, "there were no signs of a struggle, no defensive wounds."

"So, maybe she didn't kill her right away," Reagan said. "Maybe she came back later, strangled her, and burned the letter."

Olivera sighed. "I guess it could have happened that way."

"How are we going to figure this out, Chief?" Springer said.

"Evidence, Springer, evidence, unless we get lucky and get a confession. By the way, Dr. Wilson and I stopped off at the Jeremiah Java on our way back to town, and one of the women who works there, Lula Alcott, mentioned that she'd seen a red convertible in the lot the morning of the incident. Turns out it belongs to Townsend." He looked from Springer to Reagan.

Reagan's eyes widened. "My lord, reckon what that means?"

"At the very least, Townsend has got some explaining to do," Olivera said.

"I'll say, Chief. You gonna bring her in for questioning?"

"Well, I think we have to, and the sooner the better. In fact, I was going to ask you guys to pick her up. She works at the Development Office at the college, and I imagine she's there right now. You know, thinking back to our conversation this morning, I'm wondering now why she would have mentioned the letter that King was supposedly going to write to her boyfriend."

"Well, this isn't *that* letter." Reagan gestured toward the document.

"Nope, it certainly isn't. And before I do anything else, I'd better phone Jessup, see if he can confirm the age of the prints." He turned toward his computer. "I think I'd better forward these to Dr. Wilson right away."

"Don't you mean Dr. McGinnis?" Springer asked.

"Yeah, her, too," Olivera said. "I'd like to get Dr. McGinnis's opinion on the verification of the prints, but I was thinking…Well, I wonder what Dr. Wilson would say if she knew these prints belonged to Tara Townsend and Lenna Fortney."

"And by the way, Chief, how come we aren't seeing King's prints on the letter?"

"There are more prints on the letter, but these were the only readable ones. The original prints would have seriously degraded, and these look pretty new to me."

"Yeah, to me, too," Springer said.

"Okay, I'd better phone Jessup."

"You want us to pick up Townsend?"

"Not just yet. Let me see what Jessup has to say."

"We don't need a warrant?"

"Nope, not for questioning, unless, of course, she refuses, but I doubt she will."

Springer and Reagan returned to their desks, while Olivera, after taking a sip of coffee, picked up the receiver and phoned Jessup. "Jessup? Olivera here. We got a match on the fingerprints."

"Both of them?"

"Sure did. Now the question is how did they get there? Well, not so much how as when?"

"It's tricky dating prints, but in this case, obviously they're new, no more than a couple of days old."

"Okay, that's just what I needed to know. By the way, I'll drop by to pick up the evidence, if not this afternoon, tomorrow."

He hung up the receiver. "Springer."

Springer came back in.

"Jessup confirms they're new, but I tell you what. Let's hold off. I want to think through this thing before I question Townsend. Did you finish checking the alibis?"

"Everything but the trail cameras."

"Yeah, well, let's hold tight. I think I'd better get back to the morgue, fill Dr. McGinnis in on the latest."

Once Springer had stepped out, Olivera picked up his mug and wandered over to the window. "So, what next?" he mumbled under his breath. He didn't feel comfortable questioning Townsend without first running the possibilities by someone, either McGinnis or Wilson.

He was leaning toward McGinnis for some reason, although he wasn't exactly looking forward to their next meeting. Things had gotten a little touchy of late, even though they had agreed from the beginning not to allow their personal relationship to interfere with their professional interactions. Still, he needed to move past this silly bit of awkwardness. "It's better not to overthink things," he mumbled, returning to his desk. Taking up the receiver once more, he punched in the number of the morgue. "Dr. McGinnis, Olivera here."

"What can I do for you, Lieutenant?"

He thought he detected a little chill in her voice but chose to ignore it. "It looks like we've got a break in the case."

"Oh, my, that's good to hear."

"Well, I'm not sure. It's a little confusing. I'd like to run it all by you before I take the next step."

"Sure, I'll be here for a couple of hours."

"Okay, I'll be right over."

He slipped the printed sheets into his briefcase and, after speaking to Springer on his way out, drove to the morgue.

As he strode along the corridor to the end, his heart beat a tad more rapidly than usual. He guessed he was nervous with things being off between him and McGinnis. Oh, well, they'd have to sort it out eventually. He came to the door and, taking a deep breath, walked in. He hung his hat on the rack and continued toward the rear of the room, where she sat staring down at her laptop. He set his briefcase on the desk and pulled out the documents.

"What have you got?" She glanced up.

"You didn't see the email?"

"Not yet."

"Well, this." He pushed the documents in her direction.

"So, they were able to read the charred paper. That's good."

"Some were burned through, but one of the scorched pieces was still intact." He took a seat in the chair next to the desk. "I'm thinking it's important, but for the time being, it's only raising more questions."

She picked up the two sheets and, after studying the sheet with the prints, said, "These prints look new."

"I just confirmed that with Jessup."

"Lenna Fortney and Tara Townsend, huh? Bud Fortney's girlfriend."

"Right."

"She wasn't one of your people of interest, was she?"

"No, Bud Fortney was, but I'd pretty much ruled him out."

She moved on to the second sheet. "So this letter was written by Kemena King to Tara Townsend. But there's no date."

"No, but we can assume from the logo that it was written sometime after she pledged Beta Nu."

"Right." As she read on, her expression turned somber. "So this means that sometime during King's freshman year at Blanchard—"

"Yes," he interrupted, "I got some information from Townsend this morning suggesting King wrote it shortly before she drowned. Townsend was with King when she was packing for Red Oaks. Townsend even mentioned that King put in some stationery, intending to write to Trumble, breaking it off. But now this turns up, confirming that, indeed, a letter was written but not the one King said she was going to write. And besides that, did Townsend receive it? Or was it never mailed and Lenna Fortney, coming across it, drew her own conclusions and confronted Townsend?"

"Now, why would she do that?"

"Let's suppose you found this letter among someone's possessions, someone who had drowned in a mysterious boating accident. What would you do?"

"Well..." She thought for a moment. "Maybe nothing. I mean, what would be the point?"

"Yes, what would be the point?"

"I suppose, if I had a vivid imagination, I might wonder if Townsend was somehow involved in the drowning. I mean, if she had been around that day, she might have been in the boat with King, and they could have gotten in a squabble and, well, who knows?"

"That's what I've been thinking. Maybe all these years, Lenna Fortney, knowing she had nothing to do with her ward's drowning, once she'd seen this letter, wondered if maybe Townsend was involved."

"Oh, gosh. If that's what happened, it would certainly explain the presence of both prints on the letter."

"It would also explain, I'm guessing, how the letter happened to be burned. Townsend wouldn't have wanted any of this known, especially if she was involved in the drowning. So, then and there, she burned the letter."

"She didn't do a very good job of it, did she?"

"No, whoever burned the papers, probably expected the whole bundle to go up in flames. But, obviously, the flame went out a bit too soon."

"You think she killed Lenna Fortney?"

"I don't have any evidence that she actually committed the murder, but I do have a witness who can place her close to Red Oaks the morning after the murder."

"Oh, my."

"One of the servers at the Jeremiah Java Café says she saw Townsend's red convertible in the lot that morning, though she's not certain Townsend was there."

"I'd say you definitely have enough for questioning."

"Yeah, I think so."

Chapter Thirty-Two

Police Station
Wednesday, March 17, 2010, 3:30 p.m.

Earlier that day, when Olivera spoke with Tara Townsend at the Development Office, it never occurred to him he would interview her again that day. But the charred paper turned out to be central to the case, raising questions about her possible involvement not only in the murder of Lenna Fortney but also in the presumed accidental death of her friend Kemena King.

Springer and Reagan picked Townsend up at her workplace, and now she sat in the interview room waiting for Olivera. On his way in, he paused at the coffee nook to refill his mug and fix one for Townsend. He strode into the room, and before taking a seat in the captain's chair, he set the mug down in front of her. "I thought you might care for coffee."

She nodded and thanked him. "What's this about, Lieutenant?"

"We were able to retrieve some evidence from the crime scene." He opened the folder with the letter and prints. "A letter, written by Kemena King and addressed to you. Can you tell me anything about this?" He passed her the photocopy and carefully watched her reaction as she began to read.

She read for a moment, then looked up. "I don't remember ever receiving this. In fact, I'm sure I didn't."

"I thought perhaps you hadn't, considering what you told me this morning."

"If I had received it, I would remember. I mean, it contains an explicit threat, well, a rather serious threat."

"Okay, so the accusation isn't true."

"No, Lieutenant. I never dated Merritt Trumble. I mean, the idea never even crossed my mind."

"But let me ask you this. Have you ever seen the letter?"

"As I said before, I never received the letter. If I had, well, I certainly would have set Kemena straight."

Olivera passed her the second sheet. "Ms. Townsend, I am inclined to believe you never received it, but are you certain you've never seen it, because, according to our fingerprint analysis, this document contains your print. We found two prints, yours and Lenna Fortney's."

She looked startled, then dropping her head, rested her forehead against her fingertips.

He waited, fully expecting her to ask to speak to a lawyer, but she didn't. She remained silent, then raising her head, glanced his way, her expression fallen. "Okay, yes, I did see the letter, for the first time this past Saturday."

"How did you happen to see it?"

"I got a call from Ms. Fortney. I assumed she wanted to speak to me about something work-related, but when I got to the house, she was full of questions about Kemena. Had I seen her the day of the drowning, had I spoken with her, and so on. I told her everything I could remember, but she wasn't satisfied. She'd gotten it into her head that I was somehow involved. Then, she asked me about Merritt Trumble and accused me of having, well, I guess she assumed we were sneaking around behind Kemena's back. I told her I had no interest in going out with him, and even if I had, I would've never done that to Kemena. Finally, she showed me the letter, as proof, I suppose, of her suspicions. But my lord, Lieutenant, Kemena was my little sister."

"In Beta Nu, you mean?"

She nodded.

"So, how did this end—this encounter with Ms. Fortney?"

"I tried my best to convince her that Kemena had gotten the wrong idea and, if I'd had the chance, I would have made her see that. Ms. Fortney was one of the college's most generous benefactors, and I didn't want to do or say anything to upset her. I also didn't want her thinking I'd been involved in any way in Kemena's death. I am dating her nephew, for heaven's sake. More than anything, I hoped that we could get past this. When I left, she seemed somewhat doubtful about the content of the letter, and I guess that's the best I could hope for. I was thinking I could speak to Bud about it, and maybe he could shed some light on the situation."

"So, did you speak to him?"

"I did."

"Did you show him the letter?"

"No, she kept the letter."

"Do you remember where she might have put it?"

"Well, we were outside but not on the veranda. We were sitting on the lawn chairs in front of the house. When I left, she was still outside. I would guess she put it somewhere inside the house."

"But while you were there, you're sure she didn't burn the letter?"

"Not while I was there. Like I said, we were in the front yard the whole time."

"What time was it when you were there?"

"I arrived around one thirty. I must have stayed for half an hour or forty-five minutes."

"Was there anyone at the house besides you?"

"Not that I saw."

"And did you go back there, say later that day or Sunday?"

"Oh, no. I wouldn't have set foot on the place. To be honest, I was a nervous wreck. Being accused like that, it was mortifying. My intention at that point was to speak to Bud and see what he advised."

"So, what did he advise?"

"Unfortunately, Bud wasn't around. He was on the golf course. So, I left a message to call me as soon as possible."

"Did he return your call?"

"Yes, but it was later that evening, around seven. We met for drinks at Al's, though I wasn't particularly anxious to go back down to Little Smith. We talked about the letter and the whole situation, and he said not to worry, that he would deal with it."

"And did he?"

"No, he didn't. He never got a chance to speak to her."

Olivera sat there, watching Townsend, convinced that only someone telling the truth could handle that evidence so effortlessly. "Remarkable," he said. "I thought I had a conundrum." He gathered the sheets and put them back in the folder. "But now it seems I have an even greater conundrum."

"I'm not sure I know what you mean, Lieutenant."

"Well, you said earlier today that, back then, Ms. King had told you she was planning to break up with Merritt Trumble."

"That's right."

"But apparently she knew at the time that it was *he* who wanted to break up with her, no?"

"No, I don't believe that. If she had known, she'd have said something, I mean, to me when we were talking." She shook her head. "No, I don't believe she thought that for a second. Something must have happened after she left for Red Oaks. The last time I saw Kemena, we were on good terms."

"Where do you think she got such an idea?"

"I don't know, Lieutenant. Are you absolutely sure that Kemena wrote the letter?"

"Well, no, we haven't verified the handwriting, but we will, we certainly will." Olivera thought for a minute and, deciding he'd taken the questioning as far as he could, thanked Townsend for coming in. "And please, if anything occurs to you, let me know."

She assured him that she would. He offered to drop her off at the college, but she turned him down and went on her way.

Once she had left, Olivera headed to his cubicle. "Springer."

"Yeah, Chief?"

"Come in here for a second, would you?"

"Sure."

"We need to verify the handwriting. I don't know why I didn't think of that before."

"Why? You think King didn't write the letter?"

"Who knows." His voice reflected his frustration. "Townsend raised the question. She claims the accusation made in the letter isn't true and wonders if someone else could have written it. The last time she saw King, they were on friendly terms, and she is certain King would have said something if she had any suspicions about her and Trumble."

"Wow, that sure turns things around, don't it, Chief?"

"I'll say. Plus, she had a good explanation for how things went down with her and Fortney. Supposedly, Fortney called her out to Red Oaks to show her the letter, suspecting she might have been involved in the drowning. So, that explains the fingerprints. But when she left Fortney, the letter was intact, or so she claims. Oh, and by the way, she said she never entered the house. They sat in the lawn chairs out front, which explains why her prints weren't found inside."

"Gosh, that does sound convincing. You think she's telling the truth?"

"I don't know what to think, but we have to get on with the investigation. I want to speak again to two people tangentially involved in this, Merritt Trumble and Bud Fortney."

"Yeah, I'd say show Trumble the letter. See what he says."

"And I suppose Fortney might be able to support Townsend's story, since she says she told him all about it that evening at Al's."

"You gonna start with him?"

"No, I think I'll start with Trumble. In fact, let's get him in here right away."

"He's in Mound City, right?"

"Yes, his contact information is in the file."

Springer and Reagan left for the architectural firm, picked up Trumble, and made it back to the station in less than an hour. Olivera, meanwhile, set up for the questioning, arranging his notes from the interviews alongside the folder with the letter and fingerprint analysis. He studied the letter again, wondering if Trumble would be able to identify the handwriting as King's.

The front door opened, and Springer directed Trumble into the room. Olivera stood and offered him a seat. "I appreciate your willingness to come in. I have a few questions about some evidence that's just come to light."

Trumble looked somewhat concerned but not overly so. "Okay, but I hope this won't take too long. I have another appointment."

"No, it shouldn't take long at all. Mainly, I wanted to ask you about something we discovered at the crime scene." He took out the photographed letter and placed it in front of Trumble. "As you can see, this is a letter written by Kemena King and addressed to Tara Townsend. But it seems that Ms. Townsend never received it. Perhaps it was left at Red Oaks, but I can't be entirely sure of that. Have you seen it before?"

He read for a bit, then set the document on the table. He stared down at the words his deceased fiancée had apparently written to her friend. "This is preposterous." He looked up at Olivera. "There was never anything between Tara and me."

"Do you recognize the handwriting?"

"Yes, it looks like Kemena's."

"If you and Ms. Townsend are telling the truth and

no such relationship existed, between you and her, I mean, then how do you suppose King got such an idea?"

"I don't know, but I suppose somebody could have told her that."

"Why would anyone have made up such a lie?"

He thought for a moment. "To hurt Kemena? To hurt me? I don't know."

"Was there anyone back then who might have had it in for you two?"

"Had it in for us?" he repeated. "Well, Ms. Fortney wasn't in agreement with our plan to marry. I already told you that. But I can't believe she would have made this up."

"What about people your own age? Friends, classmates…?"

"I suppose this could have been somebody's idea of a joke."

"Did you know anyone like that back then—a practical joker, so to speak?"

Trumble thought again. "I can think of one person who was known for that sort of thing, I mean, practical jokes. But it's hard to believe he would have done this. He and Kemena were family, actually. Bud Fortney, Ms. Fortney's husband's nephew."

"You knew Bud Fortney back then?"

"Yes, he was around off and on, at family gatherings and such. But Bud was older, I'd say a few years older than me."

"You weren't in college together?"

"No, he graduated before I started."

"And he never showed any animosity toward you or Ms. King?"

"To the contrary, he was always friendly, though we

332

weren't that close. He was a different sort of person, not at all serious. He was more into sports, hunting."

"And you say he wasn't above playing the occasional joke on a friend?"

"He seemed to get a big kick out of that sort of thing."

"Okay, so you think it's possible that he might have made up the whole thing?"

"Possible, I guess, but I wouldn't want to accuse him of anything."

"Why do you think Ms. King didn't confront you? From the letter, it sounds like she was certainly prepared to confront Ms. Townsend."

"It wasn't true, I'm telling you."

"So, you didn't receive a letter or a call or a message of any kind?"

"Nothing."

"Interesting."

"When was the letter written?" He glanced down at the document, apparently looking for a date.

"It isn't dated," Olivera said, "but putting two and two together, we're guessing she wrote it the day of the boating accident."

"Oh, my god. That's terrible."

"Indeed."

"When you figure out whoever did this…," he trailed off, shaking his head.

"I hope we find the person and soon, because, you see, finding the burned letter at the crime scene implies that whoever made up this hurtful lie might have been involved in Ms. Fortney's murder."

"Well, I can't really imagine Bud Fortney killing anyone."

"Yeah, well, it's hard to say."

Olivera thanked Trumble for answering his questions. They stood and walked out into the entrance, where Springer and Reagan were waiting to take him back to Mound City.

Chapter Thirty-Three

Police Station
Wednesday, March 17, 2010, 5:00 p.m.

Olivera felt as if he'd stepped off a merry-go-round or, worse yet, a Ferris wheel or an octopus, spinning from one place to the next before abruptly stopping in front of a piddling piece of evidence that didn't seem to lead anywhere in particular. Earlier in the day, he'd sought McGinnis's help, and now it felt like a good time to check in with Wilson. And considering that she'd seen the letter, he wondered if her imaginative mind might have generated some ideas about how it could figure in the case. She wasn't aware, unless Jessup had filled her in, of the match they'd gotten on the latent fingerprints. What might she draw from that piece of evidence? Plus, he now had the input from Townsend and Trumble to share. "A lot to digest in a single afternoon," he muttered as he picked up his hat. He headed for the back door, and by the time he got to his vehicle, he'd already phoned Wilson and left a message to meet him at the Tavernette.

He drove to the Square but, unable to find a space, parked around the corner in front of Abboud Antiques. Nadia was locking up, and he waved his hat in her direction. "What's with all the people on a Wednesday afternoon?"

"St. Patrick's Day."

He nodded and walked on toward the Tavernette.

Inside, he greeted Ms. Tisdale in the reception area. "Ms. Tisdale—"

"Welcome, Lieutenant," she broke in. "Happy St. Patrick's Day."

"Same to you. You happen to have a booth in the back?" He glanced around the crowd, looking for Wilson.

"Follow me." She picked up a menu. "There's one table left in the entire establishment."

He trailed the hostess to the back corner. "Thanks." He removed his hat and slid into the booth.

"May I take that for you, Lieutenant?" She held out her hand.

"Yes, thanks, and should you see Dr. Wilson come in— You know who I mean?"

"Yes, of course."

"Please let her know I'm here."

Within minutes, Wilson arrived. "You need to put me on the payroll, Lieutenant." She chuckled and took a seat across from him.

"Don't think I wouldn't if the budget would allow."

"I'm getting service points, so I guess I won't complain."

"Service points?"

"You know, teaching, research, service. You have to do some of each if you expect to get tenure. They're big on community service, by the way."

"So, you're considering staying on, are you?"

"Of course, why not? Especially now," she added.

He looked puzzled, and she responded by rubbing her thumb back and forth over her fingertips.

"Oh, I see," he responded, "the new building for anthropological sciences."

"The excitement in the department is palpable."

"I've got a feeling this case is entirely about that."

"What?"

"Money." He mimicked her gesture.

"Really?"

"But before we get into that, what would you like to drink?"

"I'm game to try one of those green beers if you are."

"Not I. I know it's St. Patrick's Day and all, but I am sick of all things green."

"I've never been a fan."

"Huh?"

"My mother dressed me in it from the time I was a toddler. Gingers? The color green? Supposedly, it's our color."

"Hmm. Never heard that before." He waved to Ruby, who was passing near the booth.

"Afternoon, Lieutenant," Ruby said. "Nice to see you here, Dr. Wilson." She looked in his direction. "You want your usual?"

"Yes, please, and you can bring Dr. Wilson a mug of that green liquid."

"I'll be right back with that." Ruby grinned and collected the menus.

Wilson looked at him. "Your message sounded kinda urgent."

"I guess I'm feeling a bit of pressure, self-imposed, of course. Not that anything remarkable has happened, but we did get a match on the prints. They belong to Lenna Fortney and Tara Townsend. I went ahead and questioned Townsend, and while admitting to seeing the letter the afternoon before the murder, she'd never seen it before then. And not only that, she swore to having never dated Trumble. Never crossed her mind, she claimed."

"Was she convincing?"

"Yes, quite. So then I spoke with the other party, Merritt Trumble, who, likewise, denied any involvement with Townsend."

"You think it's possible King made up the whole thing?"

"Possibly, but not likely. Something Trumble had to say might hold water. He thinks Bud Fortney could have put that bug in King's ear."

"Why?"

"Why might he?" He raised his brow.

"Hmm. I suppose that would introduce another type into the scenario. Yeah," she added, her eyes brightening.

Ruby arrived with their drinks and asked if they cared to order food.

"Not I," Olivera said.

"We've got some nice specials, Lieutenant. Corned beef and cabbage quesadillas, Reuben nachos…"

They both shook their heads, and Ruby moved on to the next booth, where a foursome signaled for more beer with their empty mugs.

"Cheers," he said, lifting his mug to Wilson.

"Cheers." She tapped his mug with hers. "Maybe this will bring us some Irish luck."

"Are Irish people lucky?"

"I'm Irish, at least I think I am. I guess people with my coloring are thought to be Irish or Scottish, but I can't say that I consider myself especially lucky."

"I see what you mean," he said with a laugh.

"Oh, that." She chuckled, rolling her eyes. "I may have started off on the wrong foot, but I have a feeling my luck is turning around," she said with a sly smile.

"I hope so. I'm relying on you to guide me through this labyrinth."

"Ooo, I like the sound of that. So, tell me…"

"Tell you what?"

"About Bud Fortney."

"I spoke with him and Neville soon after the body was discovered, but I didn't think either of them capable of murder. Fortney, by the way, speaking of types, is your typical *puer aeternus*."

"Lieutenant, I would have never guessed…"

"Guessed what?"

"That you'd think in those terms."

"Ha, you take me for a bumpkin," he said with more surprise than affront.

"Of course, not, but I certainly didn't take you for a Jungian."

"I'm not a Jungian, but we've all seen Peter Pan, haven't we? Or maybe you haven't. You're pretty young."

"Whatever," she said with a wave of her hand. "But joking aside, this really could be a *puer* profile."

"So, that's a thing?"

"Yes, it's a thing. You know, the guy who refuses to grow up, take responsibility. As it happens, some scientists see it as physiological, considering that the brain of the *puer* prioritizes instant gratification."

"Nice," he said with a nod. "Sounds like we might be stumbling toward a motive, Dr. Wilson." He tapped his mug against her mug of green brew. "Do you suppose that Bud Fortney, in order to capitalize on his legacy more quickly, may have decided to kill his aunt? That really is quite horrible." He scrunched up his face. "Not easy to imagine."

"The world is full of people who prefer crime to hard work."

"And what about the staging, or are we still calling it 'undoing'?"

"I suppose he could suddenly have grown a conscience. But wait a second. Are we assuming that it was Bud Fortney who invented the tale about Townsend and Trumble?"

"Trumble thought it a possibility."

"If he was the one," she responded, a little excitement in her voice, "then this particular *puer* had a dark side. He might be a trickster, and tricksters take mischief to an extreme." She thought, then continued. "You know, if wealth was the goal, how better to get rich quick than to marry King and inherit the entire fortune."

"Yeah, the stakes just skyrocketed. Too bad she died in the boating accident."

"Yeah, saddling him with a very long wait. He wouldn't have liked that."

"I wonder what motivated him to make his move."

"You mean now?" she said.

"Yes. According to Townsend, she and Fortney met for drinks at Al's on the night of the murder. She told him about the letter and his aunt's reaction."

"Okay, but how would that push him to act?"

"I don't know. She said he didn't get to speak with his aunt."

"Maybe he didn't, and maybe he did. Or maybe he

just sneaked in the house in the middle of the night and throttled her in her sleep."

"Then set up the wake, cleaned up after himself, and dropped off Kemena's remains at the cemetery?" He gave his head a quick shake. "Complicated."

"Well, it kinda sounds like something a trickster might do," she said, "not out of remorse but just for the heck of it. I had a friend in grad school who did nutty stuff. He was always staging things. His apartment was like a creepy movie set with a church lectern in the living room and fake flowers strewn all about. He was a *puer*. Constantly dodged work, even though he was studying for a doctorate in psychology. I was at his place once, helping him study for an exam, and turned out he hadn't read the material and was depending on me to explain the course to him."

"Your field certainly has its share of deviants."

"Hey, talk about the pot calling the kettle black."

"Point taken." He clinked his mug against hers, then downed the last of his beer.

"But tell me this, Lieutenant. Supposing this guy is guilty, how are you gonna nail him?"

"That," he said with a groan, "is the problem, isn't it? He had opportunity. He was in the vicinity that night, but we don't have anything that places him at the scene. Not a shred of hard evidence. Springer's looking at security footage up and down Little Smith but so far hasn't found anything. I guess we could scour the property again."

"You suppose Tara Townsend suspects her boyfriend is a murderer? If anyone knows anything, it would be she, no?"

"Possibly. However, she hasn't connected him to the

lie about her and Trumble. She said she'd wracked her brain and couldn't think of anyone who might do such a thing."

"Why don't you call Fortney in, question him about the letter. If he's involved, you might detect a bit of tension."

"I suppose I must. I can't think of another way."

"Or put a notice on the local media. Maybe someone knows something."

"I was hoping not to have to do that, but maybe it's time."

Having pretty much exhausted the possibilities, Olivera and Wilson decided to retire for the evening. They said their goodbyes at the door and went their separate ways.

It was around seven, not long after Olivera reached home, that he received a call from Springer.

"Chief," Springer began, "sorry to call you at home, especially after the day we've had, but I've got something I think you're gonna want to see. But first, I oughta mention we checked the basement at Red Oaks and found a coffin without a lining, but that was about it. Not a print in sight, nothing. But then—"

"Don't keep me in suspense, Springer." Having opened a can of cat food for Grim Milly, he set it on the floor.

"Well, I reckon I can send you this."

"What is it?"

"I've been checking out surveillance near Red Oaks, and I'm seeing something pretty darn incriminating. I don't know why we didn't think of this right off the bat. They've got trail cameras in the Civil War Cemetery."

Olivera's heart fluttered with anticipation. "Send it

to me, Springer." Dang! Indeed, they should've checked the cemetery first thing but somehow overlooked the obvious.

"Okay, Chief. I'm sending it to your cellphone."

He waited a second. "Okay, I got it. Let me take a look, and I'll be right back with you."

He tapped the video, then blew it up. The picture was dark, but he could make out somebody in a hoody with the hood pulled up. He was near the statue of the unknown soldier, and it was clear what he was up to. "My god," he mumbled, "that's got to be the guy." He called Springer back. "Okay, this is about as good as it gets, Springer. Better than an eye witness, for sure. You can't tell who it is, but with an enhancement—"

"I bet that'll work," Springer cut in. "What about Jessup and Ellison? They got the best equipment around here."

"Yeah, I imagine they do. I'll phone them right away. And thanks, Springer. That's a fine piece of police work."

"You're welcome, Chief. You coming back in tonight?"

"Maybe. Let me speak to Jessup. We might have to wait till tomorrow. There's one thing we could do, though. Put some surveillance on Bud Fortney."

"Fortney? You reckon that's him?"

"Yeah, some other things are suggesting he's the one."

"What things?"

"Oh, something Dr. Wilson said."

"So, you talked to her again?"

"I did." He kept it short, hoping to avoid another discussion about Wilson's profiles. "But not just that. It was Trumble who thought Bud Fortney might have invented the story, well, what the letter suggested about Trumble and Townsend."

"Boy, this is complicated, ain't it, Chief? But I guess we suspected it would be from the get go."

"Yeah, and it hasn't disappointed. Let me get in touch with Jessup and see what he says about the video."

"Okay, Chief. I'll hold tight and wait to hear back."

Olivera clicked off and tapped Jessup's number. "Jessup, Olivera here. Hate to bother you after hours, but Springer just delivered an important piece of evidence. A video clip from a trail camera in the Civil War Cemetery."

"Okay, so what can I do for you?"

"If I send you this, you think you could enhance it? There's some footage of a guy setting a bag on the pedestal of the unknown soldier."

"Oh, wow, that does sound incriminating. I'm not at the college, but I could get back over there."

"Well, if you're willing to do that…"

"Sure, we're all anxious to see this guy behind bars."

"I'm at home, too, but Springer is at the station, waiting to hear back. If we can get a close up, we might just wrap this thing up tonight."

"Okay, I'm on it. I'll be in touch, say, in an hour?"

"Fine. Thanks, Jessup. Much appreciated."

Chapter Thirty-Four

Olivera's House
Wednesday, March 17, 2010, 8 p.m.

While waiting to hear back from Jessup, Olivera changed into sweats and running shoes. He had a feeling the hours ahead called for casual wear rather than a sports coat and tie. Milly, who'd followed him into the bedroom, looked up wistfully, as though to say, "You going out again? I've been here by myself all day."

"I know." He gave her a scratch behind the ears.

She let out a mournful, baby-doll cry. He picked her up and gave her a comforting rub. "I'll be back as soon as I can." He sat on the bed, put on his shoes, and slipped his badge and keys into the pocket of his jacket.

On his way to the station, a call from Jessup came in. "Jessup?"

"Lieutenant, we've hit the jackpot, looks like."

"What?"

"Mosey and Nadia are with Robert and me at the lab, and they were able to identify the guy in the video."

"Who is it?"

"Bud Fortney. They're sure it's him."

"As expected," Olivera said. "Things were pointing that way."

"So, what does this mean?"

"I can't say conclusively, but at the very least, Fortney better be able to explain this or, well…" He thanked Jessup and, setting the phone on the car seat, pulled into the back lot and hurried inside. "Springer," he called out.

"In here, Chief." Springer stepped out of the coffee nook. "I thought we might need a fresh pot."

"I hope you made it strong."

"Why is that?"

"I had a couple of beers earlier. I was at the Tavernette with Dr. Wilson."

"I figured as much."

"You did, eh?"

"Soon as you mentioned Dr. Wilson…"

"We were running over the new evidence, and she came up with a new profile for a so-called trickster type."

Springer shook his head. "Chief, you gotta be a dang lit major to do police work anymore."

Olivera laughed. "Having a forensic psychologist with Jungian inclinations sort of makes it that way."

Springer passed him a paper cup. "You want this black?"

Olivera nodded and Springer set the cup on the counter. "This is playing out as I thought, Springer. Jessup just called, and Frye and Abboud were with him and Ellison at the lab. They identified the guy in the video."

"Let me guess—Bud Fortney."

"Bingo."

"So, we gonna bring him in?"

"What else?"

"Reckon we'll need Reagan?"

"Yeah, let's give him a call. I don't want to go in

half-cocked. If Fortney is the guy I think he is, he's got a gun nearby and no telling what else."

Springer set his coffee down and picked up the receiver, punching in Reagan's number. "Ms. Reagan? This is Springer. Can you put your husband on the phone?"

Olivera listened as Springer gave Reagan the news: "We got a break in the case, Reagan. Don't say anything, but we got Bud Fortney dead to rights. Get down here soon as possible, okay?" He hung up the receiver. "He's coming right in."

"Good," Olivera said. "So, I've been thinking about this. We need to go over to Fortney's place and, if he's at home, bring him in. We can't do a search of the premises without a warrant, but we can arrest him for probable cause. I mean, even if he didn't murder Lenna Fortney, he had Kemena King's remains in his possession."

"You reckon he'll try to bolt?"

"No telling what he'll do, considering what he's done already."

"You're sure about this, ain't you, Chief?"

"That video is pretty darn convincing."

"Yep, sure is."

"So, let's go in prepared. Not guns at the ready, but loaded, and I have a good mind to alert Judge Hendricks, in case we end up needing a warrant."

"Good idea. We taking the SUV?"

"Yeah, let's do."

Minutes later, the back door opened, and Reagan came in still wearing his uniform.

Olivera set his coffee on the counter and checked his gun. "Check your gun, Reagan. I'm not anticipating a ruckus necessarily, but I want to be ready."

"So, here's the plan," Springer said, turning to Reagan.

While Springer filled Reagan in, Olivera, wanting to touch base with McGinnis, tapped her name on speed dial. "Dr. McGinnis."

"What's up?"

"We finally got some compelling evidence. We've got footage of Bud Fortney dropping the bag of remains at the foot of the unknown soldier. And get this. He's wearing a pair of white gloves."

"White gloves, eh? Like from the crime scene?"

"Exactly."

"I'd say that's compelling—not to mention theatrical."

"I thought you might. We're about to pick him up."

"You get a warrant?"

"No time, but we've got probable cause."

"Speaking of Fortney, I just bumped into him and Tara Townsend."

"Where?"

"Al's."

"Going in or coming out?"

"They might still be here. Let me look."

He waited till she came back on the line. "They're here, in the bar."

"Okay. Is Al around?"

"Yeah."

"Do me a favor and ask him to be on the alert. I might need him. But tell him not to say anything."

"You aren't going to approach Fortney inside the bar, are you?"

"No, I'm thinking we'll arrest him as he's leaving.

Keep an eye on him, okay?"

"I'll call or text if I need to."

"Darn," Olivera said, slipping his phone into his pocket.

"What's the matter?"

"I just spoke to Dr. McGinnis. She's at Al's and spotted Fortney and Townsend in the bar."

"Gosh, Chief…"

"I say we go ahead, but we gotta keep it safe. Let's go to Al's, but I don't want to take any chances inside the bar. Nope, don't want to do that."

"Well, darn, Lieutenant," Reagan said, "they could be in there till midnight."

"Yeah, I reckon they could, but I'll think of something. You guys ready?"

The three piled into the SUV, and Springer pulled out. "Chief, you want me to turn on the siren?"

"No need for that. McGinnis is going to alert me if there's any change. Drive fast but not too fast."

"As you say."

Springer wheeled off toward Little Smith and, about ten minutes later, pulled into the lot of the restaurant.

"Okay," Olivera said, "that's Townsend's car over there. Better park behind it."

"Block it?" Springer asked.

"Yeah. Let's hold tight for a moment, see if they show any signs of leaving. McGinnis is keeping an eye on them."

"Then what?" Reagan said.

"I'll get Al to tell Fortney he's got a phone call and can take it at the front desk. We'll be waiting for him in the foyer. But first let's go in quietly and clear the area. I'll let Al know when we're ready."

Olivera tapped in the number of the bar, and Al answered. "We're about to enter reception. Give us time to clear the area before you speak to Fortney."

"Okay, I'll wait a couple of minutes."

Olivera dropped his phone in his pocket. "Let's go."

He opened the door, and luckily, there was no one in the foyer. Fortney soon came in with Al close behind. "Bud Fortney," Olivera said, "we are arresting you in connection with the murder of Lenna Fortney."

"You're arresting *me*?"

"Sure are."

While Reagan cuffed him, Springer read him his rights. Then together they guided him toward the SUV. Olivera hung back for a second to speak to Al, then headed outside. "You frisk him, Springer?"

"Yep." He held out the gun he'd found in Fortney's pocket.

"Okay, guys, let's go."

Back at the station, Springer and Reagan put Fortney in a cell, and Olivera, once he'd gathered up his notes, went in. He began by showing Fortney the video. "You want to try to explain this?"

"Not without a lawyer present."

Olivera stood and called for Springer to bring Fortney his cellphone. Fortney made a call and got his lawyer on the phone but, unfortunately for Fortney, he wasn't in town and wouldn't be able to make it in until the next morning. In a sense, Olivera was relieved, aware that he needed more than what he had to make a murder charge stick.

He sent Springer home, leaving Reagan in charge overnight. Olivera, too, drove away but, realizing he didn't want to go home, drove back to Al's, hoping to speak with McGinnis. He wanted to ask her about Townsend, hoping she'd observed her reaction to Fortney's arrest. Besides that, he was feeling a bit of nagging jealousy. What the devil was she doing at Al's without him? Surely, she hadn't gone there on her own. So, who was she with?

When he got to Al's, Townsend's convertible was no longer on the lot, and he pulled into the space where she had been parked. He spotted McGinnis's car not far away. "Good," he muttered, "she's still here." He made his way in and spoke with Al at the end of the bar, thanking him for helping with the arrest. He caught sight of McGinnis at a corner table sitting with two guys he'd seen at the infirmary.

"Lieutenant." She rose. "Everything okay?"

"Yes, and thanks for helping out with that."

"You know these guys, don't you, Harrison Taylor and Randall Jones?"

He shook their hands. "I think I've seen you at the hospital."

"Likely," said the man she introduced as Harrison. "That's where we spend most of our time," he added with a chuckle.

"Well," Olivera said, "I don't mean to interrupt. I wanted to speak to you, Dr. McGinnis, but it'll wait."

"We were just about to call it a night," she said, "but I could stay behind if you like."

"Sure you wouldn't mind?"

"Not at all. Have a seat."

He sat in the empty bar chair, and, gesturing to the server, ordered a whiskey. "Can I get you anything?" he offered, glancing at the others at the table.

"No, thanks," Taylor said. "As Eads said, we're

about to be on our way."

As soon as they had paid their tab and departed, he gave McGinnis a searching look. "So, who are they?"

"Just friends, travelling nurses. They should be moving on soon."

"Good."

"Lieutenant, you aren't—"

"Yes, as a matter of fact I am." He picked up his whiskey and took a sip. "But enough about that. I would like to wrap this thing up soon with Fortney, and the only way I can think to do that—short of getting a confession, which isn't going to happen—is to find a piece of hard evidence, something watertight."

"That's a tall order, Lieutenant."

"I know it is."

"Well, where you want to start?"

He slipped his arm around her waist and pulled her toward him.

"Uh, I'm not sure you want to do that," she said.

"Why not?"

"Well, for one, Carlotta Humphrey just walked in, and she's staring in our direction."

He loosened his grip and sighed. "Where is she?" he asked McGinnis, not wanting to turn around.

"She's sitting at the bar, talking to the bartender. So, to rephrase the question. How do you propose we produce this irrefutable evidence?"

"I can think of a couple of things. Like question Townsend again, see what she knows that she didn't think she knew, and I will do that first thing in the morning. By the way, how did she react—"

"—when she heard you'd carried her boyfriend off in handcuffs?"

"Yes."

"I would say more calmly than I would have expected."

"Interesting."

"You don't think she was in on it, do you?"

"Oh, gosh," he said, "if she is, she played her part to perfection."

"You know, when the college hires a person to represent them, like in the top level of the administration or the Development Office, they take stuff like that into consideration."

"You mean like the ability to lie?"

"Well, I doubt they think of it that way, but the talent to dissemble, you know, in the event something that reflects badly on the college comes up."

"There's another strategy we could use." He tapped on the table. "We could play one against the other. I mean, convince each of them they had something to gain by ratting out the other."

"Not a bad approach if you can finesse it."

"That sounds like a challenge to me, Dr. McGinnis, but easier than scouring that monstrosity of a house again."

"I tell you what. Why don't you follow me home, and tomorrow I'll get busy. Maybe one of us can find that piece of damning evidence."

Chapter Thirty-Five

Police Station
Thursday, March 18, 2010, 8 a.m.

Olivera arrived early at the station and, just as he was downing the last drop of coffee, a call came in from Ed Neville. "Mr. Neville, I'm guessing you've heard we arrested Bud Fortney."

"Yes, that's what I wanted to talk to you about. Well, I said I would get back to you concerning a possible conflict. As it turns out, it involves Bud Fortney, and I'm prepared to let you know what I've found."

"Okay, uh, shall I drop by the firm?"

"Yes, I think that would be best. I'm already here. Could you come now?"

Olivera told him he'd be right over and, grabbing his hat and sports coat, headed toward the front. "Ms. Hill, I'm going to King Accounting. Let Springer and Reagan know I'll be back soon. I can't imagine it'll take long."

He drove to the firm and hurried up the stairs and into reception. "I'm here to see Mr. Neville," he said to the receptionist.

"He's waiting for you." The receptionist's tone was somber.

Olivera made his way down the corridor and tapped lightly on the door."

"Come in," Neville called from within.

He took a deep breath and entered the office.

Neville was standing by a cabinet, pulling files from the top drawer. "I don't have everything for you yet, but this should be enough to get started." He brought the files with him and set them on the desk. "Won't you have a seat, Lieutenant?" He gestured toward the chair in front of the desk. "When we last talked, I had only recently learned that we might have a problem." He rounded the desk and slipped into his chair. "Lenna suspected her nephew of illegal accounting practices, but she didn't want to say anything until she'd done a thorough search."

"What sort of illegal practices?"

"Well, transfers to unrecognized accounts, cash withdrawals, and so on. There's quite a bit."

"So, you consider the evidence compelling?"

"Indeed, I do. I've managed to collect enough for charges to be brought. I will continue to look into this, but at this point, we need to bring in an outside auditor."

"Okay, well, this may be the very piece of evidence I was looking for, and if you will make a quick list of what you have so far and email it to me, I'm planning to interrogate Fortney this morning, as soon as his attorney arrives."

"I'll do that right now, but, if you don't mind my asking, do you actually suspect him of committing this terrible murder?"

"It looks that way," Olivera said, standing.

Neville sighed and, getting out of his chair, followed Olivera to the door. "I'll keep you informed of what we discover going forward."

"I'm going to need a detailed explanation of all this. What you learned from Ms. Fortney, when, etc. But I need to get back to the station. Would you be free later on?"

"Yes, of course, and I should probably mention this. I was thinking of leaving the firm."

"I see."

"Well, Bud wants to buy me out."

Olivera thought for a second. "That sort of fits into the picture, doesn't it?"

"Indeed, it does."

Olivera returned to the station and entered through the front. Fortney's lawyer had arrived and was speaking with her client. "Did she leave her card with you?" he said to Ms. Hill.

"She did." She handed it to Olivera.

"Helen Caruthers," he said. He spotted Springer at his desk and moved in that direction. "Let's get the interrogation underway. I've just come from King Accounting." He bent down and lowered his voice before continuing. "We've got motive. Lenna Fortney was looking into her nephew's illegal accounting practices. Neville's got quite a bit of evidence already but is bringing in an outside auditor."

Springer nodded and stood. "When you wanna start, Chief?"

"Let them know I'm ready"—he nodded toward the back—"and, in about five minutes, bring them into the interrogation room."

Springer nodded again and headed toward the back.

As soon as Olivera had picked up his notes, he entered the room and took a seat across from Fortney and Caruthers. He placed a recorder in front of Fortney and began the interview. "It's come to my attention that the deceased, Lenna Fortney, was prepared to bring charges for, well, a list of fraudulent practices that most certainly would have ended in a conviction. Are you aware of that?"

Fortney glanced at his lawyer, who nodded. "No, I am not."

"I believe you *were* aware, and that was your reason for killing—let me be more precise—strangling Ms. Fortney."

He laughed. "You amuse me, Lieutenant."

"Really?" Olivera opened his computer to Neville's email and twisted the screen around. "Does this amuse you?"

Fortney looked at the list of violations and shrugged. "I'm sure all that can be explained."

"I'm not sure that it can be, nor can this." Olivera reached over and clicked on the enhancement of the video.

Fortney and Caruthers watched, then she whispered something to her client before ending the interrogation.

Nonetheless, when two days later Caruthers returned with the offer of a plea, Olivera got his wish to avoid a trial. Though the evidence in the homicide was essentially circumstantial, even if Fortney had beaten the charge, he wouldn't have eluded the myriad charges of illegal accounting practices.

Once the plea had come in, Olivera's role in the resolution of the case was pretty much over except for the tidying up. He took down the evidence boards and slipped the various photographs and notes into a couple of large manilla envelopes. Then, feeling an itch to revisit the crime scene, he hopped into the SUV and drove out to Red Oaks, where he removed the tape, gathered the cones, and double-checked to see that the doors and windows were securely locked. Just as he was leaving, a voice called out. He looked over the roof of his vehicle as Lauren Wilson wheeled around the circular drive and stopped just shy of the front steps.

"Hey," he called out. "What brings you here?"

"Nothing in particular." She stepped out of her ragtop and closed the door. "I wanted to get out of the Social Sciences building, take a drive in the country. It's the first day I've been able to put the top down."

He shaded his eyes from the intense sunlight that came from above the horizon.

"I'm surprised to see you here," she said. "I figured you'd wrapped up the case, I mean, from what I read in the paper."

"I have. I drove out to collect this stuff." He motioned toward the cones in the back of the vehicle.

She glanced at the front of the house before turning to survey the grounds. "I wonder who'll buy it."

"Why? You thinking about moving already?"

She laughed. "No way."

"Your place growing on you?" he asked.

"Yeah, and now that the weather is good, I expect I'll get started on the remodel."

"Remodel?"

"Of the cellar. I'd like to take advantage of all that extra space."

"Right. You were going to speak to Merritt Trumble, I believe."

"Yes, and now that his name has been cleared…"

"Of course." He nodded.

As a fluffy cloud floated above, dimming the brightness, Olivera looked up at the sky, then casually dragged his shoe across the brick driveway. He didn't really have anything more to say but couldn't quite bring himself to leave. The sight of Lauren in her shorts and sleeveless blouse, leaning against her convertible, was simply too captivating a view to walk away from. So, relying upon his gift of gab, he offhandedly said, "You know, this whole part of Little Smith, back before the, uh, murder"—he cleared his throat—"was all about luxury, classic luxury if you will. There was a pleasant atmosphere about this part of town, with spots like the Jeremiah Java, Al's Supper Club, and now the Red Oaks Brewery." He gestured in the direction of the most recent addition to Hembree's night scene.

She didn't say anything but looked at him, sort of studying his face.

"I imagine things will be different now," he continued, "after this terrible event. And maybe for quite some time. In years to come, I bet folks passing down Little Smith will point toward this beautiful old house and say, 'that's where one of Hembree's grand ladies met a tragic end.' " He glanced at the house, then back at Lauren.

"Yes, that's right. Stories about the owners tend to attach themselves to the houses." She tilted her head and grinned. "I never pegged you as a sentimentalist, Lieutenant." She took a step in his direction.

He chuckled nervously. "That's a surprise. Since I first laid eyes on you, I had the feeling you could see clear through me."

She took another step in his direction. "People tend to think that."

"And would they be wrong?"

"It gets a little tiring, to tell you the truth."

"Tiring?" He examined her face and realized that

she was dead serious.

"Yeah. I guess you could say too work-related. I get tired of being analytical all the time."

He chuckled. "So you do have an analytical side."

"Oh." Her voice fell. "You're referring to my take on the crime."

"Well"—he wrinkled his brow—"it got me thinking about the crime in ways that had little to do with the physical evidence."

She laughed. "That bad?"

"I had McGinnis and Springer, Reagan, too, thinking I'd slipped into temporary insanity."

"Oh, please. Was it really that far off?"

"Yes, it was." Though he could detect a slight bit of tension in the air, he was glad they were having the conversation. They'd be collaborating, and total honesty was key. Be that as it may, he chose to mask his personal interest in Wilson for the time being. He wasn't ready to admit how much he was drawn to her. It wasn't just her creative flair and spontaneous nature. She had this way of looking at him that really threw him off. He checked his watch and, taking a breath, said, "You know, it's late and I'd better get on with it."

"Yeah, me, too. It's almost dark, and I need to get back to the house. By the way, drop by when you can."

"I will. I'd like to see what Trumble does with that cellar of yours. Though, to tell you the truth, I sort of like the looks of it the way it is."

"Then you'll have to drop by before they start the demo."

He got in the SUV, cranked the engine, and, smiling back at Wilson, took off toward Hembree.

Thank you for purchasing
this publication of The Wild Rose Press, Inc.

For questions or more information
contact us at
info@thewildrosepress.com.

The Wild Rose Press, Inc.
www.thewildrosepress.com